CHAPTER OF ECHOES

AILEEN ARMITAGE is half-Irish, half-Yorkshire by birth. She began writing when failing eyesight obliged her to give up work in the outside world.

In the interests of research, she once worked her passage in the galley of a Norwegian tramp steamer. Nowadays, though loss of sight has curbed her adventures she finds it has also heightened her other senses and her instinct for atmosphere.

She is the author of *Hawksmoor, A Dark Moon Raging, Hunter's Moon, Touchstone, Hawkrise* and the first novel of her 'Chapter' series, *Chapter of Innocence*. She lives in Huddersfield, West Yorkshire.

Aileen Armitage received the Woman of the Year award for 1988.

Available in Fontana by the same author

Chapter of Innocence

AILEEN ARMITAGE

Chapter of Echoes

This edition published 1994 by
Diamond Books
77–85 Fulham Palace Road
Hammersmith, London W6 8JB

First published by William Collins Sons & Co. Ltd 1989
First issued in Fontana Paperbacks 1990

ISBN 0 261 66507 3

Printed and bound in Great Britain

To all those who loved me
and gave me faith

Shredded memories of the long-ago
Come splintering down the crowded years
Repeating reckless words best left unsaid,
Acts long forgotten in the head
But stored, unhallowed, in the heart.
Forgive the hate, absolve the dread
And let me bathe in echoes of your love.

A. ARMITAGE: Echoes

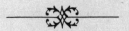

CHAPTER ONE

1956

A hazy moon slid out from behind a bank of cloud, throwing silvery light on the slate roof of Needler Hall. No sound disturbed the night air save the rustle of leaves and the bark of a distant dog. Shadowy figures crept out from behind an outbuilding and stole across the lawns towards the house.

One of the faceless creatures began to shin up a drainpipe. Another of them, creeping stealthily through the bushes, turned and hissed.

'Here, this way. There's a window open!'

One by one the figures slithered in through the opening. Inside, just under the window, a figure lay sleeping. One of the men laid a finger to his lips.

The figure sat upright. 'What the devil's going on?' a girl's voice demanded. The next moment she was leaping out of bed, her naked body glowing pearly-pale in the faint light of the moon. The men stood mesmerized.

'Who the hell are you? What do you want?' she demanded. 'Get out of here!'

No one moved. The girl hurled herself on the nearest figure. 'You heard me – get out!' she yelled.

The white of her body was somehow entangled with the blur of a man, and the next moment the two bodies were rolling on the floor. Another of the masked figures began to laugh softly.

'A wildcat,' he murmured, stepping aside as the flailing bodies writhed against his ankles. 'Come on, get up or she'll wake the whole place.'

With difficulty the man on the floor shook off the girl's clutching hands and made to scramble for the door. Suddenly he yelped and put a hand to his face.

'Someone's coming!' hissed another of the men. 'I can hear footsteps!'

As he spoke the door opened and the plump shape of a woman stood outlined against the corridor light.

'What on earth is going on here?' she snapped. The men pushed past her and ran off down the corridor, leaving the woman staring after them.

The Warden's tone was deceptively mild. 'Miss Bower, I've sometimes found one of my girls with a young man in her room at night, but this is the first time anyone has been found with seven. Would you care to explain?'

Eva stared across the desk at the Warden's unperturbed face, reddened after her early morning walk with her Siamese cat around the windswept grounds of Needler Hall, and swallowed. Miss Dow was no fool.

'Well?' prompted the Warden. 'Were you trying to break a record?'

'I just woke up, and there they were,' Eva said quietly. 'I don't know how they got there.'

'They just appeared?' Miss Dow shuffled the papers on her desk. 'You know who they were, of course.'

Eva shook her head. 'They wore masks.'

The Warden sighed. 'You have a room on the ground floor, in the north wing?'

'Yes.'

'Which faces the bicycle sheds?'

'Yes.'

'And you have frequently used the window for coming back into hall after hours?'

Eva made no attempt to deny it. The Dow knew everything that went on in her domain.

'So in all probability your window has also been used by other students returning late, after doors are locked, and perhaps even by some of the men.'

'No – I've never had a man in my room,' Eva protested. 'Not until last night, that is.'

The Warden's keen eyes surveyed her for a moment and then she nodded. 'Very well, then how did those seven men come to be there at three o'clock this morning? Are you saying they broke into the building?'

'I suppose they must have. I don't know.'

'I should report this to the police, you know, but I need names.'

Eva paled. 'Oh no, it wasn't a serious break-in, honestly it wasn't, Miss Dow. It was only a bit of fun.'

Miss Dow sighed. 'I hardly consider it to be harmless fun when damage has resulted, Miss Bower. I need names. Who were they?'

Eva straightened. 'I told you. They were wearing masks. And striped jerseys.'

Eva could swear the corners of the Dow's mouth twitched. 'No swag bags, Miss Bower?'

'No.'

Miss Dow laid down her pen. 'So the men cannot be traced and made to pay. Who is going to pay, Miss Bower?'

'I don't know.'

'I do. I rather think it will be you. The Junior Common Room will have to pay for the gutters to be repaired and the shrubs replaced. I'll pass on the estimate as soon as possible. Now you'd better go and break the news to your fellow students. Good morning, Miss Bower.'

★

The Domestic Bursar cast a curious sideways glance at the copper-headed girl as they passed in the Warden's doorway. Closing the door behind her the Bursar crossed to the desk and lowered her weight onto the chair.

'You've spoken to the Bower girl.'

'Yes. As I expected, she can give no names,' Miss Dow replied drily. 'Or at any rate, she is too loyal to give them away.'

'Furtive creature. Never liked her,' muttered the Bursar.

'Really?' murmured the Warden, 'I do. Kind of girl I'd have liked under me in the Wrens. Spirited girl, even if a bit of a handful, and bright too.'

'She had all those men in her room last night,' the Bursar remarked. 'Seven – I counted them as they ran away down the corridor. And the girl was stark naked, as I told you. It's sex rearing its ugly head again, if you ask me. Sex will drive a man farther than gunpowder can blast him.'

Miss Dow held out a hand for the papers the Bursar was holding. 'Hardly, Mrs Winthrop, not with seven of them. And being naked signifies nothing – I myself always sleep naked.'

'Do you?' The Bursar's mouth gaped.

'It was reprisals time, Mrs Winthrop – the girls ragged the men's Hall last week. Just for once I think sex was not uppermost on their minds, but revenge.'

The Bursar snorted. 'You'll see the damage itemized in my report, Miss Dow. It's going to cost a bit to clean the floor, and removing that stencil from the wall in the entrance hall.'

'I think not. They only got as far as GUA.'

'I wonder what they were going to write,' mused Mrs Winthrop. 'Something disgusting, I'll be bound.'

'*Guard thine honour*. And from the way you say you found Miss Bower hurling herself at seven men in rugby jerseys, I'd say that's just what she was doing, and very effectively too.

12

Pity they ran off so quickly or you might have seen what damage she had inflicted upon them. As I said, spirited girl that Eva Bower. She'll do well.'

The Bursar rose to leave. As she opened the door the Warden looked up from the papers in her hand. 'Oh, by the way, Mrs Winthrop, is your old gallstone problem playing you up again?'

The Bursar looked puzzled. 'No, why?'

'Oh, nothing. Just wondered how you came to be down in the north corridor at three o'clock in the morning.'

A hint of a smile played about the Warden's lips as the door closed behind the Bursar's plump figure. She laid aside her pen and, cupping her chin in her hands, stared into space.

'I wish I could have been there to see what really happened . . .'

CHAPTER TWO

'Eighty-two pounds!' Eva took a mug of coffee from Zoe and squatted on the floor against the radiator. 'How on earth do they think we can raise that much, and in our Finals year too?'

'It's just too silly for words,' said Fay. 'How tiresome.'

'Well, I'm not paying,' said Zoe, drawing deeply on a cigarette. 'I didn't want anything to do with your crazy idea to rag the men's Hall in the first place.'

'Don't be daft, we've got to pay,' said Eva.

'I haven't got any money,' said Fay. 'I haven't been to draw my allowance.'

'I haven't got any money full stop,' said Eva. 'Hell, if it hadn't been for that fat old cow prowling round in the small hours . . .'

'But what about this bill – what are we going to do about it?' said Fay.

'A dance perhaps, or a concert,' suggested Zoe, dipping a finger into her mug to retrieve a floating speck of cigarette ash.

'Perhaps I could borrow it from Mummy,' said Fay. 'I can't ask Daddy.'

'That's out,' said Eva firmly. 'No borrowing.'

Fay stretched herself on the bed. 'Did I tell you Alan Finch came and sat at my table in Refectory today?'

'Several times,' said Zoe.

Eva got to her feet and put the empty coffee cup down on the bookshelves. At the doorway she paused and a sudden glow came into her eyes. 'I think I've got it!'

'Got what?'

'A play! We'll put on a play – we'll get the men to call a truce and join in with us!'

Zoe frowned. 'Well, what's so original about that?'

Eva smiled impishly. 'Depends which play you put on, my love. What about Massinger – *A New Way to Pay Old Debts*?'

Zoe yawned. 'You're crazy. Go on, get out, you two. I'm going to bed.'

The drama tutor ran slender fingers through wavy brown hair. 'I don't know, Miss Bower. I'm not sure I can afford the time –'

'Oh, please, Mr Maynard! I've got to produce it, since I was the one who suggested it, and I'd be really grateful for your help.'

Green eyes, huge with pleading, looked up at him. 'Say you'll come? We'll work all hours, I promise. I'm holding the auditions down at the Union tomorrow teatime.'

He was frowning, one hand tracing a pattern on the chalk-covered desk. 'Miss Bower –'

'Eva, please.'

'As I was saying, I can ill afford the time, and in my opinion you are very unwise to think of doing this in your Finals year. You should be working like crazy now.'

Eva jutted her chin. 'That's for me to decide, Mr Maynard. And it's up to me to find that money. Somehow.'

'Why you? Why not somebody else who's not doing exams?'

Eva's gaze avoided his. 'Because I said I'd do the play.'

'I see. Jumping in where angels fear to tread. Well, I'd forget the whole idea, Eva. You'd be a fool to take it on.'

Fay was ecstatic over dinner in Hall. 'Alan Finch has asked me to the college hop with him tomorrow night! Imagine!'

Zoe pulled a face. 'Out of all the men you could have gone with, did it have to be that Casanova? You're luckier than me, though. I've only got four Jewish boys in the whole college to choose from and they're all hopeless.'

Fay ignored her. 'What am I going to wear?'

'Heck, with all those fancy frocks your mum brought you from Paris, you need to ask that?'

'There's the white voile . . .' Fay said tentatively.

'I wouldn't waste your time,' growled Zoe as she leaned over for the salt. 'He's not worth the effort. That bloke's too cocky by half.'

'Mature, self-confident,' said Fay. 'Living at home he doesn't have to stick to rules like us. And he's done his National Service so he's older.'

'Not really what I'd call good-looking either,' Zoe went on. 'Well, perhaps in a Heathcliff sort of way.'

'Craggy,' said Fay. 'Interesting.'

'Well, just you take care he doesn't go too far,' said Zoe. 'He's a love-'em-and-leave-'em type if ever I saw one.'

When Fay had left the table Eva heaved a sigh.

'I think it's time we had a word with her, Zoe. She's still a child in the ways of the world. A word in her ear, don't you think, before it's too late?'

'I could lend her my copy of the Kinsey Report. But I think she's smitten,' said Zoe. 'What we say won't make a blind bit of difference.'

There was always a flurry of activity in the aptly-named Squash entrance hall at lunchtime. Eva, a sheet of paper in her hand, was finding it difficult to push her way through the mass of bodies to the notice board.

A pretty, sharp-featured face suddenly presented itself between her and the board. Eva recognized Kath Davis.

'I've been trying to find you. About this play – I rather

think I could make a good job of the Lady Allworth part. I've already read it and memorized the first scene.'

Eager dark eyes scrutinized hers. Eva waved the paper. 'I'm sorry, Kath –'

The eagerness fell away, replaced by sullen disappointment. 'Oh – you've already cast it. I do think you could have waited till the auditions this afternoon.'

'No – it's not that,' Eva protested, stepping aside to let a carrot-haired youth reach over to grab a girl's arm. 'I'm just trying to put a notice up now –'

'You've given the part to one of your friends, I expect,' muttered Kath. 'I could have been word-perfect in no time. Eidetic memory.'

'No,' said Eva. 'The audition's off, that's why. The play's off.'

'Off? Why?'

'I haven't really got time to do it, what with Finals. Neither have you, come to that.'

'I don't have to worry about Finals,' the other girl retorted. 'But if that isn't typical of you, letting people down after you promised –'

'If you're so bloody clever, then you produce the thing yourself,' Eva snapped. 'And you can play the lead as well.'

She felt a touch on her shoulder and turned to see David Maynard. 'Eva – could I have a word with you?'

Instantly Kath was forgotten. 'I'm on my way to a lecture now –'

'Not now, tonight,' he said. 'Let's have a coffee. At the espresso bar down the road? Eight?'

'Fine. I'll be there.'

As Eva pushed her way towards the staircase she was completely unaware of Kath Davis's glittering black eyes watching her.

★

17

'I was too harsh when I spoke to you,' David said. 'I was rude.'

'No – you were right. I was being stubborn, but I'm glad you made me see sense.'

David Maynard was the easiest man in the world to talk to, next to Max, thought Eva. He had the same relaxed manner as her stepfather, the air of listening as if you were the most important person in the world. He was leaning over the table in the coffee bar with one hand cupped round his ear, trying to screen out the sound of the juke box in the corner where Johnny Duncan was belting out 'Last Train to San Fernando'.

He sat back, shaking his head. 'It's too noisy in here to talk comfortably – how about a drink round at my flat? It's not far.'

Eva hesitated for only a moment before pushing back her chair. They left the coffee bar and along the way he wheeled Eva's bicycle for her, propping it against the fence before they went into a large Victorian house and climbed the stairs. David unlocked a door and switched on the light.

It was a cosy flat, a living room scattered with books and empty cups, and, through the open doorway, Eva could see a further room with an unmade double bed.

He saw her expression. 'Sorry about the mess,' he said with a sheepish smile. 'But I'm sure being alone with a man doesn't bother you too much.'

'How do you mean?'

He was grinning now. 'I heard you handled seven at once with great aplomb, so one shouldn't worry you.'

She smiled back at him. 'No. I can handle you.'

He cleared a heap of books from the sofa. 'Here, sit down. Three sugars in your coffee, wasn't it? Or how about a glass of wine – do you like Beaujolais?'

'Never had it, but I'm willing to have a bash.'

He gathered up the empty cups and smiled as he went

towards the screen in the corner. 'Yes, go on, have a bash,' she heard him tease. 'A Yorkshire accent?'

Eva leaned back, stretching her arms behind her head. 'I come from Barnbeck, in the Dales – went there as an evacuee in the war. My step-parents adopted me after the war ended. My father died at sea – he was in the merchant navy – and I don't know what happened to my mum. She just disappeared.'

'Don't you ever feel you'd like to see her again?'

She shrugged. 'Maybe one day I'll try. Out of curiosity.'

David reappeared with two glasses of red wine and squatted down on the hearth before the gas fire. 'Any boyfriends?'

'None in particular, just male friends.'

There was a warm twinkle in his grey eyes. 'I hope I'm one of them.'

'Course you are – even if you are one of my tutors.'

He gave her a quizzical look. 'That doesn't bother you then?'

'Why should it? Fay's dad is quite friendly with that girl in Oates Hall he coaches privately. Nobody thinks anything about it.'

'Don't they?'

There was a curious tone in his voice that made Eva look up. 'What do you mean?'

David shrugged. 'Dr Bartram-Bates is causing something of a stir in the Senior Common Room.'

'Why?'

'Because he's behaving rather indiscreetly.'

'Why? What's he been up to? Come on, you've got to tell me now.'

David sighed. 'They say he went away with the girl for the weekend.'

Eva frowned, twirling the wineglass between her hands.

'Silly bugger,' she muttered. 'Fancy doing a daft thing like that!'

David sat silent for a moment. 'I imagine he doesn't have a very happy marriage.'

'I don't know about that,' replied Eva. 'Fay's never said anything.'

'Then perhaps we shouldn't talk about it.'

'Josie Caldwell's my age – I can't think what he sees in her,' Eva went on thoughtfully. 'People shouldn't get married if they're going to act daft like that. I'm not going to get married till I'm absolutely certain.'

David was staring into the gas fire. 'People usually think they are certain when they marry,' he murmured. 'Only sometimes things change.'

'Doesn't matter. Married people ought to be faithful.'

'Things aren't always that easy, not always stark black and white. There's shades of grey . . .'

'There's right and wrong,' said Eva firmly. She glanced up at the clock. 'Oh, my God! I'd no idea it was that late! I'll finish this wine another time.'

She put the glass down hastily, snatched up her coat and raced downstairs. In the doorway David touched her hand.

'I have enjoyed your company, Eva,' he said quietly. 'Say you'll come again.'

She cycled away, conscious of him watching from the open door. She too had enjoyed the evening, the sensation of having a mature, attractive man's attention . . .

She flung the bicycle into the shed and ran round to the front door of the hall. Miss Dow was standing in the doorway, key in hand and the Siamese cat leaning against her calf.

'Close shave, Miss Bower,' she remarked.

'A miss is as good as a mile,' smiled Eva. 'I made it, didn't I?'

The Dow nodded as she turned the key in the lock. 'I imagine your window was open anyway. Come along, Hector. Goodnight, Miss Bower.'

On Saturday evening Zoe was taking curlers out of her hair in readiness for the dance.

'Reckon I'll have to have another Toni soon, but it made a hell of a frizz last time.'

'I'll help you do it,' said Fay.

'Why aren't you steeping yourself like you usually do?' asked Eva. 'Not much time.'

'I'm not going to the dance. Alan's mending the bumper on the car – somebody ran into him and he doesn't want his father to find out.'

'You don't have to stay in just because he's not going,' Zoe pointed out. 'There's plenty of others . . .'

Fay shook her head firmly. 'I don't want the others. I'll pamper myself while you're out – have a lovely long bath and shampoo my hair. Don't worry, I'll enjoy myself.'

At midnight Zoe stood in the doorway of Eva's room.

'Somebody ought to put a stop to those rugby louts coming in sloshed after the pubs shut,' she grumbled. 'Stamping all over our toes. Just look at my new shoes!'

'You should learn to say no,' retorted Eva. 'You must have danced with the whole team. All except Alan Finch.'

'That slob! Can't think what Fay sees in him.'

'She's going to find out sooner or later. Somebody's sure to tell her about him and that student nurse.'

'Bound to,' said Zoe. 'Maybe we should break it to her gently.'

Eva shook her head. 'You can't break a heart gently.'

As she lay in bed Eva thought about Fay. She was infatuated

with Alan Finch, his exuberance, his persuasive charm. She did not appear to know about her father and his girlfriend. She had never had very much to do with her father in college, but Zoe and Eva had believed that was because it might make life difficult for both of them. How long could they hope to keep all the bad news from her?

There was a rustling sound outside the window, and then a tap at the windowpane. Eva sat up, the sheets uncovering her bare flesh.

'Who's there?' she whispered.

Pulling the sheet around her she knelt up on the bed and lifted a corner of the curtain. Beyond the window she could make out the hazy shape of a face. She unlatched the window.

'Who is it?'

The face came closer, a flash of teeth and the irregular dark features of Alan Finch. 'It's me.'

'What do you want?'

'Just to talk to you. Can I come in?'

'No you can't. Clear off.' She made to close the window.

'Hold on – I want to help you.'

'Help me? What with?'

'I heard you dropped the play. Now this money you've got to raise – maybe I could help. Let me come in – it's cold out here.'

'No. Tell me from there.'

'I wanted to thank you too.'

'What for? I've done you no favours.'

'You didn't split on us that night. You must have known who I was because you pulled my mask off. I had the scratches for days.'

'I didn't, as it happens.'

He rubbed his chin ruefully. 'There could have been a real stink over that if you'd told them . . .'

Eva was conscious of his gaze, curious as he took in the bare shoulders above the sheet. 'Oh, that. That was ages ago. I'd forgotten – and in any case it wasn't to protect you, I can assure you. You're not worth it.'

'How do you mean?'

'Cheating Fay – telling her you were fixing your car tonight. Lying bastard.'

He was grinning. 'Oh, I see. Well, I changed my mind. A man's entitled to do that, isn't he? Let me in and we'll talk about it.'

'What do you take me for? And what happened to your nurse anyway? Push off, you're drunk.'

But he did not move. Eva went to take hold of the latch, and his hand closed over hers. For several seconds neither spoke. Alan's gaze held hers and she was aware of the power of his dark eyes. She steeled herself and glared at him, and slowly he moved his hand away.

'Bugger off,' snapped Eva and, slamming the window shut, she drew the curtain back into place.

She was still shivering as she snuggled down again under the bedclothes. She could almost understand why Fay found herself irresistibly attracted towards that man . . .

CHAPTER THREE

'I don't want to hear,' said Fay. 'It's my business.'

'Now look here,' said Eva, shoving another mug of coffee into her hand, 'we agreed we'd always share everything, problems and triumphs alike. Well, Zoe and I feel we can't just let you blunder on – you're too trusting by half –'

'Too naïve,' agreed Zoe. 'Too soft an upbringing, not like us. We just want to see you right, and that Alan Finch is a scheming devil.'

'That's right,' agreed Eva. 'Chuck him before you get hurt.'

'You're too late,' said Fay quietly.

Eva heard Zoe's quick intake of breath. 'You don't mean – oh no, you haven't –'

'No,' said Fay firmly, then added, 'but he more or less said that if I wouldn't then he knew where he could go.'

'There!' said Zoe triumphantly. 'Didn't I tell you?'

Eva was watching Fay's expression. 'The sod,' she said tersely. 'Don't let him bully you, Fay love, there's better fish . . .'

Zoe sighed, pulled off her dressing gown and climbed into striped pyjamas. Fay gave a wry smile.

'Can't think why you wear those dreadful things,' she said with an attempt at a laugh. 'So unfeminine. Do let me buy you a pretty nightdress for your birthday.'

Zoe looked down at the pyjamas in surprise. 'What's wrong with them?'

'So unflattering, darling. Just suppose a man broke into your room . . .'

Zoe snorted. 'Can't be worse than Eva – she wears nothing at all.'

'There's no point trying to talk me out of it,' said Fay quietly. 'I've made up my mind. I am going to see Alan again.'

Over her bent head the other two exchanged glances. 'With his threat of blackmail?' said Zoe. 'You're a fool.'

'She's right,' said Eva. 'Ditch him quick before you get hurt.'

Fay's voice was no more than a murmur. 'I want him, Eva. I don't want anyone else.'

Kathleen Davis was standing in front of the mirror in the women's lavatories applying lipstick to her thin lips when Eva emerged from a cubicle. Catching sight of Eva's reflection she spoke with an air of innocent enquiry.

'I see there's a note in your pigeonhole from Professor Zetterling. Think perhaps he wants to have a go at you for cutting the lecture again today?'

Eva ran the cold tap and pushed the button on the soap dispenser. It was empty again. 'What's it to you what he wants?'

Kath shrugged thin shoulders and replaced the lipstick in her bag. 'I wouldn't be surprised if he did, that's all. You're a long way behind the rest of us. Oh, I know your spoken German's OK, but it ought to be when your dad's a German – it's bound to be an advantage being brought up bilingual.'

Eva sighed. Never in her life had she met anyone as petty and jealous as Kathleen Davis. 'Yep. It helps.'

'Still, language alone isn't going to get you through the exam,' mused Kath. 'You'll never pass the literature papers – you only got a C for your essay again this week.'

Eva scowled as she leaned round Kath to reach for the roller towel. 'And whose fault's that? There's only one good book in the library on *Minnesang*.'

'So?'

'We all know who had it out all week so none of us could get a look in. Selfish, I call it.'

Kath gave a satisfied smile. 'Others might call it diligent – the Prof certainly thinks I am anyway.'

'Ah well, he doesn't know you like we do. Anyway, I got a B-plus in French for the Rimbaud essay and you got C, so I reckon that makes us quits.'

The smug smile faded from Kath's face. 'Well, you would, wouldn't you?'

Eva frowned. 'What does that mean?'

Kath shrugged and moved towards the door. 'I mean, anything salacious would appeal to you.'

Eva glared. Kath went on smoothly, 'Any girl who'd let all those men into her room . . .'

'I didn't let them in! Why can't you mind your own flipping business, Kathleen Davis?'

'And butters up to one of the lecturers too . . .' Kath gave one of her enigmatic smiles. Eva fought hard to control the rage welling up inside her.

'What's it to you what I do?'

Kath gave another of her sickly-sweet smiles and went out, leaving Eva mouthing unrepeatable words at the mirror.

It was sleeting outside, splattering the windows with cold grey rain. Professor Zetterling wiped Middle High German strong verbs off the blackboard with a corner of his academic gown, now green with age, then turned to the red-headed girl standing patiently before the dais.

'I sent for you, you say? Now, why did I do that, I wonder. Who are you?'

'Eva Bower, sir. You left a note in my pigeonhole. It said you wanted to see me.'

'Bower,' Professor Zetterling repeated absently, fishing in his pocket for his spectacles. They emerged with a strip of Sellotape dangling. 'Which of my classes are you in?'

'Third year, sir. Finals.'

'Third year.' He brushed biscuit crumbs off the pile of files on his desk and opened one. 'Ah yes. Eva Jarrett-Bower. Well, according to information from one of the other students, Miss Bower, you were absent from my medieval literature class yesterday.'

'Yes, sir. I'm sorry.'

He peered closely at her over the top of his spectacles, unaware of the Sellotape hanging over his left ear. 'And that's not the only lecture you've cut lately, I'm told. Losing interest, are you?'

Pale blue eyes flickered over her. 'No, sir. I've just been busy, that's all.'

'Too busy to attend lectures in your critical Finals year? Medieval literature is not your strongest subject, Miss Bower. Your essay on the *Minnesänger* left much to be desired.'

'I know, sir. I'll try harder next time.'

Blue eyes crystallized. 'It's a little late to be promising to try, young lady. Failures are a bad reflection on me. I had better warn you that I must seriously consider talking to the Dean about your future. In view of the circumstances I think perhaps it would not be in the Department's interest to allow you to attempt Finals this year after all.'

The girl's head swung up. 'Oh no, sir, you mustn't stop me! I can pass, I know I can! I always get the things I really want. I'll work hard, I promise – I won't let you down.'

Professor Zetterling glanced at the chalkdust-shrouded clock on the wall. Any moment now afternoon tea would be brought in, and after that he would have to face that scruffy

4.30 first-year class – or was it the second-year class on Goethe? The last thing he wanted right now was an altercation with the Dean of the Arts Faculty. He drew a deep sigh.

'Very well. I shall leave the matter in abeyance for the moment, but next term I shall review the situation in the light of your work at that time. It will still not be too late to cancel your exam entry. Good afternoon, Miss Barker.'

Zoe cycled up to the bicycle sheds just as Eva was coming out. 'You going to Jane's birthday party tonight?'

Eva shook her head. 'Going down to David's.'

'David now, is it? You and Mr Maynard have got very pally lately.'

'Don't talk daft. It's only natural when we get on so well. Are you going to the party?'

'Yes – taking Colin Flaxman with me. He's quite nice, really, once you get to know him.'

Eva smiled as they made for the back door of the Hall. 'Funny lot, you Jews, your dad arranging for you to meet up with local Jewish families with suitable sons. Kind of arranged marriage set-up.'

'Not really. I don't have to marry anyone. Colin is just a nice bloke, that's all.'

'Why don't you have him up to tea so we can meet him?'

'I might – but only if you promise to mind your language. He won't think I'm such a lady if he hears the way you talk.'

'Fay'll impress him – she's a natural lady.'

Zoe shrugged. 'It's a wonder she didn't swear when she heard about Alan. I could kill that Kath Davis for telling her about the nurse.'

'She'd revel in it, the cow! I swear it was her who told the Prof about me cutting lectures too. Honest, sometimes I wish that bitch was dead.'

In the corridor they paused. Zoe opened the door of her room. 'Fay's mum's asked her down to a society coming-out ball at Claridge's. She asked if one of us wanted to go with her.'

'Not me – that's more your territory.'

Zoe tossed back dark hair. 'There's a world of difference between the West End and Golders Green. I'd never remember the right words to use, napkin for serviette and all that.'

Eva giggled. 'Me neither. All that U and non-U rubbish.'

'Keeps us yokels in our place,' agreed Zoe.

'Makes you feel like taking your knickers off and going to the ball after all. It'll do Fay good to get away for a bit.'

Zoe chewed her lip thoughtfully. 'You know, if she learnt about Alan trying to get into your room, it might just turn her off him . . .'

Eva shook her head. 'The nurse didn't, so why should that?'

'She knows he didn't go home with the nurse but she doesn't know he tried it on with you instead. Randy devil! Why leave her in ignorance? She ought to know what a Casanova he is.'

Eva shook her head even more firmly. 'There are some things it hurts too much to know – that's why I wouldn't tell her about her dad either.'

'Suit yourself – but I think you're wrong. In any event, Fay's going to suffer in the end.'

'I'm sorry, darling, I won't be going to Jane's party. Alan said he would phone tonight and I don't want to miss it.'

Fay sat in the entrance hall with a book on her lap, close to the two telephone booths. If she stayed in her own room to listen to the hit parade on her little mains radio she might miss hearing the telephone ring.

She looked up at the sound of footsteps. It was Jill Morrison, the Hall's resident hypochondriac, shuffling towards her in a pink dressing gown and clutching a hot-water bottle.

'Oh, Fay, have you got any throat lozenges? I can feel one of my throats coming on – I get them at this time every year. It's the damp climate here, Mummy says.'

'I'm sorry, no, I'm afraid I haven't.'

'I don't know where everybody is. They can't all have gone out.'

The pink figure shambled miserably away down the corridor, trying out the throat with a few exploratory coughs.

It was difficult to concentrate on reading. Every couple of minutes Fay glanced up at the clock on the wall and hoped Alan had not forgotten. More footsteps approached and she looked up to see Miss Dow crossing the hallway, closely pursued by Hector.

'Good evening, Miss Bartram-Bates. Trying to find a little peace and quiet?' she enquired.

'No. I'm waiting for a phone call.'

'And making good use of your time,' said the Dow, nodding towards the book. 'What are you reading?'

'A book about reincarnation,' murmured Fay, feeling her cheeks redden. How could she confess to the Dow, the most self-confident person she had ever met, how much comfort she derived from the book, how she feared death just as she feared the dark, how she needed a ray of hope just as she had always needed a night-light?

'Interesting,' said Miss Dow. 'That which we shall never know is always fascinating.'

She went on her smooth, imperturbable way still pursued by her sinuous, inescapable companion. Fay watched her retreating and felt envious. What did the Dow know of fear, of vague but persistent shadows that haunted the soul by day and by night, of the crying need for a soul-companion who would understand and share the terrors, would soothe and drive them away?

It was the strength of a man's shoulders she needed, a man like Alan. But he was asking of her something she knew was a sin.

'Fornication is a mortal sin,' the nuns at St Agatha's used to say, before she even knew the meaning of the word. 'No, dear, put your hands over the sheets while you sleep. That way you will not fall into temptation.'

Temptation. The word then had meant only greed for more sweets or envy of another girl's new frock. Now it had acquired a new and more powerful meaning – the desire to lie close with a warm body which promised protection from the evils of the dark. But to sin deliberately meant penance in Purgatory hereafter.

Reincarnation was far preferable, a chance for the soul to take on a new body like a new overcoat and begin again, to come back into a world where there would be no suffering in the dark alone.

Suddenly the telephone bell shrilled. Fay leapt to her feet, the book slithering to the parquet floor. Snatching up the receiver she heard her voice tremble.

'Needler Hall?'

'Can I speak to Zoe Jacob, please?' Disappointment filled her. It was a pleasant enough male voice, but not the one she was hoping to hear.

'I'm sorry, she's not here. She should be back about eleven.'

Zoe could see Colin was not even trying to stifle the yawn. Jane Halliwell's party, held in the upper room of the Crossed Keys, was quite an event compared to most people's parties in Hall, but so far it had been a disappointment as far as Colin was concerned.

31

'There must be something you can eat,' Zoe protested when he complained.

'Pork pies and sausage rolls? Doesn't she know we're Jewish?'

'She could hardly cater for two Jews she didn't even know would be here. Anyway, you like dancing and there's a live band.'

'If you like communal dancing. The hokey-cokey's not exactly my cup of tea.'

So she danced without him, and was enjoying the lively company. At ten o'clock she saw him peering at his wrist-watch in the dimmed light, the one he'd proudly displayed to her when he'd picked her up. Part of his new stock, he had said, the better-class jewellery he sold nowadays.

'I think perhaps we'd better be making a move,' he said, rising to go as she came back to her seat. 'I'll fetch your coat.'

She frowned at him. 'But I'm not ready to go yet. The party's just livening up.'

'I promised Mother –'

'Well, you go then. I'm staying.' She sat down and folded her arms.

Colin looked uncertain. 'But I ought to see you home – can you manage on your own?'

'I'm not a doll. Of course I can.'

'Well, if you're sure . . . You'll still come down on Saturday?'

He had barely left the room when the band struck up the conga. Hands pulled Zoe to her feet again and, amid laughter and confusion, bodies sorted themselves into a line in the half-light of the room. Voices struck up a raucous repetition.

'Aye, aye, conga, aye, aye, conga . . .'

The long line snaked its way along the room towards the door and in the gloom of the corridor outside Zoe felt the hands about her waist being wrenched away, and then replaced. A husky voice murmured in her ear,

'I've got you now, Zoe Jacob, and I'm not going to let you go.'

Even before she turned she recognized the voice. It was Alan Finch.

'Good party?' asked Eva. Fay's expression was remote and she didn't appear to be listening.

Zoe shrugged. 'I enjoyed it. Colin got cheesed off.'

'People who get bored are boring,' said Eva. 'But about this bloody money – what are we going to do? We need a miracle to find it.'

Fay sighed. 'I believe in miracles.'

'Did Alan ring?' asked Eva. Fay shook her head.

Zoe snorted. 'If you think Alan Finch could ever be serious about you, or anybody else for that matter, that would be a miracle and no mistake.'

'Perhaps,' said Fay quietly. 'I still believe in Santa Claus and magic.'

Eva was studying her pale face. 'What do you want out of life really, Fay?'

'I've told you. Magic and miracles.'

Next day in the Refectory Eva was carrying her tray from the serving hatch across to join Zoe and Fay at the table when Alan Finch appeared.

'Mind if I sit with you?'

'Not at all,' said Fay, and Eva could see the brilliance that leapt into her eyes.

'If you must,' said Eva. Zoe groaned and looked away.

'I've got an idea that might be of help,' he said easily, pulling out a chair. 'How much have you got to raise for that damages bill?'

Eva sighed. 'We've got to find eighty-two pounds.'

'Easy,' he said. 'I know how to do it.'

'Go on then, Mr Clever-Clogs. Tell us.'

He gave an enigmatic smile as he raised a forkful of sausage. 'What's it worth?'

'Bugger off,' said Eva.

'We'd be terribly grateful if you could help,' Fay cut in quickly. 'Really we would.'

He went on undeterred. 'If I fix it for you, will you come and watch the match on Saturday? We could do with a few supporters to cheer us on.'

His dark eyes were focused on Eva. 'Not me,' she said firmly. 'I can't for the life of me understand why eleven men –'

'Nor me,' cut in Zoe. 'There're much better ways of spending a Saturday afternoon than freezing on a muddy field.'

'I will,' said Fay. 'I'll be there. I won't let you down. I've got to go now – I've got a class. I could cut it –'

'No you won't,' said Zoe. 'I've got one too. Let's go.'

Fay smiled as they left. Eva turned to Alan. 'Well, what've you got in mind?'

Green eyes challenged brown ones. Alan smiled.

'A raffle, that's what. I've got everything organized. All you have to do is to collect the divvy when the raffle's drawn.'

Eva grunted. 'Depends what the prize is. We won't sell many tickets if it's not worth it.'

'It's worth it all right. I've got someone to donate a camera.'

He was smiling broadly, the confident smile of a man who knows he's succeeded in impressing. Eva stared.

'A camera? What sort of camera?'

He leaned forward and patted her hand. 'I told you, it's all in hand. I've got a girl to sell tickets, everything. Now, don't ask any more questions – just leave everything to me.'

He sat back, sipping coffee, and there was a light of amusement in his eyes. He really was remarkably attractive . . .

'Why are you doing this?' she asked.

'Because it was us caused the damage and because I like you.' He glanced at the clock. 'I've got to go. Maybe we can be friends now?' Dark eyes searched hers.

'Not while you treat Fay the way you do. You're a slob.'

He pushed back his chair and got up. 'The raffle's to be drawn at the dance next Saturday. I'll see you there.'

Eva looked up at him. 'I still can't understand why you're going to so much trouble,' she said suspiciously. 'Especially after the other night.'

'I told you, I like you. I like fighters, and God, I've never seen a girl fight like you did that night. I've still got the scratches to prove it,' he added ruefully, 'in places I can't show.'

'Good,' said Eva, picking up her books from the table.

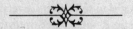

CHAPTER FOUR

The Saturday night hop was in full swing. Zoe was jiving with one of the maths students, ponytail flying and masses of petticoats swirling under her circular skirt. Eva sat by the wall, regaining her breath and watching the trumpet player, a barrel-chested young man with cheeks bellied out so far that they hung like sacks when he stopped playing. He wasn't one of the students but a local who came in every Saturday night with the band. He looked ill. Emphysema, they said he had, his lungs distended and destroyed from thousands of hours of playing his beloved trumpet.

'Talented people should always strive for excellence – don't betray your talent no matter what the cost. Don't let anything sidetrack you.'

David's words came back to her, his blue eyes serious and fingers running through tousled hair. He would approve of this boy blowing out his lungs to make music which gratified his soul, even though he knew it was costing him his life.

The number ended and the President of the Union stepped forward on the dais, one hand upraised. 'And now the moment you've been waiting for,' he announced. 'The raffle for this splendid camera. I shall now ask Kath Davis, who has spent hours of her valuable time promoting this raffle, to draw the winning ticket.'

He held up a wicker wastepaper basket overflowing with tickets. The band played a fanfare and the students began cheering and whistling. Kath Davis, her cheeks flushed and her hair scraped into a ponytail, emphasizing her angular features, held out her hand to dip into the basket.

'Green, eighty-three,' she called out. 'Green, eighty-three.'

There was a pause while people scrutinized their tickets, then a deep voice called from the crowd: 'That's me.'

Heads turned. Eva saw Martin Dempster move forward to climb the steps. He beamed as he crossed the platform and took the camera from the President, then descended the steps again and threaded his way through the dancers to where Alan stood by the door, a bright-eyed Fay beside him. Eva went across to join them.

Fay was inspecting the camera. 'How lucky you are!' she was saying to Martin. 'I'm never lucky at this sort of thing.'

'Nor am I as a rule,' smiled Martin, and Eva saw him give an almost imperceptible wink towards Alan. A sudden suspicion leapt into her mind, but then she dismissed it as an uncharitable thought.

'They won the rugby match,' said Fay. 'It was great.'

Martin smiled. 'So we're in celebratory mood. Can I walk you home tonight, Eva?'

'No thanks. I'm on my bike.'

Eva cycled home with Zoe, leaving Fay to drive back with Alan. Eva was just drifting off to sleep when she heard the tap at the window of her room. It was Alan. She pulled a wrap on quickly.

'What do you want?'

'Just to hear you say thanks. I told you I'd see to it.'

'Why should I thank you? It was you who caused the damage in the first place.'

He grinned. 'You don't mince words, do you?'

'That's the way I was brought up. So I'll ask you straight out – was there something fishy about that raffle?'

37

'How do you mean?'

She could swear she could detect amusement in his tone. 'You know what I mean – it strikes me as odd when you organize a raffle and then your best friend goes and wins it.'

'I didn't run it – Kath Davis did it all on her own. She sold every ticket – ask her.'

Eva's eyes narrowed. 'I wouldn't trust her any more than I'd trust you. She'd do anything to get in with you. You did fix it, didn't you?'

'What a suspicious devil you are.' He was still laughing at her, she could swear it.

'Didn't you?' she repeated.

'And if I did?'

'Then you're a cheat! Whoever gave that camera doesn't know you were using him. You ought to give it back, you deceitful bugger.'

Alan threw back his head and laughed, a deep, throaty laugh. 'He already knows – it was Martin's camera. His parents gave it to him last week for his birthday.'

'You mean – you rigged it so he got his own camera back?'

'He wouldn't have given it if he hadn't been sure of getting it back – it cost a ruddy fortune.'

Eva gasped. 'But all those people who believed it was genuine – you cheating, lying bastard! We'll have to give the money back!'

'And wreck Martin's reputation, and mine, and Kath Davis's?'

'She was in on it then?'

'She wanted to rescue your Junior Common Room – you let them down over the play.'

'Is that what she said?' Eva fumed inwardly. Not only had Kath Davis scored over her, the whole enterprise was shady and distasteful in the extreme.

38

'Come on now,' said Alan soothingly. 'No one's been hurt. People have only parted with sixpence and that won't break them.'

'We could have asked them to give that without cheating them,' muttered Eva.

'People don't give unless they think there's a chance they'll strike lucky. Human nature. And they'll feel a whole lot worse if they learn they've been conned – people don't like finding out they're stupid.'

He was right, she couldn't help admitting to herself. 'You conned me,' she growled. 'I still think you're mean, and deceitful.'

'Everyone's satisfied so why worry? Leave well alone,' said Alan.

'I would never have agreed to it.'

'That's why we didn't ask you. What the eye doesn't see . . . But then, you know about that.'

There was that devilish light of amusement in his eyes again, exciting and teasing. Eva was curious.

'Know about what? What do you mean?'

'Come on now, little innocent. It won't be long before the whole college knows.'

'What are you talking about?'

'About you and the drama chap. Been seeing a lot of each other on the quiet, I hear. Go for older men, do you?'

His head was cocked to one side, his fingers reaching to caress hers. Eva stood, open-mouthed, trying to assimilate his words when suddenly he swore.

'Hell! There's that woman with the bloody cat again! I'm off!'

And he was gone. Eva saw the flicker of the Dow's flashlight as her footsteps crunched along the gravel path. She drew the curtains and tried to go back to sleep.

★

Kath Davis paused as she was passing the girls' breakfast table.

'Pity you didn't buy a raffle ticket,' she said to Eva with a thin smile. 'Fay bought two whole books. Never mind, I still got enough to settle the bill.'

'Don't belt her!' Zoe muttered to Eva between clenched teeth. 'Let me smash her face in first.'

'Since when have you been so matey with Alan Finch?' Eva asked.

'Since he asked me to help. We've been seeing quite a bit of each other since.'

Kath sailed off, a satisfied smile still playing about her lips. Eva smouldered, controlling her anger with effort. 'Creep! She knew all along it was a great big fraud! I hate that girl!'

Needler Hall was steeped in the pervasive odour of camphor. Fay watched engrossed as Eva knelt on the bedroom floor pounding mothballs into a powder and then sprinkled them onto layers of hessian, then rolled the cloth around a stout stick and fastened it in place with wire.

'There you are, one torch,' she said when it was done.

'Oh, now I remember!' said Fay. 'And now we soak it in the bucket of paraffin. I never can remember these things – I'm just not practical with my hands at all.'

'Comes of having servants, I suppose,' said Eva.

'Oh no, Mummy doesn't have servants now,' replied Fay. 'Not any more.'

She went suddenly quiet. Not for the first time, Eva noted, when her family was mentioned. Had she suspected that all was not well between her parents, or had Dr Bartram-Bates's escapade been discovered?

'Let me have a go at making one now,' said Fay, 'and you can watch to see I do it right.'

Zoe stuck her head round the door. 'The world is made up of two kinds of people,' she said. 'Those who won't lend anybody their hair dryer and those who –'

'Yes, OK, you can borrow it,' said Eva. 'Anyone fancy a walk in the park?'

A November sun hung low and red over the park. Eva was listening to Fay while throwing a stick for a bedraggled mongrel who was bounding back to her with it, his stumpy tail wagging excitedly. Fay seated herself on the park bench, and Eva sat down beside her.

'Look, Fay, I wouldn't keep feeling bad about it if I were you. Forget it.'

'I hate her, Eva – she's making a play for Alan. It's a sin to hate, but I do.'

Fay seemed to shrink inside the collar of her coat, her hands digging deep into the pockets. Eva bent to take the stick from the mongrel's slavering mouth.

'Come on, Fay. She's not going to get him. Finals are what matter now.'

'I'm not going to pass, Eva. After all that's happened I'm going to let Daddy down again.'

Eva chewed her lip, ignoring the pleading look in the mongrel's eyes as he offered the stick yet again. 'Don't talk so daft. You've never let anyone down in your life.'

Fay smiled bleakly. 'Thanks. I know you're trying to make me feel better, Eva. You're a good friend.'

Eva glanced sideways at her pale profile. 'It's that blooming Catholic conscience of yours. Never gives you a minute's peace.'

'And I've let Alan down too.'

'Bloody hell! Let him down because you don't sleep with him? And how would you live with your conscience if you did, eh? Strikes me it's him who's letting you down.'

Fay withdrew a hand from her pocket and took the dog's stick. 'Don't you ever have this battle with your conscience, Eva, or is it only me? All my life I feel I've failed. Daddy most of all.'

'Rubbish!'

Fay sighed. 'I wish we weren't at the same college, Daddy and I. I wish he was a million miles away.'

'Don't say that.'

'Why not?' Fay's eyes were wide.

'Because wishes have a habit of coming true. Twice I've wished things on people and then wished like hell that I hadn't.'

Fay dropped the stick abruptly and got to her feet. 'Let's not talk about it any more. It frightens me. I'm going back to the Hall.'

Later that night Zoe poked her head round Eva's door, a jar of instant coffee and a spoon in her hand.

'I can't stand any more revision – if I look at another botany specimen I think I'll scream. Fancy a cup of coffee?'

'Fine.' Eva pushed her books away. 'I can't concentrate on a thing tonight anyway. My mind's full of idle thoughts.'

'Like what? Anything interesting?'

'I was thinking about three. You and I both came from a family of three.'

'Yes. And you, me and Fay all have three-lettered names?'

Eva considered. 'And Fay believes in the Holy Trinity too.'

Zoe licked the tip of the spoon. 'Wonder why three has always been such a mystic number?'

'Don't know, but if you're going to make that coffee now, remember I like three sugars.'

When Zoe had gone Eva leaned back, rubbing her aching

neck and letting thoughts drift through her mind. Threes. Three of a kind. *Third time lucky. The Three Bears. The fairy granting three wishes.* The magic number seemed to persist throughout folklore.

And then another thought made her fingers stiffen on her neck. *Disasters always come in threes.* There had been Ronnie that time, the evil Australian who was gored to death by the boar, and before that the cousin killed in the pit accident. And she had wished both of them dead.

Kath Davis made the third.

The torchlight procession was an event which never failed to thrill Eva, the sight and smell of hundreds of torches blazing along the street which led from Needler Hall and through the village up to the men's Hall where the bonfire lay ready. Faces glowed in the torchlight, faces half-hidden by scarves wound tightly around mouths to keep out the dense smoke trailing from the torches.

'Oh, mine's dripping!' cried Fay. 'I mustn't have fastened it tightly enough!'

By the end of the street Fay's torch was beginning to disintegrate, scattering scarlet embers over her coat. Behind them Eva could see torches glowing all the way down the village street, straggling around the corner by the pub and snaking down the hill. The mood of exhilaration seemed to spill over from the procession into the neighbouring houses, whose occupants watched from windows or came out to the gates to lean and watch.

In the grounds of the men's Hall figures, silhouetted against the firelight, already danced around the bonfire, whirling their torches and cheering as the gaudy guy on the top lurched drunkenly and then began to blaze. The orderly procession broke up into erratic, laughing groups flashing off jumping jacks and bangers. Girls shrieked and leapt out of the way. Someone struck up a song and enthusiastic voices joined in.

'Oh, not *Eskimo Nell*,' said Fay. 'It's very rude.'

'That's your rugby pals for you,' said Zoe.

Suddenly rockets began to soar skywards and Catherine wheels whizzed and spat. The air was becoming thick with smoke and it was hard to discern faces despite the scarlet glow of the bonfire. All that Eva could see clearly was the myriad lights of torches before they were flung onto the bonfire. Zoe gripped Eva's arm.

'Doesn't it make you feel good?' she shouted above the din. 'Nights like this make life exciting, don't they? You can forget all about the pressure of Finals for a bit.'

Eva too felt exhilaration rising in her. A group on the far side of the fire began to squeal, but at first Eva took little notice. The sound of girls squealing was everywhere. Then she realized that the sound was not of giggling excitement but of anxiety, and then she saw the glow.

It was a yellow flame licking high, too high for a torch. Blinking her eyes against the gritty smoke she made out that it was something ablaze, and then the breath caught in her throat. It was the wall of a cottage which was on fire, the gatehouse to the men's Hall.

'It's the Warden's house!' cried Zoe.

'Oh, God, no!' moaned Eva. 'I'm not paying for that!'

Youths were already dealing with the blaze, beating it with sticks and something that looked like a blanket. Within minutes it was out and merrymaking filled the air once more. Eva caught sight of Alan moving around the bonfire, and alongside him the triumphant face of Kath Davis. She glanced at Fay.

Fay's expression gave no sign that she had seen him. She held her torch at arm's length, trying to avoid the blazing fragments flying from it.

44

'Here,' shouted Eva. 'Give me that bloody thing – I'll sling it on the fire.'

Somehow, Eva could never quite work it out afterwards, Kath Davis chanced to walk by, tossing her ponytail with a flourish, at the precise moment that Eva snatched the torch from Fay and swung her arm back. A scream behind her made her turn, and her heart stopped. A sheet of flame was leaping up round Kath's dark head, and Eva saw the girl's eyes widen in horror, and then her screams filled the air, drowning the noise around them. Faces turned, mouths gasped as the yellow flames licked and spat shreds of hair, turning the dark head into a withered mass.

Kath was on the ground, rolling and shrieking. Someone flung a jacket over her head, and the noise subsided. A terrible, ominous silence overcame the nearest bystanders, while from under the jacket came only sobbing moans.

'Oh Christ!' cried Eva, and she fell on her knees beside the writhing figure on the ground. She was aware of Fay leaning over her as she pulled the jacket away.

Kath's hands were clasped over her face, only the frizz of scorched stumps of hair visible. With a moan she let her hands fall away, revealing a seeping mass of flesh where her face had been. Eva's heart stopped.

Someone pushed Eva aside. It was Alan. He snatched up Kath Davis's limp body and ran towards the Warden's cottage. The Warden, embroiled in a heated argument with a group of the male students over the damage to his property, took in the situation at a glance and led the way indoors. Zoe clutched Eva's arm and Fay stood, mouth agape. No one spoke, and then they heard the distant wail of the ambulance.

Some days later Eva sat in David Maynard's flat.

'It was terrible, David. I still can't believe it really happened.'

He refilled her glass. 'It wasn't your fault –'

'I wish I could be sure of that, but there's going to be an enquiry.'

'Which will clear you completely, and maybe then you'll be convinced.'

Eva sipped the wine. 'Even if it does, I still feel bad about it. Oh, David, I didn't mean to hurt her, not like that. I'd no idea she was behind me. Oh God, imagine, having to live the rest of your life with a hideous face!'

'I know you didn't mean it.'

'And people talk. They're talking now. It's awful.'

He nodded, reaching across her for a cigarette. 'I know. I've heard the whispers, but you mustn't let it upset you. College gossip – everything that happens in an insular place like this is food for gossip. It's magnified out of all proportion.'

'She didn't like me – she made that plain.'

'She was envious of your popularity, perhaps. You say she had few friends.'

'She was spreading lies about me, getting me into trouble with the Prof. It could look like revenge.'

'Only a fool would believe that. Have some more wine – it'll help you feel better.'

'I still feel responsible,' Eva said miserably. 'I wished her dead.'

David spread his hands, large, gentle-looking hands. 'Tell me anyone who hasn't wished somebody dead at some time or other. I know I have. Anyway, she didn't die.'

'It's not the same, David. When I wish it, it happens – I know, I've done it before.'

He eyed her quizzically. 'Are you saying you can hex people? I'd better tread wary.'

'Don't laugh, David. I'm serious.'

David's tone was beginning to register impatience. 'Look, you have no more responsibility for that accident than I have. I wish you'd believe that.'

Eva set down her glass and, sighing deeply, leaned towards him. 'Look, I've done it before – twice before – and I know it works. Once, when I was little, I hated my cousin because he teased me. I wished him dead, and within a few days he was killed in a pit accident.'

'Coincidence, Eva, that's all.'

'And again, in the war, there was a really vicious Australian who came to our farm. He was cruel, to Maddie and to me. I wished him dead, and a few days later our old boar tore him to bits and ate his face. His face – oh Christ!'

She closed her eyes as if to shut out the memory. David took her hand between his.

'Sometimes we see those we love harmed and we blame ourselves –'

'I hated Kath Davis! I shouldn't say it, but I did.'

She felt tears begin to prick her eyelids. David leaned closer. 'We'd like to undo what's happened, but we can't –'

Eva began to sob quietly. He put his arms around her. 'I know. I understand. But we can't live life hampered by regrets. You must forget it, Eva. That's important.'

'Forget?' She looked up angrily. 'It's easy for you to say! How can I ever forget what I did to her?'

'I'm sure your friends have told you the same. You have good friends.'

'The best.'

'I'm envious,' he murmured.

'Don't you have anyone you're close to?'

David looked down. 'Not any more,' he said quietly.

'Yes, you have,' said Eva. 'You've got me.'

She turned her face up to his and found comfort in the

warmth of the fire, the muzzy sensation of the wine in her head, and his lips gentle on hers.

Eva watched Zoe aimlessly pushing a pencil through a sheet of discarded revision notes.

'I still can't stop thinking about it, you know. I lie awake at night seeing that awful face again. She didn't deserve that.'

'No point losing sleep over it. Put you off work if you let it get to you like that. It was an accident after all, whatever they might say.'

Eva frowned. 'That hurts, people saying things.'

'Cruel,' said Zoe. 'Some rotten devil's putting it about that you set fire to her hair on purpose. I mean, can you imagine it?'

Eva paled. 'Who the hell started that?'

Zoe shrugged. 'Does it matter? I put the lie to it, of course.'

'Christ!' exclaimed Eva. 'If I find out who the bitch is I promise you she won't be saying it much longer.'

'Well, at least you know it can't be Kath Davis this time. As a matter of fact,' said Zoe, 'it was Alan Finch told me.'

'Did he now? Then I must have a serious word with him.'

'Alan, I'd like a word with you.'

He detached himself from the group of men standing chatting in Squash Hall and came across to join Eva by the notice board.

'I wanted a word with you –' Eva began.

'I know.'

'About these rumours.'

'Forget it. Nobody believes them. Anyway, I was the one responsible for what happened, not you.'

'You? I shoved the bloody torch in her face!'

Alan shook his head firmly. 'I was escorting her. I was responsible for her.'

'It was me who shoved the torch –'

'That's not the point – it wouldn't have happened if – if . . .'

'If what? Look, Alan, she got burnt by a torch – the torch I was trying to throw on the bonfire. It was my fault, and only mine.'

'No, Eva. I was with her. At least, I had been . . . I'd just left her.'

Eva gave him an icy look. 'I see. You spotted another pretty face, is that it?'

Alan's expression was sober. 'Yes, as a matter of fact. So I was trying to get rid of Kath. I left her. If I'd stayed with her, this wouldn't have happened. So you see, you can stop worrying – the responsibility is all mine.'

'And who was the tart who made you desert her?'

'Alan!' It was Martin Dempster, calling Alan back to the group. As he turned to go Alan spoke over his shoulder.

'As a matter of fact, it was you.'

CHAPTER FIVE

'Pure accident, Dr Bartram-Bates, I assure you.' The Dean glanced up at the tall figure standing by the window. 'There is no implication of any kind of malice or neglect on either Miss Bower's or your daughter's part. Pure accident.'

The Dean leaned across his desk to the chessboard and moved the white knight closer to the black queen. The man by the window straightened and turned.

'I never for one moment believed otherwise. The girl who was injured – is it very serious?'

'Serious enough. A number of plastic surgery operations will be necessary evidently, but it's amazing what they can do these days.' The Dean brought up the white bishop.

'Will she be back to continue her studies?'

'It's doubtful. But in the circumstances she can consider herself lucky not to have been killed.'

'Lucky?' murmured Bartram-Bates. 'A matter of opinion.'

'Perhaps so,' agreed the Dean, moving a pawn forward. 'But as to the other matter – you say you would like permission to take your daughter when you give a paper at the Oxford Union?'

'That's correct.'

'Well, it's certainly an honour to be invited. But is it not usual to take one's wife? Is Mrs Bartram-Bates unable to go with you?'

'Unfortunately, yes. Other commitments.'

'I see. Well, it's not the best time to take Fay from her studies –'

'I know, but I should like her to come all the same.'

'Well, you're her father and perhaps a day or two away would be beneficial after the shock she's had.'

'Thank you.'

The Dean looked up from the chessboard as the doctor turned to go. A handsome, impressive man for his forty-odd years, he thought. There could be some truth in the rumours flitting around the Senior Common Room.

'One moment, Dr Bartram-Bates. I'd like a word before you go.'

The doctor turned and came back. 'Yes?'

'You're a clever man and no doubt ambitious,' the Dean remarked quietly as the black queen relinquished her corner position. He was aware of the other man's stiffness.

'Yes.'

'And ambitious men do not allow a dalliance to prejudice their future careers.' The white knight hesitated, then yielded to the queen's advance. Dr Bartram-Bates did not move a muscle.

For long seconds there was silence in the study, then the Dean gave a deep sigh. 'It would be foolhardy for such a man to find himself dismissed in disgrace, I feel, when the whole academic world lies before him. Don't you agree?'

'Yes,' said the doctor.

'You may go,' said the Dean, and as the doctor opened the door the black queen swooped down the board on the defenceless bishop.

'You don't have to come to my lecture if you don't feel like it, Fay, but I should be very proud to have you on my arm at the ball. We don't see a great deal of each other.'

There was an uncomfortable pause before the girl replied.

'I appreciate the thought, Daddy, but I really don't feel up to going. What about Mummy?'

She could not bring herself to look him in the eye. Even now she feared he might say what she did not want to hear. Parents together spelled some kind of security; parents apart meant a world of total chaos.

'Ah, well, I don't see much of your mother these days,' he murmured. 'She has her own interests, you know.'

Bridge parties, coming-out dances for her friends' daughters, alternating with the occasional visit to a retreat to absolve her conscience – not a real life, thought Fay, but a substitute for something vague and indefinable which she knew was missing from her life.

'Well?' he prompted.

She looked up at him, aching to hear him say he cared, to believe he could feel emotions instead of being completely absorbed in his academic world. 'It could be useful, you know, my dear, the right contacts for you if you choose to take a Master's degree later.'

'Can't you take someone else?' she said quietly.

He turned away, his hand trailing across the books on his desk. Was it imagination or did she catch sight of a flush on his handsome face before he turned away?

'I thought you'd be pleased,' he murmured. 'I thought you'd be glad to get away for a while.'

She could hear the disappointment in his tone. She sprang to her feet. 'I'm sorry, Daddy – when is it, did you say?'

'Thursday next week. Stay till Saturday.'

'Oh.'

He turned back to face her. 'You mean you will come?'

She shook her head. 'I can't. I've promised Mummy –'

She saw him stiffen. 'Never mind. You must do your duty by your mother. I must get on with preparing my paper now.'

*

'Tell us about the weekend, Fay – was it a good do at Claridge's?'

Fay's eyes shone. 'Fantabulous, darling! We had Paul Adam's band playing till four o'clock in the morning, lashings of caviar and champers, and Mummy had ordered the most divine gown for me, off the shoulder –'

'Any dishy men?' asked Zoe.

Fay wrinkled her nose. 'No one to hold a candle to Alan.'

'Sounds a dead loss to me,' growled Zoe.

'Did either of you see Alan while I was gone?'

'We didn't go to the Saturday night hop.'

'No money,' said Eva.

Fay looked at her curiously. 'Do you ever mind being poor, Eva?'

'I'm not poor – it's just that I haven't any money. I'm lucky, or maybe I just chose well.'

'Chose what?'

'Friends – parents.'

'You didn't choose your parents,' objected Zoe. 'They chose you.'

Eva roared with laughter. 'They think they did, but really it was me who chose them.'

'My dad's terrific,' said Zoe, 'even if he is the lousiest businessman in London.'

Eva sat on her bed to re-read her stepmother's letter alone. Wintry sunlight slanted across the page, illuminating Maddie's large, generous handwriting. Mostly it was news about Barnbeck, about the new vicar and the gossip about Eunice Sykes's engagement to a Middlesbrough solicitor and Doreen Sykes's overflowing pride that her daughter was to marry so well.

'She says I'm to be sure to tell you that Eunice is getting

married here in Barnbeck at Easter, with her fiancé Arnold's
three sisters as bridesmaids and his nephew as pageboy, and
they hope you'll be home on vacation and will be able to come.'

Eva smiled. Eunice, companion in all those childhood
pranks, scrumping apples and chasing chickens, cheating
evacuees out of gobstoppers and comics – Eunice an Easter
bride; it didn't seem possible.

But Maddie's tone grew warm with excitement as she wrote
about her horses.

'Max and I have great hopes for our newest filly, Damsel.
She's six months old now, growing fast and every day she
reminds me more of my favourite of all time, Duster –
remember learning to ride her when you were a little girl?'

As she read, Eva could feel again the bay's great broad back
between her thighs, recall the exhilaration of sitting up so high
above the ground. How far away Barnbeck seemed, she
mused. College life was so far removed from the peaceful
tranquillity of the Yorkshire Dales where life changed little
from one generation to the next. Somehow it was reassuring to
know that it would always be there, a close-knit community
where everyone knew everyone, its squat stone cottages
seeming to have grown out of the very earth and be part of it,
giving a sense of permanency and belonging. Barnbeck. The
very name spelled stability. She never missed it while she was
away, but it was always wonderful to go home.

Home. Well, that was what it was, ever since the war had
uprooted her from Middlesbrough and her natural mother.
Eva could only dimly remember her now, a slim woman with
fair hair in a turban and a splash of scarlet lipstick, giggling
when she smothered Eva with cuddles, then lowering her
voice when she spoke of Eva's sailor father who never came
home from the war.

The war had been frightening when bombs started to fall on Middlesbrough, but once she'd been evacuated to Scapegoat Farm to live with Mr Renshaw and Maddie, the war had become only something talked about on the wireless and the reason people gave for lack of toffees. Life had become beautiful, with fields and trees and flowers.

Then Max had come into their lives, the refugee released from internment camp, billeted like herself at Scapegoat to work alongside Maddie on the farm. Everything had been light and love with Maddie and Max, until the murderous Australian had interrupted their lives, the man they said was Maddie's cousin.

Maddie had been mother and friend to Eva all these years, loving and honest, adored by Max and trusted by those great Cleveland horses who could have trampled her diminutive figure in a second. No girl could have had a better mother. Eva felt content. It would soon be Christmas. Fay, for all her advantages, was far less blessed than she was . . .

The telephone call took Eva by surprise. Alan came directly to the point.

'Will you come to the going-down ball with me?'

'Why the heck should I? Ask Fay.'

'I want to take you. Will you come?'

'Fay'll be expecting you to ask her – she's the one you've been taking out.'

'I don't have to, just because I've dated her once or twice. I'm asking you. You like me, don't you?'

'Not a lot. You always smell of beer.'

Eva heard a soft laugh at the other end of the line. 'I know why you fascinate me – you keep a man guessing.'

'I don't keep you guessing at all – I've told you flatly no, and that's it.'

'Tell you what then,' he went on smoothly, 'if you won't

come to the ball, how about letting me take you for a ride in the car?'

Eva heard her own voice, small and suspicious. 'What for? And where to?'

'Anywhere you like. Just to talk and get to know each other better. No strings, I promise.'

'You'll take Fay to the ball?'

'OK, if you say yes.'

'I'll think about it.'

'Didn't you say you live up the Dales somewhere? I could drive you up home at the end of term.'

'You're not going to stay at our house,' she said fiercely.

'I'm only suggesting taking you there. Can't be any harm in that, can there?'

Eva swallowed hard. 'I'll think about it,' she said, and hung up.

'I'm going to the ball with Alan,' Fay announced delightedly. 'I'll be able to wear the new gown I wore to Claridge's. Oh, isn't life wonderful?'

After she'd gone Zoe turned to Eva. 'She's never going to pass. Just think, Alan Finch scraped a third-class degree, yet Fay's a damn sight brighter than he is and she'll wind up failing. There ain't no justice.'

'Alan did English,' said Eva. 'Everyone knows it's a doddle.'

'He never does a stroke of work. Does nothing but play rugby, drink and chase girls. Waste of space, he is.'

'He's not bad really,' said Eva. 'He was very nice to me after Kath Davis's accident.'

Zoe's eyebrows arched. 'You're the last person I expected to hear defending Alan Finch.'

'I'm not defending him. I just don't think he's completely rotten, that's all.'

56

Zoe sighed. 'You've been taken in like all the rest. Next thing we know you'll be as smitten as Fay.'

'Don't talk so daft,' said Eva. 'He's offered me a lift home, that's all.'

Zoe looked up sharply. 'Will you tell Fay?'

'I haven't said I'll take it yet.'

'You're playing with fire, you know. You're out of your depth with that bloke.'

'Shut up,' said Eva. 'You don't know what you're talking about.'

'I've told you, you're asking for trouble. Don't come running to me when you're lovesick.'

'I won't,' said Eva, 'because it won't happen. Not for centuries yet, and even then not with Alan Finch.'

The day was sunny and mild for the time of year. Alan drove confidently, one hand on the steering wheel and dark eyes flicking to his passenger and back to the road again as they talked.

Eva relaxed against the seat, enjoying the countryside slipping past the window, feeling a gradual bloom of anticipation as grey city streets gave way to open countryside and the distant prospect of purple hills. Already she was visualizing Maddie's eager embrace and Max's smile, the familiar smell of Scapegoat Farm's kitchen, and the rub of the old sheepdog against her legs.

'Penny for 'em,' said Alan.

'Oh, nothing. Just thinking of home.'

'Miss it much? I never do.'

'You live at home – that's different.'

He shrugged. 'I didn't miss it when I was in the army – quite the opposite. Enjoyed the freedom. Don't you?'

'I suppose so, but then I always felt free at home.'

He gave her a quick sidelong glance. 'Girls usually

complain they need space to spread their wings. Too much restriction at home.'

'Not mine.'

'Parents too busy doing their own thing?'

Irritation prickled her. 'No. They love me, they understand people's needs.'

He nodded. 'Spoilt. I see.'

'You don't see at all. Change the subject.'

'All right then. Will you go out with me?'

'I am out with you.'

'I mean steady. I rather fancy you, Eva.'

'But I don't fancy you. Change of subject again.'

She heard a long, slow sigh as he negotiated a bend in the road. As he straightened up the wheel he spoke quietly. 'Look, stop mucking about, Eva. I know you like me else you wouldn't be here. I've got a car –'

'Your dad's car.'

'And loads of girls would jump at the chance –'

'Then give it to them. I don't want it.'

He sighed again. 'Look, I know you've been seeing that drama chap, but he's far too old for you.'

'Girls mature faster than boys – medical fact. We need older men.'

'Eva! For Christ's sake! I'm trying to tell you I want you – I think you're the most fascinating woman I've ever laid eyes on – I don't know what it is but you've got something –'

'And I'm keeping it,' Eva interrupted firmly. 'You're a cheat, a liar, and you've got a head the size of a bucket. Want me to spell it out any more? You make me bloody angry.'

Alan grinned. 'Now you're getting excited – that's good. But don't you know it's bad for you to get excited and then stop? People ought to satisfy their natural feelings or it becomes a strain on the heart.'

'My heart's in good shape, thank you. No, don't bother pulling up – I want to get home.'

'What's the matter with you?' he teased. 'Afraid of your natural instincts, is that it?'

Eva sighed. 'Do you ever think of anything else besides sex?'

Alan considered. 'Not since I was eight and I fell in love with Beryl – we had the record for the longest kiss in our street. Until my brother beat my record with the same girl – I never forgave him for it.'

Eva sat up. 'Look, we're coming into Agley Bridge – Barnbeck is the next village. Now, just shut up about your randy appetite and concentrate on the road.'

Alan put his foot down harder on the accelerator and smiled. 'Playing hard to get – I know you fancy me really.'

Eva turned to face him and took a deep breath. 'Now just let's get this straight, Alan Finch, before we go any further. You may think you can wrap girls round your little finger – well, Fay may think you're OK but I think you're a lazy, randy, self-centred Casanova.'

'That's a bit strong.'

'I wouldn't touch you with a barge pole if you were the last ruddy lad in college. Got it?'

He was laughing as he turned into the sharp incline that fell away from the packhorse bridge down into the valley.

'OK,' he chuckled. 'You've had your chance. I'll have Fay instead of you then. She's prettier, and richer.'

'You can do as you bloody well like. Only slow down at this crossroad or you'll have us both in the ditch.'

Alan pressed the accelerator down to the floor. At that moment Eva caught sight of the cart coming towards them, its bulk filling the centre of the narrow road.

'Watch out!'

She could see the startled face of the driver as Alan,

realizing that the space either side of the cart was too narrow to pass, swung the car sharply round into the lane to the left and careered over the bumpy road towards the dry-stone wall. The back wheels slithered and the car swung violently. Alan swore and Eva felt her heart leap into her throat as she heard the crunch of metal against stone.

The car's rear end sank into the ditch, dragging it to a halt. Alan switched off the engine. Eva pushed the car door open and jumped out.

'You stupid bugger – you could have killed us both! I'm off.'

She reached into the back seat to grab her case, then began to run downhill towards Barnbeck and the outline of Scapegoat Farm silhouetted against the moor. Behind her she could hear Alan's cry.

'Eva! Wait for me – I'm sorry!'

Maddie's keen eyes missed nothing. She looked as slim as ever in jodhpurs and riding jacket, watching Alan explaining to Max about his predicament.

Max nodded. 'A tractor's what you need. Come along with me.'

Maddie held her tongue until Max and Alan had disappeared together down the lane.

'That young man couldn't take his eyes off you,' she observed as she poured tea from the huge brown teapot. 'Is there something going off between you two?'

Eva felt the blush rising to her cheeks. 'Don't talk daft – he's Fay's boyfriend.'

'Fay's or not, he quite fancies you,' said Maddie. 'But the point is, do you fancy him?'

'No,' said Eva sharply. 'He's not my type. I just took advantage of a lift, that's all.'

*

Christmas passed in a haze of holly berries and home-made plum pudding, midnight carols in the squat old church in the village and presents under the pine tree in the parlour. The aroma of boiling ham mingled with the scent of the pine needles, and cards from friends and neighbours littered the room.

Eva felt again the sense of peace and contentment that always stole over her in Maddie and Max's company. It would have been pleasant to see Eunice again, but Mrs Sykes seemed almost proud that her daughter was away for Christmas. She stood talking to Eva outside the village church, twiddling the gleaming new ring on her finger which had been her Christmas gift from her husband.

'Arnold – that's Eunice's fiancé, you know, Arnold Butler – wanted her to spend Christmas with his family. Lovely house they've got, Eva, detached, with a built-on garage for Mr Butler's Bentley. Such a nice class of people. Family firm of solicitors. You'll be sure to come to the wedding, won't you, dear?'

'I'd love to,' said Eva. 'Where's the reception to be?'

'Otterley Hotel,' said Mrs Sykes. 'It would have been cheaper at the Co-op and there'd have been the divvy too, but as I said to Edward, our daughter only gets married once. I wouldn't want the Butlers to think we did things on the cheap.'

It was just before spring term was due to start. Eva was sitting at the kitchen table talking while Maddie ironed when Max came in, brushing sleet off his jacket and sitting down at the table. Maddie brewed tea and Eva leaned forward, elbows on table.

'I want to talk to you,' she said quietly. 'I didn't mean to, but I need to.'

Max stopped unlacing his shoes to listen. Maddie nodded. 'Talk if you want to, love.'

61

'Remember me telling you about that girl in my German class, the one I didn't like? Kath Davis?'

'I remember,' said Maddie. 'The dark girl with the biting tongue.'

'She got burnt on Bonfire Night. Torch in her face, set fire to her hair. I did it.'

Maddie looked concerned. 'What a dreadful thing to happen! Oh, love!'

'It was an accident,' said Eva.

'We know that,' murmured Max. 'But it must have upset you badly even if you didn't like her.'

'Trouble is, I wished it on her,' said Eva quietly. 'Remember Ronnie?'

Eva saw Maddie glance quickly at Max and for a moment there was silence around the table. Then Maddie smiled and patted her arm. 'That was a long time ago, love. It's pure coincidence, that's all.'

'That's right,' said Max firmly. 'Don't let's get superstitious about these things.'

Eva shook her head. 'It worries me all the same. Do you think some people can really hex other people?'

Max sighed. 'Some cultures believe that,' he admitted slowly. 'Voodoo, for instance –'

'Oh Max, I don't like being able to wish people dead – or hurt – it frightens me!'

Maddie laid a hand over Eva's. 'Eva – that's nonsense! Anyway, this girl didn't die, did she? You mustn't think such things.'

Eva covered Maddie's hand with her own. 'It really scares the hell out of me, Maddie. I seem to have this terrible power . . .'

Max leaned over towards her. 'It won't work, Eva – not unless you really believe in it. Disbelieve it, and the power cannot work.'

She stared at him for a moment, and slowly the anxiety faded from her eyes. 'Thank you, Max. You always talk sense. Anyway, forget it now. I've got over it.'

She rose quickly. Maddie's gaze fixed on her face. 'Are you sure, love? Have you really got it out of your system?'

Eva gave her a bright smile and tugged her hands. 'All gone, I promise. Let's go and see Damsel – hasn't she grown a lot since I went away?'

Zoe searched her father's face as they sat in the kosher restaurant waiting to be served. There were streaks of grey now in the black of his beard, she noticed, matching in perfect symmetry the greying temples.

'So I said to her, lady, take my word for it, be happy with what you got. If I gave you two hats, I'm asking you, wouldn't you say then you got a double headache?'

'Maybe the hat really was too tight?' said Zoe.

'So she buys a hat too small for her – am I to blame?'

'Did you change it for her?'

Louis Jacob shrugged plump shoulders. 'I ask you, here I am trying to pay off my bills and she wants to play swapping games. I got more feathers and net and flowers to buy. Kosinski asked me today when am I going to pay him and I say, what am I, a fortune-teller?'

'Business hasn't been so good lately then?'

Her father spread his hands. 'Better you don't ask, princess. What sin did I commit to have such a rotten season? Even my customers who don't pay their bills have stopped coming in.'

Zoe smiled. 'You always say that.'

'Well, now Chanukah is over, maybe business will pick up again. Your mother will soon be back in the workshop and all will be well.'

'It's not like her to stay in bed like this,' said Zoe. 'Has she complained about this pain before?'

Louis pouted thick lips. 'From time to time, but always she says it is nothing. She asks every day about you and the Flaxman boy – can't you tell her good news about him?'

Zoe shook her head. 'I'm sorry, Papa. He's no better than the Kosinski boy for me. If you want to see me well-off, you'll have to tell me the way to make my own fortune, I'm afraid.'

Her father leaned across the table, wagging a forefinger. 'You want to make a million? That's easy.'

'Easy? How?'

'You buy a million bags of flour at a pound each and sell them for two pounds each.'

He leaned back, easing his weight on the chair and smiling to see his daughter's laugh, then turned and beckoned to the waitress. 'Waitress! The menu, please.'

The waitress glanced over her shoulder, dark eyes dancing under the neat cap. 'Menus we don't serve. You want to read, go to the library.'

Valerie Bartram-Bates lay in bed, blinking against the January sunlight streaming across the satin sheets.

'Draw the curtains again, there's a dear, or I'll have one of my migraines starting.'

Fay did as she was told and then came back to stand by the bed. Every day since she had come home for Christmas her mother had had either a nervous headache or kept fanning her face with *The Times* because of her hot flushes. She seemed to be getting them far too frequently these days.

'Sit down, dear. I want us to have a little talk.'

Fay pulled the little damask dressing stool closer and sat down. Her mother heaved herself higher on the pillow.

'Have you seen much of your father this term?'

'Not a great deal. He did ask me to go to Oxford with him.'

'And did you go?'

'No.'

'Pity,' said Mrs Bartram-Bates distantly. 'He could hardly take that chit of a girl with him.'

Fay's eyebrows rose. 'What girl?'

'It's come to my ears – no matter how, as it's a roundabout story – but I've heard he's having a liaison with a first-year student. So ridiculous, at his age and with his position to uphold.'

Fay could not hide the shock she felt. 'Daddy – and a girl? Oh no, I don't believe it!'

'I agree, it's not characteristic of him, my dear. I can only imagine it must be his age. Middle-aged men are prone to indiscretions if the temptation arises.'

'Are you sure though, Mother? It could be just malicious rumour.'

'I'm afraid you'll have to believe it – my source is highly reliable. There's no doubt about it. I shall have to consider seriously what to do.'

'You're not thinking of divorcing – oh no, you can't!'

Her mother regarded her with serious eyes. 'Your brother thinks I should.'

'Oh no, you can't break up – you need him.'

'Why not? I'm quite independent, you know, despite my health. In fact, I rather suspect now that it was my private income which attracted him in the first place. We have very little else in common.'

'Daddy's not like that – he never gives a thought to money!'

'Because he hasn't needed to. But Clive feels he has played fast and loose too long on my money.'

'Fast and loose? He's never done this kind of thing before! Oh Mother, I can't think why you married him when you think so badly of him. You must have loved him once.'

Valerie Bartram-Bates sighed deeply. 'I told you, Fay. We met on a cruise before the war. What I didn't tell you was that

I let him seduce me. When I learnt I was pregnant I had very little choice in the matter.'

'I never knew. Why didn't you tell me?'

'One doesn't like such things to be generally known. Shotgun marriages are very non-U, my dear. In our circle we simply have premature babies.'

Fay took a deep breath. 'Is this what you wanted to tell me, Mother?'

'No. I wanted to know if you knew about this girl, if she was the kind who could be bought off, kept quiet in some way.'

Fay shook her head miserably. 'I knew nothing.'

'Disgusting at his age. One would think he'd be past all that by now – he's more than twice her age! It's humiliating. He leaves me no choice but to divorce him.'

Fay sat up sharply. 'But that's against the faith, Mother – the Church doesn't recognize divorce. Anyway,' she added as a thought struck her, 'even if Clive was born by accident, you had me after. Surely you loved him then?'

Her mother darted a look of scorn at her. 'Love? That was wifely duty, my dear. Your father always claimed his conjugal rights from time to time, and one has to fulfil one's duty. Even that stopped in time.'

Fay could only look at her mother in horror. Two people who bore no love for each other . . . A child born not out of love but of duty . . .

'Yes, even that stopped,' her mother murmured in a far-away voice. 'He much preferred reading all those books of his. I used to say that Lady Print was his mistress. I never thought he'd take a real one.'

'Stop it, Mother!' Fay cut in. 'I can't bear it!'

Her mother turned large, sad eyes upon her. 'Ah, you're far too trusting, Fay. You'll have to grow wise in the ways of the world, and the ways of men in particular. I hope you'll never make the mistake of trusting too far as I did.'

Tears were beginning to trickle down Fay's cheeks. 'Mother, can't you find it in your heart to forgive him? Please, try and think kindly of him.'

Her mother patted her hand. 'Even if I could forgive, my dear, I could never forget. Go now and let me sleep a while. Tell Aunt Daphne I shan't be coming down to dinner. I might have a little soup later on.'

Fay paused in the doorway and turned. 'I think you're wrong, Mummy. I think you'll regret it one day.'

CHAPTER SIX

It was Sunday afternoon in Needler Hall. A pink dressing-gowned figure came shuffling down the corridor, pale blue eyes gazing anxiously into Eva's.

'Eva, I've got to talk to someone. I've stayed in bed all morning worrying about it. It's my heart, you see. It definitely kept skipping a beat when I first woke up.'

'Imagination, Jill. Forget it.'

'Oh no, I didn't imagine it. I talked to my mother just now on the phone, and she said I definitely need it seeing to. What do you think?'

'I think she's right, Jill. Your heart definitely needs seeing to.'

The girl's face clearly registered relief. 'I am glad. I'll make an appointment to see Dr Thomas first thing tomorrow.'

She wandered off, the anxious expression now replaced by a contented smile. Eva shook her head and went on her way.

Fay danced into the entrance hall, peeling off her coat.

'I've had such a wonderful afternoon with Alan, out in the country. He says he missed me over the vac.'

Happiness glowed in her eyes and she chattered excitedly as they walked down the corridor to her room. 'I've never known anyone so tender before. I feel so happy it's ridiculous.'

She tossed her coat over a chair and then suddenly the glow faded from her face. 'Strange, but I can't help feeling sometimes that Heaven must be preparing some great unhappiness for me.'

'What the devil are you talking about?'

'Being so happy – I'm sure God will punish me later.'

Eva stared at her. 'What rubbish! I never heard anything so wicked in all my life.'

'It's wicked to enjoy yourself. That's what I was taught.'

'A fat lot of good your religion's done for you if it leaves you with a sense of sin about everything.'

Fay was staring out of the window at the sunlit garden. 'What's your vision of God then, Eva? Doesn't He punish you?'

Eva snorted. 'Not for enjoying life, that's for sure. My God's a nebulous thing – the power of good over evil.'

'Simple, uncomplicated thinking,' murmured Fay.

'Far better than your torturous sin-soaked ideas. No wonder you're mixed-up.'

Fay turned to look at her, cocking her head to one side and fair hair tumbling over her shoulders. There was a wary look in her eyes as she spoke. 'You know, sometimes you make me feel uneasy, Eva.'

'Uneasy? Why?'

There was a slight frown on Fay's forehead. 'There's just something about you that makes me shiver at times. A sort of dark power. It's the sort of thing the nuns used to warn us against.'

With an almost imperceptible movement she made the sign of the cross.

Eva felt uneasiness rising in her. 'What a load of rubbish you do talk, Fay!'

Fay shook her head. 'I can't help it – I feel it's like the power of the devil. I almost feel God will punish me for our friendship.'

Eva stood silent, feeling a shiver run down her spine. 'If you ask me, you've been watching too many horror films lately.'

Fay stood up. 'I'm sorry, Eva. I only sense it now and again.'

Slim fingers were touching the crucifix about her neck. Eva came close. 'I'd hate to lose your friendship.'

Fay hung her head. 'I've no idea why I should suddenly come out with that tonight, after I'd had such a lovely time with Alan too.'

'You're really very fond of him, aren't you?'

Fay's expression grew tender. 'He's the first man who's liked me for myself, as I am. He was telling me about how he enjoyed country life, because he'd been up in the Dales this vacation.'

'Yes. He gave me a lift home at the end of term.'

Fay sat down abruptly on the bed. 'He took you home? You didn't tell me.'

'Didn't he tell you?'

'No.' Fay's forehead rutted in thought for a moment, then she looked up. 'How could you do that, Eva? You knew he was my boyfriend.'

'I didn't think you'd mind. I'm sorry. It was only a lift. He dropped me off, and that was all.'

'I see. First Daddy, then you . . .'

'No! You've got it all wrong! Honestly.'

'Good night, Eva.'

Fay struck a match, touched it to the little night-light candle on the bedside table, then swung her legs into bed and pulled up the bedcovers. Eva stood hesitantly by the door.

'We are still friends, aren't we, Fay? I wouldn't hurt you for the world – you must believe that.'

From under the bedclothes came a small, muffled voice. 'I hardly know what to believe any more. Please go now, Eva, and let me sleep.'

'I'm not going to change my mind, I'm afraid, Fay. And it's hardly your duty to judge my actions.'

'But she's younger than I am, Daddy – what can you possibly see in her?'

Bartram-Bates sighed. 'Something that's always been lacking in my life – warmth and vitality, excitement.'

'But you were never like that! Mummy used to say you were always happy just with your books.'

'Of necessity, my dear. Your mother only knows how to give affection to Clive. But you already know that.'

Dr Bartram-Bates did not pause in his packing, conscious that his daughter was near to tears behind him. A woman's tears he could not handle.

'But what about Mummy? She needs you.'

Her voice was so faint it was almost indistinguishable. He folded a shirt neatly and laid it in the suitcase.

'She doesn't need anyone, Fay, least of all me. Just so long as she has Clive, she has all she needs. Now, hadn't you better be getting back to your books? You mustn't neglect your work.'

He was aware of her hesitant figure in the doorway. 'Are you sure about this, Daddy? Isn't there some way –'

'No,' he answered firmly. 'Your mother and I have our own lives to lead now, separately.'

He straightened and caught sight of her reflection in the mirror. He turned to his daughter, uncertain how to phrase his words. 'You'll be all right, Fay. Just do well in your examinations and the future will take care of itself.'

'Why must you go now?'

'To avoid being formally dismissed. I'd hate that.'

'Where will you go?'

'I don't know yet. I'll contact you.'

She was standing, staring at him helplessly. Again he tried to find the words he wanted to say.

'Fay – I want you to know – we have to do what we want with our lives – it's not that I don't care – about you, I mean . . . Oh hell! I do wish you well, Fay, truly I do. And I hope you do the same for me.'

She moved forward into his arms, letting her head rest on his shoulder but avoiding letting her face touch his. He could feel warmth on his shoulder, but whether of tears or not he could not tell. After a few seconds he stepped back and held her at arm's length.

'No tears now, Fay. Stiff upper lip and all that.' She almost ran from the room. John Bartram-Bates gave a deep sigh, then picked up his travelling alarm clock and placed it carefully in the suitcase.

On Saturday afternoon Eva played netball. When the match ended, exhilarated and without waiting to shower with the others, she cycled away from the courts, eager to see David.

There was a note pinned to the door of his flat.

'The key is at Bob's if you should call. I'll be back about six. Love, D.'

There was a coinbox telephone on the grimy wall of the entrance hall. Eva fished in her pocket for a couple of pennies.

'Zoe? I'm at David's. He's not in, so I think I'll have a bath and shampoo here till he get's back. Won't be in for dinner – OK?'

'What've I told you about playing with fire? Being in a lecturer's flat –'

Eva laughed. 'You know me – I like men who're mad, bad and dangerous to know. See you later. Oh – by the way – we won six-two.'

The young man in the flat next door handed over the key with a cheery smile. 'No, he didn't say where he was going. Just that he'd be back about teatime.'

David Maynard glanced up as he neared the gate. Disappointment filled him that there was no light at the window.

He climbed the stairs and unlocked the door. As he pushed it open his breath caught in his throat. The room was in darkness but for the glow of the gas fire, and sitting on the rug before it, her legs curled round to one side of her, was Eva.

She was swinging her head slowly from side to side, letting the cascade of golden-red hair sway before the fire's heat. She was incredibly beautiful. Suddenly she looked up.

'David! You're early.'

Uncurling her legs she stood up, eagerness and surprise in her eyes. David could feel his heart thumping. She glanced from him to the clock, then smiled.

'What a bloody useless clock you've got – it's stopped. Did you forget to wind it?'

She walked into the bedroom and switched on the light. He could not help admiring the graceful way she moved. He let the raincoat slide off his arm to the floor and followed her.

She sat at the dressing table and began combing her hair. He came to stand behind her, kissing the top of her head, damp and sweet-smelling with shampoo. She was enticing, so clean, so wholesome and exciting . . .

He pulled her to her feet and held her close. 'I might have caught you naked,' he murmured. 'Would you have been embarrassed?'

'Why should I be? It's natural. We never worried about it at home. I missed you, David,' she said. 'The flat seemed empty without you.'

David reached out a hand to unfasten the top button of her shirt. She laid a hand over his and he pulled her close. A strange, long-forgotten sensation rose in him, a wild excitement that was headier than wine. He could feel the warmth of her body against his and her fingers buried in the hair at the nape of his neck.

'I love you, Eva. Oh God, I never thought I'd fall in love again.'

She smiled as he bent his head to kiss her, and it delighted him that the eagerness in her kiss matched his own. When she moved away he ran his fingertips over the curve of her breast.

'Where were you today, David? I missed you. You didn't tell me you were going anywhere.'

He took a deep breath. 'I went to London. For an interview.'

She looked up at him, surprise in her clear green eyes. 'For a job? Whatever for?'

'It's with a theatre company – assistant stage manager.'

She frowned. 'That's a step down, isn't it? You've got a damn good job here. What is it, David?' She looked at him closely. 'You didn't tell me anything about it.'

'I couldn't.'

'Couldn't?' Eva stared in surprise. 'I thought we had no secrets from each other – I thought we promised.'

His voice was distant, sad as an echo on the moor. 'Some secrets are best left unsaid, Eva – they hurt too much.'

Eva shivered, filled with apprehension. *We can't tell Fay – you can't break a heart without hurting.*

He took her gently by the shoulders. For a moment they held each other's gaze and she could see the sorrow like stagnant water in the depths of his eyes.

'What is it, David? You've got to tell me.'

He took a long, slow breath. 'Eva, more than anything in the world right now I want to make love to you. I never meant it to come to this.'

'David –'

He laid a finger to her lips. 'Eva, I'm married.'

She broke away from him. 'Married? Oh God! Why the hell didn't you tell me?'

She swung away from him, shivering uncontrollably. His voice came low and penitent.

'I'm sorry. I couldn't help falling in love with you.'

74

'I see. I was just a pastime.' Her words came slowly, each one hanging heavily on the quiet evening air. 'Now you're going to run off to London to get away from me.'

'To be near her.'

She turned back to him, anger and scorn welling inside her. 'Bugger you, then. Clear off to London. You can fry in hell for all I care. I hope you bloody well do.'

She turned away abruptly and, without a backward glance, marched out of the room.

Zoe's face was pale. 'It's Fay, Eva – her dad's gone off with that Josie Caldwell. All college is talking about it, and she's locked herself in her room. Try and talk to her, for God's sake – she won't let me in.'

Fay did not answer Eva's knock at the door. Eva tried the handle, but the door was locked.

'Fay – please – let me in.'

Seconds passed, and then Eva heard the key turn in the lock. The door opened, and Fay turned away as she went in.

'Why have you locked yourself in?'

Fay's answer came in a low, strangled voice. 'I was locking the world out.'

'You haven't been near college all day,' said Eva. 'Look, I know you don't want to talk, but we are your friends, Zoe and I.'

Fay sat down wearily on the bed. 'Daddy's gone off with that girl. I tried to talk to him, but he wouldn't listen.'

'I know how you feel. He didn't mean to hurt, I'm sure.'

'He can't really love that girl – he didn't love Mother and he can't have loved me. Now I can't be sure of anything. I don't know what to believe of people any more.'

Eva sat down on the bed beside her and put her arm around the girl's slender shoulders. 'You've got to stop feeling so sorry for yourself, Fay. Other people are much worse off than you.'

Fay gave a thin smile.

'Come on now,' said Eva firmly, 'what are you afraid of?'

Fay shook her head. 'I don't know – not being loved, I suppose. Not knowing whom to trust any more. Even Alan –'

Eva stood up and walked across to the desk where a pack of cards lay. 'Trouble with you, Fay, is you don't feel worthy of being loved, and that's daft.'

Eva began building the cards into a house. Fay watched as she leaned them carefully together.

'What do you know about it, Eva? Have you ever known what it is to be let down? To have someone you really trusted suddenly run out on you?'

Eva continued piling the cards without answering. Fay went on. 'It's all very well for you – you know for a fact your father won't let you down. But mine did, Eva – running off with a girl younger than me. Imagine it!'

Eva spoke quietly. 'I do know how you feel, honestly, but you've just got to get on with life.'

Fay was not listening. 'There's no reason why tutors and students shouldn't be friends – you and David are, but there's no question of any funny business – why couldn't he have done that?' She stood up. 'Thanks for coming anyway, Eva. I know you meant it kindly.'

'I know I'm right,' said Eva fiercely. 'When you're let down, you've no one else but yourself. Life's what you make of it.'

As Eva went out the house of cards shivered in the draught, and as the door closed behind her it gave a final, shuddering quiver and collapsed into a heap on the desk.

Professor Zetterling blinked shortsightedly at his notes and then back to Eva. 'I saw you last term, according to my notes, Miss Bower.'

'You said you'd review the situation again this term.'

He gazed down again helplessly at his papers. An expert in his own field he might be, but the day-to-day practicalities of life were almost too much for him.

'My grades, sir. They have improved, haven't they? I can sit for Finals.' The eagerness in the girl's tone was most gratifying.

'Ah yes, that was it! The matter of the examinations – well, your grades are much improved now – I see no reason now why you should not sit your Finals, none at all.'

'Thank you, sir. You won't be sorry, I promise.'

He looked up again and peered at the copper-haired girl. He remembered her now, the one who always argued in class, the one who always held strong opinions which differed from received opinion. Disruptive at times; still, there was always one student who was a handful and conformity was not everything. She could argue a logical case and might well impress the external examiners at that.

'Very well. Thank you for coming, Miss Baker. Good day.'

It was as she was leaving the room that he recalled it was teatime. Now, for some reason he wanted to take tea in the Senior Common Room with his colleagues today – what was it?

And then he remembered. That seedy-looking lecturer with the buck teeth from the Physics Department had told him there had been some dreadful scandal about Dr Bartram-Bates. Something about a girl student in the Music Department. Professor Zetterling tried hard to remember the last time there had been gossip such as this in the college – the time a Maths student was found to be cheating, was it?

He shuffled his papers together and stowed them away carefully under a dusty copy of *John Bull*. Tea in the Senior Common Room should prove an interesting affair today.

The weeks passed. Eva took great care to avoid seeing David again and on the two occasions that he telephoned she refused to take the calls. A letter with his neat handwriting on the envelope was thrown, unread, into the wastepaper bin.

Despite her firmness Eva felt an aching void in her life without him. Neither Zoe nor Fay, preoccupied with their own worlds, questioned her and she buried herself in her books. When spring sunlight began to pour into the windows she could sense the gloom of winter lifting and was glad.

It was Zoe who first mentioned his name.

'Someone said David Maynard's left, gone to London or something. Haven't heard you talk about him lately,' she remarked.

'He got a job in a theatre,' Eva said shortly.

Zoe's eyes missed nothing. 'And you aren't keeping in touch? What's up?'

'He's married. End of story.'

'That explains why you haven't been going out. Why didn't you tell us?'

Eva shrugged. 'Couldn't talk about it then, don't want to now.'

Zoe was too shrewd to question further. 'Well at least there's nothing to distract us from work now.'

'Why did you finish with Colin Flaxman, Zoe?'

'He just didn't turn me on. You know what I mean.'

Eva nodded. 'Has there ever been a man who really did things for you – you know, made a shiver run down your spine whenever you looked at him?'

Zoe smiled. 'The ones who do are always either up to no good or spoken for – or both.'

Eva considered for a moment. 'Have you met Fay's mum?'

'No – why?'

Eva shrugged. 'Just wondered. What kind of woman is it that a lecturer runs out on?'

★

Easter was approaching and there was a cool freshness in the air and an atmosphere of promise. Eva sat one evening pencilling in answers to *The Times* crossword puzzle while Zoe was cutting her toenails.

'Fay seems a lot happier these days. She's working again,' Zoe commented.

'Well, she's writing a lot, but I bet it's mostly love letters to Alan.'

'Makes a change from all those short stories she used to write. Did you notice, they were always about lost fathers turning up again after years?'

'What do you make of this clue? "Tactful mad policy." I can't figure that out.'

'Diplomacy,' said Zoe quickly. 'It's an anagram.'

'Of course it is. That finishes it.'

Eva laid the newspaper aside just as Fay entered. 'What are you two doing?' she asked.

'Anagrams,' said Zoe, reaching for the nail varnish. 'You any good at them?'

'Try me,' said Fay. 'I used to be good at making words out of a long word, using all the letters – you know, trying to capture the meaning of the long word.'

Eva frowned. 'Oh, I get you. Let's all have a go – piece of paper, three minutes, no more.'

'Right,' said Zoe, replacing the stopper in the bottle. 'Longest word, best definition, wins.'

Heads bowed over papers, brows furrowed in thought. Minutes later Eva slapped her pencil down.

'Right, time's up. What've you got, Zoe?'

'I only made boredom out of bedroom, reminds me of Colin Flaxman.'

'We don't wish to know that. What about you, Fay?'

Fay cocked her fair head to one side. 'Actually, I got two. Which do you want?'

'Both,' said Eva. 'Shortest one first.'

'I got tender names – that's endearments. Eleven letters.'

'Brilliant,' said Zoe. 'What's yours, Eva?'

'Voices rant on – conversation. Twelve letters.'

'Great! You win.'

'No, you don't,' said Fay. 'I got a fourteen.'

The other two gaped. 'Fourteen? What is it?'

'Made in pint pots.'

'Made in pint pots?' repeated Zoe. 'What the hell's that?'

'Disappointment,' said Fay. 'I win.'

CHAPTER SEVEN

The Easter vacation presented a challenge Eva was little expecting. Miss Gaunt, the Barnbeck village schoolmistress, was taken ill and a replacement could not be found for the last few days of term.

'Let me suggest your name to the office, Eva – I'm sure they'd agree.'

'Marvellous opportunity,' said Maddie. 'Since you're going to be a teacher, this will be a great way of cutting your teeth.'

But what had been one of Eva's favourite games as a child, marshalling the other children to sit and obey while she held court in front of her miniature blackboard and easel, did not prove so attractive in real life.

'Sit still! Don't keep running out,' she exhorted the class of lively youngsters. 'No, Rachel, we won't be studying stick insects today – put that away.'

Miss Gaunt seemed amused as she sat up in bed listening to Eva's account.

'And if I ever see that Rachel Swallow again, it'll be too soon,' Eva concluded. 'Never stopped asking questions, and never satisfied with the answers. I just couldn't get on with what I was trying to do.'

Miss Gaunt nodded and smiled. 'There's always one like Rachel. In your day it was you. She's exactly like you were.'

By the end of the week Eva was exhausted. She wrote to Zoe:

'If there's one thing I've decided during this week, it's that

teaching is definitely not for me. What I'll do with my life I don't know now, but it emphatically won't be teaching.'

The highlight of the vacation was Eunice Sykes's wedding to Arnold Butler. Eva could scarcely recognize her harum-scarum companion in mischief, the Eunice who was ever eager to fall in with Eva's wild schemes in the old days. She looked a picture in a haze of white veiling, gazing up with adoration in her eyes at her handsome young bridegroom. Doreen Sykes could not conceal her pride that her son-in-law was a solicitor.

'Arnold is the second Butler in his father's firm of Butler, Battersby and Butler, you know. He'll be senior partner one day when his father retires. Eunice and Arnold have got a lovely house in Middlesbrough. Edward and I are going to stay with them after the honeymoon.'

Summer term began, bringing with it the imminent prospect of Finals. Most of the third-year students were immersed in work to the almost total exclusion of everything else, but Zoe seemed more distant than usual.

'You've been very quiet since we came back,' said Eva. 'What's up with you?'

Zoe shrugged. 'It's Mum – she's not well and it's not like her. Talk to Fay if you're in the mood to chat.'

'She's off out with Alan again. It's all very well for him.'

'Go and talk to Jill Morrison then if you're that stuck. She was unpacking a load of sticking plasters and iodine last I saw of her.'

Eva gave a mock shudder. 'No thanks. There's only so much the human ear can stand. Boy, can she talk!'

Fay came into Eva's room, humming a tune as she sank down on the bed.

'You sound happy,' said Eva.

Fay gave an enigmatic smile. 'I am. You know when I stayed in last night? Well, Alan said he couldn't concentrate on anything. I think he really does care, even if he hasn't actually said so.'

Zoe snorted. 'Don't believe a word of it! He tries on emotions like other men try on shirts.'

'Yes,' agreed Eva, 'usually ones that are too big for him. For heaven's sake keep your mind on the exams.'

'If Alan loves me, nothing else matters,' replied Fay. 'I know what I'm going to do with my life, and the precedent has already been set for me.'

After she'd gone Zoe pulled a face. 'She doesn't know what she's letting herself in for. I heard Alan Finch took a girl from Oates Hall off to Stratford for a dirty weekend in the vacation, but we can't tell her that.'

Eva picked up a sheet of paper from the floor. 'What's this? It must have slipped out of Fay's file.' She read aloud the one sentence written on the sheet.

'The pleasure that comes over me whenever I think of you sets my soul on fire.'

Eva grew anxious. Zoe seemed less perturbed. 'Don't worry, she never gives him the letters. She just files them.'

Eva considered. 'Do you think he's just after her money?'

'What else? I hope by the time Finals are over she'll have come to her senses.'

It was the week before Finals when the telegram arrived for Zoe.

'*MAMA SERIOUSLY ILL STOP COME AT ONCE STOP PAPA*'

As she walked beside her father along the hospital's green-and-white-tiled corridor Zoe felt as if she had been suddenly transported into an unreal world of fantasy. Mama couldn't be dying – it just wasn't possible. Her father's voice was hoarse.

'One minute she is lighting the Sabbath candle, the next she is rolling on the floor, screaming in agony. Renal failure, the doctors say. A hell of a stone blocking the kidney.'

'But she's not going to die, is she?'

'She is very weak, princess, too weak for them to operate. The doctors say there is nothing they can do.'

Miriam Jacob lay in the far bed, nearest the window, tubes from a clamp leading to a drip in her arm. She smiled wearily as her husband and daughter approached.

'Zoe,' she murmured. 'I didn't want they should bother you.'

Louis Jacob stood back, reluctant to let the tears gleaming in his dark eyes be seen. Zoe pulled a chair close to the bed and took her mother's hand. It felt cold as ice.

'Why didn't you tell us you were ill, Mama?' It was hard to keep the sound of tears out of her voice.

'I didn't want I should worry your father when he is so busy.'

'But we should have known – you never told us.'

'At a time like this? It's important you should get your exams and get a good job.'

'You're more important than a job, Mama. We want you well again.'

Miriam shook her head. 'In a laboratory you will meet doctors. I only wish God had spared me long enough to see you married to a good Jewish boy. I would die content if I could see my first grandchild.'

Louis's voice cut in roughly. 'What is this talk of dying? You want I should have to lay out good money on a funeral when I still have all these bills to pay? What kind of selfishness is this? Tell her, princess, tell her I cannot afford a funeral.'

He turned away and walked quickly down the ward. Miriam's lined face softened into a smile. 'Poor Louis. He will be lost without me. He needs a good woman. Listen, Zoe, I

84

want your father should marry again one day – after a decent interval of course. He's not the man to live alone.'

Zoe gripped her hand tightly. 'But you're going to get better, Mama. It's you he needs.'

'He's a wonderful man. Do you know, princess, when he first brought me to this country he promised he would give me diamonds and a gold watch as big as a frying pan. Such a beautiful man.'

'And he will, Mama, when you're better again.'

Miriam's eyes grew tired. 'He needs a woman, but don't let that *yenteh*, that busybody Mrs Kosinski, choose a wife for him. You see he gets a good wife, Zoe, that's all I ask, a woman who will be good to him, someone warm and kind who deserves a man like my Louis.'

A nurse tapped Zoe on the shoulder. 'I think you should go now – Mrs Jacob needs to sleep.'

Zoe bent to kiss her mother's cold cheek, but Miriam's eyes were already closed. Louis was waiting outside the ward and as the two of them walked away down the hospital corridor neither spoke. Zoe knew he was thinking the same overwhelming thought as she – that in all probability she would never see her mother alive again.

It was late that night when the telephone call came. Zoe listened apprehensively as she heard her father's muffled voice in the hallway and then watched as he shuffled back into the living room.

For long seconds he stared at the photographs on the mantelpiece, pictures of Miriam as a young bride, Miriam as a young mother with baby Zoe in her arms . . .

'She's gone,' he said hoarsely. 'She's slipped away.'

He leaned slowly across the table and snuffed out the Sabbath candle, then stood motionless and vacant-eyed. Zoe leapt to her feet.

'Oh, Papa!'

She enfolded his thick body in her arms and for a moment he stood, stiff and unyielding, then subsided gently against her and she felt him begin to shake. Anger and disbelief surged in her, and then after that came a vast, interminable sense of desolation . . .

The night before Finals Zoe came to Eva's room. She pulled off her coat with the black armband on the sleeve and tossed it on Eva's bed.

'Been for a walk to clear my head,' she murmured. 'Couldn't work. Nothing more'll go into my brain now.'

She slumped in the easy chair, gazing into space.

'Come on,' said Eva. 'Things aren't that bad. Tomorrow's the big day, remember.'

Zoe sighed. 'It's not just the exams, Eva. It's Papa – I really am worried about him. He's walking round like a ghost. I don't think he even realized what was going on at the funeral.'

'It's a terrible shame. And what a hell of a time for it to happen. I am sorry.'

'My mind's just not on exams any more. I know I'm going to fail.'

'Rubbish! Now you're talking like Fay!'

Zoe looked up. 'Have you seen her today? I thought she might be upset over Kath Davis being here. You know she's come back, do you, just to sit the papers?'

Eva went pale. 'She's back? No, I didn't know.'

'She's not staying in Needler, don't worry. Poor thing though – her face looks hideous.'

Eva pushed back her chair. Zoe looked up. 'Where are you off?'

'I want to take a walk and think too. It's a lovely warm night.'

'Don't let Kath being here bother you. Forget it.'

Eva made to open the door. 'I know you're right – we owe it to our parents, to ourselves, to do the very best we can. But it's bloody hard going.'

The air was balmy, a slight breeze rustling the leaves of the trees overhead as she walked. Eva felt uneasy, and wished that David was near. His presence had always given her a sense of calm and tranquillity, and she realized how fond she had become of him over the months, without being aware of it. He had been a good friend, had always understood her moods. He would have banished the spectre of Kath Davis's scarred face from her mind. If only he hadn't deceived her . . .

But this was no time to feel regret. David was married; he belonged to someone else and she must concentrate on her own life ahead. Eva steered her thoughts away from him. Tomorrow . . . She suddenly realized how late it was and turned to retrace her steps towards the Hall.

The lane leading up the hill towards Needler Hall was unlit. Spectral shapes of trees materialized out of the darkness and Eva became aware of footsteps behind her, heavy and uneven. She quickened her step, and the footsteps behind quickened likewise, coming closer and closer until they were hard on her heels.

'Well, hi there,' said a voice, and she recognized the deep tone of Alan Finch's voice. 'If it isn't Miss Toffee Nose herself.'

Eva half-turned, and caught the scent of beer on his breath. Before she could speak he had caught hold of her arm.

'Hold on a minute – you're not going to fob me off again,' he muttered. 'I'll teach you you can't tease me and run off. Prick-teasers, that's what we call girls like you.'

Without warning he flung himself at her, knocking her

off-balance so that she fell to the ground. Alan fell on top of her, pinning her down so hard that she gasped for breath.

'Get off, you slob! Let me go!'

His mouth clamped over hers, strangling the words. Eva struggled to free herself, but she was no match for his muscular strength. Before her inward eye she had a fleeting vision of Ronnie, all those years ago, flailing on the ground with Max in just this way and herself, a child of nine or ten, hurling her diminutive body into the fray. Alan's hand was tearing at her skirt, pulling it upwards and his fingers groping underneath.

'Stop it, you bastard, or I'll kill you!'

She was aware of his mouth close to her ear, of his heavy breathing and the sweet fumes of beer in her nostrils. Then suddenly Alan's grip loosened and he sat back on his haunches. Eva scrambled to her knees.

They were both on the ground, Alan's anxious face only inches away from her own.

'I'm sorry,' he grunted. 'I don't know what the hell came over me.'

Eva tossed the tangled mane of hair back out of her eyes and stood up, brushing grass and dust from her skirt.

'You rotten bugger,' she said coldly. 'You disgust me.'

With a coolness that belied the anger and tumult she felt inside, she began walking away towards the Hall, tossing her head as she heard Alan's voice pursuing her.

'I didn't mean it, Eva! I'm sorry!'

Hector was leaning against the Dow's lisle-stockinged leg just outside the front door of Needler Hall. He gave Eva a totally disinterested look before continuing his scrutiny of the rooftops. His mistress nodded to Eva.

'A final breath of fresh air to clear the brain ready for tomorrow?' she enquired. She appeared not to notice the hair all awry and the crumpled frock.

'That's right,' said Eva. 'Getting rid of the cobwebs and rubbish.'

The first day of the examinations dawned hot and brilliant with sunshine. Students in undergraduate gowns mustered outside the examination hall, talking in hushed whispers.

'God, what a day to have to stew in the exam hall,' complained Jill Morrison. 'I swear I can feel one of my migraines coming on, and I haven't any pills with me.'

Eva wasn't listening; she was searching for Fay and Zoe's faces in the crowd. Neither had been at breakfast and it was important to wish them both luck. The clock on the tower of the Arts Building showed five minutes to go before the doors were to open.

Suddenly Zoe's white face appeared at her side. 'Eva – have you seen Fay?'

'No – have you?'

'Not since last night. I went to her room this morning and she wasn't there – but I found this pushed under the door.'

Zoe held out a folded sheet of paper. Eva unfolded it and saw a collection of words cut out of newspapers or magazines interspersed with words printed in pencil in block capitals. Sunlight glared on the white sheet as she read.

You may be pretty, rich bitch, but you will not keep him. It is my intention to see that you fail.

'God,' said Eva. 'What a bloody thing to do, and on the day she starts Finals too.'

'Well at least she doesn't know about it,' muttered Zoe. 'Lucky I got there first. But where on earth is she? They're opening the doors.'

'Don't worry,' soothed Eva. 'They don't lock them again for fifteen minutes. She'll turn up.'

As they joined the swirl of bodies pressing into the doorway Eva squeezed Zoe's arm. 'Good luck,' she murmured.

Zoe returned the squeeze. '*Mazel tov*, my friend. Know something? I've made up my mind, the minute this lot's over I'm going to clear off out of here, go abroad for a while. Want to come with me?'

'We'll see,' said Eva. 'First things first.'

Three hours later the exam ended and Fay had not appeared. Even by nightfall there was still no sign of her and Eva and Zoe were worried.

'Maybe she's done a bunk because she did no work,' said Eva. 'Maybe she's gone home.'

Zoe shook her head. 'Fay's not a coward. Anyway, English is a doddle – she'd have walked it. Even Alan Finch said it was a doddle.'

Eva felt uneasy at the mention of his name.

'He was hanging around here last night,' she told Zoe. 'I wonder . . .'

'Around here?' repeated Zoe. 'Where?'

'Down the lane. I saw him as I was coming home.'

'Odd. She didn't go out last night. Did you talk to him?'

Eva hesitated. 'Not really. He was a bit sloshed – I could smell the beer.'

Zoe cocked her head to one side. 'You were near enough to smell the beer, but you didn't talk? What kind of story is this? What are you hiding, Eva?'

Eva blushed and laughed. 'As a matter of fact, he made a pass at me.'

Zoe rolled her eyes. 'What a Casanova! If only Fay knew. Look, Eva, it's locking-up time and she's still not back. What are we going to do?'

'Nothing,' said Eva. 'She's old enough to decide things for herself.'

'But what if she stays out all night? I know they won't send her down at this late stage, but I'm worried, Eva. And what's more,' she added, 'there's that poison-pen note. Somebody might be planning mischief.'

'Hell – I'd forgotten that,' said Eva. 'If she doesn't come back, we report it to the Dow first thing in the morning.'

Miss Dow's keen eyes narrowed as Eva told the story. 'You say she has been out all night, and there has been no message from her?'

'That's right. It's not like her, and we're worried.'

'And I am alarmed, Miss Bower. You speak of a threatening note under her door. You know, of course, that Miss Bartram-Bates is heiress to a fortune?'

Eva drew in a quick breath. 'Heiress? I hadn't thought of that. You mean – she could have been kidnapped?'

'It is not beyond the realms of possibility, Miss Bower, and I only regret that you did not come to me sooner. The police will have to be informed, and her family. Do you know where her father is now?'

'No,' said Eva miserably. 'Only that he's with Josie Caldwell somewhere.'

'Leave this matter to me, Miss Bower, and get on with your exams. Let me know at once if you hear from Miss Bartram-Bates. Good morning.'

Jill Morrison's pale blue eyes were huge with apology.

'I'm sorry – I had this dreadful migraine after the exam, you see, and I went straight to bed. I clean forgot she asked me to give this to you at dinner.'

Eva took the envelope from her outstretched hand with a shiver of apprehension and tore it open. Jill Morrison hovered behind while she read.

'Dearest Eva and Zoe, I know you will understand when

I tell you that I have gone away with Alan. For the first time in my life I am loved. We are going to Scotland to be married. Nothing in the world matters so much as love. Fay.'

'Not too important, is it?' asked Jill anxiously. 'Only I really was most dreadfully ill last night. Nervous tension, I expect – that always brings on one of my migraines.'

With a sigh Eva retraced her footsteps towards the Dow's office.

Next day in the Arts Building a shadow blocked the passageway. Eva was stepping aside when she made out the face before her in the gloom, a twisted face with a shrunken nose and dark eyes gleaming from their sockets.

'Well, well, if it isn't Miss Eva Jarrett-Bower.' There was no mistaking the mocking voice of Kath Davis. For a moment Eva stood stunned before she found her voice.

'Kath – I'm so sorry.'

'I hear your friend has run off,' Kath went on. It was her voice, but the mouth slanted awkwardly in a darkly-discoloured face. 'Shame,' she said, and the taunting tone stirred Eva to life.

Guilt and anger vied in her, then anger won. 'It wasn't your note that frightened her away,' she retorted. 'You wasted your time.'

The girl stood squarely across the passage, blocking Eva's way. 'No?' she said softly. 'But at least she's gone.'

'She's gone all right – with Alan Finch. Did you know that? They're going to be married?'

'With Alan?' Kath echoed. 'Oh, God!' The rigidity of her body slackened for an instant, and then she stiffened. Words issued from her lips in a sibilant hiss. 'She'll pay for stealing him – and you'll pay for this!'

She stabbed a finger towards the mess that was her face, then abruptly she turned and ran off down the corridor.

The evening of the last exam Eva walked with Zoe in the park as dusk stole over the flowerbeds.

'It's such a shame Fay not getting her degree when she could have walked it,' said Zoe.

'And getting stuck with a sod like Alan Finch for life. She deserved better than that.'

'It's what she wanted,' Zoe pointed out.

'It's what she thought she wanted,' Eva corrected. 'I only hope she doesn't regret it one day.'

Zoe sighed. 'I wonder if any of us knows what we really want. I wonder if we'll ever see her again.'

A deep sadness filled Eva at her words. In a few days now she would be leaving college and friends behind and returning to Barnbeck. The future looked so unclear . . .

She stopped suddenly and turned to Zoe. 'About that trip abroad you mentioned, Zoe – I've made my mind up. I'm coming with you.'

CHAPTER EIGHT

Eva and Zoe tumbled, laughing, off the back of the coal lorry, hauling their suitcases to the side of the tree-lined avenue.

'Well, at least this one didn't try to make a pass at us,' muttered Eva, then she called out to the driver, '*Merci bien, monsieur. Au revoir.*'

The lorry driver waved and drove off down the sunlit road. Zoe pointed at Eva's white shorts and broke out laughing again.

'Well,' growled Eva, 'we were lucky to get a lift at all. Other hitchhikers don't seem to carry big suitcases like us.'

'We'll need a lot of clothes if we're staying in France long. God, it's hot.' Zoe sank down on her suitcase.

'I'll have a go,' said Eva. 'Here's a car coming now.'

The sleek red sports car sped past, ignoring Eva's outstretched thumb.

'Bastard!' said Zoe. 'Lord, my language is getting as bad as yours. Try this white one.'

Behind the steering wheel of the long white limousine Eva could see a middle-aged man and beside him a fair-haired woman. Eva jerked her thumb repeatedly. The car hummed past, then drew slowly to a halt farther along the road.

'Come on,' cried Eva, grabbing her suitcase and running. Zoe tottered after her, puffing with the weight of the case. The woman smiled through the car window. She was young and incredibly elegant, fair hair piled in a smooth chignon, diamond earrings glistening in the sunlight, and an apricot poodle curled on the skirt of her white linen suit.

'Paris?' she said in a low, musical tone. Eva nodded eagerly.

'*Oui, madame. Nous allons à Paris.*'

'*Ah, vous êtes anglaises,*' she said, her pencilled eyebrows rising in pleasure. 'Please get in.'

The poodle on her lap opened one eye, gave the girls the briefest of glances, then returned to his interrupted sleep. The man at the wheel looked back over his shoulder at the immaculate white covers on the car seats, then muttered something to the woman.

'Don't fuss, Robert,' she murmured in French. 'They will be washed.'

The woman introduced herself. 'My name is Chantal Noircy and this is my husband Robert,' she said in slow, precise English. 'We go to our apartment in Paris for tonight and tomorrow we go home to our château.'

'Château?' muttered Zoe, raising her eyebrows.

'Les Pommiers is very beautiful at this time of year,' Chantal went on, 'far more pleasant than Paris. It is too hot in August in the city.'

Everything about the couple spoke of money, even the subtly heady scent of Chantal's perfume. Robert was balding and tending to plumpness, Eva noted, but his shirt and suit were expensive and a diamond pin gleamed in his tie. He must be at least fifteen years older than his wife, she calculated.

'You have a hotel in Paris?' enquired Chantal. 'No? Then you must stay with us for the night. The apartment is spacious, and it is good for me to practise my English.'

The apartment, in a shady courtyard in one of the Parisian suburbs, was indeed spacious and every bit as elegant as its owners. Chantal showed the girls to a silver-and-green bedroom with twin beds canopied with pale green satin drapes and then left them. After they had showered and changed Robert drove them all to a restaurant.

A waiter glided across the lush deep-pile carpet towards them. 'Monsieur has a reservation?' he enquired. 'If not, then I regret . . .'

Behind him appeared the maître d'hôtel. 'Monsieur Noircy, there is a table for you in the corner. This way, if you please.'

Though he spoke no English Robert was a courteous host.

'*Grenouille*? Frog – frogs' legs,' Chantal translated for Zoe. 'You will try some?'

'With what wine?' Robert asked Eva.

'No thanks, not for me.'

'Red or white?'

'No, really, I don't drink very much.'

'And your friend – what will she drink?'

It was clear he would brook no refusal. He himself drank more than he ate, Eva noticed. He poured a different wine with each course and would not take no for an answer. Chantal sipped often but drank little. Eva was beginning to feel lightheaded.

'You have never tried Armagnac?' Robert asked. 'Then you must try some with the dessert. Or cognac – this is my favourite brand.'

'What is he saying?' whispered Zoe. 'Is he saying we've got to drink more booze? I've drunk enough already to sink a battleship. We've drunk a damn good dinner, if you ask me.'

'What is this, drink a good dinner?' asked Chantal. 'I do not comprehend.'

'Just a joke,' said Eva. 'The food is fantastic.'

Chantal frowned. 'Do not allow my husband to make you drink too much. You must try one of the desserts – I recommend the *gâteau aux framboises* – it is delicious.'

'We can't eat any more, truly,' said Eva.

'Then we should go home now and sleep.' Chantal turned to her husband and spoke in rapid French. He nodded and rose, a little unsteadily, and signalled to the waiter.

Zoe stumbled as they made to leave, and giggled to Eva as they clambered into the back of the car. 'I'm tipsy – I'm sure I am. Like that night we tried to get drunk dropping fag ash into our cider, remember?'

The twin beds were blissfully comfortable and within minutes Eva and Zoe were sleeping like children.

Eva suddenly sat bolt upright, startled out of sleep by some sound she could not identify. For seconds she sat there, seeing nothing in the darkness but the high rectangular outline of the window. Then the sound was suddenly repeated – the high, shrill cry of a woman's voice.

'My God!'

Eva leapt out of bed. From the darkness came Zoe's voice. 'Don't go out, Eva. It's none of our business.'

'What do you mean? Somebody screamed – it could be Chantal – we've got to find out if she's all right!'

'No – listen.'

Eva sat on the edge of the bed, shivering in apprehension, every muscle strained for action. Then she heard the voice – a man's, and it was clearly Robert's voice, harsh and imperative, followed by a woman's low murmur.

Then came a sound Eva recognized at once. It was the thud of blows on flesh, sharp cracks and the cry of pain she could recall all too well. She let her face fall between her hands.

'Oh God, he's hitting her!' she moaned.

'I know,' said Zoe quietly. 'I've been listening.'

'But shouldn't we do something? He's much bigger than she is.'

'We have no right,' said Zoe. 'Like I said, it's none of our business. Some women enjoy it.'

'My mother didn't,' said Eva savagely. 'My real mother. She just couldn't stop it.'

'She wasn't in a position to leave, but Chantal could. If she puts up with it, there must be a reason. Now shut your ears and go back to sleep.'

Chantal was strangely composed at breakfast and there was no outward sign of the previous night's occurrence. No bruises marked her flesh that either girl could see, and her behaviour was just as coolly self-possessed as on the day before. She fed titbits from the table to the poodle on her lap.

'We shall go to Les Pommiers tomorrow,' she remarked, signalling to Robert to pass another croissant. 'What would you like to do today? You could accompany me to the fashion salon if you would like that.'

Robert murmured something. Chantal turned to him. '*Nous irons chez Balmain, ou peut-être chez le jeune Yves St Laurent.*'

'*Bien.*'

'Balmain?' repeated Zoe. 'I understood that.'

Chantal smiled. 'Robert wishes me to buy new gowns while we are here, and I would welcome a woman's help. Robert is useless in a salon.'

Zoe's eyes met Eva's and there was a second's pause. 'Yes, we'd love to, wouldn't we, Eva?'

Eva hesitated. 'We should be getting on our way.'

Chantal threw up her hands. 'Ah, but you say you wish to see Paris! Come with me and then Robert will drive us around the city to see the sights. You are not hurrying elsewhere, are you?'

Eva could not bring herself to meet Chantal's enquiring

gaze. 'We – er – we plan to go south, Chantal. We'd like to go to Provence.'

Zoe stared at her. Chantal patted Eva's hand. 'Then you must come with us as far as Les Pommiers, stay a few days, and then after that – *comme vous voulez.*'

She would hear no more excuses. In the car Eva caught sight of the bundle of banknotes Robert thrust into Chantal's hand and which she put away in her handbag without comment.

Outside the salon Robert helped his wife to alight. Eva heard her speak quietly to him in French.

'Return for us at midday, then you can take us to lunch in the Champs Elysees.'

'Wow!' whispered Zoe as they entered the salon. 'I thought the apartment was posh, but this! I'm up to my ankles in carpet!'

Chantal was smiling to see their delight in the perfume-drenched salon with its magnificent crystal chandeliers and elegant gilt *Louis Quatorze* chairs.

'I am curious to see the designs of this new couturier,' she explained, settling the poodle on her lap. 'Yves St Laurent is the new designer, the successor to Christian Dior who, alas, died recently.'

The girls sat beside her on the fragile-looking gilt chairs and watched in wonder as model after elegant model paraded before Chantal. They all wore waistless dresses and wide-brimmed hats. The stern-faced woman in black standing beside Chantal bent to murmur a commentary as each model appeared. Occasionally Chantal nodded.

'Monsieur's new line this year is the Trapeze line,' the woman was saying. 'Very original, and so becoming to all figures.'

'Looks just as shapeless as the Sack to me,' muttered Eva.

'Funny how they all look alike,' said Zoe. 'Every one of those po-faced girls looks like Barbara Goalen.'

'I wasn't looking at the faces,' replied Eva. 'Just the frocks. Didn't think much of them, even if they do cost a fortune. Not my cup of tea.'

'Nor mine,' agreed Zoe. 'But they're not meant for the likes of us.'

'Time somebody did come up with something for people like us,' muttered Eva. 'Something exciting instead of all this boring stuff.'

The final model glided down the staircase, a willowy brunette wearing a swirling, strapless, black chiffon ball-gown and long white gloves. She stood, hand on hip, staring aloofly at her audience. Chantal clapped her hands.

'*Parfait!*' she cried. 'I'll have it.' She turned to the woman in black. 'Send the gown to Les Pommiers and the account to my husband as usual.'

'Robert will be *enchanté*,' she remarked with a smile to the girls as they made to leave. 'We are to attend the Minister's ball in September where Robert is to be honoured for his services to industry. He will be so proud of me.'

Glancing at her diamond-studded wristwatch as they emerged into the sunlit street she added, 'We have still an hour to pass. Let us call a taxi.'

The taxi carried them to a less fashionable *faubourg* on the left bank of the river where small shops lined a busy street. Chantal paid off the taxi driver and led the way into a boutique where blouses and gloves and scarves were piled untidily in the window amid a profusion of potted plants.

'I love this little boutique,' she said, 'a little bohemian but so unusual. Robert would not like it at all, but he gave me money to buy some little things.'

Eva and Zoe stared in delight. The colours in the little shop hit the eyes with their brilliance, peacock blue and emerald green, purple and scarlet – colours as gaudy and electrifying as a gipsy caravan. Behind the counter a young man with tousled hair and an open-necked shirt nodded and smiled.

'*Bonjour, mesdames.*'

Above his head Eva could see a poster, a picture of a girl with an untidy mane of long blonde hair blowing in the breeze, her sea-green shirt unbuttoned to the waist and the inner curve of her breasts clearly visible. Zoe pointed.

'Look – Brigitte Bardot – the sex symbol.'

Chantal's gaze followed her pointing finger. '*Oui, elle est belle,*' she murmured. The young man turned to look, elbow leaning on the counter.

'*Magnifique,*' he agreed. 'Madame would like to try on the blouse?'

'You have it?' asked Chantal.

'One exactly the same, madame, in the very same colour.'

'Let me see!'

She handed the poodle to Eva as the young man laid the green blouse on the counter. Chantal fingered it and then, without warning, suddenly threw aside her jacket and unbuttoned her blouse. Eva and Zoe watched, amazed, as she peeled it off and stood there, naked breasts revealed. The shopkeeper's eyes gleamed, but Chantal seemed totally unconcerned, as if unaware of the livid bruises on her back and breasts.

She was about the throw the blouse around her shoulders when she caught sight of Eva's stare. She glanced down at her body ruefully.

'Everything costs,' she said softly. 'Nothing is free.'

The taxi returned them to the salon minutes before Robert arrived. He was sweating profusely.

'The city is too hot,' he grumbled to his wife in French. 'I need a drink.'

He needed several drinks before lunch, several more during lunch, and it seemed to Eva that he never stopped drinking throughout the day until bedtime. During the night she lay awake, half-expecting and half-fearing t hear those dreadful cries again.

'I think she asks for it anyway,' said Zoe before she fell asleep. 'Fancy taking her clothes off in the shop like that!'

'Don't you like her?' asked Eva.

'Yes, she's nice. But I'd be scared to death of him.'

'Like you said, it takes all sorts.'

'Are we still going to Les Pommiers with them tomorrow?'

'We don't have much choice now.'

Eva lay awake far into the small hours, but the night remained silent save for the sound of distant taxi horns and wailing cats.

Robert did not join in the conversation at breakfast. He was deeply immersed in reading a copy of *Le Figaro* while absently sipping black coffee. Eva regarded him across the table, sunlight glistening on his balding head, and marvelled how different he was from his wife. Chantal looked every inch the aristocrat, legs elegantly crossed under her satin negligée, while he looked more like her gardener than her husband.

He looked up suddenly and addressed his wife in French. 'I see those accursed terrorists have been busy again,' he remarked. 'They bombed a shop on the *rive gauche* yesterday.'

'Who, Robert?'

'The Algerians. They still do not accept French sovereignty.'

Chantal shrugged. 'Would we, in their situation?'

'Would we commit an atrocity such as this?' He pushed the newspaper across the table towards her. Chantal picked it up and glanced at the photograph, then shuddered.

'Two women killed,' Robert went on. 'Two innocent victims. They have no regard for human life.'

'*Mon Dieu!*' Eva heard Chantal's quick intake of breath and looked down at the newspaper. The photograph showed the shattered remains of a shop front, the windows blown out and the signboard hanging drunkenly.

'What is wrong?' asked Robert, his eyebrows rising.

'Nothing,' said Chantal quickly. 'I have seen this shop, that is all.'

Eva recognized it then, the little boutique where Chantal had bought the blouse. She saw too the pallor of Chantal's cheeks.

'I wonder if the proprietor was hurt,' said Chantal.

'Injured – leg blown off,' said Robert. 'Imagine, in broad daylight – just after midday! Where were the gendarmes, I ask myself, to let this thing happen? Why do we pay such high taxes?'

'Never mind, we are leaving today,' said Chantal.

'Murderers!' muttered Robert. 'I hope they are caught and executed! They ought to be maimed as they have maimed their innocent victims. There is nothing I should like more than to torture them myself.'

Eva glanced quickly across at Zoe who was completely unaware of what had taken place. Zoe smiled. 'Could I have another croissant, please?'

Chantal's fearful expression faded. 'Of course, my dear. Help yourself.'

Zoe's dark eyes grew round as Eva told her of the newspaper account of the atrocity.

'Yesterday? Just after midday? My God! An hour sooner and it could have been us!'

'Chilling thought,' said Eva. 'We were damn lucky.'

Zoe thought for a moment. 'Wouldn't Fay be amazed if

she knew? She'd never dream we'd be having such an adventure. Poor Fay – I wonder how she's getting on.'

Dr Bartram-Bates stood uneasily by the window in his wife's drawing room, looking out at the London traffic so as not to encounter her accusing face. Nothing on earth would have induced him to answer her summons to visit if it hadn't been for Fay's extraordinary behaviour.

'It's all your fault, John. You should have kept an eye on her, then this wouldn't have happened.'

The aggrieved tone in her voice inflamed him. 'You shouldn't have been so soft with the children, granting them everything they asked.'

'You were near to her all the time, but you dodged all responsibility. You left all the worrying over the children to me. What kind of father is that?'

'You had no time for her either,' he retorted, 'only for your rosary and retreats. You took no more responsibility than I did when it came to it. Really, Valerie, I fail to see what use all this accusation is.'

His wife let the rosary beads fall in her lap and sighed. 'Too preoccupied dallying with your lady friend, a chit of a thing even younger than Fay, that's why you had no time for your daughter. You could at least have let Fay live with you.'

John Bartram-Bates turned to face her, the irritation plain on his handsome face. 'No I couldn't – it was out of the question. Tell me, Valerie, you say you've talked to Fay?'

Valerie answered moodily. 'On the telephone. She rang me from Scotland.'

'Did you tell her we were going to meet?'

'Yes. She said it was pointless discussing it – it was her life and she'd live it the way she liked.'

'That doesn't sound like her.'

Valerie shrugged. 'You don't know your own daughter so

how can you tell? I told her I'd every right to speak my mind when she always comes running to me for money. I told her she'd let us down, not getting her degree and running off with an adventurer.'

John sighed. 'Well, if they marry I suppose we'll have to accept it. There's not much choice.'

Valerie sniffed. 'You may do as you please – you always do, but I won't recognize him. I told Fay that. I said, I'm not going to keep him; you're on your own now.'

'Yes,' said John thoughtfully, 'but then, I think in a way she always was.'

Château des Pommiers was a huge and once-grand edifice a couple of hours' drive south of Paris, its former magnificence now crumbling and fading from neglect. It stood in the heart of a vast wooded park, its colonnaded façade now overgrown and cracked stone urns on the steps to the portico spilling only weeds.

As they entered Eva was aware that the sultry evening air was heavy with the odour of damp and rot. Robert went straight to his study to read the post. Chantal led the girls through the huge vestibule and paused at the foot of the stairs, fingering the balustrade with a loving touch.

'Les Pommiers has been my family's home for generations,' she murmured. 'Unhappily I had not the money to restore it to perfection.'

'But your apartment in Paris is terrific,' said Eva. 'That bedroom we had –'

'That was Robert's home,' Chantal cut in. 'He is a wealthy man. We have begun work here, but there is still much to be done.'

She set the poodle down on the floor. 'Go to the kitchen, Zouzou,' she commanded. 'Marianne will have your supper ready.'

The poodle trotted away into the dark recess beyond the staircase. Chantal smiled at the girls. 'I am happy to be home. This place is part of me.'

Robert did not appear for supper. Chantal seemed dreamy and remote and the girls were willing to go to bed when she suggested it.

Zoe was rooting in her suitcase in the spacious but shabby bedroom as Eva undressed for bed. 'I'm fed up of all these rotten clothes,' she grumbled, flinging a blouse over the chair. 'I hate rotten cardigans – nobody can tell the difference between me and the Dow in them.'

Eva surveyed the contents of her suitcase. 'Me too,' she agreed, pulling out a handful of shirts. 'And this skirt' – she flung it the length of the bedroom – 'I'd be happy if I never saw it again – or these socks – or this mouldy old petticoat.'

Zoe laughed as the garments sailed through the air, then shook her head. 'Must be nice to be like Chantal. Can you imagine her wearing these scruffy shorts?'

'No. She's too classy a lady,' agreed Eva. 'Her clothes are incredible. That ballgown must have cost a fortune.'

'And I wouldn't be seen dead in it,' said Zoe. Eva laughed.

'Chance would be a fine thing. And no one would mistake you for a lady if you were.'

'They certainly won't take me for a lady in these damn shorts, that's for sure. Wouldn't you think there could be some sort of clothes anyone could wear, a young style, not just copies of what our mums wear?'

Eva sat down on the bed and hugged her knees. 'What sort would you suggest?'

Zoe shrugged. 'Something easy to wear and casual, not all boned so you can hardly breathe. You know, loose things that still look great, like gypsies wear.'

'Like shirts and trousers, big skirts, cloaks and capes. Yes, something really twentieth-century,' said Eva. 'I heard there's a shop in Chelsea where the woman sells things like that.'

'It's Chelsea, so it's dear,' said Zoe. 'I had a look – they were quite fun clothes, but a bit schoolgirly for me.'

Eva yawned as she surveyed the clothes scattered around the room. 'I'm for bed – we can clear this lot up in the morning. Hey – tell you what – why don't we swap? All my lot for yours?'

Zoe pulled a face. 'I don't fancy yours any more than my own. Oh well, anything for a change, I suppose.'

Next morning Chantal was breakfasting alone on the terrace when the girls came down. Her hair, normally coiled in a smooth chignon, was flowing loose about her shoulders. She wore no make-up, and she was lazing in a peasant-style gathered skirt, its ragged hem dipping above sun-tanned legs and bare feet. Eva could see the clear outline of her breasts under the blouse from the boutique which she wore unbuttoned to the waist. Eva stopped in the doorway, caught in admiration.

Chantal looked up and smiled. Zoe moved towards her, eyes gleaming in pleasure. 'You look terrific, Chantal. Do you often dress like this?'

Chantal shrugged and made a mock-pout. 'Whenever I am permitted.'

'Permitted?'

'For Robert's business and society I must wear Balmain or Fath or Givenchy. But here, where no one sees me, I may wear what I choose.'

'You look beautiful,' said Eva, 'every bit as good as Brigitte Bardot.'

Chantal bowed her head in acknowledgement. 'Thank you. May I pour coffee for you?'

She picked up the cafétière and poured the thick black liquid into wide cups. A wasp buzzed over the table, searching out the scent of the confiture. Chantal brushed it aside. 'After you have eaten we shall drive out into the country. Robert has agreed. You would like that?'

The white limousine purred along the country lane in the heat of the afternoon, the windows lowered so that the breeze fanned their faces. Chantal, sitting beside Robert, held on to her wide-brimmed sunhat.

Lunch had been a long and leisurely affair on the sunlit pavement outside a village bistro, charcuteries and lobster and salad washed down with copious glasses of wine. Eva gazed out over the hedgerow edging the lane across the fields where only an occasional white farmhouse gleamed amid the vast expanse of ripening corn. The sun's heat lay heavy over the land, filling the nostrils with the heady scents of summer, and Eva began to feel drowsy.

No one was talking; all four occupants of the car seemed so relaxed and content to think private thoughts that the intrusive sound of a sudden crack did not at once alarm them. Then Robert swore and braked hard. Eva opened her eyes.

The windscreen was shattered. In front of the car stood two dark-skinned men, and one of them was pointing a revolver at Robert's head.

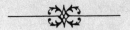

CHAPTER NINE

The car was slewed almost at right angles across the road, its engine silent. The men stood on the grass verge, one half-crouching behind the taller one who held the gun.

'My God, they shot at us!' moaned Chantal, and her lacquered fingernails clawed deep into the poodle's coat. Eva could see Zoe staring at the bullet hole in the back seat between them.

Robert sat white-faced, his hands still gripping the steering wheel. The taller figure moved round to the driver's window, and Eva could see clearly now the brown-skinned young man in a ragged shirt with a mop of tousled dark hair and black eyes gleaming with menacing determination. He jerked the gun a fraction, speaking at the same time in guttural French, but Eva could not follow his words. He was clearly of Arab origin.

'What's happened?' whispered Zoe. 'What's going on?'

'Terrorists,' muttered Chantal.

For seconds Robert did not move. Zouzou began to yap and cowered in Chantal's lap. The gunman repeated his words, but more savagely this time, hissing into Robert's face.

'Get out, Robert,' Chantal whispered. 'For the love of God, do as he says.'

Robert moved slowly, eyes staring and his movements as mechanical as a robot's. As he climbed out of the car and stood alongside it, the gunman slammed the door shut. Then he turned and beckoned to his companion before moving round to Chantal's side of the car.

'*Vous savez conduire?*'

'*Oui.*'

He jerked the pistol again, motioning her to take the driver's seat. Eva leaned forward.

'You're going to drive them?'

Chantal looked out at Robert, standing helpless by the roadside with his arms pinioned behind him, droplets of sweat gleaming on his bald head. 'I have no choice,' she murmured, then set Zouzou down on the seat beside her. Instantly the poodle leapt for the open window and out on to the dusty road.

Eva heard the tall man cry out as the dog's teeth sank into his ankle, and felt the grip of Zoe's hand on her arm. She saw the man swoop down and seize the poodle by the collar, then give it a hefty kick. Zouzou yelped, but kept on fighting to bite again. Chantal's fingers flew to her lips, but she made no sound.

Twice more the heavy boot thudded into the little dog's flank, but Zouzou did not give in. He struggled and twisted, and found a way to snap his teeth firmly into the man's wrist. The man snatched his hand away, stared down disbelievingly at the smear of blood, then cracked the poodle a ferocious blow with the gun.

Zouzou sank without a sound, sprawling on his side on the dusty road. The man raised the gun and fired, the crack of the bullet fading instantly on the afternoon breeze. Zouzou's little body twitched and lay still.

Eva sat stunned, watching the thin stream of blood ooze from above the dog's closed eyes and begin to trickle down to the dust of the road. The shorter man started to cackle. The other swore under his breath and turned back to Chantal who was sitting, mouth and eyes wide, still in the passenger seat. 'Move!' he snapped.

Suddenly Robert came to life, as if the sharpness of the

man's voice had somehow cleared the fog from his brain. His face lost its vacant expression and he shook himself free of his captor and strode towards the taller man.

'Now, look here, do you know how many hundred francs that dog cost?' he demanded. Chantal was slithering across to sit behind the wheel and Eva saw her hand reach down for the ignition key, then hesitate.

The smaller man had seized hold of Robert once more. The other waved the pistol in his face. Eva could understand enough to make out that the man was saying he was going to take Robert's car.

'Nonsense,' snapped Robert. 'You don't terrorize me. I'll have the gendarmes arrest you both.'

The taller man's lips were set in a harsh line as he nodded to his companion. The shorter man then pushed Robert roughly towards the ditch. Eva heard him snap some words she could not make out, and then Robert knelt down on the grass. The gunman held the pistol to the back of Robert's head.

'Oh no!' Chantal's voice was no more than a hoarse whisper and then Eva, horrified, heard the sound of the pistol shot.

Robert's body sagged and fell. For seconds no one moved. It was a grisly tableau, three women in a car watching two Arabs looking down on the body of a man they had just slaughtered in cold blood, while several feet away a tiny apricot body lay bathed in a widening pool of its own crimson blood.

Eva heard Chantal make a kind of choking sound, and then the engine roared into life.

'Go for it, Chantal!' cried Eva. 'Put your foot down!'

Zoe's fingers were digging deep into Eva's arm, her eyes huge with horror at what had just taken place. The car was already in motion, but the taller terrorist's reaction was swift.

Through the shattered windscreen Eva saw him hurl himself across the bonnet of the car, gun waving. The move was so swift that the impetus carried him sideways straight through the windscreen, fragments of glass hurtling into the car with him. His legs smashed hard against Chantal, knocking her backwards as she flung up her hands to protect herself.

The car jerked to a juddering halt. He lay sprawled across the front seats, the gun still in his hand. Eva leaned over, scratching and clawing, trying to wrest the gun from his fingers, but to no avail. With a huge effort he scrambled upright, Eva's hands still clawing at his hair.

Breathing heavily, he brought the gun up to Chantal's head. Eva's hands fell away abruptly and, through the windscreen, she saw the smaller man come running. He jerked open the back door and climbed in to sit down heavily between Eva and Zoe, the bulk of his stocky body now obscuring the bullet hole.

At this close range Eva could smell them, the stench of old sweat mingled with a strange, rancid smell. Involuntarily she shrank back. Zoe, too, sat crouched against the far corner.

'No more nonsense,' rasped the gunman in French. 'Drive.'

Chantal made no argument. She brushed slivers of glass from her skirt and smoothed back her hair. Eva could see her profile, small scratches standing out lividly on her pale cheek and her lips set as she re-started the car and drove on.

Confused thoughts were running through Eva's mind, a patchwork of jumbled images of a tiny dog fighting bravely, of the terrorist hurtling through the windscreen, of Robert keeling over into the ditch . . . The whole afternoon seemed to have taken on the strange, surreal quality of a nightmare.

Zoe found her voice at last, tiny and tentative. 'What are they going to do with us, Chantal?'

'Hold us as hostages until they get way, I imagine.' Chantal's tone was curiously matter-of-fact. The gunman alongside her was studying her profile with interest.

'Get away where?' asked Eva.

'Home to Algeria.'

The gunman jabbed the pistol against Chantal's shoulder. '*Taisez-vous*,' he commanded. 'Speak only in French.'

Eva's mind was racing. If they were heading for Algeria then they wanted to reach the south coast – a full day's drive at least, she calculated. Surely the chance must come in that time to trick or elude them . . .

Dusk came swiftly and by nightfall they had passed through only villages, at the gunman's direction. Zoe was looking pale.

'I'm dying to spend a penny, Eva,' she said plaintively. 'I'm beginning to feel sick with it.'

'So must they,' Eva replied. 'They must stop soon.'

'And get more petrol,' remarked Chantal, nodding towards the petrol gauge.

'Not on these country roads, they won't,' said Eva. 'We'll have to get to civilization sooner or later.'

The stocky man jabbed her with his elbow to be silent, but she could see he was growing drowsy for his head kept drooping and then he would jerk it suddenly upright again. The gunman pointed to a long, low building silhouetted against the darkening sky and told Chantal to drive up the lane towards it.

As the car pulled up he spoke to the stocky man who jumped out and went to investigate. He came back, nodding, and the gunman motioned to the girls to get out. He waited to follow behind Chantal.

The building was a large barn, stocked now with newly-gathered hay which filled the nostrils with its rich, warm sweetness. The stocky man flung himself down, his swarthy face breaking into a smile.

Chantal turned and spoke to the gunman. He listened and nodded.

'Come,' said Chantal to the girls. 'We may go and relieve ourselves now.'

The shorter man scrambled to his feet and followed them outside. It was useless to argue; he was not going to leave them alone. It was humiliating, but the sensation of relief was almost worth it, Eva decided. So the fellow stood where he got a glimpse of backsides – so what? In this atmosphere of dreamlike unreality and sudden death it hardly seemed to matter.

The hay was scratchy on skin which had little in the way of clothing to protect it, but the two men were deep in conversation in some foreign tongue and Chantal seemed to welcome the respite, lying back on the hay as if it were her own satin-draped bed. Eva lay down, and Zoe crawled close beside her.

'I'm scared,' she murmured. 'They don't need us, only the car. Look what they did to Robert.'

Chantal overheard. 'They evidently need a driver.'

'But not us,' said Eva. 'Zoe's right.'

'Girls make useful hostages. You need not worry.'

Chantal's matter-of-factness unnerved Eva. She must know these were men who had brutally bombed and maimed the shopkeeper in Paris; her husband lay dead in a ditch a hundred miles north of here, maybe undiscovered for days, and yet she could remain outwardly cool and self-possessed. Either she was a superb actress or, like their captors, totally dispassionate.

The two men were still talking, glancing across now and again to keep an eye on their captives. Chantal lay, eyes half-closed, and murmured under her breath in English.

'The farm must be close to the barn, not more than a kilometre away. If only one of us could get away . . . Somehow we must distract their attention.'

'How?' muttered Eva.

'I think the opportunity may present itself,' said Chantal. 'We must be patient.'

Time passed, and Zoe's eyelids began to droop. Eva could see the men looking their way, openly now. The stocky man's eyes gleamed, taking in the curve under Zoe's open-necked shirt as she lay on her side in the hay, and there was unmistakable intent in his eyes. He got to his knees and crawled to her side.

No sooner had his fingers intruded their way under her shirt and Zoe's eyes snapped open, wide with alarm, than Chantal spoke.

'Leave the child alone,' she said quietly in French. 'You would not soil yourself with a Jewess, would you?'

The man's hand stopped suddenly, then withdrew as if he had been bitten by a rattlesnake. '*Elle est juive?*' he echoed. '*Mon Dieu!*'

'*Oui, elle est juive. Elle est sale.*'

The stocky man sank back on his haunches. The taller man rolled over on the hay to face Chantal. '*Taisez-vous,*' he snapped.

Chantal put her hands behind her head and shut her eyes as he crawled across and lay down beside her. 'Be silent, woman,' he hissed. 'I know how to make you stay silent.'

Eva saw his mouth come down on Chantal's lips, his body slithering over hers. Chantal did not move. The other man sat up, cross-legged, and began to chuckle.

The gunman moved aside off Chantal's inert body for a moment, and Eva saw his grimy hand pulling at Chantal's skirt, jerking it up to reveal the expanse of naked thigh. His

115

face was buried now in Chantal's neck, and over his shoulder Eva could see her face in the gloom, pale but set as his hands tore at her underclothing.

Eva made to go for him, but Chantal saw the move. 'No!' she whispered. 'Don't interfere!'

Eva drew back and lowered her hand. Zoe's eyes were wide with fear and the stocky man was intent on the couple, leaning forward to watch more closely. Zoe shrank back in the shadows. Suddenly Eva realized Chantal's intention – the distraction she spoke of, the chance to get away and raise the alarm . . .

Zoe was behind the stocky man's back, almost indistinguishable in the gloom. Eva made a slight movement of the head, jerking it towards the door. Zoe nodded.

Eva was not aware of the moment when Zoe actually slipped away. She only knew that she was obliged to watch, powerless, as the gunman forced himself upon the unresisting Chantal. Nausea overwhelmed her; every fibre of her longed to lash out at the foul beast, to tear his face and break his bloody neck . . .

Eva closed her eyes against the loathsome scene being enacted before her, digging her nails hard into her thighs to try to distract her brain, but it was impossible to close her ears to the sound of the gunman's grunts and laboured breathing, the sound of the other man's delight. The nightmare unreality of this hideous fantasy still persisted . . .

'*Leave me alone, Bert – you'll wake the kid! For Christ's sake, Bert, leave off!*'

First my mother, then Maddie . . . God knows what women have had to suffer at the hands of evil men . . .

'*La petite – la juive – ou est-elle?*'

The stocky man's cry startled Eva into reality. She saw him dart for the door, the gunman scrambling to his feet and fastening his trousers. Chantal still lay motionless.

The men gabbled anxiously. 'The Jewish bitch has escaped – go and look for her.'

'We don't know which way she's gone.'

'To the farm, idiot. We must stop her before she alerts them. You go and get her. I'll take care of these.'

The stocky man disappeared out into the darkness.

Zoe crouched in the shadow of the trees in the little copse, panting for breath. She strained her ears, trying to catch any sound which might mean they were after her, and then it came. A dog barked in the distance; it must be at the farm.

She scrambled to her feet and began running again towards the sound, stumbling every now and again as her foot caught the roots of a tree. Her lungs were beginning to ache. She reached the edge of the copse, rounded the last tree, and suddenly a shadow leapt at her.

She cried out as powerful arms caught her round the knees and brought her down; a heavy body fell across hers and drove all the breath from her. A hand clamped tightly over her mouth, and then came the deafening sound of a shot . . .

The tall man motioned Eva to sit by Chantal then stood looking anxiously out of the door.

For long minutes no one had spoken, and the silence was becoming oppressive. Suddenly there came the sound of a distant crack. Eva's hand flew to her mouth. 'Oh my God! He's shot her!'

'No,' said Chantal. 'That was a rifle shot, not a pistol.'

The man by the door was half-crouching now, pistol in hand, as he peered out into the darkness. He turned suddenly and grabbed hold of Chantal's arm.

'Come. We must leave, fast.'

Seizing hold of Eva he shoved them both roughly out of the door. Chantal's face was as expressionless as a corpse as she let herself be bundled into the driving seat without a murmur. The gunman pushed Eva into the back seat then climbed in beside Chantal.

'Drive!' he snapped, digging the gun into Chantal's shoulder. 'Drive fast.'

She drove fast, the car bumping and lurching over potholes. With the windscreen gone, cool night air blew directly into their faces. Eva could feel fronds of Chantal's long hair flipping her cheek as she leaned over the seat. The car's headlamps picked out the dusty surface of the track ahead.

'I ought to have killed the Jewish bitch,' the gunman grunted, then suddenly his eyes dilated and he pointed ahead to the outer reaches of the car's headlamps. 'Brake! Gendarmes!'

Chantal jammed her foot on the brake and there was a screech of rubber gripping metal. Eva could see now the car drawn across the rutted lane where it joined the main road, the uniformed figures of men grouped close to it, the marksman leaning, rifle in hand, over the bonnet . . .

The gunman forgot Chantal and turned his pistol towards the gendarmes, taking aim at the marksman. Instantly Chantal acted. She banged her foot down on the accelerator and drove straight for the police car.

Eva braced herself for the inevitable impact. There was a sudden crashing sound of metal and simultaneously the crack of a gunshot. Everything seemed to be hurtling through the air. Eva's nose hit the seat in front and then she felt her head being jerked backwards out of her spine. She fell to the floor as the engine spluttered and died.

Feet came running, and the car doors were wrenched open. Eva raised her head slowly and the first thing she saw, to her relief, was Chantal's face looking back at her. The gunman was no longer in the car – and then she saw him, lying along the car bonnet, his feet hooked over the dashboard. The impact had evidently hurled him out through the open windscreen. His head lay twisted at a strange angle and she could see the bullet hole between his eyes.

There was a gleam of life returning to Chantal's eyes as the gendarme helped her out.

'Madame Noircy?' he said. 'We found your husband's body. The farmer saw your car here. We guessed.'

'My husband?' echoed Chantal.

'You know he is dead.'

'Yes. And my dog?' Chantal's voice was vague. 'You found Zouzou? What have you done with him?'

Eva cut in between them. 'Zoe – what happened to Zoe?'

'We grabbed her – we were waiting for the men.'

The gendarme turned, indicating a police car half-screened by the bushes. Through the window Eva saw a figure sitting hunched, shrouded in a blanket. It was Zoe.

Two uniformed figures passed, carrying between them a stocky, dark-skinned body which they pushed into the back of a van. Chantal looked back at the body lying on the car bonnet.

'Come away,' said the officer, taking her arm. 'Sit in the car.'

'No, I want to look at him. He raped me.'

Eva watched her, her face impassive as she looked down at the crumpled, bloodstained figure. Silhouetted against the light from the car headlamps Chantal looked fragile and vulnerable as a child.

'Well, he went out the way he came in,' said Eva.

Zoe's face was animated as she sat in the huge pastel green bath at Les Pommiers.

'Fancy making me go for help,' she grumbled, 'when I

don't know a word of French. It was lucky for me they shot the other Arab.'

'We were all very lucky,' said Chantal as she sat before the mirror combing out her long hair. Eva looked up from the washbowl, shampoo running down her face.

'You? After what happened to you?' she said quietly.

Chantal shrugged. 'I have only a few scratches. It could have been much worse. These Algerians have been known to commit the most terrible mutilations . . .'

'I wonder,' murmured Zoe. 'They knew I was Jewish . . .'

Eva was silent for a moment as she rinsed her hair and then straightened. 'I hate men,' she muttered, wrapping a towel round her head. 'My mother, my stepmother, and you – you've all suffered because of lousy men. You say you didn't love Robert, and I think we know why.'

'Ah, you overheard. It was only sometimes like that, and there were reasons.'

Eva scowled. 'There are no good reasons for cruelty, Chantal. You don't have to speak well of him, just because he's dead.'

Chantal shook her head. 'You don't know all, Eva. Robert's first wife denounced him to the Nazis. They tortured him. Sometimes, only sometimes, he had terrible dreams.'

'I didn't know that, but even so he shouldn't have taken it out on you. Why didn't you leave him?'

Chantal caught her hand as she passed. 'Listen to me, Eva. I could bear it. Robert was rich and the château meant a great deal to me – Robert was a diamond merchant who wanted a woman he could present anywhere. It was business. I opened my château to him and his money because it was my job.'

'I hope I never become that cynical.'

'Practical, Eva. Once I was a romantic like you, looking for my knight in shining armour, but I found only the trades-man. It had to suffice.'

She smiled ruefully, then reached for her perfume spray. 'But it is not always like that, my dear,' believe me. With the right man it is wonderful. One day you will discover . . .'

Eva shuddered. 'I doubt it. Their greedy hands on your body . . .'

Chantal shook her head. 'No, Eva. Once I loved a man with all my heart, and that was wonderful. I wanted to spend my whole life with him.'

'Why didn't you marry him then?'

Zoe climbed out of the bath and reached for a towel. 'Yes, why didn't you?'

Chantal spread her hands. 'He had no money. We would have struggled together, lost Les Pommiers, and gradually love would have died.'

'Not if you really loved him.'

'What a little idealist you are! Women have to be tough, *ma chère*, stronger than men. The human race depends on it. Women carry history on their backs.'

For several seconds the girls remained silent. Then Chantal gave a deep sigh.

'What is it?' asked Eva.

Chantal shook her head. 'I was just thinking about my poor Zouzou – what a dear, brave little thing he was. I shall miss him.'

The newspapers were full of the story of a rich diamond merchant kidnapped and assassinated by Algerian terrorists in a remote country lane, but to Chantal's relief she was granted the right to have his body interred in the family vault of the chapel in the grounds of Les Pommiers.

'Robert would be proud to know he is to be laid to rest alongside my ancestors,' Chantal remarked to the girls. 'And mercifully we shall be spared the morbid sightseers and the prying reporters. The only stranger at the funeral will be Robert's son, Luc.'

Eva and Zoe accompanied Chantal to the funeral service on a fine but overcast morning. She wore a neat black suit and gloves and a veiled hat, and smiled as she took a final glimpse in the mirror.

'I think Robert would have approved,' she commented.

Then she went downstairs to where the dark-eyed young man waited. Luc Noircy was a tall, good-looking young man in his early twenties, Eva guessed.

In the coolness of the little chapel Eva stood in the front pew between Chantal on one side and Zoe and Luc on the other. Behind them sat the members of the château staff. Apart from the muted sound of organ music and the priest intoning Latin words, there was no sound. No tears were shed at Robert Noircy's departure from this world.

Eva stared at the coffin, visualizing his body in a white shroud, the hole glaring in the back of his head. It seemed hard to believe that only three days ago he had been so alive, polite and thoughtful by day but a bullying tyrant to Chantal by night. Life was so unpredictably changeable.

She glanced across Zoe at Luc Noircy. His mother was dead, and now he had lost his father too. Did he feel bereft, an orphan isolated and alone? His expressionless face gave no sign of any emotion at all. In his shoes she would have been desolate.

For once she allowed herself to think of David. Where was he now, and what was he doing? If life could be so unpredictably short – would she ever see him again? Suppose she learnt one day that something had happened to him . . . She tried to brush away the regret that leapt in her. It would have been wrong whatever the circumstances.

It was a strange feeling, realizing that one portion of her

life was gone forever, her student days over and done. Never to see David again was bad enough, but never to see Fay or any of the others . . . Never to see Alan Finch . . .

After the ceremony was ended Luc Noircy bade Chantal a formal farewell, bowing to kiss her fingertips, then he turned to bow slightly to the girls. Eva saw the quick, grave smile to Zoe, and then he made for a waiting car. Chantal watched him go.

'*Tant qu'il ressemble à son père*,' she murmured. 'The first time I have seen him, but he is handsome, so very like his father when he was young.'

The clouds were drifting away, giving way to the sun when they returned to the château. Chantal kicked off her stiletto-heeled shoes in the vestibule and gave orders to Marianne to serve the midday meal on the terrace.

At the foot of the stairs she trailed one slender gloved hand over the newel post as she began to climb. Her voice came back over her shoulder to the girls behind her.

'I am going upstairs to change,' she remarked quietly. 'I shall not wear mourning, because I do not mourn. The ordeal is over, and now a new life may begin.'

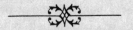

CHAPTER TEN

Eva and Zoe debated what to do.

'We can't very well move on yet and leave Chantal on her own,' Zoe commented. 'Not till she's got used to being a widow anyway.'

'No. We'll stay as long as she wants us,' agreed Eva.

But if the girls expected an atmosphere of sadness or regret to permeate the château over the succeeding days, they were quickly disabused of the notion. Chantal busied herself about the place, drawing innumerable sketches of the alterations and renovations to the château she intended to carry out and clearing cupboards of Robert's clothes.

'All these can go to the nuns – they'll find a use for them,' she said, sweeping up an armful of suits and laying them on top of the shirts and socks in a large trunk. 'I'm sure Luc won't want them either.'

Turning, she caught sight of the girls' faces and smiled. 'No hypocrisy, *mes chères* – I want no souvenirs. Our marriage lasted only eight years. Luc will not weep for him either, I know. He and I will both benefit from Robert's death.'

Zoe looked puzzled. 'You didn't know Luc before the funeral? That's funny, isn't it?'

Chantal held up a shirt to the light. 'Not really. His mother was dead and Robert sent him to boarding school. He studies photography now. He never visited Robert.'

'He looked lonely,' remarked Zoe. 'He came alone.'

Chantal flung the shirt into the trunk. 'Then perhaps I was

124

right to invite him to come and stay at Les Pommiers. He said he would write to me.'

Zoe cocked her head to one side. 'He looked almost Jewish to me,' she ventured. 'Such dark eyes and hair . . .'

'He is,' said Chantal. 'His mother was Jewish.'

'Married to a Gentile?'

'She fled from Austria in '36 and settled here. Perhaps she hoped her marriage would protect her when the Nazis came. I don't know – Robert only told me how she betrayed him – told the Nazis that he was in the Resistance. Perhaps that was to save her own skin, who knows?'

Zoe was staring out of the window. 'So maybe Luc too lost his relatives in the concentration camps like my mother and father did. Poor man.'

'He would have been only a baby then. He won't remember,' said Chantal. 'He has been well cared for – Robert saw to that.'

She dropped the lid of the trunk and fastened it. 'There. That's done.' As she straightened she caught sight of Zoe's far-away expression. 'Don't worry about Luc. He is well provided for. Soon he will inherit a great fortune from his father.'

'I was thinking of Robert,' said Eva. 'No one seems to have loved him.'

Chantal sighed. 'He got what he wanted. He wanted his name allied to that of de Lessigny – my family – and the estate. And a gracious wife. He did not complain.'

She opened the door in the far wall of the bedroom. 'Here is my dressing room. There are clothes here from many years back. I do not want them any more. Please help yourselves to any of them that you choose. Please – take as many as you wish for I shall throw the rest away.'

The dressing room was lined with wardrobes on every wall. Chantal flung open the doors, revealing a mass of colours and fabrics. 'There. I shall leave you to inspect them at your leisure. I shall be on the terrace, drawing up the plans for another bedroom to my own design.'

Chantal left a waft of perfume on the still heat of the afternoon air as she left the room. Zoe seized a peacock blue silk kimono from the wardrobe.

'Just look at this, Eva – it must have cost a fortune!' She pulled it on over her frock, tying the belt tightly about her waist, and pirouetted before the cheval mirror. 'You've had it, Eva – this is mine!'

'OK, then I'll have this.'

Eva pulled out a twenties-style dress of black georgette, covered with long silky white fringes from neck to hem. Pulling off her shirt she put it on, then snatched up a black silk scarf and tied it, pirate-fashion, around her forehead. 'All I need now is a long rope of crystal beads,' she laughed, twirling round and kicking up her heels in a mock Charleston. 'Boy, if they could see me now at college!'

'Here's a feather boa to go with it,' said Zoe, handing her a scarlet tumble of feathers. Dust flew in the air, caught in the sunlight from the window, and Eva coughed.

'These things must have been here ages – long before Chantal's time. God, wouldn't it be marvellous if we could take the lot?'

For the next hour the girls revelled in trying on hundreds of garments, from formal black suits to magnificent crimson ballgowns, from ethereal shell-pink nightdresses and negligées to exotic beach suits and swimwear.

'Hell, it's almost impossible to choose from this lot,' said Eva at last, flinging herself down on a velvet chair. 'We can only take what we can carry so I suppose we'll have to be sensible and take just things we can actually wear.'

'I'm not leaving this kimono, sensible or not,' said Zoe with emphasis. 'Or this fantastic skirt.'

'And I'm going to take this gypsy-type dress,' said Eva. 'And the boots and cloak.'

'They don't go together,' frowned Zoe. 'They look daft. So does that shirt and trousers of Robert's you're wearing, especially with the shirt open like that and a red string tie around your neck. Nobody wears things like that.'

'I'll start the fashion then,' said Eva firmly. 'Like Chantal I'm going to wear what I want, fashionable or not.'

'Here, you mean, while we're in France?'

'And when we go back home. Why not?'

'Yeah – it's growing on me.'

'I'll chuck all my old lot away – make a bonfire of it – and have only Chantal's stuff now.'

'Good idea. So will I.'

It was while they were making a giant heap of all their old clothes and refilling their cases with new clothes from the wardrobes that Eva sighed and sat back on her haunches.

'Such a shame the rest's going to get thrown away,' she murmured. 'Labels like these – Balenciaga, Balmain, Dior – I wish we could take the whole lot back home with us.'

Zoe sighed too. 'So do I,' she breathed. 'I'd give anything to be able to take them all.'

Behind them Eva heard a sound and turned. Chantal was leaning against the doorframe, smiling as she watched them. Fair hair tumbling about her shoulders, she looked delightfully *gamine*, fresh and cool with her white blouse tied high under her breasts leaving her midriff exposed and a pair of faded cotton trousers cut off and fraying just below the knee.

'Take them all?' she repeated in her husky, musical voice. 'That is no problem. I shall arrange it.' She led the way downstairs, and in the vestibule she picked up the telephone.

From the window Zoe stared out into the darkness. 'I can just see the last embers of our bonfire,' she told Eva. 'Just imagine, those sparks are all that's left of my grotty old shorts.'

'Gone, but not forgotten,' said Eva. 'No one who's ever seen you in those things will ever forget.'

'No worse that your ropey old cardigan,' retorted Zoe. 'Heaven alone knows how you ever got a date in that thing.'

'I didn't.'

'What's Chantal doing?'

'She's still got the architect here. Work starts on the new bedroom next week.'

'Should we move on then, do you think? We've been here ages now.'

Eva shrugged. 'Hardly enough time left to go south now – results will be out soon. I reckon we'd better head for home.'

Zoe pulled a face. 'Results! Waste of time me going home for them!'

The telephone bell shrilled in the hall, and then came the sound of Chantal's voice. A minute passed, and then she called out:

'Eva! Zoe! Descend at once!'

She still held the telephone in her hand as they reached the bottom of the stairs. She smiled as she put her hand over the receiver. 'It's Luc – he wants to come and stay here next month. Will you be here then, he wants to know?'

Eva shook her head. 'We must get back to England now.'

'Perhaps we can meet some other time,' said Zoe.

Uncovering the mouthpiece again Chantal chattered away in rapid French. *'Oui, oui, merci, Luc. À bientôt.'*

She put the telephone down and turned to the girls. 'Luc regrets you will not be here, but hopes he will see you again.'

'Great,' said Zoe. 'I'll look forward to that.'

Eva sighed. 'I've so enjoyed staying with you, Chantal, but we'd better start packing to go home. I wonder if Zoe's father's received our consignment of boxes yet – I wonder what he's saying.'

Zoe rolled her eyes. 'I can just imagine. "What is this? All these boxes and not a feather or a ribbon for my hats among them?" I only hope he got my letter before they all turned up on his doorstep.'

'Come,' said Chantal. 'Let us go riding. You may choose whichever of Robert's horses you wish.'

'Not me,' said Zoe. 'Eva will go.'

'I'd love to. I haven't ridden in months.'

Chantal was standing on the jetty at Calais to wave the girls goodbye. To Eva and Zoe up on deck she looked a tiny, fragile figure, her cotton skirt blowing about her knees in the breeze and her long hair flapping in her face. Eva waved, wondering if she would ever hear the calm sweetness of her voice or see the perfection of her profile again, or whether yet another chapter in her life was ended.

Zoe seemed to sense her thoughts. 'I liked Chantal,' she murmured. 'I've never known anyone quite like her before.'

'Me too,' agreed Eva. 'Tiny, but tough. Just think of all she's been through.'

Zoe nodded. 'We've been through quite a bit ourselves lately – kidnap, and murder.'

And watching what they did to Chantal in the barn, thought Eva, and a sense of bitterness welled in her. 'Yep,' she muttered. 'I don't think anything will ever throw me into a panic again.'

'I know what you mean – as if we've grown up overnight. Come on, she's out of sight now – let's go below and see if we can find a seat.'

Louis Jacob's little hat shop in a side street in Golders Green was thrown into complete confusion. In the basement workroom two sweaty, dishevelled machinists were on the verge of rebellion.

'I been struggling with this rotten material all day, Mr Jacob. It's terrible stuff to sew,' complained Patsy.

Louis wiped droplets of sweat from his forehead. 'More excuses for being slow I cannot take. The order must be ready tomorrow, you hear me? No order, no wage packet come Friday.'

'It's not her fault,' protested the older machinist. 'The damn machine keeps breaking the thread. You ought to get this tension seen to.'

Louis turned to her. 'Do I need you to tell me what I got to do? I got an order to get out and only two girls to do the work. Patsy, ask Ella if you need help.'

'So do I get supervisor's pay while Rosa's off?' Ella asked between clenched teeth as she snapped off the thread. 'And do we get the machines looked at before they break down altogether like they did last week?'

Louis muttered something under his breath. 'I'll look at them tonight.'

'You looked at them last night. That's why we need a mechanic now,' said Ella. 'And how much longer are these boxes going to be left here? We've hardly room to breathe as it is.'

Louis threw up his hands. 'What am I? A fortune-teller? How do I know how long before my daughter fetches them?'

'What's in them anyway?'

'I can see through cardboard? Suddenly I got X-ray eyes? Let's all get back to work now, I got a shop to run.'

He clambered laboriously up the narrow staircase to the small room at street level where his hats were displayed. Sweat was trickling into his eyes and he wiped it away with his sleeve. If only Rosa would come back. Half an hour extra on her lunch break, she had said, and it was half-past two already. She could keep the girls in order. Her cheerful plump figure and easy-going manner were indispensable to keep the atmosphere happy. True, she could erupt occasionally into volcanic outbursts of Italian temper if the girls provoked her too far, but they usually vanished again as suddenly as they were born.

She too was a foreigner in a strange land like himself, thrust here by the war and then suddenly widowed while still comparatively young. What age would she be, he wondered? Fortyish? Forty-five? Italian women tended to grow plump early and appear middle-aged. But she was warm, maternal and Jewish, and he had never had a better supervisor.

The doorbell clanged and two women entered the shop. Louis's quick eyes took in the older woman's felt hat trimmed with a single feather and the rings on her fingers. The younger woman, hatless, was unmistakably her daughter and wore a similar well-cut coat. These could be worthwhile customers, and he moved out from behind the counter towards them with a warm smile.

'Can I help you, ladies?'

The older woman indicated a blue hat in the window and Louis was carefully interposing his bulk between the wax heads when he saw the young man outside in the street. He was looking into Louis's window, but beyond the display to the women at the counter. He saw Louis and came to the door.

'Mr Jacob?'

'That's what it says over my door.' He was clearly not a customer; probably just asking the way to another shop in the busy street.

'Is Zoe here – or Eva?'

Louis clicked his tongue irritably. The blue felt was proving difficult to reach without knocking over one of the wax heads. 'Why would young girls be in a place like this when they can be on holiday in France, I ask you?'

The young man seemed embarrassed, shifting from one foot to the other. Louis regretted his sharpness; he was a respectable-looking enough fellow, not like many of the young people today. And he might have a mother who appreciated a good hat.

'But I expect them tomorrow,' Louis added as he managed to retrieve the blue felt at last. 'Is this the model you wish to try? You got good taste, lady – I only make one of these. Never another like it in the whole of London.'

Rosa was full of concern when she got back to the shop. 'You not eat lunch again today,' she remarked. 'You grow thin and ugly and who will want to come to your shop then?'

'About me you got nothing to worry, Rosa. I got enough fat,' Louis replied, but he was glad she'd noticed. 'I'm not hungry.'

'You come to my house tonight and I give you good meal. A man should have meat on his bones.'

He smiled at her. 'Maybe by tonight I could eat a little something.'

Rosa pouted full lips. 'I make you a big plate of spaghetti, maybe? Or do you lose your appetite because of the letter, ha? You got to tell Zoe she fail the exam, ha? What she do now?'

Louis sighed and pulled a cigarette packet out of his pocket. 'I don't know, Rosa.'

He drew out a cigarette and struck a match to light it, inhaling deeply. Rosa fanned the air in front of her face. 'Not good for a man to smoke too much. The girls complain you fill the air with bad smell.'

Louis was not listening. 'What are all these boxes, I ask myself? Zoe has not the money to buy so much.'

Rosa smiled. 'You have not looked? You are not the man I know.'

Louis pulled himself upright. 'Would I do such a thing to my own daughter? What kind of a man do you take me for, Rosa Petrucci? I am ashamed of you!'

Rosa took hold of his elbow. 'OK, now you go back to the workroom and leave me to manage the shop. I'll have your spaghetti on the table at seven.'

Zoe was far more philosophical than Louis expected when, once the hugs and embraces of reunion were over, he broke the news to her. Eva watched Zoe's set expression as she listened.

'I didn't expect to pass anyway, Papa. I'm sorry. I was never as bright as you thought.'

'Nonsense, princess. You were the prettiest and the cleverest girl in the school! But don't think I am disappointed, sweetheart – I know you will succeed – you, the shrewdest little businesswoman this side of Vienna – next to your dear Mama, of course. You will do well, I know it.'

'What about Eva? Can she telephone home to find out how she's gone on? She's going home anyway, but the sooner she finds out . . .'

'Of course.'

The moment they were alone Louis seized his daughter by the shoulders. 'What you trying to do, eh? You trying to make a crook out of your own father? Is that what you want?'

Zoe stared at him in amazement. 'What are you talking about, Papa?'

'Those boxes – where did you get them? They cannot be yours – tell me they are not stolen?'

'Papa! What are you saying?'

'Only I got to know if I got stolen goods on my property, don't I?'

Zoe cut in hotly. 'They're not stolen – they're mine.'

Louis wagged a finger. 'You don't buy those, princess – Balmain, Dior, Balenciaga?' Then Louis's eyes gleamed. 'Ah, you buy them cheap, maybe – tell me you buy them cheap.'

Zoe smiled impishly. 'Yes, Papa – very cheap.'

'What they cost you, eh? Next to nothing?'

'Hardly anything at all, Papa.'

Louis clapped her on the shoulder. 'That's my girl! I make a businesswoman of you yet. How much?'

'I didn't pay anything.'

'What? Not a penny?'

'Not a penny. They were given to me.'

Louis flopped into a nearby chair. 'Paris model gowns for nothing? You got a better business brain than I thought. Wait a minute,' he added, a dull gleam starting to glow in his eyes, 'if you pay nothing, what you do to get them, eh? You do something you don't want to tell your papa?' He sprang to his feet again and looked deep into her eyes. 'What you do, princess, that someone should give you such an expensive gift?'

Zoe's shocked expression made him regret the words at once. At the same moment he became aware of the red-haired girl, Eva, standing in the doorway. He turned to her with an effort to smile.

'You hear the result? You pass?'

Eva's reply was quiet. 'I got a lower second.'

'Such a pity,' soothed Louis. 'Both of you.'

'That's great,' said Zoe, hurrying across to hug her. 'Well done!'

'A lower second is good?' said Louis with raised eyebrows. 'Then I congratulate you.'

'And we did nothing to get the clothes,' said Eva. 'They were given out of friendship.'

'Right,' said Louis. 'But so many boxes – how many hundred dresses? What you do with them all?'

'Wear some, sell the rest probably,' said Zoe. 'Labels like those have got to be a good investment.' She turned eagerly to Eva again. 'You will come back, won't you? The sooner we get started the better. We've got a living to earn.'

'You bet I'll be back. Leave you with this lot all to yourself? Not blooming likely!'

Eva was about to leave the room when Louis remembered. 'Ah, there was a young man here yesterday, Zoe. He asked for you – and for Eva.'

He was aware of the two sets of eyes suddenly focusing on him. 'Who?' said Zoe. 'Did he give his name?'

Louis spread thick fingers. 'I am busy, two customers waiting. Cash customers, princess – do I stop to chat with young men when there is business to be done?'

Zoe came closer. 'What did he look like? A student, would you say?'

Louis shrugged. 'Maybe. A good-looking young fellow, very dark and very smart. I cannot guess his age. But I tell him you both be here today. He will come back.'

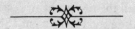

CHAPTER ELEVEN

There was something unbelievably reassuring about being home again, the familiar smell of hay and horses in the farmyard and Lassie's warm body lying across her feet. Eva rode in the early morning along the ridge above Barnbeck with Maddie. At Thunder Crags they reined in the horses.

Far below she could see the lower slopes of the hills swathed in woods sweeping down to the river and the squat stone cottages of Barnbeck clustered about the church. Once again she had the old familiar feeling of permanence, of unchanging stability. Maddie was watching her.

'Lovely, isn't it? Whenever I was troubled I used to come up here just to look down at that view. Made me feel much better somehow.'

'You think I'm troubled then?' said Eva.

Maddie turned to look back at her. 'You've changed. You're not quite the same as you were before – grown up, maybe, after all that happened in France.'

'Maybe.' Eva thought of Chantal crying out in the night, of the kidnap and Robert's murder. And before that there had been the thrill of Alan and the hurt of David, but of these she had not spoken to Maddie.

'I can't help thinking how sad it is that Robert died unmourned,' Maddie said softly. 'It must be life's greatest tragedy not to be loved. God has been good to us.'

Eva turned the thought over in her mind. That Max adored Maddie and she him was evident in their every look and gesture. She remembered the little book of poetry Max had given Maddie for her birthday and the inscription he had written in the flyleaf.

'*The mountains may crumble and the hills depart, but my love for you remains for ever.*'

It must be wonderful to know beyond a shadow of doubt that one person's love remained constant and unchanging for all time; that total honesty and truth existed in that love. Not the half-truths and evasions of David, the calculating acceptance and compromise of Chantal. Maddie and Max were fortunate indeed.

'I wonder you haven't had a baby, you and Max,' Eva said.

Maddie slithered down out of the saddle and stood looking over the valley. 'There's nothing I'd have liked more,' she murmured.

'It's not too late – you're only twelve years older than me. Don't you wish you had a son to carry on the farm?'

Maddie smiled. 'We've got you. I don't expect you to take over my livery stables, but it would be nice. You're good with horses.'

Eva dismounted and came to stand by her. 'No, I meant your own flesh and blood. Mr Renshaw used to say he was the eighth Renshaw to own Scapegoat Farm, and he was really proud of that.'

'I know. It was always a disappointment to him that I wasn't a son.'

Eva was silent for a moment. 'You know, Maddie,' she said quietly, 'I remember telling him once that he was so crabby he didn't deserve a grandson. I've often wished since that I'd never said it.'

Maddie turned around abruptly and took up the horse's reins again. 'Now stop it – no more of this hexing nonsense, Eva. I just refuse to believe it.'

'After Ronnie?'

'After Ronnie, after Kath Davis, everything. Come on, let's get back and see if Max is home yet.'

As they were riding back along the ridge Eva spoke again. 'Maddie, don't bank on me coming back to run Scapegoat, will you? I haven't decided yet what I want to do with my life.'

'You'll be going back to London, I know, about those clothes, but after –'

'I don't know what comes after, Maddie, only that it won't be teaching.'

It was as they were picking their way carefully down the rock-strewn path towards the farm that Maddie spoke again. 'You know, ever since you first came to us I knew you'd make us proud of you.'

Eva smiled. 'When I first came – it seems such a long time ago now – you and me and Mr Renshaw and Ronnie . . .'

A shadow fell across Maddie's face. 'Ronnie – ah, yes. You know, Eva, I've always been so glad that he died that time the boar got him. If he hadn't, I'd have spent the rest of my life worrying that he'd turn up again one day with his face all disfigured and hatred in his heart. Many's the time I've had bad dreams about that.'

The shadows lifted from Maddie's pretty face when they rode into the farmyard and she caught sight of Max leading a black colt into the stables.

His darkly handsome face crinkled into a smile. 'I've just been putting Thane through his paces again,' he said. 'Put the kettle on, love. I'll be in in a minute.'

The tea was brewing in the pot by the time he came in. 'How's he doing?' Maddie asked. 'Still swinging his back end on the half pass?'

'He's improving,' said Max, flinging himself into a chair. 'He seems to have got the hang of the pirouette – circled his hind legs well today.'

'Good,' pronounced Maddie. 'He certainly has the right temperament. He could do well for us.'

Eva leaned her elbows on the table and watched as Maddie poured tea. 'Will he be up to dressage standard soon?' she asked, slipping Lassie a biscuit under the table.

Maddie laughed. 'Not by a long chalk – piaffe, flying changes – he's got a long way to go and a lot to learn yet. But he's certainly very promising.'

'Like you,' said Max. 'He's bright. He's got a great future ahead of him.'

Eva saw the quick look Maddie flashed at him, then she smiled at Eva. 'It's all right, love,' she said quietly. 'We want you to know that whatever you decide to do, it will be all right with Max and me.'

Max's voice followed hers, slow and deep. 'That's right, Eva. More than anything in the world, we want you to be happy.'

Eva could hear her own voice, husky with feeling as she took the cup of tea from Maddie's hand. 'I know, and I'm grateful. And one way or another I'll make you proud of me yet, I swear I will.'

Back in Golders Green once more Eva found Zoe deep in earnest debate with her father about the boxes of clothes. Louis Jacob sat in his armchair smoking a cigarette, a burst of bristles on his chin and reeking of tobacco.

'Heaven forbid I should be unhelpful to my own child but those boxes are taking over my workshop, princess,' Louis was complaining. 'Where to put the new materials Kosinski is sending, I ask myself? In the lavatory?'

'Don't worry, Mr Jacob,' Eva soothed. 'We plan to go into business as soon as we possibly can. Perhaps you could help us find premises.'

'Premises?' he echoed, throwing up his hands in disbelief.

'Have you any idea how much it costs to rent premises in London? Not to mention the rates. You got money?'

Eva shook her head. 'I'm skint. But never mind the cost for the moment – if we did raise the money, what's the first move we have to make?'

'Experience you need, and judgement. I've known lots of women set up small gown shops and they can never make a go of it. The killer instinct, that's what you need.'

Eva was aware of Zoe's dark eyes on her. 'Those women failed because they weren't different; but we are. Anyway, experience comes with trying.'

Louis's eyes gleamed. 'Ah, trial and error, eh? That's no way to run a business, young lady. You got to be sure you make money.'

'And how will we ever know if we never try? It seems to me you've got to think big to be big.'

'You got a stock, yes?'

'Yes – terrific stuff.'

'But it won't last forever. What you do then, eh?'

'By then we'll know something about the business and be in a better position to decide than we are right now.'

Louis was rubbing his bristly chin thoughtfully. 'You're like babies in the woods, wolves and cheats all around you. How you hope to survive? Men I know in the business who will tear you limb from limb – men like Kosinski – such a thief, you have to count your fingers after you shake hands with him.'

'I can smell a cheat a mile off,' said Eva. 'We'll survive.'

Louis could not resist a smile. 'You're a very confident young woman, and very straight-talking. I like that.'

'I was told it was always best to be direct, not give people false ideas. I learnt that when I was young. I'm the way I am. I'll never change.'

Louis got up from his chair. 'Have you had supper?'

'No.'

'Come, we'll talk more in the restaurant. One way or another I got to get those boxes out of my shop.'

Over the meal the conversation produced no firm plan. Rent for premises was the stumbling block, and Louis could think of nowhere the girls could use. The discussion dwindled and died over coffee.

'That young man,' said Zoe at last. 'The one who came to the shop that day asking for us – has he been back?'

'Young man? Ah, him – no, Rosa has not said so.'

'Pity. I'm dying with curiosity to know who it was,' sighed Zoe. 'I hope he does come back.'

Louis signalled for the bill. When the waitress laid it before him he picked it up and scrutinized it carefully.

'Cover charge?' he said in amazement, pointing at the item. 'What is this cover charge? I come to eat, not to sleep.'

The waitress set her lips in a pained expression. 'It's a set charge, sir. Everyone has to pay it.'

Louis plunged his hand in his pocket and laid money on the plate. 'I pay for what I get, young lady. I get no cover. There's for the food.' He pulled out more coins. 'And there's for you. Good night.'

'I haven't been in an espresso coffee bar like this,' said Eva some days later, leaning across the table towards Zoe. 'Nice and bright, isn't it?'

She fingered the red formica table top, touched the plastic daffodils in the white pottery vase.

Zoe looked around. 'It's never full, though. Just look at that big space beyond the pillar – not a soul there. It's only used by the skiffle band when they come in on Saturday nights. Dad would say that's an expensive waste of space. Not that he's such a wizard in business – he's been bankrupted twice. But for my mother . . .'

Her voice tailed away and her eyes misted in recollection,

but Eva's thoughts were already racing. She leaned across the table eagerly. 'Just think what we could do with that lovely big area, Zoe. It'd be perfect for us.'

Zoe took a deep breath. 'Yes! But do you think – ?'

'No harm in asking.' Eva turned in her chair and called out to the large-boned girl behind the counter, 'Could we see the manager, please?'

The girl frowned. 'Something wrong with your coffee?'

Eva shook her head. 'Just tell him we'd like a word with him.'

The girl lumbered slowly into the back of the shop. Zoe's eyes were gleaming. 'He's bound to say no. He knows as well as we do how much a square foot rented property is. We can't afford it.'

'No harm in trying,' said Eva firmly. 'Like we say up in Yorkshire, them as don't ask, don't get.'

A deep voice behind her made Eva jump. 'I am the owner here. Who wants me?'

Eva saw Zoe's eyes widen before she too turned to see the owner of the voice. He was tall and his shoulders as broad as an ox. His thickened nose and ears were those of a boxer and his greying hair was plastered with Brylcreem. He stood, shirt-sleeved arms akimbo, and Eva could not help noticing the heavy gold identity bracelet about his thick wrist.

'I didn't know you were there – you made me jump,' she said accusingly. The man pulled out a chair and sat down.

'I'm Reg Fowler,' he said shortly. 'Now, who are you and what do you want?'

'My name's Eva Bower,' she said, 'and this is my friend Zoe Jacob. We'd like to talk to you about that wasted space.'

'Jacob?' he repeated, turning his head to look at Zoe. 'Any relation of Louis Jacob, the milliner?'

Zoe took a quick breath. 'You know my father?'

'Know him?' growled Reg. 'He went bankrupt owing me

142

four hundred quid, he did. I remember Louis Jacob all right.'

'Oh,' said Zoe in a small voice.

'One of the nicest men I ever dealt with,' said Reg. 'That was in the days I was wholesaling fabric, before I took on this little goldmine. Now, what can I do for you girls?'

'Let us make use of that wasted space,' said Eva promptly, pointing beyond the pillars. Reg's mouth gaped.

'Make use of it? For selling, you mean?'

'Why not? You aren't using it.'

'What for? Nothing shady, no bent stuff?'

'We've got dresses to sell – high quality goods. Unusual stuff too – it'll pull customers in like crazy,' said Eva. 'Women'll love it – and I bet there isn't another coffee bar –'

'Espresso,' interjected Reg.

'– with a gimmick like that. Just think, women coming in and buying, then coming back with their friends.'

Reg turned to look over his shoulder at the far room. 'How much you prepared to pay for it? Five quid a day?'

Zoe gasped. Eva shook her head. 'Out of the question. We haven't got that kind of money.'

'We couldn't manage five pounds a week,' said Zoe.

'That's probably the most generous offer you'll get,' said Reg, leaning his elbows on the table and linking his hands under his chin.

'All our capital's tied up in the stock,' said Eva, gathering together her gloves and handbag. 'We've a limited quantity of rare and high-quality goods so it shouldn't be a long-term thing. Still, if you can't see the good business sense of having a great attraction like ours in the shop –'

Zoe took the signal and rose to leave. Reg sat up sharply. 'Hold on a minute – give me a chance to think before you go rushing off.'

The girls hesitated but neither sat down. Reg gave a deep sigh. 'Look – how often do you need it?'

'One night to start with – what's the slowest night of the week?'

'Tuesday, without a doubt. Just the space and the tables?'

'And somewhere for a fitting room – a screen, anything.'

He was eyeing her up and down. 'How much does this mean to you, eh?'

Eva took a deep breath. 'I'd give my eye teeth for the chance,' she murmured, 'but if you don't give it to us, someone will. Even Mary Quant had to start somewhere.'

'Mary who?'

'In the King's Road,' said Zoe.

Reg rubbed his chin for a moment. 'Your eye teeth, eh?' he murmured, looking hard at Eva. Then he sat back and slapped his thighs. 'Tell you what, you give it a try. If my takings on Tuesday rise by fifty per cent, you can keep it going. If they don't, you're out. How's that suit you?'

'OK, and no rent if your takings are good,' said Eva. 'And we get free coffee whenever we want it.'

Reg threw back his head and laughed. Eva could see the gold fillings glinting in his back teeth. 'You're a tough little customer and no mistake,' he roared. 'You'll do well in business.'

'You won't regret it,' said Eva firmly. 'We'll bring the boxes in tomorrow, eight of them, and see about the fitting room. You find somewhere safe to store them till Tuesday.'

He was still laughing as he made his way back behind the counter, tweaking the plump bottom of the pudgy-faced girl washing cups as he passed.

'Reg Fowler?' repeated Louis when the girls found him down in the stockroom with Rosa, and Eva could swear his swarthy complexion paled visibly. 'In Dover Street?'

'Deal Street, Papa,' said Zoe. 'And yes, it is the same fellow you owe money to.'

Louis frowned. 'He has a coffee bar now? As well as the bookie's shop and the dry-cleaner's? Not to mention all the other little ventures of his . . .'

'He certainly seems successful – he wore a gold bracelet as thick as your arm,' said Zoe. 'But he was willing to let us have it rent-free.'

Louis shook his head slowly. 'If Reg Fowler does a favour he has something up his sleeve besides his arm. I don't like it, princess.' He looked at his daughter curiously. 'He said I was the nicest man he's ever known?' he asked dubiously.

Zoe laughed. 'He said you're the nicest man who ever went bankrupt on him.'

Louis groaned. 'So better I keep out of his way. He has boys who deal with people for him – people like me. Perhaps it is better you girls handle this business alone without me, eh?'

'That's what we want to do, Papa – so long as you let us use your typewriter.'

'It's yours.'

'And find out where we can lay our hands on hangers and a dress rail.'

Louis wagged a knowing finger. 'I know just the man.'

'And help us get these boxes round to Deal Street tomorrow.'

Louis's eyes widened as he looked down at the crates. 'What am I? A furniture remover already? This is not a box, princess – this is a bungalow. I was born in a house smaller than this box.'

He gave a deep sigh, shaking his head. 'So like your mother – do this for me, Louis, do that. All right, so type your cards for the windows and I will see what I can do.'

Zoe gave him a quick hug. 'Thanks, Papa. We've still got to get the ad in the paper yet.'

The girls left the stockroom and Louis turned to the corner

where Rosa bent over a ledger, frowning and licking a stub of pencil. She looked up.

'God help them with that old typewriter of yours, Louis – the keys are all rusted together.'

He shrugged. 'Do I have money for a new machine suddenly? It's nothing a drop of oil won't cure.'

'You need money, yet you tell the girls they must not pay you board and lodging – I heard. How you pay the bills if you feeding two more mouths?'

'I charge my own daughter? What kind of father am I to charge my own flesh? Things are not so bad, Rosa. Soon they will make money, and then they will pay.'

Rosa eyed him curiously. 'Your daughter – yes. But the other one – you have always the eye for the pretty ones, Louis.'

Louis snorted. 'She has a good head. I like her. Now, have you learned at last how to do my books properly? Three weeks I teach you, and still you keep rubbing out the figures. Are you an idiot, Rosa, or a very clever crook?'

Rosa chewed the tip of the pencil and looked down at the ledger. 'I not very clever, Louis. Still I not understand what is creditor and what is debtor. Which is people who owe money to you?'

She was looking up at him shyly, the vulnerable woman peeping from under layers of heavy flesh.

Louis threw up his hands, but there was patient tenderness in his tone. 'A million times I tell you and a million times you forget. I am the creditor when people owe money to me.'

'So the debtor is the man who doesn't pay you.'

'You got it.'

Rosa looked down again at the ledger. 'Louis,' she said quietly, 'I think we got trouble.'

Louis sighed deeply. 'So what else is new?'

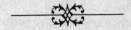

CHAPTER TWELVE

Zoe laid the iron aside and was lifting the navy linen dress carefully to put it on a hanger when Eva burst into the Jacobs' kitchen.

'I've done it!' she cried excitedly. 'It'll be in the *Gazette* this week!'

Zoe examined the dress critically. 'So what's so exciting about getting an ad in the local paper?'

'Not the ad – a feature article! I shot them a line – they're sending a reporter round to meet us at Reg's in half an hour! Get your war-paint on, Zoe – the battle begins!'

As they changed and put on make-up hastily Eva explained. 'I guessed they wouldn't be very interested in a couple of girls starting up in business, so I told them instead that two local girls had been caught up in a hair-raising escapade in France, terrorists, bombs, murder, the lot.'

Zoe frowned. 'Stretching it a bit, isn't it? Anyway, we can't give away Chantal's personal secrets, Eva – it wouldn't be fair.'

'I've thought of that. Leave it to me.'

The young man was waiting in Espresso Rico, notepad and pencil in hand. He adjusted his metal-rimmed spectacles which kept sliding down his thin nose and left his coffee to go cold while he questioned.

'You say you narrowly escaped death in a shop which was blown up by Algerian terrorists in Paris?' he asked.

'By inches,' said Eva. 'We were very lucky.' She noticed Reg hovering nearby, ears pricked.

'You met this lady when she gave you a lift, is that right? Can you give me her name?'

'Sorry,' said Eva. 'Classified information. Suffice it to say that she was an aristocrat, a lady of very ancient family.'

'I see. Then I can take it that it was her high position which made her a target for the terrorists?'

'Very possibly. Who knows?'

'They took the chauffeur and shot him – out of hand?'

'And her pet poodle,' cut in Zoe. 'They were quite ruthless.'

'Then they took the three of you to a remote farmhouse and kept you bound and gagged until the shoot-out with the police? How did the police come to be there?'

Eva indicated Zoe. 'They got there just in the nick of time because of my friend's bravery – she managed to escape the thugs and raise the alarm. If she hadn't . . .' Eva shuddered.

The reporter sighed. 'This lady – this important lady – only escaped certain death at the terrorists' hands because of your timely intervention. A good story, but can't you tell me her name?'

Zoe sat, her back straight and nose in the air. 'We are not at liberty to disclose that information. My friend has already told you.'

'Official Secrets Act?'

Zoe compressed her lips and Eva signalled for more coffee. The reporter looked down at his notes.

'Hundreds of Paris gowns, Balmain, Dior, Givenchy, Balenciaga – she must be incredibly rich to have made you a gift of all these,' he prompted.

'Yes,' said Eva, 'far more than we can use so we plan to sell most of them.' Then she added in a loud whisper to

Zoe, 'I don't think the Countess would mind us saying that, do you?'

'Countess,' repeated the reporter, and scribbled furiously. 'Is she young? Pretty?'

'As a matter of fact,' said Eva, delving in her handbag, 'I have a snap of her here somewhere – ah yes, here it is. That's Zoe . . . and that's me with the lady. You can just see the steps of the château behind us.'

The young reporter's eyes gleamed as he bent over the photograph. 'May I borrow this? I'll see you get it back.'

He tucked it away in his wallet. 'Now, let's see I've got your names spelt right. Zoe –'

'With a diaeresis over the e,' cut in Eva.

'A what?'

'I don't use it,' said Zoe, 'any more than Eva uses the hyphen in her name.'

The reporter wrote laboriously, then added in a persuasive tone, 'You sure you can't tell me the lady's name?'

'Emphatically not,' said Eva.

Reg intruded his large body between the reporter and the girls. 'You heard, mate,' he said gruffly. 'Confidential is that. You got enough – I know about these two girls. They're being very modest – they tackled them terrorists single-handed, you know. Never gave a thought to their own safety. You got a story for the headlines and no mistake, so don't you go bothering them, or else –'

The young reporter rose quickly and adjusted his spectacles again. 'No – right – I've got plenty to go on. Thanks very much.'

As he was going out of the door a pink-faced youth came in, sweating profusely. 'I got a couple of boxes here,' he panted. 'Where do you want me to put them?'

He indicated the handcart outside at the pavement edge. Eva saw Reg's jaw drop.

'Jesus!' he exclaimed. 'You said you got eight boxes, but Christ! I thought you meant dress boxes! Where the hell am I to put that lot?'

'Stack them down the end – we'll unload on to rails later,' said Eva. 'Now, what about curtains for a screen?'

It took most of the day to unload the boxes and hang the dresses on the rails. Zoe surveyed them mournfully.

'Just look at the creases – and after all the time we spent ironing them,' she groaned.

'They'll hang out,' Eva reassured her. 'But they look pretty dreary, all on a rail like that. They'd look a lot better if we had models parading them.'

'And what on earth are we going to ask for them? We've no idea what they cost.'

'Models,' Eva was murmuring. 'Hang on a minute.'

She poked her head round the screen to survey the area where the pudgy-faced girl and a bosomy blonde were serving coffee. 'Well, they're no use,' muttered Eva, 'but look at that pretty brunette in the window – and her fair-haired friend. They must be size thirty-four, both of them.'

Zoe's mouth opened wide. 'You can't ask them to model – they're the debby sort,' she protested.

'So what? They might well leap at the chance to wear Dior, if only for five minutes. I'll ask them.'

Zoe could hear Eva's opening gambit. 'Fancy having a shot at being a model on Tuesday night?' She saw the brunette's haughty stare, and then Eva pulled out a chair and sat down. Five minutes later she came back.

'That's two settled. Harriet and Adele. A couple more and we're in business.'

She looked across to the centre table where a young man was chatting to a dizzy-looking blonde. 'Can't have her,' said

Eva emphatically. 'She's easily WX. Never mind, there'll be more in before long.'

'Prices,' said Zoe. 'What are we going to charge?'

Eva shrugged. 'Let's say twenty pounds apiece to start with. We'll see how they go.'

'Twenty pounds?' gasped Zoe. 'That's nearly as much as Papa pays Patsy per month.'

'Patsy isn't in the market for Dior. And anyway, I've got to pay my way. I've got to pay your dad for rent and board same as any other working girl. Now, let's start listing the dresses in the order we're going to show them.'

The next day Louis could hardly believe his eyes. He looked up from the newspaper, holding it out at arm's length.

'What is this I read? My daughter in the paper?'

Zoe smiled as she buttered toast. 'It's just to advertise the sale, Papa. Good move, don't you think? All Eva's idea.'

Louis was staring at the paper. 'A countess,' he murmured. 'You did not tell me your friend was of royal blood?'

'Poetic licence,' said Zoe. 'Don't believe all you read.'

'But it says here you were bound and gagged – tied up in a farmhouse! Oh, princess! I knew nothing of this!'

'It's all exaggerated, Papa. Don't worry.'

'Don't worry, and my daughter in the hands of villains? What kind of father am I if I don't worry?'

'It's over, Papa, and it wasn't as bad as that at all.'

Louis returned to the paper. '*Heroic girls Eva Jarrett-Bower, daughter of horse-breeder Maximilian Bower* – hey princess, we got a hyphen in the house – *and Zoe Jacob, daughter of Louis Jacob, exclusive millinery designer to the peerage –*' He looked up blankly at his daughter. Zoe shrugged.

'You once gave a hat to my friend Charlotte, when we were in the sixth form.'

'That was a sample, princess, a damaged one. Charlotte was going to a tramps' ball.'

'She was the Honourable Charlotte, daughter of a peer, wasn't she? And you supplied her with a hat, didn't you?'

Louis looked back at the newspaper. '*Louis Jacob, exclusive millinery designer*. You hear that, princess? I am exclusive. They don't get everything wrong.'

The kitchen door opened and Eva burst in. 'Has the paper come? I'm dying to see it – what do they say?'

Louis handed over the newspaper. Eva took it, then her eyes widened. 'The *News of the World*? We gave the story to the *Gazette* reporter. How on earth –'

Louis swallowed down his toast. 'Slater, the editor. He would never miss a chance to feed a good story to the nationals, and why not? Business is business, and it must be good for us too. Exclusive designer, eh?'

Eva gripped Zoe's arm. 'Fantastic! Couldn't be better! If we don't get them flocking in now . . . !'

On Tuesday evening Reg Fowler surveyed the rows of dresses hanging on rails at the far end of his coffee bar and the half-dressed girls he could glimpse between them. Well, if it achieved nothing else, it would certainly enliven his evening.

Customers were beginning to trickle in already, far earlier than usual, and they were heading for the area beyond the pillars. There were the usual kind, the young ladies about town and smart office girls with their current boyfriends, but along with them came women he rarely saw in the Espresso Rico, well-dressed matrons heavily loaded with jewellery and some carrying lapdogs. The place was filling up fast. Reg sent a girl to the storeroom to fetch more chairs.

'This is where the haute couture show is to take place, is it not?' asked a plump, well-heeled bottle-blonde. Reg put on his most gracious smile.

'That's right, madam. Let me find you a seat.'

It was amazing. One after another they were coming, the narrow street outside beginning to choke with gleaming Bentleys and Daimlers. Deal Street had never seen anything like it. Reg strolled among the tables, chatting here and there with clearly excited ladies.

'I agree, events like this are unusual, madam, but we never turn down the opportunity to be different. We pride ourselves on being original,' he said contentedly. Already he had calculated the takings at one coffee a head; an extra penny a cup tonight would go unnoticed by this class of clientele. If only he'd thought of charging an entrance fee . . .

By the time Eva stood in the centre of the room and held up her hand to quell the chatter, the coffee bar was already full to overflowing. Newcomers were having to stand, and over their heads Reg could see girls emerge from behind the dress rails, mince around the minute clearing in the centre, then disappear again.

The customers were visibly eager, reaching forward to touch a hem, asking questions of Eva, and some following Zoe behind the curtains to try on. Above all the chatter he could hear Eva's clear voice outlining the features of the gown now on display.

'Harriet is wearing the latest Paris shape, the Trapeze line, in this afternoon frock of beige linen with mother-of-pearl buttons, designed by Yves St Laurent. This was one of the Countess's favourites – she actually wore it twice. Normally she only wore everything once,' said Eva.

The rails were emptying fast. Zoe could hardly find room to breathe, let alone write, while bodies pressed around her, coats and suits and dresses flying in all directions as one customer snatched discarded garments from another. The list of names and figures in her hand filled page after page;

Adele and Harriet and their two debutante friends looked exhausted from struggling into one outfit after another; and still the audience waited breathlessly for more. Zoe looked at the rapidly depleting rail and signalled to Eva.

Eva poked her head round the screen. 'How's it going back here?'

Zoe wiped her wrist across her brow. 'Frantic. They're going too fast, Eva. I reckon we underpriced them. There's only ballgowns left.'

Eva went back. 'Right, ladies, now we come to our really exclusive and therefore more expensive stock, the ballgowns worn by the Countess to the most elegant soirées in Paris.'

Eyes gleamed and hands clutched feverishly. By the time Eva announced the coffee break nothing remained on the rails but one white linen suit.

'Open another box,' said Eva. 'Never mind if they're creased.'

Zoe bent to open the next box. 'Hey – this isn't Dior, it's Chantal's country stuff, the casual things.'

'Oh Lord, I meant to pick through those myself. Never mind, it's all we've got. Let's see how they go.'

As the second half of the show began the models delved into the box.

'Fantastic!' cried Harriet as she pulled out a full gathered peasant skirt. 'I'm not going to parade this – I'm booking it, Zoe – it's mine.'

Adele lifted from the box a gingham frock with a low neckline, laced bodice and puff sleeves. 'Oh boy! This is mine!' she cried. 'Just like Brigitte Bardot!'

Eva overheard. 'The clothes you are about to see were the Countess's favourite clothes of all, the ones she could wear when she was well out of reach of the public eye. The style, you will observe, is very similar to the style worn by the film actress Brigitte Bardot, and this is not surprising when you learn that Brigitte and the Countess patronize the same Left Bank designer.'

And then came bedlam. If the more mature customers had vied for Dior and Balmain, the younger ones fought now for the Bardot look. Banknotes and cheques poured into Zoe's hands and the paper bags ran out. Adele was modelling an embroidered off-the-shoulder peasant frock.

'Beautiful!' cried a tow-haired dumpling of a woman. 'I'll buy that!'

Eva looked across at her, her ample breasts splayed out along the table top. 'It's a size thirty-four, madam.'

'Never mind,' said the lady. 'I'll take it. If it's a good make it will let out.'

Eva glanced back at the rails. Everything had gone except the white linen suit.

'And now, ladies,' Eva announced, 'I regret that we have come to the end of the evening. Nothing now remains but this one suit, the simple yet elegant lines of Chanel. To tell the truth I am not anxious to part with it since it is the suit the Countess chose especially to accompany her husband to his last resting place in the ancient family mausoleum, a symbol of her purity and piety.'

Eva stood motionless, hands clasped before her and eyes downcast. For a moment there was absolute silence in the coffee bar, so complete that the only sound to be heard was the whistling of an impatient chauffeur out in the street.

'I'll give you forty pounds for it,' a voice called.

'And I'll pay fifty,' called another. Eva looked up and held out her hands.

'Sixty!'

'Eighty!'

'One hundred pounds!'

Eva clapped her hands and smiled. 'Done! Ladies, thank you all for coming, and good night.'

There was a sigh of disappointment as bodies began to rise, gathering bags and poodles to depart. Reg hurried across to Eva.

'You ain't sold out, have you? Not already? My girl Rita'd give her eye teeth for gowns like you got there.'

'We sold what we brought. There's more at home.'

Reg's crumbled face eased into relief. 'Thank Gawd for that. Same again next Tuesday then? I'll arrange a few smoked salmon sandwiches if we gonna get this class of customer again.'

Eva glanced back at Zoe. She was surrounded by a knot of young women, all eager to catch her attention.

'Do at least give us your telephone number, or take mine in case you come across another one like that.'

'I'll see what I can do,' Zoe was promising, 'but actually I wanted that particular model for myself.'

'I'll pay double if you can get one for me.'

At last Eva was able to speak to her alone. 'Well – what did we take?'

Zoe looked rapturous. 'You'll never believe this, Eva – almost fourteen hundred pounds!'

Reg was nearby. Eva took a five-pound note from Zoe's hand and held it out to him. 'Five pounds a day, I think you said, Reg – here you are.'

Reg waved it aside. 'I said if I was fifty per cent up – well, I wouldn't tell this to anyone else, but –' He came closer and lowered his voice. 'The takings are three hundred per cent up.' He beamed broadly. 'Girls, you don't owe me no rent so long as you'll do it again next week.'

Adele and Harriet, clutching their parcels in delight, had gone home. The last customers had dribbled out into the night. Reg and his girls disappeared into the back. Eva and Zoe bagged up bundles of coins and cheques and notes and then put on their coats.

'I'm clapped out,' said Zoe. 'Dying for a good cup of tea.'

As they neared the door of the coffee bar two men in dark suits and slouch hats came in. Hugely built and bristled, eyes gleaming amid folds of swarthy flesh, they made Eva think of escaped gorillas. Without a word they advanced slowly towards the two girls.

Eva glanced at Zoe and saw the alarm in her eyes and the involuntary movement to clutch the money bag closer to her body.

Reg appeared from the back and stood there, elbows on the counter. For a moment no one moved, then Reg chuckled.

'It's OK, girls,' he said smoothly. 'I reckoned the lads ought to see you two safe home, you with all that money on you and all. This ain't no neighbourhood for girls to be out late on their own, especially with so much loot on them.'

'No, really, it's very good of you, Reg,' said Eva, 'but there's really no need. It's not far.'

'Bollocks,' said Reg. 'Babes in arms, you two. My boys'll see you're OK, won't you, lads?'

Louis was completely bemused. He sank onto a kitchen chair, overcome by the sight of so much money.

'So rich already,' he was murmuring. 'I never saw women so anxious to part with their gelt.'

'You saw?' said Zoe. 'How come?'

'Would I not watch my daughter's triumph? Did I not see it all from outside in the street? Ninety-seven of my bags I counted coming out, ninety-seven bags with Louis Jacob on them. Good for business, that.'

His eyes glowed as he pictured ladies of wealth in their bedrooms, even now opening their parcels and noting the name on the bag. Next time he must remember to get them printed *Exclusive Milliner*.

'Why didn't you come in?' said Eva. 'We could have done with some help.'

Louis shuddered. 'I see the boys come. I leave.'

Eva gave a laugh. 'I don't blame you – they frightened me to death.'

'And me,' said Zoe. 'I thought Reg was going to take the money for what Papa owed him.'

Louis shook his head. 'I wouldn't put it past him – there's nothing that wide boy won't do for money.'

He touched the pile of banknotes on the table with reverence. 'Such a good businesswoman you are, princess. From your Mama you get that, not from me. She always used to say I was a *shlemazl*, always running into trouble, and it's true.'

'Maybe you should have gone into partnership, Papa, like Eva and me.'

Louis sighed. 'The millinery trade is dying, princess – people aren't wearing hats so much these days.' He reached over to touch the pile of cheques and frowned. 'One thing I tell you, princess – try always to take cash, not cheques.'

Eva's lips were moving as she counted silently. At length she laid the last coin down and sat back.

'I make it thirteen hundred and eighty-five,' she breathed. 'Isn't that incredible? Never in my wildest dreams did I think we could do that well.'

'And,' said Zoe, her face aglow with pleasure, 'we've got at least as much again to sell. Roll on next Tuesday!'

They were heaping the money together when Louis suddenly remembered. He clapped his hands to his head.

'What a *shlemiel* I am! I forgot the telephone call – the young man – he rang again for you.'

Zoe and Eva looked up. 'What young man?'

'The one who came looking for you. He said he must speak with you. He says his name is Finch, Alan Finch.'

Eva sat down abruptly. 'Alan?' she murmured. 'What the devil can he want with us?'

CHAPTER THIRTEEN

'You know,' said Zoe as the girls got into bed, 'if it hadn't been for what he did to Fay, I'd have quite liked Alan Finch. Interesting sort of bloke, I thought, even if you couldn't trust him as far as you could throw him.'

Eva said nothing, sitting up with her arms around her knees and watching the reflection of the neon light flashing somewhere out in the night.

'You quite fancied him once, as I recall,' Zoe mused. 'And he definitely had his eye on you. You never mention that now – or David Maynard.'

Eva busied herself plumping up the pillow. 'No. That's all dead and gone.'

'You don't still hanker for David then? It looked like a real big thing once.'

'I thought it might have been. I was wrong. Funny how distance lends objectivity.'

'Distance lends enchantment, I always thought.'

'Couldn't be more wrong,' said Eva. 'It makes you realize how you could have wasted your life on the wrong things. Gilbert Murray learnt all the Greek tragedies by heart. What a waste of a life.'

She was just drifting off when Zoe suddenly turned over. 'You gave a great spiel tonight, Eva. They really lapped it up, every word of it.'

'Thanks.'

Zoe chuckled. 'Chantal only wore everything once – what a whopper!'

'Didn't I say once a night? I thought I did. Now shut up and go to sleep.'

Louis was waiting for Eva at breakfast.

'Zoe tells me you didn't know what to charge last night,' he said as he passed her the pot of tea. 'It's important you should know the original cost so you can charge a percentage.'

Eva poured a cup of tea. 'We're not complaining, Mr Jacob – we came out of it very well.'

'But maybe better next time – maybe it was the customers came out well yesterday. You ought to get at least fifty per cent of the cost price.'

'But we've no way of knowing that, Mr Jacob, short of going back to Paris to find out.'

Louis rubbed his nose, muttering. 'There must be some way to find out the going rate for Balmain. I see what I can do.'

Rosa stood hesitantly at the portico of Harrods. Her plump face was pink and her full lips quivering.

'No, no, Louis, I cannot – I am not dressed for town – I not know when I come to work today you would want to go to Knightsbridge. I am so ashamed.'

'Nonsense, Rosa – you look charming, and we must find out. The label says Balmain but like all expensive stores, they put no price ticket. Would you have me disappoint my daughter, Rosa? Would you make me do that?'

She saw the pleading in his eyes and gave a brave little smile. 'OK, Louis. I do this for you I would do for no one else.'

Smiling he drew her arm through his and led her into the store and across its carpeted floor towards the staircase. 'Hold your head up high, Rosa,' he murmured. 'No woman in London is better than you.'

In the dress department Rosa shrank into the background as Louis advanced to the counter.

'We want to look at the gown in the window, the one that says Balmain,' he said to the superbly-coiffeured assistant. The woman's face betrayed no surprise.

'Certainly, sir. Would madam care to try it?'

'First we want to look,' said Louis. 'It is possible Mrs Petrucci does not like the texture of the cloth.'

'It's the purest silk georgette, sir,' the assistant assured him. 'At four hundred pounds one would expect the very best.'

Rosa paled and shrank further from the counter. 'What you expect is not always what you get,' said Louis. 'But if it is too much trouble –'

'Not at all, sir. I'll have it fetched at once.'

Louis saw Rosa shaking her head in terror. 'No matter,' he told the assistant. 'Mrs Petrucci has changed her mind. I think she is in need of a cup of coffee. Tell me, which way to the restaurant?'

'Four hundred pounds!' exclaimed Rosa as they caught the bus to go home. 'A man could almost buy a house with four hundred pounds!'

'Sometimes I am amazed at human nature,' muttered Louis, 'but fifty per cent – *oh, vay!*'

'The girls cannot ask so much,' protested Rosa. 'They too will have many creditors – debtors.'

Louis brightened. 'But ten per cent is not unreasonable! At forty pounds a dress . . .'

His mind was racing, trying to estimate the number of gowns still remaining in the unopened boxes at forty pounds a time . . . Even at a guess, the resulting figure was phenomenal. His head began to spin.

'Here is our stop, Louis,' Rosa said with relief. 'I am so glad to be back.'

At the corner of the street Rosa stopped. 'You come back to my place for a bite to eat, Louis? I got a good apple dumpling.'

He smiled and shook his head. 'Thank you, no, I gotta get back.' Seeing the look of disappointment which crossed her face he caught hold of her sleeve. 'You are a good woman, Rosa,' he said softly. 'Tomorrow I take you shopping for a new coat, eh?'

She looked down at her shabby working coat, then caught her breath. 'Not Harrods, Louis? Surely –'

Louis clicked his tongue. 'Harrods – schmarrods! Tomorrow I take you to my friend Henry Bernstein in Soho – he will make you a coat fit for a queen. Henry Bernstein gives the best value for money in London – Miriam always said so.'

Zoe was ironing in the kitchen. Louis seized his daughter and spun her round the table in a frenzied waltz.

'Princess, you are a millionairess!' he cried. 'Oh, that I should live to see my child a rich woman, and not even through a rich husband!'

Zoe eyed him curiously. 'Where were you, Papa? The girls have been asking for you all day, and for Rosa. They needed more veiling for the new model. Where have you been?'

'Shopping, princess, to Harrods.'

Zoe rolled her eyes. 'You wouldn't shop at Harrods if it was the last store on earth. You must be drunk.'

Louis spread his hands, his face a picture of injured innocence. 'Would I drink when there is business to be done? I went for you, princess, to discover the price of Balmain. Four hundred pounds, no less? Daylight robbery!'

Eva dropped her shopping bag on the chair and shouted,
    'Zoe, where are you?'

Zoe came in from the kitchen. 'I was ironing. Did you get the fruit and stuff?'

'Never mind that – listen! Guess who I saw in the market?'

Zoe nodded. 'I know. I saw him too when I went out to get some veiling. Isn't it amazing?'

Eva sank down in the armchair. 'Of all people – him, the last person I ever expected to run into like that. I can't get over it.'

Zoe squatted on the floor by the fire, her eyes gleaming in the firelight. 'Me too. It's quite incredible. I wonder why he's here? Did you get a chance to speak to him?'

'No – I only saw him from the top of the bus.'

'Neither did I. He must have just come over. I wonder where he's staying. I'm dying to get in touch.'

Eva frowned. 'Just come over? What are you talking about?'

Zoe twisted round to look up at her. 'Luc, of course – he must have just come over from France. Who did you think I was talking about?'

Eva shook her head. 'I was talking about Alan Finch – I saw him in the market this afternoon. He was with a girl – and it wasn't Fay.'

Reg Fowler's girlfriend was already sitting in the Espresso Rico when the girls began their preparations the following Tuesday afternoon. She put away her lipstick and stood up.

'I'm Rita,' she told them with a broad, tooth-whitened smile. 'I'm a part-time model, actually, so Reg thought maybe I could help you show the stuff.'

Eva and Zoe's gaze travelled down her voluptuous body with its pouter-pigeon breasts and nipped-in waist, its generous hips and ample thighs. Zoe turned beseeching eyes on Eva.

Eva swallowed. 'The only frocks we have left now are the tiny ones, Rita, from the days when the Countess was on a crazy diet. She only got a good figure back again when she got over the craze. But it's very kind of you to offer.'

She could see Zoe begin to breathe again. 'Yes it is,' she said. 'Maybe you'd like to help me with the orders and the money? If we're as busy as we were last time –'

'Fantastic!' said Rita. 'I never make a mistake with change – comes of working in a shop when I first left school. I didn't stick it long – like Reg says, with my looks and figure I could do better. You have to have a good figure in my profession – I'm a photographic model, you know.'

From the kitchen recesses Eva could hear Reg's chuckle. 'One of the best,' he called out. 'The lads at the photographic club don't get many like her to the pound.'

Rita dimpled. 'Now, leave off, Reg,' she called back, 'or you'll have the girls wondering what I get up to. It's all strictly legal, you know,' she added confidentially. 'Nothing the vice squad would be after me for, nothing like that. I'm a decent girl, I am.'

Reg sauntered out from the back and draped his arm over Rita's shoulders. 'She's a bit of all right, is our Rita. Do anything for anybody, she would.'

Rita gave him a playful dig in the ribs. 'Here, hark at that rain,' she said. Eva could hear it, pattering hard against the café windows. Reg glanced over his shoulder.

'Gonna be another bloody rotten night by the sound of it,' he commented. 'Same as it's been a bloody rotten summer. Just hope the punters keep coming in.'

They came, despite the teeming rain which made the streets shine like rippled glass, shaking off soggy umbrellas and dripping mackintoshes as they came in. The air in Espresso Rico was heavy with the mingled smells of cigarette smoke and fragrant coffee, wet hair and steaming damp coats. Mostly, Eva noticed, it was the younger girls who came this time, not their Dior-dressed mothers.

But the rain did not seem to have dampened their enthusiasm. Customers and models Adele and Harriet alike were fighting to try on Chantal's peasant clothes, chattering excitedly all the time.

'I say, this skirt doesn't seem to look quite like it did on the model – or is it just the light, do you think?'

'You're right, it's all wrong – get it off.'

The second girl snatched the skirt eagerly and began struggling her way into it. The first one tried to tug it back.

'No, no – I haven't seen anything like it since Mary Quant opened.'

'You can keep Quant,' puffed her friend, 'and her little girl look. Kneesocks and flat chests . . .'

The other gave up. 'This Bardot look is definitely for me – far more sexy. If you decide not to have it I'll have it.'

'It's what we call the *gamine* look,' said Eva. 'It's going to be all the rage.'

There was no stopping them. The demand for Chantal's casual clothes owed far less to her courtesy title than to the fresh, wholesome freedom of her wardrobe. By the time Reg sent out trays of coffee the rails were almost empty once more.

'I didn't bother with the smoked salmon sandwiches,' he confided to Eva. 'Now, if their mums had come . . .'

The demand for clothes continued unabated during the second half of the sale until the very last item was gone. Still customers pleaded.

'Tell me where I can ring you – I want a frock just like that one you sold to my friend.'

'Can you get one of those peasant skirts made up for me in green? I'll give you my phone number.'

'What did you say?' Eva asked Zoe as the last lingerers headed for the door.

'Gave them Papa's number. I don't know what we'll do when they ring.'

A paunchy man in a grey mackintosh spattered with cigarette ash pushed his way through the tables to where Eva stood with Zoe by the screen.

'Slater,' he said tersely without removing the cigarette from his mouth. 'Editor of *The Gazette*.'

'No more interviews, please,' said Eva. 'Can't you see we're busy?'

'No interview, miss. Just wanted to say I thought yours was a damn good story. Seems to have done you a bit of good tonight. Did us both a bit of good, in fact.'

'I'm glad to hear it,' said Eva.

'And it could benefit us both to keep the Countess story going – even if she was only Madame Noircy.'

Eva could see the knowing gleam in his grey eyes. 'Yes,' he went on smoothly. 'A great pity to let it lapse. I'm sure there's some angle we can use –'

'You can tell your readers what a success our sale has been,' said Eva.

Slater wasn't listening. 'Like the heroines of the terrorist drama now consorting with known gangsters, for example,' he went on undeterred. 'Yes, that could be a novel angle . . .'

'Gangsters?' echoed Eva in surprise. Reg's craggy face appeared behind Slater's back as the editor went on. 'Crooks like Reg Fowler. Small-time, admittedly, but a known member of the underground fraternity nevertheless. You two and him – fragrance mixing with foulness . . .'

'Here,' said Reg gruffly. 'Who are you calling a small-time crook? Just you take care what you say, Mr Slater, or I'll do you.'

The cigarette quivered in the editor's mouth. 'Ah, Reg, I was only saying –'

'I heard what you said, Mr Slater. Say what you like about me, but you call me small-time and there's trouble, right?'

'I'm sorry, Reg, I wouldn't dream –'

'I'm sure you wouldn't, Mr Slater. Say good night, Eva – Mr Slater's leaving.'

The editor's flabby body seemed to rise a clear foot off the floor as Reg grabbed a handful of raincoat and steered him towards the door. All that remained was a smouldering cigarette end on the floor.

Reg came back. 'You can forget him,' he said cheerily. 'If he gives you any more bother, just you tip me the wink. Anybody bothers you anytime, me and the boys'll soon sort 'em out.'

Eva smiled, and it was as she was turning back to Zoe that she caught sight of the young woman in a fawn mackintosh sitting alone in the corner. She rose and came across to them.

Zoe's mouth opened wide. 'Fay! What on earth are you doing here?'

Fay's smile was as crooked and attractive as Eva remembered. 'I read about you in the papers, darling. I couldn't resist coming to see for myself.'

'Oh, I'm so glad to see you!' Zoe hugged her close and over her shoulder Eva's gaze met Fay's.

'Hello, Eva,' she said.

Eva hung back. 'Hello, Fay. You're the last person in the world I expected to see here, but I'm awfully glad you came.'

Rita came across to join them. 'You a friend of theirs?' she asked Fay brightly. 'I'll get Reg to send some more coffee then. Reg asks did it go all right, Zoe?'

'The takings are lower but we did OK.'

Rita grinned. 'He says the same, so everybody's happy.'

'Come and sit down,' said Zoe, taking Fay's arm. 'I want to

know everything. Did you go away to Scotland with Alan? Is he with you?'

Fay seated herself, then leaned across the table. 'No, that's all over. We didn't get married, Zoe. We parted.'

'He let you down? Oh, Fay!'

'It didn't work out, that's all.' Fay spoke quietly, tracing a ring of spilt coffee on the plastic table surface. 'Anyway, I came back to London.'

Zoe looked across at Eva and for a moment there was silence. The pudgy-faced girl brought a tray of coffee, sniffed, and went away.

'I was nearly out of my mind at first,' Fay went on softly, as if talking to herself. 'Mother wouldn't have me back at home and stopped my allowance. Daddy was God-knows-where with his girlfriend. I felt so alone. I thought of all kinds of crazy things, throwing myself under a tube train, going into a convent – I was really quite barmy for a bit.'

'Poor Fay,' murmured Zoe. 'We had no idea.'

'I'm so sorry,' said Eva. 'Maybe we could have helped if we'd known.'

Fay straightened. 'Still, I got through it. Life's for living, I told myself. You can't waste it sitting alone in one spot, wishing for things to change, because that way they won't. Like Eva once said, you've got to shape life the way you want it to be.'

'Good for you,' said Eva. 'So what did you do?'

'I had no money, so first I had to get myself a job. And would you believe it, fate played right into my hands. I got in touch with a bridge friend of Mummy's who owns a magazine. He gave me a job.'

'Well done,' said Zoe. 'Doing what?'

'Writing fashion articles for *Trend*, and I love it.'

'*Trend?* That's a super glossy mag – I've read it at the dentist's,' said Zoe. 'Gosh! You'll be famous.'

Fay smiled. 'Maybe one day – I'd like to be a leading fashion writer like Carmel Snow is for *Harper's Bazaar*. And I'll do it too.'

Eva sat silent. This was a new Fay, a woman who spoke with quiet confidence and resolve. Somehow she had grown up dramatically over the past few months.

'Did you know Alan's in London?' Eva asked.

'No,' said Fay, 'and I don't care. If I never see him again it will be too soon.'

Zoe changed the subject. 'If you and your mum don't get on now, where are you staying?'

'I've got digs in the Finchley Road – nothing spectacular, but a junior feature writer doesn't earn enough for Mayfair – not yet, anyway.' Fay glanced at her watch. 'I'd better be going or my landlady will be sending out the police – she's very sweet really, but a trifle over-protective at times.'

'We must see you again soon though,' said Zoe. 'There's so much to talk about –'

'Like what you're going to do next,' said Fay. 'I want to hear all about it. You're not going to stop at tonight, are you? The kids were going crazy for the Bardot look. It'll make a nice piece for the magazine.'

'We're out of stock,' said Eva. 'We'll have to talk about future plans.'

'You have a phone number?' asked Fay. 'Here's mine. We'll meet again soon.'

Eva watched her slim figure as she made for the door. Even in Fay's walk there was a new decisiveness.

Reg appeared with Rita behind him. 'Who's your friend?' he asked with a roguish grin on his craggy face. 'She's a real looker and no mistake.'

'Here,' said Rita with a mock frown. 'You got all you can handle with me. You ain't in the first flush of youth now, you know.'

He turned to pinch her bottom and she squealed. 'There's hidden depths in me, girl. You'll find out.'

In the kitchen the girls found Louis standing waiting for the kettle to boil. His eyes were red-rimmed and he kept sneezing.

'Well, how you go on tonight?' he rasped. 'God, I got a hell of a cold starting.'

Eva stacked the takings on the table. 'Six hundred and forty pounds – that makes just over two thousand altogether! Who'd have believed it?'

Zoe's eyes were shining. 'And if we'd had more we could have sold them ten times over. I've never known people go so crazy for stuff.'

'Where there's demand, you fill it,' said Louis, lifting the steaming kettle. 'That's business. Just think, if you got two thousand at roughly ten per cent of cost –'

'That means Chantal spent a fortune,' said Zoe, 'but we haven't any left to sell and we can't get more. That's the end of that little business, but now we've got capital to start something else.'

'Achoo! More frocks from the wholesaler, princess? I got a good friend –'

'At least we can pay for our board now,' said Eva, 'but we have to think carefully how we're going to invest the rest.'

'Why not your own shop?' suggested Louis. 'This place maybe? The hat trade is dying, and I think maybe I am dying too. It is time I retire to a nice little house in Westcliff.'

He sneezed loudly again. Zoe looked at him in concern. 'You've got a bad cold, Papa. What have you been doing?'

He spread his hands mournfully. 'All night it rains. Out in the street is no place for an old man like me.'

'You weren't standing outside the coffee bar again?' exclaimed Zoe. 'Oh, Papa!'

'Why not, princess? It gives an old man great pleasure to see his daughter taking money like there was no tomorrow – and you know what, Zoe? I see fifty-three more of my bags come out of the shop. Fifty-three – that's more than come out of my shop in a year!'

Zoe gave him an affectionate hug. 'Get off to bed now, Papa, and I'll bring you a hot toddy.'

He was making for the door when he turned, a crafty gleam in his eye. 'What you think, princess – you and Eva like to buy my shop, eh?'

'I don't know, Papa. We'd need to know more first, value of fittings and stock, things like that.'

'And we'd have to have a look at the books,' said Eva.

'Anyway,' said Zoe, 'as I remember you put the business in my name because of the bankruptcy thing.'

Louis shrugged. 'Just a thought.'

CHAPTER FOURTEEN

A week later the telephone was still ringing in Louis Jacob's hallway. Order after order was piling up.

'Just look at this, six peasant skirts, two blouses and three off-the-shoulder frocks,' said Zoe from the list in her hand, 'and also a lined cloak and a pair of frayed shorts.'

'Frayed?' echoed Louis. 'So now the rich want used goods?'

Eva sat, chin cupped in hands, deep in thought. 'We got to think of a way out – it's too good an opening to miss. There's the clothes we kept for ourselves and the things Adele and Harriet took – is there any way we could copy them if we borrowed them back?'

'Copy?' said Louis. 'No problem. Once when I was making lingerie I took a Marks and Spencer nightdress to pieces. I sold hundreds that season,' he said proudly, then added as an afterthought, 'and I sewed the original back together and took it back to the shop. I got my money back.'

'So if we buy material and thread,' said Zoe thoughtfully, 'use the models as patterns and then put them back together –'

'My girls would sew for you. They need more work,' said Louis.

Eva jumped up, eyes shining. 'You're a genius, Mr Jacob – can I use your phone?'

Ella and Patsy sat at their sewing machines and stared at the lengths of coloured cotton and silk in amazement. Ella raised disbelieving eyes to Louis.

'You want us to sew up *blouses*?' she said. 'Never in my life before have I sewn blouses.'

'Nor me skirts,' said Patsy. 'Only the ones I make meself out of me mum's leftovers.'

'So now you get industrial training at my expense,' said Louis. 'Do you throw generosity in my face?'

He sneezed as if to indicate what such an action would do. Ella pulled a face. 'You ought to be home in bed before your cold turns into something worse.'

'Yes,' said Patsy. 'This room'll be full of your germs swimming around the place.'

Rosa came down the stairs and went to peer closely at his flushed face. 'You're running a temperature, Louis. You should be tucked up warm in your bed with some Beechams Powders. Go home, Louis.'

Louis's red eyes widened. 'With all these things to get ready for the girls, how am I to go home?'

Rosa took the pattern pieces from his hand and laid them on the bench. 'No work today, Mr Jacob. Now we have the chance to show you how well we can get by without you, Ella and Patsy and me. We'll show him, won't we?'

Zoe pulled the blue cotton frock from the pile of clothes on the bed and held it up against her body.

'Guess which, Eva – the original or the copy?'

Eva fingered it for a moment. 'It's the original, I know it is.'

'Wrong! It's one of the copies, in almost identical material. Now let's see how it fits.'

As she pulled it over her head Eva reached for a linen shirt. 'This is a copy too? I'll try it on.'

She pulled off her own blouse. 'Don't you ever wear a bra?' asked Zoe.

'Nope,' said Eva. 'I like to feel free and unfettered.'

They both stood before the mirror, twisting about to inspect every detail. 'It's fantastic,' cried Eva. 'This shirt fits like a glove.'

'And this frock – though maybe it's a tiny bit longer than Chantal's.'

The girls grabbed hold of each other and whooped round the room in delight. 'Who'd ever guess?' cried Eva. 'They've done an incredible job. Now all that remains is to see if our customers can spot the difference!'

'Maddie? It's Eva.'

It was gratifying to be able to tell her the news over the telephone, hear the glow of pleasure in her voice as she listened.

'Two thousand, Maddie – it would have taken four years of teaching salary to get that much!'

'And what do you and Zoe plan to do with it, love?'

'Stay in the fashion business if we can. There's no satisfying the demand for our sort of stuff. We're thinking how best to invest our money, rent premises and machinists maybe.'

'Or buy wholesale clothes to sell?'

'We'd much rather manufacture our own – the ones we copied have gone like hot cakes. Whatever we do, it's got to be different.'

She could hear Maddie's smile. 'As always. If ever we could count on you for anything, Eva, it was to be different.'

'But if we do, we'll need our own name. Got any ideas for what we could call our company, Maddie?'

There was a pause while Maddie considered. 'What about Chantal – or Countess? She's the one who started all this.'

'Too posh.' Eva could hear Maddie murmuring to Max.

'Max suggests a French word – an endearment, perhaps, like *Chérie* or *Mignonne*.'

'Too twee. It's got to sound young and fresh and new. Something that has the Bardot ring about it.'

Maddie sighed. 'You're on your own, love. I'll ring you back if we come up with anything.'

Louis leaned on the counter at Henry Bernstein's retail office in Soho.

'I tell you, Henry, she is going a long way, my princess – she gets her good head for business from me.'

Henry rubbed his long nose, his dark eyes huge and mournful as a spaniel's, and tapped the sample of cloth on the counter. 'This coat for Mrs Petrucci, Louis – are you sure this is the fabric she will want?'

'She will like it. By when will you make it up for me?'

Bernstein shrugged thin shoulders. 'By Friday?'

'So soon? I thought this was your busy season.'

'What difference for a friend?' Bernstein leaned confidentially across the counter. 'I tell you truth, Louis – times is bad. Even Rosenberg finish with me. Not good enough, they say – me, Henry Bernstein, not good enough for Marcus Rosenberg!'

'*Oh, vay*,' murmured Louis. 'What you do now, Henry?'

'Who knows? Maybe I sell and go join my nephews in Liverpool – they got a good little business. You hear of anyone wants a good business . . .'

'How much?' said Louis, 'to a friend?'

Bernstein stared, leaned forward again. 'Settle the debts, it's yours.'

'That bad? How much?'

'A couple of thousand maybe.'

'I'll put the word around,' said Louis. 'Now, the coat – I want a good satin lining and good deep pockets, you hear?'

'I've been thinking,' said Zoe. 'If we were to buy or rent a

176

place like Bernstein's, don't you think it might be a good idea to get Fay to come into business with us? She'll get all kinds of contacts in her job.'

Eva cocked her head to one side and thought. 'Maybe. You'd have to ask her first.'

'You don't think she'd leap at it? Well, perhaps not. But she wrote a super piece about our show in *Trend* – she'll back us all the way. Yes, maybe you're right.'

'Put it to her if you like. And I'd like a word with her after.'

Eva could hear Zoe's voice in the hallway, chattering excitedly on the telephone. After a while Eva went out to listen.

'Eva's here now – she wants to talk to you.'

Eva took the receiver. 'Hello, Fay.'

'Hello.'

'I'd like to talk to you sometime, Fay. On our own.'

There was a silence on the other end of the line. 'Can it possibly wait?' Fay's voice came stiffly. 'I'm due to meet someone now.'

Eva tried to hide the disappointment she felt. 'OK – I'll catch you later then.'

'Do that. Goodbye.'

Zoe was waiting in the living room. 'She won't join us, she said. She said we were the ones with talent and ideas, but she'd promote us and try and find contacts. She'll do an interview with us for *Trend* just as soon as we get started.'

'Great,' said Eva. 'Now, how about seeing an accountant about these Bernstein debts?'

Reg Fowler sat open-mouthed. 'You wanna make a bid for this Jew boy's premises, machines, the lot?' he gasped as he sat with Eva over a cup of coffee in Espresso Rico. 'You sure think big, I give you that. But where'll you get that kind of money, eh? It'll take more than you've got.'

'We know what we're doing,' said Eva confidently.

Reg sighed. 'I wish I had a pound for every time I've heard that. But tell you what, sweetheart, I can put you in a line of business that would earn you a bomb in no time – no risk either. You don't have to put up no capital, just work for me.'

Eva raised her eyebrows. 'Work for you? Doing what?'

'Plenty of added bonuses too, if you play your cards right.'

'Doing what?' repeated Eva. 'Not that I'm interested . . .'

'You got a bit of life about you,' Reg was saying, cocking his head to one side to assess her thoroughly. 'A bit of vitality is what the business needs.'

'Not like your dead-beat waitresses – they look like zombies floating around,' retorted Eva. 'Anyway, I don't know what business you're talking about, but it could be shady for all I know.'

Reg chuckled. 'No, straight as a die. Honesty is not incompatible with amassing a large fortune, somebody once said.' He lowered his voice. 'I could make it worth your while, Eva. Come in with me and you won't regret it.'

'Who said that – about honesty?' asked Eva in amazement.

'How the hell should I know? I only remember things I want to remember, not who said them. Now, are you interested?'

'No,' said Eva firmly. 'I can read between the lines.'

'Meaning?'

'I'm not in the market for personal services. If I want money that's not the way I'll get it. Whatever the job is I'm not interested in sleeping with the boss. I don't want a lover, I want a backer.'

Reg was laughing out loud now. 'You're a right one and no mistake! Do you make a habit of being so blunt?' he asked.

'Do you make a habit of making up to a woman without being encouraged?'

'Only if it's you, sweetheart – I never could resist a woman with spirit.'

'Bugger off, Reg. Find another playmate – I've got a fortune to make.'

It was easy to find Fay's digs in the Finchley Road. A bemused-looking landlady came to answer Eva's knock.

'Fay?' she repeated absently, and Eva could see her bosom heaving in a strange, volcanic movement. 'I'll see if she's in.'

She removed a cat from under her jumper and let it fall to the linoed floor. Moments later Fay came down.

'I was just going out,' she told Eva. 'Walk with me to the bus if you like.'

Eva turned and fell into step beside her. 'Come on, Fay, out with it,' she said. 'I could feel that atmosphere the moment you came to the Espresso Rico the other night. What's up?'

Fay shrugged and gave a faint smile. 'I was embarrassed, that's all – it was a bit strained last time we met, if you remember. I had some peculiar ideas about you then – feelings I couldn't explain.'

'Is that all?' said Eva. 'Then forget it. We're friends again. Where are you going?'

'Home. My mother seems to have changed her mind about me. Why don't you come with me – it'll make things easier.'

'OK, if you think it will help. I'm so glad, for your sake.'

'It hasn't been easy. Have you ever tried living on a budget of four shillings a day? I'm sick of the sight of spaghetti and meat loaf. Here's the bus.'

'Maybe today's your lucky day,' said Eva as they climbed the stairs to the top deck.

'According to my stars in the magazine I'm in the spotlight today; don't let opportunities slip through your fingers, it said.'

'If your mum wants you back in the fold –'

'If she does, it's only because the divorce is going through,' said Fay. 'I still can't believe they've done it.'

'Does it upset you very much?'

Fay sighed. 'There was no other way. It was best for everybody.' After a moment she added, 'Daddy certainly seems much happier. He says Josie gives him space; she demands no commitment from him. I think he always feared intimacy, being devoured by someone.'

'And how did your mum take it?'

'Not quite so well. She's the kind of woman who needs a lot of attention to stop her going inside herself. Daddy paid no attention to anything but his books. Ah, here's our stop.'

Valerie Bartram-Bates was lying on a chaise-longue in her drawing room cradling a minute Pekinese in her lap. She received Fay's kiss on her cheek and then turned curious eyes on Eva.

'My friend from college, Mummy – Eva Jarrett-Bower.'

'Jarrett-Bower?' repeated her mother. 'I don't think I know your family, do I, dear?'

'I don't think so. Not unless you've come across them at horse shows,' replied Eva.

'Ah, they ride? With which hunt?'

Eva frowned. 'The Garthdale Hunt, as a matter of fact. Do you know that dog is dribbling?'

Mrs Bartram-Bates held the dog up to inspect her dress. 'Good Lord, it's wet me again,' she cried. 'Take it away, Fay, there's a dear – the damn thing's like a leaky hot-water bottle. I wish I'd never let Clive persuade me to have it.'

She dabbed at the small stain on her frock with her handkerchief then turned her attention again to Eva. 'Where do you live, Eva?'

'In the Yorkshire Dales. A village called Barnbeck.'

'Really?' Blue eyes widened. 'Don't you find life terribly boring in a small village so far away from the city?'

Eva could feel her face grow hot. 'No, I don't, as a matter of fact. I find it very reassuring to know everyone, and everyone knows me.'

'I'm sure. Do you play bridge?'

Eva couldn't resist it. 'No, but I'm a dab hand at cribbage.'

Fay leapt in. 'Eva's going to start her own business, with Zoe – you remember me talking about Zoe?'

Her mother's forehead creased in thought. 'Hats,' she said at last. 'Her father is a milliner. I don't know his hats myself – I always wear Aage Thaarup.'

'No, you wouldn't have heard of him,' said Eva. 'His clientele is very small and exclusive.'

Mrs Bartram-Bates ignored the slight and picked up the newspaper. 'Have you seen this, Fay? Lady Lewisham, talking to reporters, says Lord Lewisham won't dream of doing a hand's turn in the house. He won't even pick his clothes up off the floor. Doesn't that remind you of someone? Really, I think women make rods for their own backs.'

'Mummy,' said Fay quietly, 'I thought you wanted to talk to me.'

'I only wanted to say you can move back in here if you like, everything will be as it was before. Well, almost.'

'Things won't ever be the same, Mummy. You'll have to get used to it.'

Mrs Bartram-Bates pursed her lips. 'Men! They're so unimaginative! A husband only wants his wife to be fertile and unfulfilled – it's very unsatisfying for a woman.'

'But now you have all the freedom in the world to do whatever will fulfil you,' Fay pointed out. 'Look on it as a new start. Not everyone gets that chance.'

Her mother's tone was bitter. 'It's all very well for him – he's got what he wanted. A girl of that age! I used to say his mistress was Lady Print – he'd read anything in print, even the writing on the sauce bottle. Believe me, Fay, Nemesis will catch up with him one day. He'll pay for his sins, please God he will. I'll spend my days praying for it.'

Eva leapt up in alarm. 'Don't say that, Mrs Bartram-Bates! Don't ever say things like that!'

The woman looked startled. Fay cut in quickly.

'I'll move my things in at the weekend. We'd better be going now, Mummy. We've got a living to earn.'

'Ah, yes,' sighed her mother. 'You and Clive. Everyone seems to have a mission in life but me. Mine must be praying for grace for everyone.'

On the ride home Fay gazed out of the bus window. 'Maybe you can see now why I felt so shut out, Eva, so alone as a child. Mine was an ectopic kind of upbringing, out of the bosom of the family.'

Eva thought for a moment. 'But that's a kind of freedom, in a way.'

Fay snorted. 'Don't you believe it – I was dead, I was coffined by class and religion. If I hadn't had my father . . .'

'You did feel close to him, didn't you, even if he wasn't the demonstrative sort?'

Fay sighed. 'It's not always men who use women, Eva. Sometimes it's the other way round.'

'Your mother? I feel sorry for her too.'

'I've found one thing by experience, Eva – I don't need Alan or anyone else to make life worth living. She'll never find that.'

'Money must be some comfort. I've never seen such a vulgar display of wealth!'

Fay turned startled eyes on her, then laughed. 'Some day that tongue of yours will land you in a load of trouble.'

'Well, it is a bit much. But all the same I wish I knew where she got that fabulous fabric on the loose covers – it'd make a fantastic skirt.'

'I'll tell you, darling – Harrods.'

'The blooming telephone's never stopped ringing since you went out,' complained Zoe. 'First some bloke called Cavendish and then Alan Finch. He's coming round to see us.'

'What, now? Oh no!'

'Why not? Now's our chance to tell him what we think of him. Anyway, you've got to ring this Cavendish chap back right away. Number's on the pad in the hall.'

Mr Cavendish had a suave and gentle voice. 'You don't know me, Miss Bower, but I'm the buyer for Ferris and Stocks.'

'Ferris and Stocks? The one on the high street?'

'The one on every high street in every large city in the country. I've been reading about you in *Trend* magazine, and I've also just been looking at a most unusual skirt. Blue cotton, peasant style, laced up the front. Is it one of yours?'

'It sounds like one of ours. But why do you ask?'

'Is it original? That's what I want to know, and are you manufacturing in quantity? Because if so, we ought to meet for a little chat.'

Eva thought fast. 'That style's catching on fast in Europe right now, Mr Cavendish. The fabrics are completely original – no one else uses them. So far we've manufactured only a limited quantity, to special order.'

'I see. Well, if you should decide to go into full-scale production, let me know. I'd be very interested.'

Eva felt her heart leap. 'Tell me one thing, Mr Cavendish – is this a definite offer, because if not . . .'

'Let me assure you, Miss Bower, my interest is genuine.

And if we do business, you will not find Ferris and Stocks unreasonable. We pride ourselves that we deal very fairly with our suppliers.'

Back in the living room Zoe was laying the table. 'Alan should be here any minute.'

Eva seized her by the shoulders, making her drop the knives in her hand. 'Bugger Alan – listen, Zoe, we've got to decide whether we're buying Bernstein's or not. Our whole future depends on it.'

CHAPTER FIFTEEN

'Why did you tell this Mr Cavendish our materials were original?'

'Because I saw this stuff on Fay's mum's sofa, furnishing stuff from Harrods, and I want to try doing one of our skirts in it. We'll get one made up and I'll take it to Cavendish as a sample if it's OK.'

'And if he likes it? What then?'

'We go into the wholesale business!'

'Are you crazy? We've got two machinists, part-time.'

'That's why we've got to think seriously about Bernstein's. Listen, Zoe, this could be the start of something really big. We could become international – I could buy and sell in three languages.'

'Hold on, let's think this thing through.'

'Could we pay off Bernstein's debts and still have enough to buy material, do you think?'

'What do we pay the salaries with? Bobbins? Eva, you're letting enthusiasm carry you away. It just isn't feasible.'

'I guess we need a loan,' grumbled Eva. 'Or one of us must find a rich husband like Chantal. You did say you saw Luc around, didn't you?'

'Eva – that's not funny!'

'I'm sorry – I was only joking. But I'm not joking about the sample – I'm determined to have it made up and see what Mr Cavendish thinks of it.'

The doorbell rang. 'That's Alan,' said Zoe. 'I'm going to leave you to it.'

'I'm on my way out,' said Eva. 'Just remembered a sudden appointment at Reg's.'

Alan looked somehow larger and darker than she remembered him as he took up half the settee in the Jacobs' living room. He sat with easy grace, one foot on the other knee, watching Eva as she put on lipstick at the sideboard mirror.

'I got Zoe's address from your stepmother,' he said conversationally. 'I called first in August, but you weren't back from France then.'

'Why were you looking for me?' she asked without turning round.

'I didn't know where to find Fay. I wanted to make sure she was OK.'

'You didn't try her mother's then?'

'I knew her mother kicked her out.'

'Because of you. She's back there now.'

'And is she all right?'

Eva turned to face him. 'Yes, she is – but no thanks to you. You were a bastard to her.'

She heard his deep sigh. 'I'm glad she's happy. Is she working now?'

'Yes, she has a very good job. Are you going to see her?'

'No. It's best to let the past remain dead and buried. I don't want to hurt her any more.'

'You won't,' said Eva firmly. 'She's got over you. She's made something of her life.'

'Has she forgiven me?'

'Who knows? I haven't.'

'It was stupid of me, I didn't realize what a selfish oaf I was being, but now I do and I'm sorry. I'd like Fay to know that.'

'The best thing you can do for her is clear off and leave her alone – don't sour it up again. Good night, Alan – I'm going out now.'

He rose as she made to pass the settee. It wasn't only his size and height that filled the room; it was a kind of physical charge that surrounded him, flooding the room with the power of his personality. Like Max he could dominate a room without speaking a word.

'Can I give you a lift? My car's pretty clapped-out but it's going.'

'No, thanks. I prefer to walk.'

'Can I walk with you?'

'No.'

'Why not? My shirt's clean, I haven't got dandruff – I'm really quite presentable.'

She turned to him, looking up into his dark eyes and his mouth twisted into a good-humoured smile. 'You arrogant devil,' she said fiercely. 'I don't care how you look – I don't want to be seen with you. People judge you by the company you keep.'

'Eva – I only –'

'Sod off! Make a fool of some other girl, but leave us alone. Try the one you had in the market.'

Dark eyebrows rose in surprise at her outburst, and then he laughed. 'You're jealous.'

'The hell I am.' Eva called back. 'Just bugger off and leave us in peace.'

He heard the front door slam and pulled a wry face. Zoe's father came into the room.

'The girls gone out, Mr Finch? Left you alone? Goodness me, what bad manners the young people got these days. Not like when I was a boy.' Louis shook his head ruefully.

'That's right, Mr Jacob,' said Alan. 'Urchins, the lot of them.'

Eva stood in the centre of the room in the plush office suite of Ferris and Stocks, waiting for the buying manager to put down the newspaper he was reading. On the desk, alongside the neat blotting pad Eva could see a telephone, a silver cigarette box and a table lighter, but of the buying manager she could see nothing but the glistening grey hair on top of his head.

Minutes passed, and he took no notice of her. Eva pulled forward a chair and sat down. Still she could not see the face behind the newspaper. She coughed. No reaction. She crossed her legs. The newspaper rustled. She began opening the box on her lap. Still no reaction. Eva noticed the hanging thread on her sleeve. A button was coming loose. She grew restless. She coughed again.

The voice behind the paper was indistinct. 'I'll be with you in a moment.'

Another minute passed. She tried again. 'Our appointment was for eleven – it's now twenty past.'

The newspaper did not move. Eva stared at her distorted reflection in the curved surface of the cigarette lighter, feeling the vexation beginning to rise.

With slow deliberation she leaned forward and pressed down the lever on the cigarette lighter. The flame licked up the newspaper and flakes of black ash fluttered to the desk. Calmly Mr Cavendish crumpled the paper and dropped it into the metal waste bin beside his desk, watching as the flames died. Eva swallowed hard. What the devil had possessed her?

Mr Cavendish turned to look at her. 'You have my full attention, Miss Bower. I take it you are in a hurry?'

His coolness surprised her. Eva held out the skirt. 'I brought a sample of the skirt you asked to see – the one we talked about on the phone.'

Mr Cavendish held the skirt up to the light of the window. Eva held her breath until he turned back to her.

'This is furnishing fabric, isn't it?' he asked smoothly.

'Yes.'

'Who supplied it?'

'Harrods.'

He blinked. 'Harrods? At how much a yard?'

'Thirteen and six.'

Mr Cavendish took a deep breath. 'You do realize that what you are asking us for the skirt is about a pound more than we would expect to charge the customer? Your costings are far too high, Miss Bower.'

'But it only represents a very small profit on what it cost us,' Eva protested.

'Buying fabric from the manufacturer is far cheaper, Miss Bower. Cut that cost and your rate would be far more attractive.'

'I'll look into it.'

'Now, about quantity – if we can establish a fair price, do you think you could meet an order for, say, two dozen a week?'

'I'm sure we can, Mr Cavendish.'

'In each of three colours?'

Six dozen – better still.

'In small, medium and large?'

Eva made a quick calculation. 'You mean – eighteen dozen in all? Oh my God!'

'That would supply the group of stores in one area only, of course. Outside your scope, is it?'

Eva nodded unhappily. 'Eighteen dozen would stretch our present resources too far, Mr Cavendish. When we're able to get larger premises . . .'

Mr Cavendish re-folded the skirt and pushed it across his desk. 'I'm afraid we can't do business just yet, Miss Bower. One day in the future perhaps. Thank you for coming to see me.'

Eva was not to be beaten easily. 'Even if we can't supply a

large order yet, couldn't we supply just one store in the meantime – you have one major store in town, don't you?'

He smiled. 'I like your designs, Miss Bower, and I like your spirit, but I'm afraid we cannot do business yet.'

He reached for a sheet of paper and wrote, then pushed it across to Eva. 'Take this. Go and see Mr Fleming at this address about material. I think you'll find you can save a lot of money.'

Eva looked down at the paper. 'Is this a wholesaler, Mr Cavendish?' she asked.

'A manufacturer. Good afternoon, Miss Bower. Do keep in touch.' As Eva rose he added with a wry smile, 'Who knows, one day you may set the whole world on fire.'

Eva held out her hand. 'Thanks, Mr Cavendish. You'll hear from me.'

That evening there was a board meeting around Louis Jacob's kitchen table. The air was heavy with the solemnity of the occasion. A pall of cigarette smoke hung over Louis's head.

'He's right,' said Zoe. 'We're still babes – we're not ready for the big time yet. We should meet all the orders we've already got and then think about making our own original designs. We haven't got the capacity yet.'

Louis drew deeply on his cigarette. 'You could still buy the Bernstein place. My accountant has checked out the debts.'

Zoe groaned. 'Papa, your accountant's advice led you into bankruptcy. You don't still listen to him?'

'I would make an offer if I had the money, princess. Imagine, a factory with a retail shop in Soho!'

'It would mean plunging all we've got into buying and we'd have nothing left,' said Eva. 'I'd like to work up to that, but Zoe's right – first we've got to establish the demand.'

'You got a cheap place for fabric now, I hear?' said Louis.

Eva nodded. 'Terrific – this place Mr Cavendish sent me to – super stuff at a good price. Much cheaper than Harrods.'

Zoe was leaning on her elbows, frowning as she gazed into space. 'Why don't we use our own shop and put the work out to Bernstein on a CMT basis? That would save buying more machines.'

Louis's eyes glistened as he ground out his cigarette in the ashtray. 'Zoe, you're a genius! There is room for frocks as well as hats in my shop and it would keep Bernstein in business too – why did I not think of that?'

Eva frowned. 'You lost me – what's CMT?'

'Contract out to someone else the cutting, making and trimming. That leaves us free to do the designing and marketing,' said Zoe.

'Brilliant!' exclaimed Eva. 'Let's talk to Mr Bernstein tomorrow. If he agrees, we can tell Fay to get cracking and spread us all over the magazine.'

Paper patterns lay scattered around Louis's workshop, patterns made up from the original French garments now resewn and returned to Adele and Harriet. Zoe and Eva were excitedly discussing plans for the redecoration of Louis's shop to catch the public eye.

'You're the one with the dramatic flair,' said Eva. 'Do something really stunning like one of your college stage sets and I'll help with the painting or whatever.'

Louis was elated with his new role of overseer. No more did he have to concern himself unduly with full order books for his hats; they now took second place to the chaos of his daughter's new business. Now he could act the inspector, checking that all was as it should be.

Ella and Patsy delighted in sewing fashion garments as well as hats and were reluctant to let unknown machinists down at Bernstein's share in the new work.

'Not to worry,' said Louis. 'I will watch them like a hawk to see they do the goods as fine as you. I show them your work so they know what they must do.'

Eva chose fabric for forty dresses from Mr Fleming's factory and Louis carried it ceremoniously down to Soho. Henry Bernstein eyed it critically as he laid it up ready for cutting.

'Only forty frocks, Louis?' he asked. 'This is not going to keep me in business.'

'It's a start, Henry – give it time.'

'You know,' Bernstein said thoughtfully, rubbing his long nose, 'the pattern is made too generous if you ask me. Now if we cut the skirt panels just a little narrower – just a little off here and here, then I could lay them so, and save a good half yard.'

Louis put his head to one side and surveyed the lay. 'A half yard? To each dress?'

'So I could make five to every four your daughter allows for.'

'No cabbage. You don't even think about cabbage, Henry. This is important.'

'Would I cheat your daughter?' Bernstein fingered the material. 'This is very good stuff – it must have cost.'

'Of course she uses good stuff to be like Balmain,' said Louis proudly. 'None of your market rubbish, this.'

'Balmain, eh?' echoed Bernstein. 'Your daughter send me no labels for the collar. She have no name, eh?'

'How many dresses have we got, Papa?'

Louis cleared a space on the cutting table and laid the package on it with a broad smile. 'We have forty-eight.'

'Oh, great!' cried Eva. 'That's better than we thought.'

'Henry knows how to cut.'

Eagerly the girls tore open the first carton. Each dress lay neatly packaged in tissue. Eva lifted the collar of the top dress.

'What's this? It's got a label in it – they've all got labels.'

Louis shrugged. 'Would Henry Bernstein send unfinished garments? Of course they have labels.'

Zoe leaned round Eva to look. '*Balmoral* – what's this *Balmoral*, Papa?'

Louis squared his shoulders and beamed at his daughter. 'My idea, princess. Watch this.'

He picked up a pair of scissors from the workbench with a flourish. 'First, we remove the *oral*.' The scissors snipped at the label and a piece fluttered to the floor. Louis held the dress out to Eva. 'You see?'

Eva looked at it, mouth wide. 'It only says *Balm* now – I don't get it.'

'Seconds,' said Louis proudly. 'You got Balmain seconds to sell.'

Eva stared at him, thunderstruck. 'You mean pass these off as Balmain? We can't do that!'

Louis frowned. 'And why not? Balmain has to get rid of his seconds some place, same as anybody else.'

'They don't look anything like Balmain's designs, and anyway it's cheating, that's why,' said Zoe.

'Cheating? So what is taking apart a model garment and copying it if not cheating?'

'There's a difference,' said Zoe. 'One's good business.'

Louis pouted. 'So is selling Balmain seconds, princess. All it takes is a little *chutzpah*.'

Drawing a deep breath Eva turned to Zoe. 'I know your father means well and is only trying to help, but this is blooming ridiculous.'

Louis looked from one girl to the other, bewildered. 'So what is wrong? Dressmakers I know who make *schmatter* do it all the time.'

'Now we're going to have to cut out all those damn labels,' said Zoe, sighing. 'Really, Papa, you should have asked.'

'I try to help you,' said Louis, still at a loss to understand. 'A man should help his own flesh and blood.'

Zoe was holding up one of the dresses. 'Eva,' she said with a frown, 'there's something wrong. This frock is terribly skimpy.'

Eva lifted out another dress. 'And this, and this – oh God, what have they done?'

Louis brightened. 'I tell you Henry is a good cutter – forty-eight dresses he get you instead of forty. So maybe the skirt is a shade narrower –'

'Narrower?' Eva almost shouted at him. 'They're supposed to be peasant dresses and they're damn near pencil skirts, you idiot! What the devil were you playing at?'

'Eva – that's my father you're talking to!' Zoe's voice was sharp.

'I'm sorry.'

Zoe rounded on her father. 'But you have cocked the whole thing up. First the labels, now the cut – you're a pain in the neck! No wonder your own business went for a burton.'

'Don't mention that name,' muttered Louis miserably. 'That man becomes a millionaire, while I am only a struggling father who is not appreciated by his own child.'

Zoe's face softened. 'He was only trying to help, Eva.'

'I got you eight extra dresses,' Louis murmured. 'This is using your head. Forty-eight dresses has got to be better than forty.'

'But you ruined the whole lot – now we've got forty-eight useless frocks.'

'Yes we have,' agreed Zoe then, turning to Louis, she said,

194

'This is a disaster – what the hell do you think we're going to do with all this lot? We're not going to sell them, that's for sure. It'd ruin our name.'

'All that good money down the drain,' muttered Eva.

Louis straightened and reached for his hat. 'I'm going out.'

Zoe looked alarmed. 'Where to?'

'I'm going to have a strong word with Henry Bernstein. He won't get away with this. I teach him he can't make a fool of us.'

The girls watched his short, plump figure stride purposefully out of the door. Zoe lifted a frock and let it fall on the counter.

'What on earth are we going to do? This lot's only fit for the market, but we'd get very little for them.'

Eva's lips set in a tight line. 'We're going to sort this out somehow. We're not beaten yet. The market, eh? We've got to get some of our bloody money back . . .'

Zoe looked scandalized. 'We're not going to take a stall on the market as well as the shop.'

Eva folded the dress back into the box and snapped the lid back on. 'You get on with redecorating the shop, Zoe – I've got to pop out for a while.'

The market was seething with shoppers in search of bargains and the weather-tanned little man behind the blouse and skirt stall was wary of the red-haired girl anxious to show him her bundle.

'You got how many? Forty-eight? Where did you get them from?'

'You don't ask and you don't tell people,' said Eva. 'But if you've got an eye for a bargain you'll snap 'em up. If you don't, I know others who will.'

'Let's have a see.'

He shook out one of the frocks and fingered the cloth. 'You say Reg sent you?'

'He said you were one of the shrewdest fellows he knew. They're Balmoral, you know.'

The stallholder screwed his eyes up to inspect the label. 'Balmoral? I ain't never heard of them.'

'You've never heard of Balmoral? I thought everyone in the trade knew them.'

The stallholder took a woman customer's pound note and dipped in his pouch. 'I seen one like it – there's a lady round the corner reads palms wears one like this.'

'Palm-reading must pay then – I'm in the wrong job. But that's Balmoral's feature – the gipsy look.'

'Yeah, sure, but I can't take forty-eight of 'em.' He handed the woman her change and Eva waited till she had gone.

'It's all or nothing,' said Eva.

The stallholder rubbed his unshaven chin. 'Me brother might take some – he's got a stall in Petticoat Lane. I could split them with him if the price is right.'

'Fifty pounds,' said Eva. 'And a damn good bargain at that.'

The stallholder nodded. 'Tell you what, why don't you drop 'em off at my warehouse at teatime?'

'I can arrange that. Where's your warehouse?'

'Lock-up garage in Pym Street. Green one with the tin roof.'

Eva dropped the cartons at his feet outside the garage door.

'Two more packages to come – my driver's just bringing them.'

The man dug in his inside pocket and pulled out a bundle of notes. 'Let's see, forty quid, wasn't it?'

'Fifty,' said Eva.

'I reckon forty's about enough. I ain't asking no questions about where they come from.' He peeled off notes, licking his fingers to separate them.

'They're not stolen if that's what you think,' said Eva. 'Fifty is what we agreed, and fifty is what I want.'

He held out the money. 'Take it or leave it, girl. It's up to you.'

'I'll just ask my driver what he thinks – here he is now.'

The man glanced back over his shoulder. Reg Fowler was puffing as he lumbered up and dropped two cartons on the ground. He looked at the money in the man's hand.

'How much you offering my friend?' he enquired mildly.

The man started. 'Reg! Hallo, mate – oh, fifty wasn't it? Here you are, miss.'

'Fifty pounds!' exclaimed Zoe. 'That's great. It's fifty pounds more than I could have got.'

'At least it's not a complete loss,' said Eva. 'We've learnt something. Now we'll start doing our own things to order.'

'We do need our own label,' said Zoe with emphasis. 'What shall we have for our name? Something significant.'

'Maddie suggested *Chantal*, since she triggered off the idea in our minds, and *Countess*, all kinds of *femme fatale* words, but I think we really need a name that suggests the vagabond look.'

'What's wrong with *Vagabond* then?'

'No, but it's near. We want to suggest a kind of ragged Audrey Hepburn. *Gamine* perhaps – that suggests the urchin look we want.'

Suddenly the two girls looked at each other and simultaneously they shrieked. 'That's it!' cried Zoe. 'It's perfect!'

'*Urchin*.' Eva rolled the word round her tongue. 'No one's going to mistake us for anyone else with a name like that. Yes, that's what we are, urchins.'

CHAPTER SIXTEEN

Zoe was singing at the top of the ladder to the accompaniment of Fats Domino on the wireless. Eva, standing amid a jumble of paint tins and rags, stuffed her fingers in her ears.

'I can hardly recognize this place now,' she called out above the din.

Zoe stopped singing and, lowering her paintbrush, made a mock bow. 'I'm a bloody genius. Can't say Papa's so chuffed about it though.'

'You'd hardly expect him to rave over orange and purple – it's rather different from the olive green he had.'

'If it's supposed to make customers think of a gipsy encampment it's got to be colourful,' said Zoe.

'I'm not arguing – I think it's fantabulous. And when you get all that netting and stuff up it won't be recognizable as Louis Jacob, milliners, any more.'

'He cried, you know. He actually wept.'

'Who did? Your dad?'

'When he saw me painting his name out over the door and painting Urchin over it. He didn't want me to see, but I did. I felt a real swine. Pass me that piece of chalk, will you?'

'What you going to do?'

'I've just had an idea. See where those two steps stick out under the door to upstairs? I could draw a gipsy caravan and those steps could be the caravan steps. Hey, I could saw the door in half and make it a stable-type door like they have on caravans! Bright orange with purple looped curtains inside the top half!'

'This gets more like one of your stage sets every minute.'

'You complaining?'

'No, it's just what we need. This shop is going to be the showpiece of London. By the way, the Urchin labels will be ready tomorrow.'

'Oh yes, and Fay rang. She's coming over to see how we're getting on. And she said she's going to bring this photographer who wants to take some shots of our models when we open.'

'Then we've got to impress her. Does she know we exaggerated the French story a bit?'

'She guessed Chantal wasn't really a countess. She said she remembered what a liar you were back at college.'

By the time Zoe had put the final touches to the shop even the staff could hardly recognize it. The evening before they were to open Louis couldn't wait to bring Ella and Patsy up from the basement workroom to inspect it.

'Just look what my daughter do with my shop – and it did not cost a fortune either,' he enthused.

'Cripes!' gasped Ella. 'It's like the Christmas grotto at the Co-op.'

Rosa stood behind Louis, arms folded across her plump bosom and a smile of pride on her amiable face. Patsy stood speechless, mouth gaping wide as she gazed up at the green netting covering ceiling and walls. Plastic flowers bloomed in profusion overhead, intertwining between asymmetrically scattered blouses and skirts, while around the netted walls hung dresses at zany angles. In one corner a gipsy tent concealed the changing area, and in the centre of the room three poles leaned together to form a tripod over an unlit camp fire.

'See the copper cauldron over the fire?' exclaimed Louis delightedly. 'That was my Miriam's preserving pan – in it she has made many pounds of jam for us when my princess was a little girl. I never thought to see it filled with scarves.'

Rosa beamed. 'They are mine, from Italy. Zoe ask to borrow them.'

Patsy turned slowly, taking it all in. 'Here,' she said, pointing at the door to the stairs. 'How did that caravan get in here? It weren't here before.'

Rosa chuckled. 'It's not a real caravan, Patsy. Zoe is clever girl. It only looks like a caravan.'

The girl took a step closer. 'It is – the door's open – I can see the curtains. But why's its wheel up there on the wall?'

Ella jerked a thumb towards the trestle table. 'You gonna get that pasting table out of here now you've finished?'

'No,' said Eva. 'That's the counter.'

Rosa ushered her staff off home and then bore Louis away to supper at her house.

'Your daughter have no time to cook for you tonight – you come eat cannelloni with me.'

Until late into the night Zoe and Eva busied themselves in the shop, arranging and re-arranging, reluctant to leave. Zoe kept taking a dress down off the wall and looking inside the collar.

'*Urchin* – doesn't it look great! Every time I look at it it gives me a kick.'

'I felt the same when I came down the street and saw the name over the door. It's ours, Zoe, all ours! Tomorrow we've got to open a bottle of wine to celebrate the opening, and wish luck and prosperity on the place.'

Louis came home at midnight, tired but still excited. 'You two girls should wear your own frocks in the shop, the ones you make. You both have good shape like mannequins. Then the customers will see how attractive are the goods.'

'We already decided that,' said Zoe sleepily.

'You gonna make outsize? You need outsize – there's a lotta big women in the world – you only got to look around Golders Green to see that.'

'Later, perhaps,' said Zoe. 'I'm for bed now.'

But Louis hadn't finished with good advice. 'You know for retail trade you must add fifty per cent to cost to get one third profit? You know that, eh? If you mark up only a third, you make only twenty-five per cent profit.'

Eva could hardly keep her eyes open. 'You already told us, Mr Jacob, lots of times. My brain can't take in any more tonight.'

'Nor mine.'

Louis threw up his hands. 'Paper bags? You remember to get paper bags, Zoe?'

Zoe sighed. 'Yes, Papa. Plain brown ones, no name. Now, good night, Papa.'

'Good night, princess. I shall be up early – I shall be the first in the shop to welcome all the customers. I have told all my friends.'

As soon as Louis had left the room Zoe turned to Eva. 'Just think, tomorrow somebody could be wearing an Urchin frock, showing it off proudly and telling people she bought it at our place. I can't wait for tomorrow!'

'It's gone midday already and not a soul's set foot in the place,' muttered Zoe. 'Do you think it could be my window display? A pile of bricks and netting is not quite what people expect of a dress shop. Maybe they don't know what we are.'

'They'll come, don't fuss, they'll come.'

An old lady opened the door. 'Excuse me, miss,' she said apologetically, 'but I'm trying to find Jacob's, the milliner's. It used to be around here somewhere, I'm sure it was, but I've been up and down this street till me feet's sore.'

Two office girls fingered skirts and inspected the price tickets.

'Here, I didn't know this place was here, did you?' said one to the other. 'Nice, ain't it? Funny, but nice.'

Three more young women talked to each other with the assured confidence of Mayfair.

'It was Amanda who told me about it, darling. She went to this quaint little sale with her mother in some espresso bar. I just had to come and see for myself.'

'It's charming – so quaint. I'll have it.'

One of the office girls had fallen in love with one of Rosa's scarves. 'But there ain't no price on it.'

'It's not for sale, but we could get one for you for Friday.'

'Where from?' whispered Zoe.

'I'll get the fabric – Patsy can sew 'em up.'

'Oh good,' said the office girl. 'Pay day – I'll have a scarf and one of them blouses then.'

Just after six Louis appeared, his nose rising slowly above the level of the basement stairs. His eyebrows rose at the sight of so many customers.

'Are you going to close tonight, princess, or am I to sleep on the cutting table?'

'Not yet, Papa. It's going so well.'

Fay rushed in, fair hair windblown and her pretty face flushed.

'Thank goodness – I thought you'd be closed. I've been waiting for the photographer and he's only just come. He's paying off the taxi – nice young man, got in touch with us to say he wanted to do the photos of your set-up. He's very well spoken of, actually. Here he comes now.'

Zoe was staring dumbly at the young man who had just walked in and was smiling at her.

'Luc,' she croaked. 'Luc.'

Fay looked astonished. 'You two have met?' she asked. Eva, seeing Zoe's bemused expression, stepped in.

'We met Luc in France – I am delighted to meet you again,' she said, holding out her hand. He took it in a firm grip, but she noted his eyes moved back to Zoe. Zoe recovered sufficiently to shake hands, her dark eyes wide and a glow beginning to suffuse her face.

'Well,' said Fay. 'They told me you wanted to do the shoot, but they didn't tell me you knew the girls.'

'We met briefly,' he answered in a deep, low voice with only a trace of a French accent, 'but I felt we should meet again.'

'Are you working in England now?'

He shrugged, an expressive Gallic gesture that made Eva think of Chantal. 'At the moment, I go where my work takes me.' He glanced around the shop. 'Your work is most impressive. Are you ready to model the gowns for me?'

'Tonight?' said Zoe. 'We're exhausted.'

'We're ready,' said Eva. 'Just give us a minute.'

The shoot was a crazy, befuddled experience, a babel of laughter and orders and glasses of wine, customers looking on while Zoe and Eva changed from one outfit to another. At last Luc declared he was satisfied.

'We have some very good pictures,' he said. 'So full of life. Everyone will take notice when this issue of *Trend* comes out.'

Louis's nose appeared above the basement stairs yet again. Seeing people still there, he hovered.

'Now, let me take you for a meal,' said Luc. 'You must be hungry.'

'I'd love to – you can lock up now, Papa.'

Fay picked up her handbag. 'I have other arrangements,

but I'll make sure you get a copy when the next issue comes out.'

Luc turned to Zoe. 'You know a good place to eat?'

'I know a smashing kosher restaurant, and I'm famished.'

'Kosher?' echoed Eva. 'I'm going home. See you later.'

'You got on well with Luc tonight?'

'Oh yes! At least I think we did. I'm a bit muzzy about it all really.'

'I told you we shouldn't have drunk so much wine with the customers.'

'I remember he kept looking at me in a funny way that made me go all shivery, like gooseflesh – know what I mean?'

'Yes.'

'Do you really? Have you had that feeling?'

'Yes –'

'Who was it?'

'Long time ago – I've forgotten.'

'It wasn't David, was it – it was Alan Finch.'

'We did a damn good day's trade today, don't you think?'

'Which is a polite way of telling me to mind my own business.'

'Who's polite? Mind your own bloody business.'

For the rest of the week the shop continued to throb with activity. The doorbell never seemed to stop clanging and the sound was music to Louis's ears. Customers came, customers stayed till all hours, and Louis no longer asked to lock up.

'The wine was a wonderful idea,' he told the girls, 'for special customers only, of course. This we must do regularly.'

Sometimes the same customers reappeared bringing friends, flinging off clothes in abandon if the fitting room was already occupied and trying on more clothes. On Friday afternoon a woman returned to collect the dark blue skirt she had ordered.

'Hell!' Eva exclaimed to Zoe. 'It's not ready – I forgot to tell Patsy it had to be finished for today.'

'Give her a glass of wine – I'll tell Patsy to get a move on.'

Half an hour later the woman was still sitting waiting, a third glass of wine in her hand. 'Isn't it ready yet?' she slurred. 'I'll be drunk at this rate by the time I get it.'

'It's the butterfly appliqué taking the time,' said Eva. 'Have some more wine.'

At last the skirt arrived, and the woman took it eagerly, holding it up to inspect it. 'This butterfly is askew,' she said with a frown. 'It's cock-eyed.'

Eva saw Zoe trying to keep the smile from her face. 'It's the fashion, madam. If it's set square, it's square.'

The lady's face registered relief, and then pleasure. 'Oh, that's all right then. Will you take a cheque?'

She signed with a flourish and needed only a little help to pour her into a taxi.

The week's takings lay on the kitchen table. 'I can hardly believe it,' breathed Zoe. 'Who'd have thought it?'

Eva fingered the notes. 'Fay's friends turning up in droves like that was a bonus. I've been thinking – we ought to pay your dad a wage for all he's been doing for us.'

'No, no,' protested Louis. 'Wait until you get on your feet.'

'How much?' said Zoe.

Louis sighed. 'I tell you what, you pay me what I was earning out of the shop before, eh?'

'Sounds reasonable,' said Eva. 'How much was that?'

Louis started ticking off the fingers of one hand. 'Let me see, what with rates, wages, heat and light deducted – I was losing twenty pounds a week.'

*

In a dingy bedsit lit only by a single unshaded light bulb a girl sat on the edge of the bed, cutting carefully from a magazine. On the patchwork counterpane lay an open scrapbook.

She put down the scissors and was reaching for a tube of glue when the door opened and a burly young man came in.

'Look what I found in *Trend*, Joe. It's her.'

Joe took the cutting from her and scrutinized it. 'She's got a lovely figure, hasn't she?' said the girl.

He grunted. 'Not as good as yours.' He let one hand fall on her shoulder then ran it down her back in a caressing movement.

'She's beautiful too,' the girl murmured. 'Just look at that red hair. I used to have lovely long hair once . . .'

Joe turned the girl round to face him, looking deep into her eyes as if unaware of the vivid scarring, the misshapen nose and puckered skin. 'She's not as beautiful as you are, Kathy,' he muttered, his finger tracing the line of her ravaged cheek and, bending, he kissed her lovingly. For a moment she clung to him, then stood back with a sigh.

'Of all the people in that place, you were always the one who made me feel good, Joe. I don't know what I'd have done without you.'

She picked up the cutting again. 'She deserves to be punished for what she did, Joe. She's got it coming to her.'

He stared at her blankly for a second, then understanding dawned in his eyes and he nodded. 'Yes, Kathy. I'm gonna do for her – so long as it's not tomorrow.'

She looked at him, wide-eyed. 'Why, Joe?'

'I'm going to see Danny Blanchflower – Spurs are at home to Arsenal. Can't miss that.'

'No, not tomorrow, Joe. I want you to do it on Guy Fawkes Night. I want you to see she gets it then.'

'Yeah, OK, she deserves everything that's coming to her.'

The girl smiled. 'Good boy, Joe. You'll show how you love your Kathy, won't you?'

It was as Eva was coming home with a fresh supply of buttons and lace that she caught sight of the man standing on the corner of the street. There was something in his stance that suggested unease or uncertainty, and she looked again, feeling a faint stir of recognition.

Then he turned and saw her. 'Eva!'

It was David Maynard moving towards her, his face alight in a smile of pleasure. She stared.

'David – what are you doing here?'

'Aren't you pleased to see me? I've missed you.'

'Of course I am.' She could not help the lame tone in her voice. She felt shaken, as if a ghost from the past had caught her off-guard.

'Eva, there's so much we have to talk about. Why didn't you answer my letters?'

'You told me you were married. There was nothing else to be said.'

'Look, is there somewhere we can talk – a café or something? We can't talk on the street.'

David waited until the waitress had brought the pot of tea and left. 'What you never gave me a chance to tell you, Eva, is that my wife is ill – very ill – in hospital. I took this job so that I could be near her. I had to, Eva – I wasn't running away from you. That's the last thing I wanted. You must believe me.'

Eva was staring dumbly at the red check tablecloth. Curious, she thought, but he had said 'I' five times in that speech. In the old days she would never have noticed.

'She's very ill?' she murmured, feeling words necessary to fill the gap.

'Very, and not likely to recover. It's been a long, painful business.'

'You never told me – and we said we told each other everything.' It wasn't meant to sound like an accusation but that's how it came out. David looked hurt.

He poured tea into two cups and passed one cup to Eva. 'You might not have understood – a man needs female company – he can't afford to frighten it away.'

'How little you trusted me, David. It doesn't matter now.'

He frowned. 'Somehow I thought you'd have understood my problem and been sympathetic. The old Eva would have been.'

'The old Eva wasn't told. But I do sympathize, David, truly I do. It can't be easy for you.'

'It's been bloody hard, doing my work at the theatre and visiting Phyllis every day.' His face brightened. 'But it'll be a lot better if I can see you now and again, take you out for a meal – would you like to come and see my theatre? It's no great shakes, mind you, just a little place out in the East End.'

'Sounds great.'

He leaned across the table towards her, his expression earnest and intense, just as she remembered. 'Look, Eva, I've got an awful fight to stop myself feeling guilty because I'm with you here while Phyllis is lying so ill in hospital. Don't make me feel worse, Eva, please.'

'I'm not trying to make you feel anything. It's your conscience that's troubling you.'

David's face darkened angrily. 'I didn't ask to be married to a cripple, for God's sake, but it's draining the life out of me watching her misery. I love her, Eva, but there's nothing I can do but be her strength. She needs me, but I need the vitality only you can give me. For heaven's sake, Eva, let me meet you now and again.'

She looked at him as if at a stranger, seeing him for the first time. 'Funny, but I used to think you so mature, so worldly-wise,' she murmured. 'I wanted you so much, a stable relationship with you, not just a will o' the wisp who flew in and out of my life.'

David leaned forward eagerly. 'More than anything I'd like a country life, living with you in your village with books and dogs and tranquillity. Maybe some day . . .'

Eva stood up, her tea undrunk. 'Not now, David. Things are very different now. Like you said, I'm not the old Eva.'

He stared at her, a disbelieving look in his eyes. 'You won't? You don't want to see me?'

'Sometimes, perhaps. As a friend.'

He stared down gloomily at his cup. 'I've suffered torment such as you'll never know. Your last words to me came true, Eva. You wished me to fry in hell.'

Zoe's tone was matter-of-fact. 'I saw him walk you up the street. He's going very grey, isn't he?'

Eva thought for a moment. 'Funny how you look at things, isn't it? Once I would have argued with you that it made him look distinguished.'

'I hope you told him to bugger off – him a married man and all. Because if you didn't, I will. Did you?'

'Not in so many words.'

'You never had any problem telling blokes to sod off before.'

Eva sighed. 'I've changed, Zoe. All the certainty I had at eighteen has somehow been knocked out of me. You know, sometimes I think growing up is changing, becoming a sort of composite of the original you and all the people we've ever met and liked and been influenced by.'

Zoe looked at her askance. 'And does that bother you?'

'Not really. I think I'm getting to know what I really want now.'

CHAPTER SEVENTEEN

Some weeks later the girls sat with Louis in the Jacobs' parlour, watching the grey November drizzle through the window.

'What a lousy night for the kids and their bonfires,' said Eva. 'They'll never get their fireworks to light in this rotten rain.'

'Bonfire Night again,' said Zoe. 'I'd almost forgotten.'

Louis pointed out of the window at a couple passing by. 'My God! Look at that woman's hat! Zoe, promise me, if ever I make such a hat, you will have me shot. And just look at her husband – an accountant he must be, he looks so shifty. What fools to go out on such a night.'

'I'm going out,' said Eva.

'So am I,' said Zoe. 'I'm going to see an Italian film.'

'Italian? Then you should take Rosa with you. She would enjoy to hear her own tongue.'

'I'm going with Luc, Papa.'

Louis's expression softened. 'Ah, a good Jewish boy. I am happy. I did not like the *goy* who kept hanging around you last year.'

'Because he was a *goy*?'

'Because he was stupid, princess. Put money in his outstretched hand and he was too stupid to clench his fist. Such a man is no good to a woman.'

Zoe smiled. 'You've no need to worry, Papa. Luc is a fine man and we get on very well.'

Louis shrugged. 'Your mama would be so happy that all is

going well for you. Me too, I am happy, but you know how I am – everything is going so right, something must be wrong. Where are you going, Eva?'

'To meet a friend, David Maynard.'

Zoe's eyebrows rose. 'David? I thought you said –'

'I said I'd see him sometimes. I won't be late back.'

'Nor me. These arty Italian films always give me a massive inferiority complex. Have you seen the size of Silvana Mangano's bosom?'

Louis stood up. 'So you two are going to be out for the evening. I think I tidy up one or two things in the workshop and maybe go to see Rosa. Don't forget to take your keys.'

'Not going out tonight in all this rain, are you, dear?' Valerie Bartram-Bates asked her daughter.

'No, Mummy. We can have a game of chess if you like.'

Her mother shuddered. 'Not chess. Any game but chess.'

'Mummy, you have to face up to things squarely, not hide your head in the sand.'

Valerie's reply was stiff. 'I prefer bridge, you know that.'

'Because chess was Daddy's game? Listen, Mummy, I've been thinking. You can beat any man at his own game . . .'

'I really don't know what you're talking about, darling. Get out the pack of cards.'

'I think we ought to invite Mr McIntyre to dinner one evening. It can't be much fun for a bachelor magazine owner all on his own in London.'

'Very well,' said her mother. 'Only we'll still need a fourth to play bridge.'

The streets still gleamed wet in the lamplight as Eva and David emerged from the restaurant, but the flash and bang of fireworks had long since ceased.

'Are you sure you won't come back to my place for a glass of wine?' David was urging. 'I've got some new records you could hear.'

'No, David, it's late and I want to get back. Thanks for the meal – it was lovely.'

He looked crestfallen. 'I'll call a taxi then.'

'No, let's walk. It's not far, and I can show you the shop on the way.'

He slid his arm through hers and fell into step beside her. 'About those costumes – I can still talk the producer into it if you're interested.'

Something in his tone and the proprietorial way he had taken her arm irritated Eva. 'Don't bother, David, we've got enough on at the moment. Look, the shop's just around the next corner.'

In the distance a bell clanged, coming closer and filling the still night air with its insistent sound. Headlights suddenly beamed round the corner and a fire engine swept past them, the sound of its strident bell diminishing to a lower note as it swung away into the next street. David squeezed her arm.

'A fire somewhere. It's always the same on Guy Fawkes Night. Bet the casualty wards are busy.'

Eva pulled her arm free of his and quickened her pace. 'That's our street,' she muttered, 'and the fire bell's stopped.'

Turning the corner Eva saw the fire engine on the far side of the street, half-way down, and the knot of people clustered nearby. Then she saw the shop, and her heart seemed to lurch into her throat. Black smoke was billowing from the windows and wreathing around the lamp post.

'Oh God, no!' she cried out, and began to run, David hurrying after her. From the engine firemen were unravelling a length of hose. Eva pushed past them and rushed up to the door, digging for the keys in her pocket.

'Here, you can't go in there!'

Arms seized her and pulled her back. Eva struggled, crying out in protest.

'It's my shop!'

'Nobody's going in there yet, miss. The blaze has got hold of the door – we got to get that out first.'

The hose was fully extended now and a burst of water sprang from the nozzle. Suddenly the window cracked and glass shivered and crashed. Inside flames were clearly visible, licking and leaping around one of the blouses Zoe had so carefully displayed.

'Mr Jacob!' Eva shrieked. 'David, Mr Jacob's in there – we've got to get him out!'

'If he's gone upstairs,' muttered the fireman, holding Eva, 'then God help 'im. The smoke'll have got 'im by now.'

The firemen were playing the hose on the door, then one of them took an axe and smashed. The door gave way instantly, smoke pouring out to engulf him as he went in. There was a cry, and under the smoke Eva could see him, his head and shoulders protruding through a gaping hole in the floor. One of his comrades pulled him out, and he disappeared into the shop. Eva, still pinioned in the sturdy fireman's grip, looked round helplessly at David.

'Mr Jacob's in the cellar, David – he must be!'

David was staring at the scene and appeared deaf to her words. Suddenly the firemen let go of Eva and rushed into the smoke, jumping across the hole. Beyond him flames amid the black smoke showed that the floor was already alight. Zoe's blouse in the window was now no more than a charred rag clinging to a wire.

Eva snatched David's hand. 'Round the back – the basement door!' she shouted. Pulling his arm she ran to the alley a couple of doors away which led to the rear of the terrace.

★

Louis was singing happily to the strains of Max Bygraves on Zoe's portable wireless set.

He gathered up all the remnants of fabric which had got kicked under the cutting bench, ready for a good clean start in the morning. Nothing like a clear deck to start the day, and he felt so happy the way things were going that he could afford to forgo a cigarette while he worked and sang.

Nothing like a good loud singing session to clear the lungs of all the accumulated cigarette smoke of the day. Louis was accompanying Alma Cogan on the wireless.

Nice Jewish girl, that Alma Cogan – beat all your Eartha Kitts and Tommy Steeles into a cocked hat. What was that?

Louis stopped and straightened. He was sure he'd heard a crackling sound. Nothing. Must have been a mouse. He'd have to put down traps again. Or maybe get a cat. Yes, a cat would be nice.

He was fetching the broom from the corner to sweep up all the stray fragments of cotton when the bump came, and Louis stiffened. The noise had come from upstairs. It couldn't be the girls – an intruder, perhaps?

And there was a crackling – he could hear it clearly now, and it was no mouse. Curiously, he propped the broom against the wall and climbed the cellar stairs.

As he neared the door at the top Louis heard an almighty crash behind him. Startled, he looked back and saw a gaping hole in the ceiling and a pair of trousered legs. At the same time he caught a whiff of a foul smell and recognized smoke.

He rushed to the top of the steps and pulled the door open, then gasped. Scarlet flames leapt at him, searing heat paining his eyes and thick black smoke swirling around him, filling his lungs so that he could not breathe. Tears sprang to his eyes. Choking, he reeled backwards, and found himself tumbling head-over-heels down the stone steps.

Eva raced to the basement door and tugged at the handle.

'It's locked, and I haven't got the key. David – the window – smash it, for God's sake!'

David was standing behind her, shaking his head. 'Waste of time,' he muttered. 'It's barred.'

He was right. Iron bars only a few inches apart ran down the length of the window. Eva thumped his arm.

'Get something to break the door down – don't just stand there!'

She peered through the window and could make out the crumpled figure lying at the foot of the stairs.

'He's there – he's in there – I can see him! Hurry, David – the ceiling's on fire!'

David had found something and was battering at the door. Eva jumped up and down, urging him on. 'Go on, the fire hasn't reached him – oh hell, give it to me!'

At that moment the door gave way. Pushing David aside Eva dashed in, coughing as she ran, dodging the blazing fragments of wood as they fell. As she reached Louis's prostrate body and bent over him a uniformed figure appeared at the top of the stairs and came running down.

'Get out,' the fireman yelled. 'I'll see to him – you get out quick – the floor's going to give way!'

Eva stood beside David on the pavement edge and watched the men lifting Louis into the ambulance.

'Is he going to be all right?' she asked anxiously.

'Right as rain, miss. Doesn't seem as if there's any bones broken, only a bit of smoke and shock. Don't you worry, your old dad'll be right as ninepence in the morning.'

She watched the ambulance move away. The firemen were

winding their hoses back on to the reels, pulling off their helmets to wipe black fists across blackened faces. One of them, who appeared to be the officer in charge, was scribbling in a notebook.

'Could I have your name please, miss, before you go, and the gentleman who was hurt?'

'I'm Eva Bower, and his name is Louis Jacob.'

'He's the owner of the shop?'

'Yes. His daughter and I manage a business here.' She glanced back at the blackened building. 'Or at least, we did.'

The chief fireman was eyeing her quizzically. 'You have any enemies that you know of, miss?'

'No – why?'

'Or any money troubles?'

'I don't know what you mean. Why are you asking me this?'

'Because it doesn't look like this fire was an accident. I'm afraid the police will have to be informed.'

'Not an accident?' Eva echoed. 'Are you saying that somebody started it on purpose? Oh no, not when there was someone in there, they couldn't have!'

The officer put his notebook away. 'Evidence seems to indicate that it was deliberate I'm afraid, miss. I'll notify the police and they'll be in touch with you very shortly. Same address as Mr Jacob, isn't it?'

'Wait a minute,' said Eva sharply. 'What evidence? You're saying somebody deliberately set fire to the shop, even though it could have killed Mr Jacob? How do you know that?'

'Rags, miss. Charred remains of rags just inside. Strong smell of petrol. And the hole burnt through the floor. Looks like someone soaked the rags in petrol and pushed them through the letterbox, then a lighted match,'

Eva's fingers flew to her lips. 'Oh no! Who could do a thing like that? I can't believe it!'

The officer shrugged. 'It's not the first time it's happened. Kids sometimes, bent on mischief, and it *is* Bonfire Night. But arson isn't uncommon, specially when folk are short of cash and need the insurance money.'

Eva felt the anger that flooded her cheeks. 'You think we could have done this? After all the work we put into building the business up? You must be off your chump!'

She felt David's embarrassed nudge and turned on him. 'Well, he must, to think we'd be so crazy as to throw away all we've worked so hard to build up!'

The officer coughed. 'I only said some people have been known to do that, miss. Other times it's a grudge. The police'll want to know if there's anyone who held a grudge against you.'

'Grudge? You mean someone did this out of spite?'

'Could have. Do you know anyone who hates you that much?'

Eva stared dumbly as the firemen climbed aboard the engine and drove away down the street. David was still standing silent beside her.

She spoke in a small voice. 'I feel sick, David.'

He murmured something, then took her arm. 'I'll get that taxi now.'

She shook him off angrily. 'I don't want a taxi – come to that, I don't want you. I'm going home alone.'

She strode off up the street, conscious of his footsteps pattering after her. 'Come on now, Eva, you're upset,' he murmured soothingly. 'And not surprising.'

She stopped and turned. 'Upset? Our shop burnt out, Mr Jacob in hospital, suspicion of arson and fraud, or somebody hates us enough to kill? Upset? I should think I bloody well am!'

217

'Calm down, Eva, we'll soon get a nice hot cup of coffee inside you.'

'Sod off, David! You're useless! Feet of clay, that's what you've got – you're a drip.'

She turned again to walk away. David moved hesitantly after her. 'Eva, love – let me see you home, please.'

Seeing the anger blazing in her eyes he let his hand fall from her sleeve. Eva marched on, but over her shoulder he could hear her furious tone.

'Go home, David – I never want to see you again.'

The girl was sitting in the dark, watching out of the window for his return. As Joe opened the door she went forward eagerly to meet him.

'Well? Did you do it?'

He closed the door behind him and grinned. 'Yeah. It were dead easy.'

She moved round him as he took off his jacket and flung it on the chair. 'But was she there though – did you see her?'

'I saw the light on in the cellar – I'm not daft, I went round to see first.'

Her face was only a pale blur to him in the darkness, but he could hear the excitement in her tone. 'And did you see if it started all right? Did you actually see flames?'

'Yeah. Smoke first, then flames after. I stayed and watched.'

Her tone grew apprehensive. 'How long? Nobody saw you, did they? I told you to make sure no one saw you.'

He shook his head. 'There was lots of people watching, Kathy, me and lots more. Hey, you should have seen it – the fire engine bell ringing away and the firemen squirting water – it was fabulous. And flames as high as the houses – it were the best bonfire I've ever been to, Kathy. It were great.'

'It was burnt out, was it?'

'Yeah. I went back after. Pity it had to stop burning. I liked it.'

'And they didn't get her out?'

'I don't know. I weren't there all the time, but I saw holes in the floor and flames right up to the roof.'

'Good. I'm proud of you, Joe.'

She sat down on the edge of the bed. He could hear the satisfaction in her tone now and knew he had done well.

'I'm a good boy, aren't I, Kathy? Dr Spencer would give me a gold star, wouldn't he?'

She stood up again and reached up to touch his cheek. 'Yes, Joe – he would say you've done very well indeed.'

He felt he could burst with pride and, taking hold of her hand, he kissed the palm gently. 'Lovely Kathy,' he murmured. 'Beautiful Kathy.'

Zoe flung her handbag down on the kitchen table and turned to Eva.

'Well, Papa's OK – only shock and a bit of smoke on his chest so they'll probably let him out tomorrow,' she said with evident relief.

'You didn't tell him about the rags in the door, did you?'

'No. He's worrying like hell as it is.'

'What about? You reassured him the cash was all in the bank, didn't you?'

'It's the shop – he never insured it. Shop and stock all gone, and no compensation to come. He's kicking himself now, and feels guilt-ridden about us.'

'No need,' said Eva. 'There's fabric left – the fire didn't reach the cellar. And there's the patterns.'

Zoe shook her head. 'Smoke-damaged fabric. We can't use that. Let's face it, Eva, we're wiped out. Finished.'

Eva stood up abruptly. 'No, we're not. I don't know who the sod was who wanted to put us out of business, but I'm damned if we're going to let him beat us. We've got our takings, we've got our patterns, and we've got our ideas. We can start again. We *will* start again.'

Zoe stared. 'I approve your fighting spirit, my love, but let's be practical about this. We've got no premises, for a start.'

'We'll have to look for some then. What about Bernstein's?'

'No good, Papa said he's found a customer. But a place in Soho would be super.'

'Or Chelsea – that's where it's all happening these days, what with students and all kinds of arty people there. I keep reading about all their frantic parties.'

Zoe looked thoughtful. 'Chelsea would be fantastic. Right then, let's start looking.'

Rosa was surprisingly emphatic for a normally equable lady.

'No, I insist, it is no trouble at all to cook and clean here for you and your papa. He will need rest and good food to build him up. Such a terrible thing to happen! I will care for him – after all, I have no job to go to now,' she added ruefully.

Louis sat in the armchair, surrounded by cushions and newspapers, cigarettes and ashtray carefully placed within his reach. His eyes were moist as he watched Rosa's ample figure bustling back and forth to the kitchen.

'To be in my own home again is wonderful,' he croaked. 'I am a fortunate man indeed.'

Rosa hurried back into the room. 'Don't talk so much, Louis. You must rest your lungs. I bring you nice cup of tea.'

She flicked crumbs from his lap and hurried out again. Louis looked down at the packet of Passing Cloud.

'So much good money I pay out all these years to fill my lungs with smoke,' he murmured. 'I am the fool no longer.'

He pushed the packet off the arm of the chair. Rosa's cat looked up in surprise. At that moment the door opened and the two girls came in. Louis's face brightened.

'Where have you been all the day, princess? You look still for a new place?'

Eva came across and dropped a kiss on his cheek. 'We've walked our feet off, Mr Jacob. We've found nothing yet, but Chelsea it's got to be, we've decided.'

Zoe seated herself on the arm of his chair and bent to kiss him. 'That's right – Chelsea or nothing.'

'Chelsea?' he murmured. 'I knew a nice woman had a good little millinery business in Chelsea. Mrs Beckett, a thriving little shop, good area. No more though – hat trade is dying fast. They sell the building and Mrs Beckett closes down. A restaurant is there now, they tell me. Everybody wants to eat.'

'Trouble is,' said Zoe, 'Chelsea is so expensive to rent. We're going to have to talk to the bank about a loan.'

'A restaurant,' Louis was muttering, 'but Mrs Beckett said the rest of the building was empty still. It would not harm to ask.'

'This must be the place,' said Zoe, closing her umbrella and pointing up at the *For Sale* sign over the whitewashed window of the ground floor. From the basement restaurant beneath came the sound of a trumpet playing traditional jazz.

'Sounds OK,' said Eva. 'Let's go down out of this rain anyway and see how expensive it is.'

The moment they opened the door and the full sound of the trumpet blared in their ears it was evident the place was popular. Every table was occupied, mostly by students and young professional people deep in animated conversation, hands cupped round ears to listen to each other above the sound of the trumpet.

A couple at a side table rose to leave and Zoe plumped her handbag down on one of the chairs. 'Cosy here – what you might call intimate,' she said loudly. 'At least it's different.'

Eva shook the raindrops from her hair and then took the menu from the table. 'Not so pricey as you might think for Chelsea,' she remarked. 'Let's eat first and ask to see the manager after about the empty space upstairs.'

'The sign outside said it was for sale, not to let,' said Zoe.

'No harm in enquiring. Now, what do you fancy?' Eva looked around for a waitress. 'Funny, not a cap or apron in sight.'

A voice at her elbow made her jump. 'Can I take your order?'

Even before she looked up she had placed the voice. Alan Finch stood smiling beside her, shirt-sleeved and a napkin draped over his arm. Suddenly all the greyness vanished from the day.

CHAPTER EIGHTEEN

Zoe found her voice first. 'What on earth are you doing here? Teaching not paying well enough?'

'I decided teaching wasn't for me,' Alan replied cheerily. 'I wanted something more challenging.'

'At least we've got something in common,' said Eva.

He looked down at Eva's rain-sodden cloak. 'You two off to a fancy dress party?'

'Bollocks,' said Eva. 'You look pretty fancy yourself – like waiting on, do you?'

'The Italians regard it as a very honourable profession. Why shouldn't I? How's things with you two?'

'Didn't you read about us in the papers? We got burnt out.'

'No – hard cheese. What happened?'

Briefly Eva recounted the incident while he listened and nodded. 'And the worst of it was,' she concluded, 'we had to put up with a lot of damn silly questions from the police. As if we'd burn down our own place! Anyway, they're satisfied now it wasn't us, but they still think maybe somebody had a grudge against us.'

'They even suggested it could be anti-Semitism,' cut in Zoe. 'They don't know how well-liked Papa is.'

'So you need new premises,' Alan remarked. 'Pity you couldn't afford to buy the place upstairs – it'd be ideal.'

'Do you think they'd let it to us?'

Alan shook his head. 'No, the owner definitely wants to sell. I can't afford to buy or I would.'

Zoe looked around. 'Nice place. Nice idea having jazz too.'

Alan glanced over his shoulder. 'It'd be great to see real topliners like Chris Barber up on that dais some day. Just look at that trumpet-player. Doesn't he remind you of –'

'Of the boy at the Saturday night college hop,' Eva cut in quietly. 'I was just thinking that.'

The blues number ended. The pianist stepped down off the little dais and pushed his way between the tables to stop in front of Alan.

'What d'yer think then?'

Alan nodded. 'I'm happy.'

'The whole week?'

'I don't see why not.'

'How much?'

Alan took a breath before answering. 'We'll talk money in my office later. OK?'

The pianist hurried, beaming, back to the dais, muttered a few words to his colleagues, and sat down again at the piano. The triumphant sound of *When The Saints Go Marching In* filled the air.

Eva turned back to stare at Alan. 'You the manager here then?' she asked.

'The owner, actually. Bit of an entrepreneur, me.'

'Oh.' Eva looked around her. 'What's that thing in the middle of the room?'

'A china dog. Gives the place atmosphere.'

'With a pipe in its mouth? And what's that up there?'

'It's a sewing machine, of course.'

'Hanging from the ceiling! And you think we're odd?'

'So it's different, but it's mine. Sold all I had to find the money.'

'It's terrific,' said Zoe. 'And it takes courage.'

He gave a crooked smile. 'Not really – not when that's where your heart is.'

'I know what you mean,' said Eva. 'And that's what we're going to do.'

Zoe looked up and then smiled. 'Here's Luc – I told him where we'd be. Luc – come and meet an old college friend of ours. He owns this restaurant.'

Alan rose and held out a hand. 'We were just planning how to steal a fortune so we could buy this building,' he said with an easy smile.

Luc gave an equally mischievous smile as he shook hands and then pulled out a chair. 'Really? Then you must let me join the conspiracy. I could do with premises in London too.'

'Why?' asked Alan.

'He wants his own studio,' said Zoe. 'Wouldn't it be great if we all worked here – you down here, us on the ground floor and Luc up the top. You'd like that, wouldn't you, Eva?'

Eva saw Alan's gaze swing across to search hers curiously. 'Great,' she said. 'It'd be terrific.'

'How much?' asked Luc, looking directly at Alan.

'Eight thousand, freehold. If it was eight hundred it'd still be too much for me.'

'Can you put up anything?'

Alan shrugged. 'All I have is already tied up in this place.'

Luc looked thoughtfully at Zoe. 'Eight thousand, eh? We should look into it and see what could be done.'

'Eight thousand,' Eva repeated. 'Where on earth do you think we could get that? The most Zoe and I could raise would be – what, Zoe? A thousand at the *very* most.'

'We'd need a loan,' said Alan. 'Each of us to repay equally.'

'But who'd give us a loan?' Eva argued. 'We've no security to offer. I suppose we could try . . .'

'That's the spirit,' said Luc. 'Let's see what can be done.'

*

Joe was moody tonight. The girl knelt before him with a mug of tea in her hand, and for once he did not caress her hair before he took it from her.

'It is good, Joe. You did well, honestly you did.'

He slurped a mouthful of tea before answering in a surly tone. 'The paper says only the shop was destroyed.'

'Yes, Joe. That is good.'

'But not that she was hurt.'

'It doesn't matter, Joe. Her shop is gone, she's out of business now, and that makes me happy.'

His dark eyes surveyed her in the gloom. 'She hurt you, Kathy. I wanted her hurt too. I let you down.'

The girl's hand was gentle on his knee. 'No, Joe. You've never let me down. I'm very pleased with you.'

'Really?'

'Honestly, Joe.'

His voice sounded mollified. 'I only want you happy, Kathy.'

'I know.'

His tone suddenly became bright. 'And I did like the fire, Kathy – all the sparks and the flames. Can I do it again, Kathy? Please?'

'Some time, maybe. Not tonight, Joe. Now, drink your tea.'

He drank deeply then laid the mug aside. 'One day, Kathy, one day I'll really hurt her for you. I'll burn her like she burnt you – just you see.'

Mr Lawrence looked across the wide mahogany expanse of his desk, neatly arranged the way he liked it with blotting pad and inkwell, precisely ordered notepaper and silver pen. He flicked a speck of dust from his impeccable navy pinstriped knee and sat back in his deep leather chair.

The girl sitting opposite puzzled him. Her dress was

unusual, to say the least, a man's suit, a shirt and a necktie tied in a bow round her neck and another tying up her long red hair, yet she sat there as composed and erect as if it were completely normal. He was certain he had seen her around Golders Green somewhere before, and she'd caught his eye because she'd been wearing something outrageous then.

'I'm sorry, Miss Bower,' he said smoothly, 'but though I appreciate your keenness I do not feel I am in a position to risk the bank's money on your venture.'

'But we'll succeed, Mr Lawrence – we've already proved the demand for our things. Our place was terrifically popular.'

Urchin, the girls had called it – he remembered now. Ruth had mentioned she had come across the place one afternoon while out shopping.

'Such an appalling place, darling. Looked like a children's playground. No taste at all.'

'I'm sure, Miss Bower, but as you pointed out yourself, you have no security to offer. Come to me again once you are established and can show me your accounts, and perhaps then I can review the matter more favourably.'

The girl rose abruptly. 'When we don't need you, you mean? Thank you very much, Mr Lawrence. I wish I hadn't wasted your time – or mine.'

He watched her sweep from the room, red head high, and could not help admiring her. Then he picked up the silver pen and began to list, as Ruth had instructed, the gifts he must buy for Christmas.

'Stupid bastard! What a waste of bloody time,' Eva exploded to Zoe later.

'Eva –'

'I bet he thought I was just a student playing a joke on him. One day he'll be sorry he didn't want our business.'

'Eva –'

'One day he'll be begging for our account, and then I'll tell him –'

'Eva!'

'What?'

'We've got the money! Luc's got it for us! Your precious Mr Lawrence can do what he wants – we don't need him.'

Eva's eyes rounded, then she grabbed hold of Zoe and whirled her, dancing, round the room. At last she flopped into a chair. 'We've got it! Fantastic! I don't believe it!'

Zoe smiled contentedly. 'I knew I could trust Luc to sort it out.'

'I keep forgetting he's rich – he's so nice,' Eva commented.

'Not yet he isn't. He inherits when he's twenty-five, but he got a loan on that security.'

'That's terrific. You know what amazes me? The way he and Alan have taken to each other. They've hardly known each other five minutes and they're dying to get started in this thing together.'

'Some men seem to have a knack of recognizing who they can trust.'

Eva glanced at her and smiled. 'Is this the girl I once remember telling me she wouldn't trust Alan Finch any farther than she could throw him?'

'I was right then – he let Fay down, didn't he? But remember, Eva, this is business. Nothing else.'

Eva turned away, reluctant to let Zoe see her expression. 'This jazz place means a hell of a lot to him.'

Zoe twisted round to look at her thoughtfully. 'You used to hate him. Boy, you have changed – you've gone soft – I noticed it when the police were saying it was arson too – you started shouting something about wishing the rotten bugger who did it would – then you suddenly went all quiet. When the policeman asked would what, you said you wished he'd find peace.'

'Well, it must have been some crank who had problems.'

'I thought you were going to say something else.'

Eva shook her head. 'Not any more. Now, I thought we were talking about the money and the new shop.'

'It's ours, Eva. It'll take a bit of time, of course, but we need time to do the place up ready and organize everything – who's going to do the sewing for us and all that. Once Christmas is over we'll have our hands full.'

'And maybe new designs,' said Eva. 'Hell, isn't it exciting? Mr Lawrence, watch out, here we come!'

In the tiny office glass-partitioned off from the factory floor Louis sat perched on a stool facing Bernstein's desk. 'Listen to me, Henry, you have no work coming in so it makes good sense. And you get to keep four girls you don't have to pay any longer.'

Bernstein looked mournful. 'Such a thing to do, Louis, backing out on the deal just as I planned to take Naomi to Italy for a fine holiday. Such a disaster.'

Louis shrugged. 'Be patient, my friend, the right buyer will come for you. Meantime it makes sense to let my princess rent a corner from you, eh?'

'I suppose you are right. I'd be very happy to be rid of this whole damn business and retire.'

'And Henry,' Louis added in a conspiratorial whisper, 'I shall be here every day – we can talk over old times together.'

Barnbeck seemed like an oasis of peace after the bustle of London. Eva soaked up the tranquillity surrounding her in the farmhouse, revelling in the traditional turkey and chestnut stuffing and carols in the church and presents under the tree. It was wonderful to watch the glow of affection in the glances between Maddie and Max and to know that wherever she might go, she would always be a part of that love.

They wanted to know everything about the new venture, every detail down to the last reel of cotton.

'Who is this Luc?' Maddie asked when the supper dishes had been cleared away and the three of them still sat around the kitchen table. Lassie came to lie across Eva's feet.

'Chantal's stepson. He's nice, and rich too. You must come down to the opening and see our new place – it'll be fabulous when Zoe's finished.'

'Such a nice girl, that Zoe,' remarked Maddie. 'And that Alan who had his eye on you. Who's going to do the sewing for you?'

'We lost our machines because of the fire so Zoe's dad arranged for us to rent a corner of Bernstein's factory.'

'So how many machines have you got?' asked Max.

'Four now, and the girls Henry was going to have to lay off.'

'He wasn't doing very well then?'

'He wants to sell out really. His only son died in the war so he's lost interest in it.'

Maddie was fingering the tablecover. 'If you'll be working in the shop in Chelsea, who's keeping an eye on things in the factory?'

'Zoe's dad. He's more or less recovered now and there won't be any hard work for him to do, only see the girls have enough fabric and things.'

'And you'll still be doing your own designs – the patterns were saved, weren't they?'

'Most of them, but I want to get stock from the wholesalers as well, and fresh designs too. Zoe's terrific at sketching ideas, but I need more. I'm going to check out the art college as soon as I get back.'

Get back. Eva was reluctant to confess, even to herself, that the inactivity was beginning to pall. Now the New Year had begun she was anxious to get back to London and start on the thousand and one things that still had to be done. By now Zoe would be in the shop and starting on the cleaning up . . .

Eva saw the quick exchange of glances between husband and wife, and then Maddie rested a hand on Eva's shoulder. 'Tell you what, darling – why don't you go back a few days early? Then Max and I can get started again. You'd be doing us a favour.'

Louis's hand rested on Rosa's shoulder as he announced his news to the girls. 'We have had a long talk, Rosa and me, and we think it would be nice if Rosa comes to live here and keep house for me.'

Rosa dimpled. 'I like to stay here and cook and clean for you, Louis. It is not good to cook only for me.'

'Rosa needs work, and what sense is there to pay two rents and rates when one will do? And two gas and electricity bills? It makes good sense, princess, don't you agree?'

'Absolutely, Papa – I'm delighted.'

Louis's pudgy face registered relief. He turned to Rosa. 'There, did I not tell you? My daughter is a businesswoman, I say, she will understand.' He turned back excitedly to his daughter. 'Now tell Rosa, princess, about the fine building you buy in Chelsea. Chelsea, mark you, Rosa – no Camden Town for my daughter, but Chelsea, where the big money is.'

'There's a lot of work to be done first, Papa, altering and decorating the place.'

Louis spread his thick hands. 'But this is where you shine, princess! Just look what miracles you did to my shop – who else but you would have dreamt up the idea to make it a gipsy camp? Brilliant, you are, princess.'

Alan appeared from the cellar doorway and dumped a rusty old bicycle on the shop floor, wiping the sweat from his forehead with a grimy hand. 'There's a heck of a lot of junk I've got to get out of there before the bin men come. What a load of old crap!'

Zoe frowned. 'Don't you dare throw anything out. I want it.'

Alan's dark eyebrows rose. 'What for? What the devil are you going to do with a rusty old bike and a pram that must have belonged to Queen Anne?'

Zoe spread her hands in a gesture reminiscent of Louis. 'You ask that question of me? You, the man who hangs sewing machines from the ceiling?'

Luc appeared from the cellar carrying a battered rocking chair with broken spindles. 'Look at this!' he exclaimed in evident delight. 'Now I'll have somewhere to sit as well as the bed.'

'You're not having it,' said Zoe firmly, taking it from him. 'It's my window display.'

'But I need it,' Luc protested. 'For the studio flat.'

Zoe compressed her lips into an expression of indulgence. 'OK, when I'm not using it. In between you can use the pram.'

Luc put his arm around her and smiled. 'You are too good to me, Zoe. I shall begin to suspect that you're in love with me.'

Alan glanced at his watch. 'I've got to meet Eva off the train – I'd better go.'

It was easy to spot the red hair topped with a black sombrero and the flowing green cloak striding out through the ticket barrier. Alan stood motionless behind the pillar, admiring the confidence of her walk and noting the way heads turned to follow her. Like Fay, she was a stunner. But unlike Fay, the pale beauty with an ethereal quality that every man longed to worship, this girl had an earthy quality, an unconscious sensuality a man could not put from his mind.

A young businessman, briefcase in hand, lifted his bowler hat and smiled as she passed. Eva made no acknowledgement and the young man hesitated for a second, as if debating whether to follow her.

'Hands off, mate. That one's mine,' Alan muttered to himself as he emerged from behind the pillar and went forward to meet her.

Alan's battered old car wove its devious journey through the London traffic towards Chelsea. Eva had taken off her sombrero and was sitting beside him watching the confusion of cars and taxis ahead.

'Stupid clot!' she shouted as a taxi driver cut in front of them.

Alan smiled. Her vitality was one of her most attractive features. That and her enthusiasm for everything in life. No studied expression of boredom like so many modern girls. No strange, far-away expression that kept you guessing . . .

'Do anything special over Christmas?' Eva asked.

'Not a lot. And you – good journey?' he enquired.

'Great. I sat next to this fabulous old lady who'd travelled the world – she told me about living in Nepal, of all places. Wouldn't it be great to travel?'

'You can, while you're free and unattached.'

'I intend to. But we've got to have money to do it.'

Alan kept his tone as casual as possible. 'See anything of that lecturer fellow these days?'

'David? Yes, I've seen him.'

'And?'

'And nothing. He's a drip. Didn't measure up.'

'What do you want of a man, Eva?'

She shrugged. 'Don't know, really. But I'll recognize it

when I see it. Watch out – you nearly had that cyclist's sandwiches out of his pocket!'

'I'm clapped out,' Zoe announced, flinging aside the paint-brush. 'Who's for fish and chips?'

'All of us,' said Eva. 'Luc and Alan must be starving too.'

Alan put his head round the door. 'Dinner is served, ladies. Come on down and eat while it's hot, and give Luc a shout too.'

'This is great,' said Eva as they sat at a candle-lit corner table in the café eating spaghetti bolognese. From the record player the sound of Benny Goodman's orchestra floated on the air. 'Do you always eat at your own place, Alan?'

'Where else? This is my home.'

'You mean you live here? Whereabouts?'

He waved a fork in the direction of the kitchen. 'In the back. I couldn't afford digs as well as this place, and anyway, it's the best kitchen in Chelsea, so why not?'

'Why not indeed?' agreed Luc. 'And when I move in too I shall eat here.'

Eva looked across the table at Zoe. 'I didn't realize we'd all be living above the shop, so to speak.'

'We're going to put camp beds in the back room while we're doing the place up to save on fares,' Zoe told them.

'Your father won't mind?' asked Alan.

Zoe shook her head. 'Not now, with Rosa there.'

'How do you feel about that – so soon after your mum, I mean?' asked Eva.

'Whatever makes him happy is all right by me. Neither of us is going to forget her.'

Eva smiled happily. 'So it looks like we'll all be eating together every night.'

Alan swallowed a mouthful of spaghetti. 'Have you two chosen what name you're going to put over the window?'

'*Urchin*, of course. What'll you do, Luc? A name-plate beside the front door?'

'Yes, with *Luc's Studios*,' said Luc. 'Excuse me.'

'What's up?' said Eva. 'Why are you looking at me like that?'

He gave an apologetic smile. 'I'd like to finish my spaghetti.'

'Well?'

'I can't until you take that big floating sleeve of yours out of it.'

Alan was laughing openly. 'How the devil can you scrub and paint in clothes like that? Don't you two ever wear jumpers and cardigans like most people?'

Zoe shook her head firmly. 'We can't. Not since the day we made a bonfire of all our old stuff in France.'

'We like it this way, so don't mock because you're stuck with it,' said Eva.

Alan grinned. 'I'm not complaining. Now who's for chocolate *bombe*?'

As he rose to go to the kitchen, he suddenly turned. 'Oh, by the way, guess who I saw in town today?'

'Who?'

'Kath Davis.'

Both girls stopped eating to stare at him. 'Kath?' echoed Eva, coiling in with her tongue the strand of spaghetti snaking down her chin. 'Are you sure?'

'I'm certain of it. There's no mistaking Kath Davis.'

Eva stared at the candle burning in the centre of the table and wondered why the restaurant suddenly seemed to grow very cold.

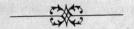

CHAPTER NINETEEN

Zoe sat at the corner table one morning when the restaurant was still closed, surrounded by sheaves of paper. Eva, dressed to go out, leaned over her shoulder watching her pencil glide across the paper.

'Alan gone off to the Regent's Palace yet?'

'Regent's Palace? He's meeting Martin at the Strand. Went half an hour ago.'

Eva shrugged. 'I thought he said Regent's Palace. Hey, what terrific designs. Let's have a look.' Eva picked up the sketches. 'Tell you what – why don't I take some of them with me up to the art college?'

'What for?'

'See if someone can draw up patterns from them. Wouldn't do any harm to try.'

Without waiting for an answer Eva singled out three of the sketches and tucked them into her handbag.

Students were spilling in and out of the door of the Students' Union. Eva did not hesitate. If that was where the students congregated, that was where she too must go. Another knot of students arrived, laughing and joking, and she tagged on with them and walked boldly in.

The bar was alive with them, sitting and standing and squatting everywhere, glasses in hand and scarves slung around their necks. Eva made her way across to the bar where the liveliest group stood, bantering and teasing. A girl with Cleopatra-like dark hair and a classic face broke off her

236

conversation with a tow-haired young man to turn and stare at Eva.

'Hullo,' said the young man, moving aside to make room for her, 'I like your dress.'

'Thanks,' said Eva. 'It's French.'

'Balenciaga,' the girl said thoughtfully.

Eva stared. 'How'd you know that?'

The girl shrugged. 'I've loved French clothes since I was a kid, long before I decided to take up fashion.'

'You study fashion then?'

'Top student in the third year is Natalie,' the young man informed her. 'Brilliant ideas she has.'

'Really?' Eva delved into her handbag and took out Zoe's sketches.

Faces craned over her shoulder to look. 'Not bad,' said the girl. 'Original, but not very straightforward to draft.'

'Could you do it?'

The girl curled her lip. 'Of course I could.'

The young man chuckled. 'If Natalie can't, no one can.'

Eva shuffled the papers and produced another of Zoe's sketches. 'Could you draft that? Fancy having a go for me?'

Natalie gave a mischievous grin. 'What's it worth? A rum and coke?'

Eva smiled. 'I think I could rise to that. And it could be worth more in time. Help out with the grant.'

'Let's have a look.' The girl took the sketch and sat down at a table to study it. The young man sat with her. Eva pushed a pound note across the table towards him.

'Get Natalie her rum and coke, will you? And a dry sherry for me, and whatever you're having.'

He brought back three glasses and sat down, laying the change in front of Eva. Natalie jerked a thumb at him.

'He's Gerry Ingram, specializes in jewellery. Who are you?'

'Eva Bower's my name.'

'And you're looking for a designer? I could do some brilliant ones for you.'

'As good as these?'

Natalie looked down at the sketches. 'These are very good. But I can design stuff like you've never seen.'

'Draft the patterns and bring some of your ideas to my place. We'll talk then.'

By the time Eva left she felt she had done quite well for a first foraging trip. Not only had Natalie Vanning promised to deliver the patterns and her own ideas by the weekend, but Gerry Ingram too was eager to show Eva some of his jewellery, ethnic designs of African wooden bead necklaces and twisted snake bracelets. The sight of them had sparked off a whole new train of thought. Urchin clothes, with their own accessories and cheap costume jewellery to go with them . . . Eva couldn't wait to spill the idea to Zoe.

'They're bloody good,' pronounced Zoe some days later, poring over the pattern drafts and sketches. 'We can extend our whole range of clothes. And I liked that Natalie.'

'So do I, and I've got an idea maybe we could use her to model some of our things at the opening. I'm sure she'd agree. What about Gerry? What did you think of his jewellery?'

'Terrific. I loved those bangles and earrings. It's a great idea to have a whole collection of Urchin stuff – I don't know of anyone else who does that.'

Eva began scooping the pattern pieces together. Zoe stayed her hand, pulled a lip, and then withdrew a mass of shredded paper from the drawer. 'Look.'

Eva stared at the chewed tangle. 'What the hell's that?'

'Our patterns – the ones that didn't get burnt.'

'What happened?'

'Rosa's cat happened. I didn't know till now that paper patterns were made of some kind of fish-powder. So it's a blessing you found Natalie what's-her-name.'

Both girls were laughing hysterically when Alan came in. 'Eva – I want you,' he said sternly. 'Come outside.'

'By the way how was Martin?' asked Zoe.

'Martin?'

'You met him at the Strand the other day, didn't you?'

'Oh yes – he was fine. He sent his love.'

Eva followed him out into the street. He stood on the pavement, pointing. Eva followed the direction of his finger and saw an antiquated bicycle propped up against the basement railings.

'It's not – no, it can't be that old thing you found in the cellar?' she gasped. 'Oh Alan – you've made a fantastic job of it.'

He took the handlebars and flung one leg over the crossbar. 'Come on, what are you waiting for? Get on.'

Eva did not hesitate. Turning round, she eased herself on to the crossbar in front of him, gathering up her skirt to clear the pedals. Swaying and wobbling he pushed off, to the raucous laughter of a passing street-sweeper.

'God, I never noticed this street was cobbled till now,' Eva breathed. 'I've never had such a bumpy ride in my life.'

'Don't think it's any better on the saddle,' laughed Alan. 'I think I'm ruined for life.'

They managed a wavering journey to the corner of the street and then he turned a complete circle to come back. Then somehow Eva's skirt became entangled in the front spokes and she shrieked. There was a sound of ripping, the wheel jammed and the bicycle lurched drunkenly. Eva felt herself falling, and then somehow she was sprawled on the ground, Alan half-lying across her, and the old bike on its side in the middle of the road.

A pair of dark eyes smiled into hers. 'May I have the next dance please, Miss Bower?'

The weeks passed in a flurry of activity. Luc's studio was equipped and he was beginning to take orders for assignments. The fact that his dark room had to double as his bedroom bothered him not at all.

'A red light gives a romantic atmosphere,' he declared. 'I shall always have red lighting in my bedroom however rich and famous I become.'

Alan was busy too, re-painting and re-arranging the seating in the restaurant to build a proper dais for musicians. Day after day the girls could hear the sound of jazz floating up from the basement as he auditioned players, often joining in himself on the piano.

'Notice how his eyes shine when he's been playing?' Eva remarked to Zoe. 'I didn't know he was so talented.'

'Hidden depths,' said Zoe. 'I didn't know he could be so much fun. Wonder where he goes when he goes off on his own?'

Almost every day Natalie came to the shop after lectures, bringing more ideas and patterns and listening excitedly to the plans for the opening.

'Me model for you? You bet I will – and my friends would give their eye teeth for the chance. Just tell us what you want . . .'

Louis came often to see how the shop was progressing, exclaiming in delight over his daughter's skill and artistry.

'A bicycle in the window? I would not believe this if someone told me of it, but you, princess – you make a picture even of rubbish. A pile of bricks too – my God!'

Alan took to the old man instantly. 'You must be very proud of your daughter, Mr Jacob. Why don't you stay and have supper with us, and we can talk about the open-ing?'

'A party? And out on the street?' gasped Louis. 'Whoever heard of such a thing to open a shop?'

'That's just it, Mr Jacob, it's unusual, and that's what we want,' said Eva. 'The press will be bound to take notice.'

'But at this time of year – what if it should rain? You cannot prepare food in the street.'

'I'm doing the food,' said Alan. 'From the restaurant. And only part of it's going on in the street – the main part is indoors.'

Louis's eyes widened even further. 'And who is to come to this party? You cannot know who will be your customers yet.'

'Important people, Papa,' said Zoe. 'You, for a start, and Fay, and Eva's mum and dad too.'

'Your parents? Then they must stay with me. Rosa will see they are well cared for. And who else?'

'What about looking in the papers?' suggested Eva. 'I'll go and get my magazines from upstairs too.'

The girls pored over the columns. Zoe pointed a finger. 'What about her?'

Eva considered. 'Not film stars. We've got to ask people who might accept.'

'OK. What about him?'

'Could be. He's got a hell of a reputation for the ladies so he could be a good customer. Put him on the list.'

Louis could not believe his ears when the girls read out their final list. 'My God, if half those people come it will make the Duchess of Essex herself green with envy,' he muttered.

'Kent, Papa. There is no Duchess of Essex.'

'So who's worried about a few miles? Oh, princess, this is going to be the finest shop in London, I can see it! And to think I am the father of such a clever woman!'

Alan smiled. 'I know Luc would agree with you if he were here, Mr Jacob. Very clever, the pair of them. Either that or crazy.'

Valerie Bartram-Bates eyed her daughter curiously. 'Who is it tonight then, Fay? You never tell me these things.'

Fay smiled. 'Just supper with a friend.'

'Donald McIntyre, perhaps?'

'You see more than is good for you, Mummy.'

'I'm learning, darling. I know how you dislike that fashion editor of yours.'

'Well?'

Valerie shrugged and stroked the little dog on her lap. 'I'm saying nothing. Your methods are your own affair.'

'Then you don't disapprove?'

'Why should I? As you rightly said, men should be used.'

Eva stood with hands on hips. 'I said a caravan, Alan, and a caravan's what I want. I want the students to come out of a gipsy caravan in the street and come into the shop. Do you think you could get hold of one for me?'

'A genuine gipsy one? You're not asking much, are you? Tell you what, if I see what I can do – and I'm not promising anything, mind you – will you go with me to the zoo? I've always wanted to go to a zoo and never had the chance. Humour me, Eva, and I'll do my level best about that caravan.'

'It's a deal. Saturday?'

Zoe was singing loudly in one of the back rooms of the shop.

'Belt up!' shouted Eva. 'Three days left and I'm trying to make lists of what I've still got to do.'

Zoe came through the doorway, happiness radiating from her pretty face. 'Who's being a grumpy old thing then when everything's going so well? Do you realize how many people would give their eye teeth to have a place like ours? A huge shop and changing room, a stockroom big enough for us to live in, and our own toilet and sink. It's fantastic.'

Eva put down her pencil. 'You've done a terrific job, Zoe, but we haven't got half the stuff we want for the party.'

'Give Papa the lists – he's so excited he'd love to fetch everything for you.'

Eva grunted. 'I did that. That's why I've still got it all to do. Oh heck! I just hope it doesn't rain!'

On the big day somehow everything clicked into place. At midday the sun came out and suddenly March seemed to turn into May. The dazzling colours of the gipsy caravan parked on the forecourt in front of the shop gleamed brilliantly in the sunlight. Natalie and Gerry kept their promise and pressed all their student friends to come in fancy dress. Clowns and Columbines, monkeys and teddy bears, bearded ladies and fairy queens seethed around the caravan, approaching passers-by with balloons and lollipops for their children.

Zoe stood in the window, hugging Eva as she whispered, 'Oh God, please let it be a success!'

'At least the weather stayed fine for us.'

Crowds began to gather in the street, curious about the colourful spectacle. By the basement railings Alan, resplendent in lion-tamer's tailcoat and topper, acted as barker, inviting the spectators inside to sample the delights of novel clothes and a bite to eat.

Eva caught sight of Reg Fowler with Rita beside him, exclaiming in delight at everything she saw. Maddie and Max were overwhelmed. They stood close together in the window, watching in amazement. Louis, in his brand-new suit bought specially for the occasion, felt he could burst with pride.

'So hard they have worked, your daughter and mine,' he

said to Maddie, 'they deserve to succeed. Just listen – I hear French and German spoken here today as well as English.'

'And Italian,' murmured Rosa shyly. 'Everyone is here.' Girl students, led by Natalie, began dancing down the steps of the caravan, pirouetting in multi-coloured peasant frocks before the assembled onlookers, and skipping into the shop.

Fay made no secret of the fact that she was impressed. 'It's a terrific idea having students doing the modelling instead of fashion models – it's the wackiest fashion show I've ever seen, but it's certainly novel! You'll start a new vogue. My mother is so impressed she's speechless – for the moment.'

'Where is she?' asked Zoe.

'There, at the table, drinking wine with Rosa. Don't let her drink too much or she starts getting maudlin.'

Mrs Bartram-Bates was starting to feel dizzy. Too many customers were milling around in the shop so she sat down on a stool and watched the student who came dancing in. 'Just look at that frock,' she murmured to her daughter. 'It looks just like a patchwork quilt.'

'It is,' said Eva. 'Or it was. It's a one-off, not another like it in England. Very exclusive, only for someone discriminating and with flair.'

'Oh,' said Valerie Bartram-Bates thoughtfully.

'I'll have it,' cried Rita. 'If there's one thing I like, it's being different from everybody else, don't I, Reg?'

'Take it off, Natalie – I'll wrap it,' said Eva.

Alan was standing by as Natalie took off the frock in the changing room. He carried it over to Eva who parcelled it up, her fingers fumbling with excitement. Louis pushed through the throng of customers to tug her sleeve, his dark eyes brilliant. 'Come, Eva – newspaper reporters are here – they want to talk to you. Come!'

Outside, the forecourt was still a crush of bodies and colour, more and more people arriving as word spread.

Inside the shop Valerie Bartram-Bates sat, glass in hand, pouring out her vexations to Rosa.

'So mortifying, my dear. As a divorcee I am no longer able to go to Ascot. We're shunned, you know.'

Zoe nudged Eva's arm. 'There's a girl going out with one of my blouses – did she pay for it?'

'I dunno – yes – no, the tall one did.'

Valerie's voice shrilled above the rest. 'Do you know, even the Mothers' Union wouldn't have me as a member now.'

'Such a shame,' said Rosa. 'Another glass of wine? It is from my own country.'

'The tall girl's got hers in a bag, Eva – the short one didn't pay, I'm sure.'

'Well, you go after her – I'm busy.'

'It is the women who suffer most,' Valerie went on. 'And the humiliation of the court hearing – one feels as if one is being charged with shoplifting.'

'I know nothing of divorce,' said Rosa. 'I am a widow.'

'I am sorry. Oh, I say, have you seen these pretty bangles?'

'It's all right,' said Zoe, pushing her way back through the massed bodies to Eva. 'I got the money off her – she said she forgot.'

'Well, keep your eyes open now for any more shoplifters – and tell the others to watch out too. And for heaven's sake, get Fay's mother out of here, or at least get her drunk. She'll bore everyone to death.'

Valerie accepted the glass of wine Zoe handed to her. 'So kind, my dear.' Then from outside in the street came the sound of a jazz band playing *When The Saints Go Marching In*. Rosa jumped to her feet and pushed through the customers to the window.

'A band coming to here,' she cried. 'Oh, and they are marching down into the cellar?'

Valerie put a hand to her head. 'What a dreadful racket! No wonder I have a headache.'

For Eva the day passed in a euphoric haze of compliments and sales, of pouring wine for everyone, of delighted smiles from Zoe and passing hugs from Alan. By nightfall it was all over and the last reluctant guests and students gone. Louis and Rosa had taken Maddie and Max home. 'Such nice people, it will be a pleasure,' said Louis. Fay had helped her stumbling mother into a taxi and only the girls and Luc remained amid a morass of uneaten food and empty wine bottles.

'I took some terrific shots today,' murmured Luc from where he sat next to Zoe on the floor, leaning against the wall. 'Fay's going to use some with the piece she's gone home to write. Have another glass of wine to celebrate until Alan comes back.'

'I couldn't,' said Zoe. 'I'm afloat.'

'I think I'm blitzed too,' said Eva, sitting on the floor with her head in her hands. 'Where is Alan anyway?'

'I don't know – he slipped out a couple of hours ago.'

A loud banging started and Eva muttered, 'Oh God, the hangover's starting already.'

Zoe raised her head and listened. 'There's someone knocking at the door, you dope.'

'Who locked it?' said Eva, stumbling to her feet. She struggled to open the lock, and Alan stood there, beaming.

'Well? A good day's work, I'd say,' he said. 'And I've brought back some of your goods.' He held out a handful of coloured bangles.

'I wondered where they'd gone,' said Zoe. 'Where did you find them?'

'Mrs Bartram-Bates – she was wearing them all the way up to her elbow.'

'She was even squiffier than us,' said Eva. 'Thanks.'

246

'Thanks? Is that all I get, after scouring the Home Counties for a gipsy caravan too? I want a little more thanks than that, Eva.'

'Like what?' She tried to focus her eyes.

'We've had a bike ride, now I fancy we ought to christen the pram – it's ready out here. Jump in.'

He wasn't joking. Under the lamplight stood the deep-bodied old pram, still in its dilapidated state of peeling maroon paint and with rusting hinges on the torn hood. Leaving the door wide open behind her Eva weaved her way across the pavement, past the caravan surrounded by a litter of paper streamers and burst balloons, and climbed in.

'You are looking very smart, my friend,' said Bernstein as Louis bounded into his office and sat down on the high stool. 'A good suit you do not wear often.'

'Would I not wear a good suit to represent a business like Urchin?' replied Louis proudly.

'Business is good then?' asked Bernstein.

'So good they need to hire more of your machines from you. Again this week they take so many orders they run out of stock.'

Bernstein shrugged. 'They will learn, in time.'

Louis felt piqued. 'Listen, I tell you something. A hundred pounds they expect to take last week, and you know how much they took?' Louis's chest filled out with pride. 'Five hundred pounds, no less. All London is wanting to buy Urchin clothes.'

Bernstein nodded. 'The rent will be higher this time – another ten pounds a week.'

Louis's plump face registered shock. 'Henry – I am surprised at you – have you no shame, no gratitude?'

'No,' said Bernstein. 'I too have bills to pay. Why don't you buy me out?'

Louis sighed. 'The time may come, my friend. You drive a hard bargain, but for old times' sake . . .'

The tiny bedsit reeked of the smell of fish and chips. Joe squatted on the floor, licking his fingers free of the last traces of vinegar.

'You should have seen them, Kathy, her and that Jew girl. Running around like a couple of kids with all those clowns and things. Balloons and stuff, just like when I was at school.'

The girl did not turn, but continued staring out of the window. 'You told me, Joe, dozens of times already.'

'She must be making a lot of money,' Joe mused.

'I wish I had a job. Who wants a girl with a face like this? Maybe after the next op . . .'

'I know where she is now, Kathy. I'll get her.'

The girl turned slowly. 'All that matters to me is getting back to East Grinstead to get my face fixed. That's all I'm bothered about now.'

Joe screwed up the paper and threw it on the floor. 'You told me, after what she done to you . . .'

'You burnt her shop. That must have hurt.'

'We could hurt her more.'

The girl sighed. 'Yes, I'd like to see her suffer.'

He uncurled himself and stood up, taking her shoulders to turn her towards him. His hand touched her face, and she felt the broken fingernails catching on her cheek. 'She's going to get burnt like you, Kathy.'

He heard her catch her breath. 'Joe, you'll be going back to Penston Hall soon and I'll be going for that op. Just be patient now, there's a good boy.'

Anger leapt in him, the red glow he remembered so well from the old days, the vexation that they never understood. 'I'm not going back to that place,' he muttered furiously. 'They keep me locked up.'

'Only for your own good, Joe. Dr Spencer knows best. He let me go when I got better.'

She tried to move away from him, but Joe held on to her face. 'I gotta get that wicked girl first,' he muttered. 'You said I gotta get her, and I will. I want to see the burning, Kathy.' His voice filled with excitement. 'Burning is good, Kathy – flames and smoke and sparkles like Bonfire Night.'

She tried to break away and he could not bear it. His fingers sank into the flesh of her cheek and he heard her moan. 'Joe – don't! You're hurting me!'

One hand fell away, but the other remained tightly holding her chin. 'Kathy, lovely Kathy,' he murmured. 'But you mustn't be cruel to Joe. Joe wants a burning.'

CHAPTER TWENTY

'Hey, guess what?'

Luc came downstairs into the shop, his handsome face aglow. Zoe looked up eagerly. 'What is it?'

'I've got a terrific assignment – a load of fashion pictures to take, and they want me to pick the locations for the shots. I've got a great idea!'

'Tell us then.'

He grinned happily. 'All in good time, but it could be good for you. Come and have a coffee with me, *chérie*.'

As soon as he had taken Zoe away up the street Alan came up from the basement, waving to Eva as he passed the window and came into the shop.

'Telephone call from Mr Jacob,' he said, lowering himself on to the stool. 'Where's the lovebirds?'

'Just gone out. What did he want?'

'To tell you and Zoe he's heard from some chap who wants more frocks from you.'

'Who? Not the one who still owes us?'

'He didn't tell me the name – he was laughing too much. He just said to tell you the guy says if you could let him have any more Balmorals, he'll take all you've got. The last lot went like hot cakes. What are you laughing at?'

'It's a long story. How's business downstairs?'

'Never better. Your customers come down to me for a bite to eat, mine come up here to look at your wacky designs. We make good team mates, don't we?'

Eva looked away, avoiding his probing gaze. 'So does Luc

– he's good for our trade too. He's got something up his sleeve right now.'

Alan was watching her as she busied herself checking the stock on the rails. 'You don't need any help really, Eva. You've got what it takes – good sense, acumen, good designs.'

'I'm not just selling design, I'm selling talent. Zoe's brilliant, and Natalie and Gerry are incredibly talented too. Hold on a minute, let me just check these accounts.'

He watched her as she bent over the ledger, saw the frown that appeared as she read. 'What is it, Eva?'

'This chap who still owes us a hundred pounds and keeps giving excuses why he can't pay. I'm not so sure we should have trusted him.'

'No problem, sweetheart. Just give me his name and address and I'll soon sort him out for you.'

'Would you? Maybe if you ask he'll see he can't just keep palming us off.'

'Any time you get problems, just you tell me.'

Later that week Louis came to deliver more dresses from the factory. 'Three dozen, like you ask, princess, and every stitch perfect – I make sure of that.'

'Thanks, Papa.'

'Henry I must watch like a hawk. Know what he say to me today? Cloth like this he can get for cheaper he says, cut the cost by nearly half.'

'No, Papa, we've had this out –'

'No, I tell him loudly. Would a firm like Urchin cheat our clients, the highest levels of London society? We have our reputation to consider, I tell him. We cannot afford to recognize our reputation.'

'Jeopardize, Papa. I hope you made that clear to him.'

'Of course, princess. Did I not tell you? Can we go eat in the restaurant now?'

Alan came to serve them lunch and Zoe touched his sleeve. 'Guess what?' she said mischievously. 'Luc's doing a fashion shoot this afternoon – and he's taking the pictures outside here.'

'Here? In the street?'

She nodded. 'The magazine'll never notice, he says, but all the readers will see Urchin and Finch's in the background.'

'Cunning devil – if he gets away with it.'

Louis was still eating when Zoe returned to the shop. Eva took her turn to go down to eat. As she entered she saw Alan's broad back and beyond him, Louis's excited face.

'Are you sure?' Louis was saying. 'I could do with the extra money. It is true I supervise for the girls, but so much time I have on my hands now I am retired.'

'You'd be doing me a great favour,' Alan replied. 'I need a man of your personality – not just anyone could do it.'

'Then I accept with pleasure,' said Louis, and hurried past Eva beaming.

As Eva seated herself Alan turned and saw her. He smiled in welcome. 'And what can I serve madame today?'

'You gave Louis a job?'

'I thought the place could use a cheerful maître d'hôtel, so to speak, someone to welcome guests and see they get everything they need.'

'Which you usually do yourself,' said Eva. 'You didn't need him at all. You just thought he needed money.'

Alan shrugged. 'Who doesn't these days?'

She smiled. 'You're a nice bloke. I think I rather like being team mates with you. You going to watch Luc's shoot this afternoon?'

Alan's gaze slid away. 'Ah, not this afternoon, I can't. Spot of business to see to.'

Eva felt a sense of disappointment.

*

Natalie turned up at the shop just in time to see Luc taking the last of the fashion shots in the street outside.

'Sorry I'm late – got caught by one of the lecturers just as I was leaving. Here are the patterns I promised.'

She laid a bundle of newspapers on the counter in front of Eva then eyed the model girls outside critically.

'Gerry would have a fit if I ever got as skinny as that,' she remarked. 'Is it true they eat like pigs between shoots, then starve and even make themselves sick to get skinny again?'

'No idea,' said Eva, 'but I agree they all look like they could do with a damn good bowl of Alan's spaghetti. What've you got here?'

Natalie unrolled the pieces of newspaper. 'Patterns for that Cossack sketch I showed you last week – skirt and chemise.'

'Newspaper?' said Eva. 'Well, at least the cat won't fancy printer's ink.'

Natalie laid the sketch alongside the pattern pieces. Eva's eyes gleamed. 'With boots and a cummerbund – terrific!'

'And maybe I could design a long, full-skirted coat for you to go with it – and maybe a cossack hat.'

'I can just see it at our next showing,' Eva mused. 'Dancing across stage, with a record of a balalaika in the background. Great – go ahead, Natalie, do the coat pattern. I'm sure Zoe will approve.'

Eva had no intention of eavesdropping but as she was preparing to close shop at midday on Wednesday she became aware of Zoe's voice, shrill outside on the basement steps.

'Messing people about – it's not right! Once it was me, but I'm not going to stand by and watch this!'

Alan's voice came soft and soothing. 'Come on, Zoe . . .'

'You've got to make your mind up and stop fooling people around. You're not playing fair.'

'It's not that easy – how could anyone choose?'

253

'You can't string people along like that – it's cheating. Somebody's bound to get hurt.'

Eva walked out on to the doorstep. Zoe stood, hands on hips, on the basement steps. She turned round as she heard the sound of the door and Alan disappeared back into the restaurant.

'What's up?' asked Eva. 'I heard the shouting.'

'Nothing.' Zoe took Eva's arm and ushered her back inside the shop. 'Now, what's all this I hear about Natalie? I'm not having that girl muscling in and taking over my territory. You could at least have consulted me.'

She sounded unusually petulant. Eva tried to reassure her.

'But it's a brilliant idea, Zoe. Cossack is just as bohemian as gipsy. It's right up our alley.'

'Nowadays you seem to accept Natalie as chief designer here. Till she came it was all my ideas. You've had it all your own way over publicity stunts like the opening party, Eva – but original design was my department.'

'But Natalie has terrific ideas –'

'Natalie, Natalie – that's all I ever hear! I'm fed up of hearing Natalie.'

Eva looked at her in concern. 'What's up, Zoe? It's not like you –'

'Shut up! Nothing's wrong with me.'

Eva spoke quietly. 'You are brilliant, Zoe, and I'd never dream of having Natalie or anyone impose their ideas on you, but when someone comes up with an idea which reinforces yours –'

'Leave it, Eva. You stick to promoting and selling Urchin – you're good at that – and leave the rest to me.'

Eva sat quiet for a moment. 'And what about Natalie? I feel a sense of responsibility towards her – after all, I persuaded her to work for us.'

Zoe shrugged. 'We're under no contract with her. Let her bring her work if she wants.'

Biting her lip to hold back the angry words, Eva walked out of the shop into the street, pushing past the sallow young man outside looking at the window display.

A late afternoon shower was spattering the pavement, turning the matt cobblestones into a gleaming grey patchwork. Eva walked on regardless until, after a time, she became aware of her frock clinging wetly to her back. A bus shelter stood empty in the square. She went inside and sat down, trying still to quell the tumult in her.

It was so unlike Zoe, always the calmest of the three friends in the old days, to turn temperamental. Something must be wrong to make her take this unreasonable attitude.

A shadow passed outside the steamed window of the shelter. Eva looked up as Alan appeared at the doorway, stood looking at her quizzically for a moment and then came and sat down on the slatted bench beside her.

'I saw you go off,' he murmured. 'You OK?'

'It's Zoe – she was acting all strange with me. It's not like her. What was she having a go at you about?'

He shrugged. 'You know Zoe – she tries to run everyone's life for them. Forget it. Female moods, tiff with Luc – could be anything.'

Eva looked up at his profile. His strong face had an air of concern, and she was touched. It was good having him around.

'Where were you this afternoon? Spot of business, you said.'

There was a pause before he answered quietly, 'I met Fay. She wanted to talk.'

'Oh.' Eva could not explain her feeling of disappointment. 'You were a sod to her. She was dotty about you once.'

'I know.'

'You left her stranded. That was a bloody thing to do.'

He gave a wry smile. 'Actually she left me, almost as soon as we got to Scotland. Can't say I blame her.'

Eva was staring at him. 'Are you saying you never seduced her? She was crazy about you.'

He shook his dark head ruefully. 'I wish I had. The whole thing was crazy. She realized it first. She senses when things aren't right.'

Eva shivered. *There's something evil about you, Eva.*

'I'm surprised she wanted to see you. What did she want to talk about?'

He looked away out of the window of the shelter. 'Oh, her feelings, how mixed up she felt, that sort of thing. Her father's girlfriend has left him.'

Eva nodded. 'She always had a hang-up about her relationship with her parents. She's a lot better now she's back at home and got her life together. I'm so glad for her.'

'Me too.'

'You only made things worse for her. Still, she got you out of her system long ago.'

It was only then that Eva noticed that Alan was not wearing a jacket. 'Just look at you, your shirt is soaking,' she said, lifting her hand to touch a finger to the nape of his neck. He shuddered.

'You shouldn't do that,' he teased. 'You're asking for trouble,' and he bent forward and kissed her. Then almost immediately his manner became business-like again. 'Fay said she's writing about the Urchin fashion shows, pictures of your models alongside the Barbara Goalen type. She's going to make sure everyone gets to know of you.'

There was a pause, and then Alan started to hum a tune. Eva looked up at him. 'I heard you playing the piano late last night. A beautiful piece. I always thought you played jazz.'

'It was my mother's favourite tune. I used to have to play it a lot for her.'

Eva could hear a wariness in his tone, and was puzzled. She frowned. 'Used to? You talk as if she were dead.'

'She is. You remember I wanted you to come to our house once when my parents were away on holiday?'

'That was ages ago.'

'They never got back from that holiday. They were both killed only a mile away from home. Ironic, isn't it?'

'Oh, Alan!' She reached out a hand to his. After a moment his other hand reached out to cover hers, squeezing hard, and she could sense his loneliness. His lips were compressed and his eyes tightly closed. Eva's heart swelled in sympathy. 'And you never said a word,' she murmured.

'Never any point sharing misery with others. But you see now why I sold up and went away.'

'But that business with Fay – that must have been just after the accident?'

He gave a shrug. 'I needed to be close to someone. And you've done me a power of good, Eva.'

Gently pulling her face to his, he kissed her. For Eva the effect was electrifying, a strange madness leaping in her and a lunatic feeling that she wanted to hold him close and block the rest of the world out. His lips were warm and hard, and at the same time infinitely tender. She was in no hurry for the kiss to end, but at last he let her go, and she sat back, uncertain what to do. Alan was looking at her, his dark eyes searching hers, and she felt confused.

'Hey,' she said in a bantering tone. 'You shouldn't do things like that. You're asking for trouble.'

'Perhaps it's time I did.'

She laughed. 'That time you asked me to your house . . .' she said in a deliberately lighter tone.

'What about it?'

'What would you have done if I'd come?'

'Filled you up with wine probably.'

'And then?'

He shrugged. 'Let nature take its course, I expect.'

She chuckled. 'I bet. I remember your reputation.'

He leaned towards her. 'And what would you have done, Eva?'

'Would you really like to know?'

'Of course.'

'Then it's a pity you didn't find out. You might have liked it.'

'Maybe I could still find out.'

There was an intensity in the darkness of his eyes that made her feel giddy. Eva smiled.

'No – you haven't got a house now.'

He was laughing. 'Oh, Eva – you're an idiot! A lovely idiot. One day I'll have that house,' he said.

Eva got up from the bench. 'Hey look, the rain's stopped.'

Alan rose and took her arm. As they walked along the street the sun came out again, its warmth on their backs emphasizing the dampness of their clothes. Holding his arm Eva could feel the warmth of Alan's body through the wet shirt and revelled in the closeness between them. All vexation was gone; the radiance had come back into the day.

As they reached the shop Alan turned to look down at her, one hand on the railing as he made to go down the basement steps. 'You should do that more often, you know.'

'Do what?'

'Run out in the rain. You look incredible with raindrops sparkling in your hair.'

The look in his eyes, the tone in his voice exhilarated Eva, but curiously this feeling was mingled with a tinge of apprehension.

★

'What was all that about, Zoe? You seemed really upset.'

'Oh, nothing. Sorry I snapped at you, Eva. I didn't mean all that about Natalie. I was just feeling a bit out of sorts.'

Zoe's tone was genuinely contrite. Eva put her arm around her waist. 'No harm done. Heard you bawling Alan out though – what had he done?'

'Nothing. He bugs me at times.'

'How?'

Zoe shrugged. 'Oh, I just don't trust him. Never did, if you remember.'

'But I thought things had changed.'

'In business. Nothing else.'

As Bernstein made his way between the rows of clattering machines towards his office he caught sight of the head inside, and the half dozen strands of hair combed carefully across the scalp told him it was Louis.

Louis, seated behind Bernstein's desk, looked up with a bright smile encircling his pink face.

'Henry – I've been waiting for you – sit, sit.' He waved an arm in the direction of the stool. 'My princess needs more machines.'

'More machines? More of my girls?'

'Aristocracy now we have for customers, Henry – a Lady, no less. Soon there will be more.'

Bernstein looked gloomy. 'Soon I will have only a corner of my own factory left.'

Louis rose and came round the desk. 'Maybe soon we shall put *By Royal Appointment* over the door. Impressive, yes?'

Bernstein shot him a scathing glance. 'The Princess Margaret Rose is a customer already?'

Louis was unperturbed. 'She will be, my friend. She is a very fashion-conscious lady. Soon the whole world will know of my little princess. Soon she will buy you out.'

Bernstein looked at his friend's face in concern. 'You look tired, my friend. Sit down and I ask the girl to make coffee and fetch a bagel for you, yes?'

The girl was waiting on the doorstep when Joe came home. 'Well?' she asked.

He shook his head, glancing at his reflection in the flyblown mirror in the hallway. 'Nobody wanted me. No qualification, they said.'

She sighed. 'We got to get money somewhere, Joe. Mine's nearly all gone.'

She turned and walked wearily ahead of him up the uncarpeted stairs. In the doorway to the bedsit Joe pushed past her and grabbed the handbag on the mantelpiece.

'Here – what are you doing?'

He continued rifling through the contents. 'I want money for chips. Where's your purse?'

Involuntarily she looked across at the windowsill and he followed her gaze. 'Right,' he said, snatching up the purse. 'Got enough for two, have yer, or only me?'

'Joe – please! That's for the rent!'

He took no notice, only rammed the pound note into his pocket and rushed past her out of the room. She looked down at the purse lying on the floor, pennies spilling out onto the bare floorboards, and sighed deeply.

Crossing to the empty fire grate she stared at the reflection of her scarred face in the mirror above. Outside London's traffic rumbled in the distance, hurtling on uncaring on its business, and above its hum the girl's voice throbbed with hatred.

'Damn you, Eva Bower, damn you!'

Fay came to the shop one evening at closing time, poised and relaxed and looking every inch the sophisticated business woman. 'Come down and have something to eat with me, and you can tell me how things are going.'

'OK,' said Eva. 'Luc and Alan are out for a walk along the Embankment. Come on, we haven't seen you for weeks.'

'Saw your last article about us,' said Zoe as they sat down at their usual table. 'You've done a lot about Urchin.'

Fay smiled. 'I'm lucky, I guess. The fashion editor is not very popular at the moment, so I'm getting the plum jobs. Urchin is the talk of the town.'

'You called us amateurs,' said Eva.

'Amateurs who've been lucky enough to put their finger on the pulse of the fashion-conscious young,' said Fay. 'It's true, isn't it? And I was being very complimentary.'

'We were very proud,' said Zoe.

'But you hoped we had staying power,' said Eva. 'As if you doubted it.'

'On the contrary, darling – I'm sure of it.'

Eva nodded. 'So am I. We've got our work cut out to keep up with orders but we'll get more machines –'

'We'll buy Bernstein out when we can afford it,' said Zoe.

'You've missed the point,' said Fay, shaking her head. 'I'm not just talking about production. I mean keeping at the forefront of fashion, continually coming up with fresh ideas, finding new young designers like Natalie every year, finding fresh ways to promote – that kind of thing.'

'We'll do it,' said Eva quietly.

'I'm sure,' said Fay.

It was at that moment that Luc and Alan arrived. Fay's face expressed no emotion as Luc pulled a chair close to Zoe's.

'Cooking up a plot, you three?' Alan enquired as he pulled up a chair alongside Fay.

Eva smiled. 'We were teasing Fay – she's making her reputation in the fashion world by writing about us.'

Fay cupped her chin in her hands, looking down at the table. 'I'd love to be the first to bring Urchin to the world. Then after that, maybe I can find other young British designers. It's high time the French were ousted from their lead.'

Fay's long fair hair was swinging dangerously close over the candle and Eva saw Alan's hand rise quickly to brush it clear. Fay did not look at him as she pushed her hair back behind her shoulders.

Eva watched Alan's profile as they talked, the glow in his dark eyes and the way his mouth curved crookedly when he smiled. He wasn't at all handsome in film star style, but craggy and interesting, as Zoe once described him, and there was strength and resolution in the set of his lips and at the same time generosity in his mouth. Then suddenly a movement caught her eye.

'Don't you think it's a great idea, Eva? Eva?'

Zoe's hand was touching her elbow, but Eva was no longer listening. Behind Alan's head a man's face peered through the barred basement window, and she thought she recognized the face – where had she seen it before?

'That man – he keeps looking in at us,' she whispered. As Alan turned his head to look, Eva saw trousered legs run up the basement steps into the street.

'I can't see anyone,' said Zoe. 'Are you sure you saw someone?'

Alan was already getting up from the table and crossing to the door. Fay was staring at Eva's face.

'It's there again,' she said huskily. 'Oh God!'

Eva felt a sense of chill. Zoe frowned. 'What is? What are you talking about?'

Fay shivered. 'Just like the clouds always block out the sun at three o'clock on Good Friday – it's an omen.'

'Fay – you're giving me goose-pimples – what is it?'

262

'That feeling I had before – evil. There's evil around you, Eva, and I'm afraid.'

Zoe was staring open-mouthed. Fay was making the sign of the cross. Alan came back to stand beside Luc.

'There's nobody there,' he muttered. 'You must be imagining things.'

CHAPTER TWENTY-ONE

Over the succeeding days the sun beat down on hot London pavements and Eva forgot about Fay's premonition. Her friendship with Alan had taken on a kind of conspiratorial air tinged with electricity, each of them aware of the new relationship blossoming between them and everyone, it seemed to Eva, was happy.

Trade was good for Urchin, for Alan's restaurant and for Luc. Natalie was buzzing in and out of the shop almost daily with more patterns.

'Just as soon as my exams are over I'll be able to spend more time on ideas,' she bubbled happily. 'Until I get a job, that is.'

Eva had just gone into the stockroom when she heard the shop doorbell clang, then Alan's deep voice. 'Hi, Natalie. Going to give me a break and let me take you out one night?'

Eva stiffened. 'No,' said Natalie emphatically. 'For the tenth and last time, Gerry's my boyfriend and I'm just not interested in older men.'

Was he just teasing, Eva wondered. Speculation was postponed by Maddie's telephone call.

'I've got two bits of news for you, Eva – one good, one rather sad, I'm afraid.'

Eva felt her heart lurch. 'Tell me the bad news first,' she said quietly, taking a deep breath.

'It's Lassie, I'm afraid. He died last night.'

For several moments Eva could not speak. Lassie, the loyal old sheepdog who'd been her companion in many a childhood prank, the confidant of girlish tears and grumbles. She could see him now, faithful to his crabby master, old Mr Renshaw, to the bitter end.

'*He's called Dog, I tell you. You can't call a dog Lassie when he's a lad.*'

She swallowed hard. 'Was he in pain, Maddie?'

'No. Max saw to that. But he was very old and very sick, love. He'd had a good innings, and I think he was ready to go.'

Lassie gone. It was hard to believe. In Eva's memory he would always be waiting for her to come home at the farm gate, tail wagging and liquid eyes eager. The mental picture brought a lump to her throat, and she tried to banish it before the tears came.

'And the other piece of news – the good news?'

It was Maddie's turn to pause. Eva could hear the intake of breath before she spoke. 'I'm pregnant, Eva. At last, Max and I are going to have a baby.'

Eva awoke with a start, unable to move and her skin prickling with cold sweat. For long seconds she lay as if paralysed, terror still ripping through her and unwilling to open her eyes for fear of what she might see there. Even her lungs refused to work.

It was only a dream, she realized with relief, but even as reluctant eyelids yielded and opened to the darkness of the room, she could still hear the pounding of her own heartbeat and the terror was slow to recede.

It had been so vividly real, standing listening to the rumble and crackle of a house on fire and the terrifying knowledge that she could not help whoever was inside. And then the growing awareness that she was not alone in the darkness of the street, that there was something shapeless and unrecognizable hovering near her, triumphant and threatening.

And then suddenly the hideous, threatening shape had flung itself upon her, throwing her down and covering her, and she recognized the leering Algerian who had raped Chantal, now forcing himself upon her. Over his shoulder she could see Alan and Natalie, side by side, pointing and laughing in the shadows. Nausea and terror filled her.

Eva took a deep breath and sat up slowly, straining her eyes against the gloom to convince herself that she was really awake, really sharing a bedroom with Zoe and that all was well. A hump in the far bed and slow, even breathing reassured her. There was no fire, no bogeyman waiting to pounce, no evil hands on her body. Chantal's words came back to her.

'With the right man, it's wonderful.'

Light, and a cup of tea – that would banish the last of the shivers, she decided. Not the bedroom light – no point in disturbing Zoe. She'd creep out quietly into the little kitchen.

Now if this were a horror film, thought Eva as she closed the bedroom door softly behind her, the heroine would reach the kitchen safely only to be pounced upon as she opened a cupboard door. The background music would swell from lyrical to menacing just as she moved towards it.

Background music? Eva stopped, kettle in hand, and listened. There was music, someone softly playing a piano, and the sound came from the restaurant downstairs. It must be Alan, playing his mother's music again. At quarter past three in the morning? He must be feeling low.

For a moment she hesitated what to do. Alan, the mocking, unheeding Alan of her dream was not the real Alan. The real man was vulnerable like anyone else. Reaching down her cloak from the hook behind the door, she threw it around her shoulders and went out.

Her bare feet made no sound on the steps as she crept down and peered through the basement window. The restaurant was in darkness. Only a shaft of light from the kitchen beyond fell aslant the tables, and just at the edge of its reach she could make out the dark-headed figure of Alan sitting at the piano.

The door was unlocked. As she slipped inside he continued playing, unaware of her. The music was entrancing, gentle as a caress and at the same time the pathos of its minor chords sang of sadness and loss. Eva leaned against the wall in the darkness and listened, enraptured.

As the last chord faded away on the silent air Alan sat motionless, his hands still on the keys. Then he straightened, closed the lid of the piano and stood up.

'I couldn't sleep. I was dreaming,' said Eva, moving across to him.

She saw his sudden, startled movement and the quick glance over his shoulder. 'Oh, Eva. I'm sorry,' he said stiffly. 'I was miles away. Did I waken you?'

'I'm glad I did wake up – it was a rotten dream. That was lovely music you were playing.'

He stood uncertainly by the piano, making no move to come to her. Eva felt a sudden inexplicable shiver, and at that moment a sound came to her ears. Footsteps in the kitchen, bare feet slapping on the tiled floor, and a slim silhouette stood framed in the shaft of light in the doorway.

'What's keeping you, darling?'

Fay was leaning nonchalantly against the doorframe, peering out into the darkness of the restaurant. 'I thought I heard voices. Who's that out there with you?' she asked. 'Oh, it's you, Eva – what on earth are you doing awake at this time of night?'

Eva suddenly became conscious of her nakedness under the cloak, and felt shame flood her cheeks. 'I'm sorry,' she blurted. The words came out stiff and awkward, a barrier between them. Fay was still smiling in the doorway.

Alan cleared his throat. 'Don't misunderstand, Eva – Fay and I had to talk –'

'No need to explain. I'm sorry I intruded.'

She was turning to go when Alan touched her arm.

Instinctively she jerked her arm away.

'Eva, darling,' said Fay smoothly, 'don't jump to con-
clusions. I'm sorry if —'

'Don't apologize,' snapped Eva. 'It's my fault for barging
in. Good night.'

Head held high, Eva marched with all the dignity she
could muster out into the street, vexation and bitter disappointment vying with humiliation inside her.

Fay and Alan! Why hadn't she seen it? What a fool she'd
been! Eva's mind shied away from scenes she preferred not to
visualize. He'd said he'd been seeing Fay, but Eva had
thought never like this.

Zoe had known — untrustworthy, she'd called him —
perhaps she knew he'd been chatting Natalie up too, and
she'd been telling him off, hadn't she? And then Eva
remembered all the other times he'd been missing. And
Valerie Bartram-Bates and the bangles . . .

Fay and Alan together, and in her ignorance she had
walked in on them — what a crass, unsuspecting idiot she'd
been!

Eva slept no more that night, lying awake unable to rid her
mind of scenes which filled her with a venomous feeling of
jealousy.

In the shop next day Zoe cocked her head to one side. 'I just
don't understand you, Eva. Why are you going around with a
face like a wet weekend? All these years you've been saying
they ought to have a baby. If that's you pleased, God help us
when you're miserable.'

'I am pleased for them. It's not that.'

'Then what the devil is it?'

268

Eva took a deep breath. 'You knew about Alan and Fay, didn't you?' she said quietly. Zoe darted her an uneasy glance.

'Oh, that.'

'I walked in on them last night. Is that why you were having a go at him the other day?'

'I can't stand cheats.'

'Then why the hell didn't you tell me?'

Zoe shrugged. 'I was going to, but he told me to mind my own business and not interfere. I thought you'd see for yourself anyway, the way he was looking at Fay.'

'It was Fay who wanted to see him – he told me.'

'Then he's a liar as well as a cheat. Honestly, Eva, you know what he is – he'll never change. Alan Finch was born a Casanova, and that's what he'll always be. You're fooling yourself if you think otherwise. I warned you he wasn't to be trusted.'

'I'd no idea he was two-timing.'

'So now you know he's not worth worrying about.'

Eva sighed. 'I wish I did think that. Trouble is, I fancy him, more than I've ever wanted anybody. I could hate Fay for taking him.'

'I told you, it wasn't her, it was him. He's hardly let her out of his sight. So stop fretting over a man who just isn't worth it.'

Eva fell silent. She couldn't explain even to herself why she felt so much bitterness mingled with jealousy. It was something bigger and more indefinable than just losing Alan to Fay which troubled her, though that was a large part of it. It was a feeling of desperate loneliness, of being dispossessed. And it wasn't that the new baby might usurp her place in the family either – no, that was one thing she was sure of, Max and Maddie's love for her. But it was something to do with belonging . . .

*

It was the day Zoe and her father came home from Watford, after placing a pebble on her mother's grave in the Jewish cemetery, that it became clear to Eva. Zoe and Louis talked fondly of Miriam.

'So like your dear mother you are,' said Louis softly, making no effort to hide the tears that glistened in his eyes. 'The very same eyes and mouth, just like your grandmother too, God rest her soul.'

That was it, thought Eva, it was a sense of identity, a feeling of belonging she lacked, of knowing where one's roots were. A matter of genes, really, of knowing one's inheritance through blood. For the first time in years she found herself thinking of her natural mother, the hazily-remembered woman who had sent her to Barnbeck and to Maddie during the war. And of her father, the merchant seaman who never came home from the sea – all she could remember of him was rough serge trousers held up by a leather belt, and the way both she and her mother had cowered when they saw the belt come off. And screams in the night from the next bedroom . . .

Eva shuddered, pushing the memory firmly from her mind and turning her thoughts to her mother. Max had said he'd tried to trace her, in vain, but was she still somewhere up there in Middlesbrough, remorseful and even pining for her lost daughter? She could not be too remorseful, never having made contact in all these years since the war.

If she was still in the area. There was just a chance there might be some way to find her which Max had overlooked. Now it was no longer just curiosity which impelled Eva, but need . . .

'Go north and look for your mum?' said Zoe. 'Why not? I'd have done it long ago.'

The late evening sun was dipping down behind London's grey rooftops as Joe looked out of the grimy window. Kath was

270

nowhere around and he felt restless. He turned away from the window, jingling the pennies in his pocket and frowning.

He'd pass the time till she got back looking at her picture book, the one she kept in the case under the bed. It wasn't as pretty as the ones with coloured pictures of animals they used to give him to look at in Penston Hall, but it was better than those books she read, with only pages and pages of words in them. Boring.

He pulled out the suitcase and opened it, found the scrapbook and turned it to catch the light of the setting sun through the window. Lots of pieces of newspaper she'd stuck in there, lots of them with only words on them, but there were snapshots and newspaper with pictures on too. The snaps were pictures of herself at college, and there weren't any marks on her face then. The newspaper pictures showed that nasty girl who'd burnt Kath's face with another girl. Kath had told him their names. The nasty one he was going to burn was Eva, and the other was called Zoe.

Kath had shown him the pictures often in the old days, telling him all about it so he could recognize the bad girl. Joe screwed up his eyes to try to read some of the words by the picture.

'Ki-d-na-p, that's kidnap,' he said aloud proudly. He knew about kidnap. He'd seen on the films when the baddies took somebody away and then asked for money before they would give the person back. Kidnap was clever, a way to get money without having to go to work.

He put the scrapbook down and thought hard. He and Kath both needed money. He hadn't had any chips for days now, and his stomach was rumbling for them. Kidnap meant taking somebody away – he could take that nasty Eva away; he could ask for money to send her back.

And then the full brilliance of his idea struck him. Not only was it a very clever way to get money, but he would have the girl in his power too. And then he could hurt her as much as he liked.

Joe frowned. He had to be very clever about this. Kath must not know of his plan because she might stop him. He pushed the scrapbook back into the suitcase and shoved it under the bed.

'No, love, there's no Mrs Jarrett hereabouts – I know everybody in this street and there's no one by that name.'

'We used to live at number twelve,' said Eva, but it was clear from the woman's compressed lips and folded arms that she was going to find out nothing from her. She tried another tack.

'She could have remarried – she was keeping company with a Mr Bakewell, foreman up at Garside,' she said, and saw the woman's brow furrow under the row of metal curlers.

'Bakewell, that rings a bell,' muttered the woman. 'Bakewell – him that went off to Canada way back? Aye, I remember him now I think of it. Flashy fellow – and aye, I recall the woman you mean – lived down the bottom, sailor's wife, wasn't she?'

'That's right,' said Eva. 'You say they went to Canada? Are you sure?'

The woman shook her head firmly. 'He did – not her. She were no better than she ought to be, that one. Bakewell's tart, folk called her.'

Eva felt a wave of anger beginning to ripple but fought it back. 'So she's still somewhere here? You wouldn't happen to know where I could find her, would you?'

The woman was rubbing the long hairs on her chin, lost in reverie. 'Had a little lass, as I recall. Terrible do, that.'

'What was?'

'Bonny little lass, hair as red as yours. Right little bugger she were and all, but it were a shame all the same. Terrible things, them tractors.'

A cold chill ran down Eva's spine. She was turning to leave when the woman suddenly jerked back to life. 'Married a steelworker from up Church Street, she did. Big lad with curly hair. Didn't have much of it left last time I saw him down the Red Lion.'

Church Street was a row of terrace houses with peeling paint and a seedy air of having seen better days. Two women in print aprons stood gossiping over a front garden fence and as Eva approached they stopped talking to watch, curiosity apparent in their defensive eyes.

'Excuse me,' said Eva, 'I'm trying to find a Mrs Jarrett – at least, that was her name, but I believe she's married again. A steelworker. Do you know who I mean?'

She could see their gaze travelling up and down her, the hostile look of women wary of an outsider, a stranger not of their class.

'What do you want her for?' asked the older of the two women.

'Private business,' said Eva.

The younger woman cocked her head to one side. 'You from the court?' she enquired. 'I seen a lawyer in one of them.' She pointed at Eva's cloak. 'You'll find her down that end, number ten.'

There was a woman weeding in the garden of number ten. She looked round sharply as Eva opened the gate.

'If you're selling, I don't want nowt,' she said, picking up a basket and going towards the house.

'I'm Eva.' She saw the woman stiffen.

'Then you'd better come inside.'

The back kitchen was dingy but neat. Carrots and potatoes

lay waiting alongside a paring knife on the enamel sink; a pile of folded, newly-laundered clothes lay on a red formica-topped table with a clutch of pegs and the atmosphere held lingering traces of cabbage and Jeyes Fluid.

But Eva was aware only of the woman standing uncertainly before her, the hair she remembered as fair now faded grey and crimped into a merciless perm; the once-pretty face now careworn and creasing round lips and eyes. It was the kind of middle-aged face one passed every day in the street without a second glance, for it had nothing to redeem its ageing anonymity. This was her mother, she told herself, the woman who had given her birth . . .

'Want a cup of tea?' her mother said. She was clearly flustered, too embarrassed to meet Eva's gaze.

'No, thanks,' said Eva quietly. 'I just wanted to see you again.'

'How did you find me?'

'Does it matter? Aren't you glad to see me?'

Still the woman's eyes would not meet hers. She shrugged and sank down dispiritedly onto a wooden chair and then looked up at Eva. There was no warmth, no love in those eyes, only anxiety.

'You won't be staying long, will you? Only he'll be home for his tea in half an hour and I can't have you here then. It'd be more than my life's worth.'

Eva sat down at the table opposite the woman. 'Mother, it's me – Eva – you haven't seen me for years. I thought you'd gone abroad.'

The woman shrugged again. 'Pity you didn't go on thinking that. It was best all round.'

Eva was shaking, angry and disbelieving still. 'How did you explain me away? What did you tell him?'

'I told him I never had no kids. He hates them.'

'You told other people I'd been killed by a tractor.' The

274

woman's gaze slid away and Eva saw her work-roughened fingers plucking at her skirt. 'Didn't you ever wonder how I was going on? Didn't you care?'

'I had no choice, Eva. I was broke – I had myself to see to.'

'And Mr Bakewell – what happened to him?'

'Colin Bakewell?' She gave a dry laugh. 'He buggered off to Canada. I had to fend for meself. I knew the Renshaws could give you a better life than I could. I did what I thought was best for you, Eva.'

Eva stood up angrily and turned away. She could not bear to look at this weak, helpless woman and think of her as her mother. The woman was kneading her fists together, twisting her wedding ring.

'I couldn't have you back here, can't you see that? I didn't want you – you'd have ruined everything. He'd have knocked the living daylights out of me if he knew about you! Go away, Eva – go back where you come from and leave me be.'

Eva turned slowly, blinking back tears. 'Do you want me to keep in touch, Mother – just to know you're all right?'

The woman got up sharply, pale eyes angry now. 'Sod off, Eva – can't you see you're not wanted here? He'll be in for his tea any minute now, so bugger off.'

She snatched up the paring knife and began peeling the potatoes with long, savage strokes. Eva picked up her bag and made for the door. As she lifted the latch of the garden gate she was aware of pale eyes watching her from the doorstep. A black cat loped slowly along the path towards the woman, stretching its lean body in the sunlight.

'Eva,' she heard her mother's voice call softly. Eva turned. The woman was holding the cat in her arms, stroking its back. 'Don't think too bad of your mother. I did the best I could. I did love you, honest.'

*

Home. Eva felt a terrible need to see Barnbeck again, and the welcoming faces of Maddie and Max. It was no difficult matter to break the train journey there on the way back to London; it only entailed one change.

The station lay grey and uninviting despite the brilliance of the sun as she waited for the connection. Eva paused on the station bridge as she crossed to the far platform. Below her a local train was chuffing its way out to the distant moors, steam rising to envelop her as it rumbled beneath. Enclosed in its hot, steamy breath she felt removed to another world where she was the only being, exiled for her misdeeds, condemned to isolation.

But she was not alone. The disappointment of not being welcomed back was nothing compared to her mother's loneliness, an abject creature passing her days in mindless routine and living in fear of her husband's displeasure. Deep and genuine pity welled in Eva. Her mother was weak not wicked, a woman too shallow to carry the responsibility of motherhood.

Whereas Maddie . . . With a rush of warmth Eva remembered her stepmother's countless acts of love, the gentle smile, the reassuring touch, the welcoming embrace. One memory stood out in her mind like a silk marker in an old book, the first day of school when they had made their way down to the village. The morning mist was still wreathing slowly from the still waters of the lake, she remembered, and she had tried so hard to mask her apprehension under a cloak of bravado. Maddie had not been fooled.

'*They might be bigger than you, Eva, and talk differently, but they're just as nervous as you are. They want to know you really – you're special, you see – you're an evacuee.*'

Maddie had always made her feel special, as if she were grateful for the pleasure of her. And the new baby would make no difference to that. It was essential, she realized, to feel special to somebody. Alan too had the gift of doing just that, but Alan was not to be trusted.

When the train pulled in at Barnbeck station she smiled at the old station master. 'Hello, Mr Fearnley – the old leg still playing you up?'

He touched the peak of his cap. 'Middling,' he said gruffly. 'Mr Bower's up at home today – expecting you, were he?'

'I don't think so – surprise visit.'

'Aye well, he'll be right glad all the same.'

It seemed the most natural thing in the world to be sitting at table with two loving faces watching and listening, taking in every word and reacting predictably. Eva began to feel peace stealing over her. Alan belonged to Fay. Home and love were here.

'Yes, I knew she was still there,' Max was nodding. 'I hoped you wouldn't find out.'

'We didn't want you hurt,' Maddie added. 'That's the only reason we kept it from you. We wouldn't do that –'

Hurt? If only they knew. *I think that young man rather fancies you,* Maddie had said.

Eva laid a hand over hers. 'I know. I appreciate that. I wouldn't want any other mother but you – even if you are too young.'

'So you don't mind –'

'About the baby? I think it was very thoughtful of you and Max to find me another playmate, someone to take for walks instead of Lassie. I'll show him where the best apples are for scrumping.'

'Oh, no,' groaned Maddie. 'I don't think I could go through all that again!'

Joe was perturbed. For three days now he had kept visiting the dress shop, hanging around where he couldn't be seen, and not once had that girl come in. The dark one was there all the time, but not the one he wanted.

He was growing anxious but he could not voice his anxiety to Kathy. Suppose something had happened to her? Oh no, please let her be safe!

CHAPTER TWENTY-TWO

'Going out tonight, darling?'

Fay smiled at her mother's reflection in the drawing room mirror as she tidied her hair. 'Not tonight, Mummy.'

'Not seeing Donald McIntyre again then?'

'No need at the moment. I've got this assignment out of him. I'll get the editor's job yet.'

'And Alan Finch? Aren't you seeing any more of him?'

Fay turned away from the mirror. 'Not for the time being. I'll reel him in again when I feel like it.'

'He really seems to have quite a soft spot for you. I could almost begin to pity him.'

Fay laughed. 'He doesn't need pity – he takes what he wants from life. He wants me only because I'm unattainable but he'll soon find a consolation, if I know him.'

Her mother smiled. 'And now you're playing the same game. You know, darling, I rather approve of the new you. I'm really beginning to enjoy this game.'

Zoe shut up shop for the day and went to wash and change. Luc would be down any minute, kissing and teasing her, the two of them passing the time rapturously as lovers do until they went down to Alan's place to eat with the others.

Not Eva, of course. She wasn't back yet but she was expected home tonight. Zoe sighed. If only Eva could be happy, not tormented with restlessness the way she was . . . It would make it so much easier to tell her then that Luc had asked her to marry him.

Not straight away, of course. She wouldn't want to walk out on the business just as it was taking off so brilliantly. But in a year or so, when Luc's photographs were known worldwide, when he came into his inheritance. They would make France their home then, maybe in the beautiful apartment in Paris where she and Eva had once stayed with Chantal. If only Eva was settled with the right man by then, not still pining for Alan Finch.

Fay had him fascinated. How different she was from the shy, guilt-ridden girl at college, the girl who slept with a night-light for fear of the dark. So poised, so self-assured she had become these days. But then, all three of them had grown up in a very short time . . . They'd had to.

It was growing late. The street lamp threw a pool of light on the pavement outside Urchin and the man watched from a doorway as couples came along, laughing as they went down the steps. Jazz music spilled out into the street as the door opened to let them in and became muted again as it closed behind them.

A glorious smell of food drifted to his nostrils and hunger pangs made him fretful. Cautiously he sidled along the railings to the head of the steps and crept down far enough to be able to bend and look through the window.

He could see them now, at a table in the corner, the tall, dark-haired man, the little Jew girl and the fat man who was often with her in the shop, but still no Eva. Frustration mounted into anger as he watched forkfuls of food going into open mouths.

'What do you think you're doing?'

The voice startled him. He leapt forward towards the tall, cloaked figure at the top of the steps, coming down towards him. It was her – Eva, the nasty one, dressed just like the Wicked Witch of the West who tried to stop the Tin Man getting his heart from the Wizard of Oz. She was standing in front of him now, barring his way.

'I know you, don't I?' she demanded. 'You're the one who keeps spying on me. What do you want?'

She came down another step. Without thinking his hand rose to hit her, punching her hard so that she fell backwards, and he heard the thud as her head hit the step. She lay still, her eyes closed and her mouth parted.

He lifted her inert body and the handbag lying at her feet and half-carried, half-dragged her up on to the street, propping her up against the railings, then looked about him, panting. A sudden swell of music showed that the restaurant door had opened again, and he saw a young man's head rise above the railings, his arm around a girl who swayed and staggered and finally fell down on the top step.

'Hold on, I'll call a taxi,' said the young man. Joe watched him go to the edge of the pavement and raise his hand. Instantly a black car glided to a halt in front of him, and Joe watched how he supported the tottering figure of the girl as they climbed in. The black car glided away into the darkness.

He looked at Eva's face. Her eyes were still closed. He let her weight slide down the railings until she was in a sitting position, then propped her head between two bars. Then, just as he had seen, he went to the pavement edge and raised his hand. The magic worked. The taxi engine purred as the driver leaned across to wind down the window.

'Where to, mate?'

'Duke Street,' said Joe, and went back to pick up Eva. The driver watched incuriously.

'Had a drop too much to drink, has she? Love-a-duck, these girls never learn.'

Eva's head leaned against his shoulder as the car made its way across town. In no time at all Joe recognized Duke Street, and was surprised how quickly they had got home.

'That'll be four and six, mate.'

Joe stared for a moment, uncomprehending, then understanding dawned. 'Oh – yes.' Money. He had no money. But Eva had a handbag, like Kathy.

He found a pound note in the purse. The driver counted out the change slowly, and Joe pocketed it. Eva's weight seemed to have doubled during the drive, and it was no easy matter dragging her from the car to the front door, then propping her up against the doorjamb while he fumbled with the key. But he felt happy. Kath would be so pleased with him when she found out . . .

She was waiting at the top of the stairs. 'Where on earth have you been till now?' she demanded, then her voice faltered. 'And who've you got with you?'

'It's her,' he said proudly, half-carrying the girl into the room and tossing her on to the bed. 'It's Eva.'

Kath was staring, open-mouthed. 'I can see it's her – what on earth have you done, Joe? She's unconscious – she isn't dead, is she?'

'I only hit her. I brought her home for you, Kathy.' He waited for the words of gratitude, of admiration.

'But what are we going to do with her?'

Joe stood erect, pride filling him out like John Wayne faced with a showdown. 'I done it for you, kid. Nobody's going to hurt my Kathy and get away with it.'

The bits of Kath's face that weren't purpled with scars went pale. 'That's stupid, Joe – you can't get away with it either. You'll have the police after us.'

The pride began to filter away. 'Nobody saw me, Kath. I was very careful.'

'But what are you going to do with her now you've got her here?'

'I've got it all planned, Kathy. She's a kidnap victim – they'll have to pay a ransom for her. You said we need money.'

She'd see the cleverness of his plan now. Kath threw up her hands. 'Oh, Joe, we can't feed her, we can't keep her – she'll run away as soon as she wakes up – she'll bring the police.'

'I thought about that too – I got rope here.' He pulled out the coil of rope from under the bed where he'd hidden it.

'Where did you get that?'

'Pinched it from the ironmonger's down the road.'

'Even if you tie her up, she'll scream when she wakes up. People will hear.'

'No, she won't.' He unfastened the cloak and tied the limp arms to the headrail. The rope was too long, and he needed more for her feet. He remembered the carving knife in the box on the floor. Minutes later she lay spreadeagled and tethered, her face as peaceful as a sleeping baby's. Kathy watched as he folded one of her hankies and used it to gag the girl.

'Look,' said Kath, 'I appreciate this, Joe, but it's stupid. It can't work. They'll only take you back to Penston Hall when they get you.'

He looked up at her, hurt making him angry. 'I thought you'd be pleased with me, Kathy. You always said you wanted her hurt like you was.'

'I know, Joe, but not like this.'

The girl's eyes were still closed but she was moaning now. Joe ignored her. 'And we want money, Kath. They'll give us some. I thought we could ask for a lot – fifty pounds even.' Kath turned away with a deep sigh. 'We could get the money first, and then hurt her,' Joe said coaxingly. 'You could watch me burn her, just like you was. I want to burn her, Kathy.'

He saw the girl's eyes were open wide now as she listened. She was frightened of him, and the sense of power made him feel good. 'You hear me?' he said to her. 'I'm going to burn you.'

She made a gurgling sound and struggled to free herself, but she couldn't. He'd made sure of that. He'd frighten her some more. He produced the blowlamp and the tin of petrol from the cupboard.

'See that?' he said proudly. 'That's my blowlamp, and it can't half burn. Goes for hours when it's filled.'

Kath was staring at him. 'You can't use that – she'll need to go to hospital! Oh, Joe – put it away, please!'

He shook his head. 'It took a lot of planning to get her, Kathy – I'm not stopping now. Where's the thing for pricking my blowlamp?'

She seized hold of his hand. 'Joe – burning is horrible – I know – you can't do it – she'd have to go to hospital and everyone would know. We'll be caught.'

He looked down into her agitated face and tried to be patient. She was being very slow to understand.

'We get money this way, Kathy. We need money.'

'Yes, all right. Have you already sent the note?'

'What note?'

'For the ransom, of course.'

'Oh. I forgot.'

He heard her sigh, and then she caught her breath. 'Shall I deliver it for you, Joe? I could take it round.'

He brightened. 'Yeah – that's a good idea.' As he spoke he saw Kath's gaze shift towards the girl, and suddenly he sensed danger. 'Here – what you going to do? How do I know I can trust you, eh?'

She looked up at him from under her lashes, that shy way she used to in Penston Hall. 'Oh, come on now, Joe – an old friend like me? How can you say that? And how are you going to deliver the note if I don't go?'

'Yeah, well . . .'

'After all, the money's more important than anything else, isn't it?'

'Yeah, fifty pounds – we'll be rich with fifty pounds, won't we?' He paused a moment, then frowned. 'You seen my pricker anywhere? I know it was here yesterday, 'cos I saw it.'

She wasn't looking at him as she answered. 'What pricker, Joe?' She was looking at Eva again, and Eva's eyes blinked.

'That bit of metal with a spike on – it's to clean the jet of my blowlamp. It gets blocked and then it won't burn proper. I like to keep my blowlamp in good nick – the boss always said I did that right anyway.'

'Did he, Joe?' She still wasn't looking at him.

'Yeah. Rotten sod he were. Good painter, but a real mean devil. Wouldn't let me do no painting – not him. Only let me burn off the old paint and rub down. I got sick to the back teeth of rubbing down rusty old gutters with that sodding wire brush.'

'I bet you did, Joe.'

'That's why I stole this blowlamp when he sacked me. I'd burn his sodding face off if I had me hands on him now. Where's the matches?'

'We haven't got any.'

'Liar. He swung his fist in her face and saw her wince as she staggered back. 'Get 'em for me.'

She put a hand to her face. 'I told you,' she said in a whisper, 'we haven't got any. We used the last this morning.'

Angrily he pushed her aside. It was no use; wherever he looked he found none. Kath was watching him nervously, her eyes wide in alarm, and her attitude gave him pleasure. It was nice to give orders instead of obeying them.

'You wanna make me angry?' he demanded loudly. The girl on the bed kept shifting her gaze from Kathy to him and back again. 'What you looking at?' he shouted. 'You shut your eyes or else –'

She shut them. He turned back to Kath. 'Find me some matches,' he said fiercely. 'Find them, or I'll be angry.'

She was looking at him with that pitiful look in her eyes, like the puppy he found in the park and tied up and fastened to a tree, then whacked it with a heavy stick till it squealed. After a while it had stopped squealing and lay down. It wasn't interesting any more so he'd left it there.

A thought struck him, and he was surprised at his own cleverness. 'How did you light the gas cooker this morning then if we've no matches? You've hidden them, haven't you?'

'No, Joe. That was the last one.'

Anger began to seethe in him, the kind of angry feeling that usually got worse until he was sick and they took him back to hospital again. Kath's eyes were searching his face.

'Look, Joe,' she said quietly, 'we only want to hurt her. There's no need to burn her.'

Joe was baffled. This was the nasty girl, the cruel one who had burnt Kathy's lovely face. She deserved burning; that was why he'd planned everything so carefully. He took a step nearer Kath.

'We can hurt her without her having to live with a face like this.' Kath pointed to her cheek. 'I'm ugly – nobody wants to look at me any more.'

He stared at her disbelievingly. 'You're breaking our promise, Kathy. You're letting me down.'

'No, Joe – I just don't think we need to hurt her that badly.'

There were tears in her eyes. Joe stepped closer and touched her cheek. 'I like to look at you, Kathy. I don't think you're ugly.'

'Thank you, Joe.' Her voice was tender, the way it used to be. She took up the carving knife and went to the bed. Joe watched in horror.

'No!' he yelled, seizing hold of her arm and twisting it so that the knife fell to the floor. 'You stupid bitch, after all my plans you bloody won't let her go!'

He slapped her hard across the cheek and saw her hand rise to her face. The open mouth irritated him, and he cracked his fist hard into her mouth. Blood appeared on her lip and began to trickle down her chin. He grabbed hold of her arm and screwed it up behind her back until she screamed.

'I wasn't – oh, Joe! Stop – you're hurting me!'

He hissed into her ear, 'How'm I supposed to light the bloody lamp without bloody matches, eh? You got a lighter?'

'No,' she sobbed. 'You know I don't smoke, Joe. Oh please let me go – I could go and get some for you – there's a tobacconist's on the corner.'

He released her and thought. The shop on the corner was a sweet shop. The thought of bull's eyes and liquorice allsorts made him feel hungry again.

'Yeah,' he breathed. 'And you could get me some sweets – and some pop. Chocolate I want, the sort with cream in the middle.'

Throwing her aside he searched for the girl's handbag – there was money in there. He found another pound note. Nasty girls had no right to be rich. He shoved the note in Kath's hand and ushered her towards the door.

'Go on, hurry up – and get some ice cream too.' An afterthought struck him. He turned towards the girl on the bed. 'Would you like some ice cream too, Eva? Yeah, let's all have some ice cream.'

Eva watched as the door closed behind Kath. Joe turned back to her.

'Ice cream cools you down,' he said softly. 'But I'll soon warm you up again, I promise.'

He picked up a piece of metal from the mantelpiece and, taking up the blowlamp, he sat down on the one rickety chair and began poking the spiked piece of metal into the petrol jet. He was humming as he worked and seemed as if he had completely forgotten her. Eva wriggled, trying to loosen the rope around her ankles and wrists, but it only chafed her more.

The cloth in her mouth was shifting though. Repeatedly she arched her neck back in an attempt to pull her mouth clear of it, and all the time her mind was racing. Had she read Kath's glances correctly? They seemed to be saying, 'Don't worry, I'll get you out of this. Don't rub him up the wrong way, just be patient.' That seemed to be the way Kath was playing it – but was she only fooling herself?

Joe was pouring petrol from the tin into the blowlamp now. The pervasive smell of petrol fumes began to seep through the small room. He set the can aside and blew on the jet, then poked it again with the spike.

'Awkward buggers these lamps,' he was muttering. 'Sometimes they'll work for you, sometimes they won't.'

Eva was frightened. At least he had no means of lighting the damn thing when it was primed, but suppose she had misread Kath's intention and she reappeared with the matches?

'That's it, can't do no more.' Joe set the blowlamp down and looked around. Ignoring her he began searching in cupboards and drawers. Suddenly she heard his quick intake of breath and saw him hold his hand up in the air. Between the grubby fingertips was a box of Swan Vestas.

'She was lying, the bitch – we got some after all!'

Eva closed her eyes. She heard the rasp of the match against the box and then the hiss as it flared into life. Hardly able to breathe, she opened her eyes and saw him applying the blazing match to the blowlamp's jet.

Seconds passed, and the lamp did not ignite. Joe swore as the match burned his fingertips and he flung it away.

'Sodding rotten thing,' he said savagely. 'I said they could be buggers, them sodding things. Come on, you bastard, light!'

But though he tried match after match, the lamp seemed to be on Eva's side. She began to breathe again, and renewed her efforts to wriggle free. The rope around her right wrist seemed to be getting looser. Just so long as he was occupied she would keep on wriggling.

He flung the blowlamp down on the floorboards. 'Bloody thing,' he muttered then, turning to Eva, he said, 'Got any sweets?'

She nodded, and saw him look around for her handbag again. There was only chewing gum in there, bought to while away the train journey and then forgotten, but it might suffice. He found it, tossed the handbag aside and began tearing the wrapper off the first strip. He shoved it into his mouth and immediately began tearing open the second and third. All were thrust into his mouth and the wrapping papers dropped on the floor.

'I got a comic today,' he told her. 'From the sweet shop. I like the *Dandy*.'

It was lying on the bed by her feet, half-hidden by her cloak. As he picked it up Eva shivered at his closeness. Even from here she could smell the stale sweat that spoke of days of neglect. But she was grateful for the delay which could give Kath time to summon help. For Christ's sake, Kath – get a move on before he tires of the *Dandy*!

He was still chewing gum when her right hand finally slithered free of the rope. Making certain he was still engrossed, chewing with loud squelching sounds, she flexed the aching wrist and then moved the hand slowly across to try and unknot the rope around her left hand. Joe was chuckling aloud, his knees wide-spread and his arms supported on his thighs.

'Good, this,' he reported over his shoulder. 'They're going to smoke the baddy out.'

Smoke. Eva stiffened. He was sure to remember now. She

saw the tousled fair hair rise slowly. He turned and looked at her thoughtfully over his shoulder.

'Kath's been gone a long time,' he observed. 'Must be a queue at the shop. Or else . . .' He dropped the comic to the floor and stood up. 'I wonder . . . Maybe she's gone for the ransom money.'

He passed by the bed to look out of the grimy window, rattling the matches in his pocket, then withdrew them and looked at them in wonder as if he were seeing them for the first time.

'It makes no odds to me, Eva,' he said with a slow smile. 'You're going to go back hurt, you are. Even if they pay, you're still going to go back burnt.'

Once more a match flared; once more he applied it to the blowlamp. From the bed Eva could see only his half-averted face, the eyes gleaming and the mouth sagging in expectancy. Suddenly she heard the blowlamp roar into life and he turned back towards her, grinning broadly at the spitting flames.

Alan was in the restaurant kitchen, taking off his apron to go and join Zoe and Luc at the table for supper. For once the place was quiet, no jazz group playing on the dais tonight. Later, perhaps, when everyone had gone he would play the piano if his present mood of restlessness persisted.

The swing door suddenly opened to admit Louis. The old man smiled broadly, depositing his hat and a cardboard box on the counter.

He stood there, proudly indicating the box. 'A small gift I bring you, Alan, a small token of my gratitude.'

Alan spread his hands. 'Oh, really, there's no need . . .' He looked curiously at the box. It seemed to be moving. Louis stepped forward and opened the lid.

'Behold, my friend, a cat!'

Inside the box a ginger kitten stared, bright-eyed and its ears pricked. It lifted its nose to sniff its new surroundings and, evidently considering them worthy of inspection, tried to climb out, and failed. Alan lifted it in his arms and instantly it began to purr.

'He likes you!' Louis exclaimed in delight. 'It is good. Rosa will be happy one of the babies has found a good home. We cannot keep all the beautiful kittens her cat has just produced.'

Alan struggled to find words. 'I appreciate the thought, Louis, but a cat – in a restaurant?'

'He is a gourmet kitten, this one. He will appreciate everything you cook. Besides, he will earn his keep – he will chase the mice away.' Louis eased his weight on to a stool. 'Me too – I have taken one. Now that Zoe and Eva are to buy out Henry Bernstein I take on today, for the factory, two more girls and the big tom kitten.'

Alan could not resist a smile. 'I shall be sorry to lose you here, Louis – you've been a great help.'

Louis's chest filled out with pride. 'A factory manager at my time of life – who would have thought it? Rosa is so proud.'

'She's a fine lady,' said Alan. 'You and she get on very well.'

'She is so like my mother,' Louis mused. 'So kind. And big too. A woman should be like an easy chair, don't you agree? Well-upholstered and comfortable. Big thighs and breasts – that is healthy.'

He looked the picture of health himself in that case, thought Alan, his ample body folding down, layer upon layer, to his thick thighs.

'My mother was a good woman like Rosa,' Louis murmured. 'She loved me too – I remember every slap from her hand. And proud too. Even though my father died she

291

saw to it I had my bar mitzvah like everyone else when I was fourteen. Henry was there – he will tell you what a fine bar mitzvah it was.'

The kitten, curled against his chest, sniffed at his ear as Alan glanced at the clock. Eva still had not telephoned for him to meet her. She must be staying on in Middlesbrough or maybe calling at Barnbeck to see Maddie.

'Any phone calls today?' asked Louis, as if he had read Alan's mind. Alan shook his head. 'Only the one I told you about.' The kitten climbed around his neck and settled down there, still purring.

'The bank – that Mr Lawrence wants their business, eh?' said Louis. 'Eva said some day he would come crawling.'

The swing door opened and Roy, the new waiter, looked at Alan with an apologetic half-smile. 'I'm sorry to interrupt, but there's this woman outside – she's demanding to see you.'

Alan frowned. 'Demanding? Is it a complaint?'

Roy shook his head. 'She's not a customer – she's just come in.'

Alan uncurled the kitten from his neck and put it back in the box. 'What sort of woman? What does she look like?'

'She's pretty awful, actually – she's got a terribly scarred –'

Before he could finish the door swung open. Kath Davis stood there, her dark eyes wide in fear and the scars on her face standing out livid against the pale surrounding skin.

'Alan, for God's sake, come quickly – it's Eva!'

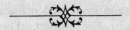

CHAPTER TWENTY-THREE

This was no time to question. Zoe and Luc watched from their table in bewilderment as Alan raced out of the restaurant and up the steps two at a time with Kath close behind, leaving Louis to explain. A taxi stood waiting, its engine running. On the way Kath explained.

'He's crazy, Alan. Dr Spencer tried to warn me but I didn't understand. Joe was the only one who was kind to me.'

'The blowlamp – you say he can't light it – are you sure?'

'Only if he found the matches. I hid them when I realized what he was up to.'

'Tell me the layout – whereabouts is your flat?'

'It's one room, at the top of the stairs, and it's locked.'

'Is there any other way in? The window – can I get in there?'

'It overlooks the street, on the first floor.'

'Then you'll have to get him to open the door.'

'He won't if there's anyone with me.'

'Pretend you're alone.'

'Driver, we'll get out here.'

'You said Duke Street, miss – it's round the corner.'

'I know. It's OK.'

'Four and six each way, that makes –'

Alan was already out and sprinting towards the house. Kath jumped out and ran after him, shouting to the driver, 'Wait here!'

Eva lay motionless, watching Joe's eager expression as he

moved the lamp up and down the doorframe, finding pleasure in the blistering paint. For the moment he was absorbed but any second his mood might change inexplicably once again.

'It's not easy, this,' he was saying. 'The big bit of wood isn't the problem – it's the beading that's tricky – you got to be dead careful.'

He bent closer to the frame, directing the roaring flame with infinite care. 'If I had me scraper with me I could show you how it's done. It's got a pointed bit that goes in the beading and a flat bit for doing the door.'

He stood back to admire his handiwork, adjusting the blowlamp down to a quiet blue flame. 'Good, isn't it?'

Mercifully he seemed to expect no reply, and Eva was glad. With the blasted gag still stuck in her mouth she had no way of talking to him, trying to soothe or placate, not unless she removed it herself and that would draw attention to the fact that her hands were untied. If only she could reach her feet without him seeing . . .

The game seemed to have lost its interest for him. He turned away from the blackened doorframe and she held her breath as he came towards her.

'Watch,' he said, turning up the flame again. Eva closed her eyes. Every muscle of her body ached with strain and the foul-smelling hiss coming so close made her stiffen with fear. He bent over the bed and pulled the gag from her mouth.

'Watch,' he said again. 'Isn't it clever how I can make it burn big or little?' He was turning the screw on the side of the lamp back and forth so that the flame flared up and died down, then flared again. 'I could set fire to a house with this. Or a shop. I burnt your shop.'

Eva caught her breath. Everything was becoming clear now – but how would Kath Davis get someone to do this in revenge? He must be her brother or something – a simple-minded brother.

She saw the flicker gleam in his eye, the sudden leap of light. 'Yeah,' he murmured. 'Burnt your shop, I did, for Kathy, 'cos of what you did to her. And I'm going to burn you. Yeah, that's it.'

Eva's tongue felt as if it had swollen too large for her mouth. 'No,' she croaked. 'That's silly, Joe. Don't do anything silly.'

He came and stood beside her, his legs touching the side of the bed as he looked down. She saw the glow of anticipation, the mouth curved into a cretinous smile. He brought the blowlamp down, so near she could feel its heat.

'Hot, isn't it?' said Joe. 'I'm going to like this game, Eva. I been wanting to burn you for a long, long time.'

At the top of the stairs Kath laid a finger to her lips and Alan stood back against the wall, out of sight.

'Joe,' she called softly. 'Let me in.'

There was a pause before he answered gruffly, 'Who is it?'

'It's me, Kathy. Open the door, Joe.'

She sniffed. There was a curious smell in the air, something more than the usual decaying smell of the house – something was burning. Alan had caught the scent of it too and was jerking his head towards the door. She knocked loudly.

'Joe, come on, let me in – stop messing about.'

There was a shuffling sound and then he spoke in a low voice. 'I don't need you, Kathy. Go away. I don't want you no more.'

She saw the alarm on Alan's face and he moved forward to push her aside. She pushed him back. 'Joe,' she said in a wheedling tone, 'I got chocolate for you – nice chocolate with cream in the middle.'

'Shove it under the door then.'

She looked helplessly at Alan. Joe's voice came again, gruff and petulant as a child's.

'Don't want it anyway,' he growled. 'Go away. You spoil things.'

'I got money too, Joe. I got the fifty pounds.'

There was a pause, no sound at all from within the room. She saw Alan set his lips in a tight line.

'Fifty pounds, Joe. You're rich.'

'Let me see it.'

Alan reached into his back pocket and took out his wallet. He pulled out a bundle of notes and passed them wordlessly to Kath. She peeled off a pound note and, bending, pushed it under the door. It shot suddenly out of sight. She pushed another under, and then a five-pound note, and they all vanished with the same speed.

Eva lay on the bed, craning her neck to watch Joe snatching the money as it kept appearing. Beside him on the floor the blowlamp stood blazing, for the moment forgotten. The bunch of notes in his grimy hand was thickening into a wad, Joe's eyes gleaming bright. Stealthily she reached down to the ropes around her ankles.

He was staring at the crack under the door, waiting for the next note to slither under.

'Go on,' he said.

Eva heard Kath's murmured reply. 'That's it, Joe.'

He looked disbelievingly at the wad. 'There ain't fifty here. What you done with it?'

'Open the door, Joe, and I'll give you the rest.'

The rope came loose. Eva's right foot was free. Joe lifted one dirt-stained fingertip to the bubbled paintwork of the doorframe. Eva lay half back, waiting for his next move. She saw him press a broken fingernail into a blister of paint, cracking it, then flicking the loosened flake away.

'Know what, Kath?' he muttered. 'There's blue paint under this brown stuff.'

'Let me see.'

'Yeah, and there's green under that. This lot's going to take time to burn off.'

There was a pause before Kath answered. 'I know you'll do a good job of it, Joe. Let me have a look.'

Eva cautiously reached for the rope around her left foot.

'Blisters, Kathy,' he murmured dreamily, pricking yet another with his fingernail. 'Blisters just like what you had in the hospital. Poor Kathy.'

He was turning away from the door, a glazed expression in his eyes, and Eva let go of the rope. 'Wicked,' he muttered. 'Lovely Kathy.' He looked down at the blowlamp. Eva's breath caught in her throat.

'Joe,' the voice called softly from beyond the door. 'I'm all better now, Joe. Open the door and see.'

He had picked up the lamp and was staring at Eva, hatred etched all over his young face as he stepped towards her. 'Wicked, nasty!' he shouted.

'Joe, I'm beautiful,' the voice cried out. 'I'm beautiful again – open the door, Joe, and you'll see!'

His head swung back towards the door but the blowlamp was still directed towards Eva, the evil-smelling flame roaring so close she could feel its heat. Eva shrank back. If only she'd had time to free her left foot . . .

'Beautiful?' he repeated in a murmur. Eva held her breath as he turned slowly towards the door and lifted the latch, pulling the door back a few inches. Kath's slim figure edged in sideways through the opening and stopped. Eva saw Joe stare at the swollen, misshapen features and the purple scars.

'You're not beautiful – she did that to you, Kathy. Now I'm going to do it to her for you.'

Then suddenly he was flying through the air towards the bed, banknotes scattering everywhere and the blowlamp still clutched tightly in his hand. The door stood open wide, and Alan was hurtling in.

Eva reacted without conscious thought, throwing herself sideways so violently that she fell heavily off the bed on to her back on the floor, jammed in the gap between bed and wall. Joe lay sprawled across the bed, a maniacal gleam in his eyes as he reached out towards her. Wedged in the gap and her left foot still fettered to the bedpost Eva was trapped, with no way of turning over to protect her face or of crawling out of the blowlamp's reach. She threw up her arms to cover her face and felt the heat searing the back of her hands.

Suddenly Alan's face appeared above her, his body lying full-length along Joe's across the bed. Eva felt the sweat pouring from her as the blowlamp swung menacingly close, its flame swaying wildly as Alan's left arm crushed down on the back of Joe's neck while his right reached to wrench Joe's arm up and clear of Eva. Eva could hear grunted breathing and Kath's moans, but above it all roared the threatening flame.

The heat receded. Eva peeped cautiously between her fingers. Above her a long flame was licking its way up the peeling wallpaper and Alan, still face-down on top of Joe, had weakened Joe's grip on the blowlamp so that its spout was wavering, swinging slowly round backwards.

'Go it, Alan!' Eva shouted. 'You've got the bugger – go on!'

She struggled to sit up, desperate to release her other foot. As she did so she caught sight of the breadknife on the floor, forgotten since Joe had bound her. Eva caught her breath; Kath had seen it too and was crawling towards it. For a second the girls' eyes met.

Eva heard the gasp, the thud, and then caught the acrid smell of burning. From the far side of the bed smoke was rising. Alan had forced the blowlamp out of Joe's powerful grip, only for it to fall by the bedside. The smouldering eiderdown was already catching fire, and the stench of burning feathers made her stomach heave.

Kath was kneeling amid banknotes, staring at the blaze as if mesmerized, the knife in her right hand, while the fingers of her left caressed her purple cheek. Suddenly Joe threw off Alan's weight and struggled to rise from the bed, but Alan brought him crashing to the floor. Heedless of the flailing bodies, Kath knelt and began hacking through the rope around Eva's ankle. Eva winced as the blade cut into her flesh.

Flames from the eiderdown were scorching across the bed to where the two girls crouched. Kath let the knife fall and raced across to the sink and ran water into a saucepan. Eva snatched up the knife and hacked at the remaining strands of rope, tossing back her hair out of reach of the flames. Suddenly, somehow, Joe was wriggling under the bed towards her but again Alan leapt on top of him. The knife flew out of Eva's hand. She shrieked under the weight of the men's bodies, digging her nails into the hardness of what she hoped was Joe's body.

She heard the hiss as Kath threw water on the blazing bed, then heard the saucepan crash on the floorboards beside her. Instinctively she reached out a hand to grab it. For a second the bodies rolled clear and, raising the pan high in the air, Eva brought it crashing down on Joe's head.

'Belt the sod, Alan! Beat hell out of him!'

Kath was on her knees beyond the bed, her dark eyes staring wide. Eva scrambled clear and stumbled to her feet, feeling her knees go weak. As she did so Joe suddenly dodged clear of Alan's grip and slithered, with all the speed and agility of a rat, towards the open door.

Afterwards Eva could recall the picture in detail, as if somehow frozen in time, Joe's burly body almost horizontal in flight, the tousled fair hair framing his dazed, wild face, Alan on his knees preparing to spring, the black hair now touched with white about his temples, and behind him the billowing smoke rising from the bed and the orange tongues of flame licking hungrily up the hanging shreds of wallpaper towards the blackened ceiling. Afterwards it remained crystal-clear in her memory . . .

She found herself lying full-length on the floor, her arms firmly clenched around the knees of Joe's prostrate figure. Alan hurled himself down on Joe's body, and Eva heard the explosion of breath from Joe's lungs. Then he was lying, eyes closed and his expression as peaceful as a sleeping child's as blood trickled from the corner of his mouth.

Alan was panting. 'Get the rope,' he muttered. Kath fetched a length from where it lay by the bed. Alan gave Eva a searching look. 'You OK?'

'I'm fine. But what kept you?'

Alan pulled Joe's arms behind his back and knotted the rope tightly about his wrists then gave Eva a rueful smile.

'I always wondered why my rugby team lost so many matches. We could have done with you.'

The wallpaper behind the bed was now no more than a blackened mess. The eiderdown still smouldered gently. Eva fetched more water and soaked the bed until the smoke no longer rose. Kath dipped a rag in the water and was wiping the blood from Joe's mouth. 'Poor Joe,' she whispered. 'Poor Joe.'

Eva reached out a hand to touch the girl's shoulder. 'He'll be taken care of,' she murmured. 'Are you all right?'

The scarred face turned to her. 'Are you?' Her gaze travelled down to the cut on Eva's ankle and she reached to dab the rag to it.

Eva laid a hand over hers and smiled. 'I'm OK, thanks to you.'

A lopsided smile flickered on Kath's face. Suddenly a broad figure blocked the doorway.

'Hey, what the devil's going on up here?' a man demanded. 'I can't sleep with all this racket going on.'

'Sorry,' said Alan, rising to his feet. 'We're going now – we've got a taxi waiting.'

It took until midnight for Eva and Alan to finish with the routine business at the police station. Zoe and Luc stayed on for Kath to finish making her statement.

'You go home now,' urged Zoe. 'We'll see Kath is all right.'

Louis was waiting still in the restaurant. Roy in the kitchen, volunteering to work on, had hot soup and a meal ready.

Louis was shocked and horrified by what had occurred. He made Eva sit down, fetched hot water and disinfectant, and knelt by the table to bathe the cut on her ankle while she ate.

'So the girl is to go back to hospital?' he asked.

'To East Grinstead,' said Alan. 'They specialise in plastic surgery there.'

'The crazy man – he too is in hospital, you say? What a country, putting a madman in hospital – he should be in prison for what he done.'

'He's sick,' said Eva wearily. 'A psychopath – he probably won't be allowed out for a long, long time. If ever.'

The ginger kitten wandered in from the kitchen and, seeing Louis, flung itself at his ankle where it clung, limpet-like, trying to bite his shoelace. Louis disentangled its needle-like claws gently from his sock and put it down on the floor, then placed a strip of adhesive tape on Eva's cut ankle.

'My dear,' he murmured, 'such a terrible thing to happen. Is there any more damage?'

It was only then that Eva became aware of the stinging pain

on the backs of her hands, the reddening which spread up her forearms. She held up an arm, and Alan rose.

'Bicarb. I've got some in the kitchen. Come on.'

He reached out a hand to help her to her feet. Eva looked up at him and gave a thin smile.

'Tomorrow I'll thank you properly, Alan, but not tonight – I'm too shattered.'

As they went out to the kitchen Louis sat back on his haunches. The kitten tried to balance on its diminutive hind legs to attack his tie. Louis heard the sound of a car pulling up outside and then the door to the street opened. Louis half-turned.

'I am so sorry, we are closed,' he began, then caught sight of the shirt-sleeved figure in the doorway. It was Reg Fowler.

'What's this I hear?' growled Reg. 'Who's been messing with our little Eva?'

Louis gaped. 'How did you know? It only happened tonight.'

Reg glowered. 'I hear everything that goes on in my patch. Kidnap and attempted extortion, I hear. Who was it, eh? Wasn't one of my lot – they wouldn't dare. Not our kind of business. So who was it? I'll nobble anybody who goes for our Eva.'

'Not to worry, Reg,' Louis said urgently. 'They've got him – he's in custody.'

'I know they've got him, but I want his name – who's he with?'

'He's just a nutter, Reg. He's not a professional. Go home, please.' Louis felt apprehensive. The copper on the Chelsea beat would raise his eyebrows if he caught sight of Reg Fowler in such unfamiliar territory.

Reg looked around. 'You sure she's OK?'

'She is fine. I tell her you call to ask. You like a whisky before you go, just to keep out the cold?'

'No thanks, mate. I got my motor outside.'

As Louis watched him go the kitten took the opportunity to clamber up his trouser leg again and hung, eyes huge with amazement at its feat, from the front of his waistcoat. Louis cupped one pudgy hand under its bottom and carried it away, back to the kitchen.

Eva lay half-awake into the night, jerking fully awake from time to time in fear, sweat breaking out on her forehead. It's over, she kept telling herself, it's over and I'm safe. And so, thank God, was Alan. If he hadn't been in time . . .

But though she slept at last, it was a sleep threaded with dreams of a hissing serpent slithering through tongues of flame. Peace came only with the soothing tones of Alan's voice.

'No more worry, Eva, no more pain. I am here.'

CHAPTER TWENTY-FOUR

Fay smiled at Donald McIntyre as he walked into her office.

'Ah, I'm so glad you came in, Donald. I'm having a job persuading Violetta to drop the Urchin theme for a while. Perhaps you could persuade her we've rather flogged it to death?'

Donald sat on the edge of her desk, swinging a well-tailored leg and eyeing her thoughtfully. 'Violetta at fault again?'

Fay shrugged. 'It's not really her fault, but thirty-nine is a teensy bit old to be *au fait* with all the innovations in the fashion world, isn't it? There's lots of bright young things emerging these days, like Mary Quant and this young Natalie I spoke to you about. She really ought to open her own place, I told her.'

Donald's eyes gleamed as he smiled. 'You're something of a manipulator, aren't you, Fay? Let me tell you something – I am not going to get rid of Violetta.'

'Oh, I wasn't suggesting –'

'Yes, you were. But it's plain you and she can't work together, so I have a suggestion to make. How about a job in New York?'

Fay's poise slipped away. 'New York? But you'll be here, in London –'

'That's right, but I'll keep my eye on you. Working with *Vogue*, it's important you reflect well on me after I've recommended you.'

'You'll be going over there though?'

'Now and again. Well? Aren't you pleased?'

'Of course. Thanks.'

A windy drizzle blew against the shop windows. Alan stood leaning against the counter but Eva still found it hard to meet his gaze. He watched her slow, stiff movements, the marks of the rope still visible around her ankles, and her forearms still bandaged.

'You were fantastic, Alan,' Zoe was enthusing. 'Eva told me all about it.'

'Yes, you saved my life,' said Eva gruffly. It was too hard to put into words just how grateful she felt, and at the same time how confused.

'How are you feeling now?' Alan asked. 'Think maybe you should put off the show for a week or two?'

'No, the show goes on,' Eva retorted.

Luc arrived, ushering in a group of girls. 'I've brought the models,' he called out. 'Come and see.'

Eva eyed them over appreciatively. They were pretty girls, long-haired and with bright, lively faces. 'They're smashing,' she murmured. 'They're just what I wanted – completely natural.'

'Where did you get them?' asked Alan.

'They're photographic models,' said Eva. 'I wanted natural movement and expression.'

'They're a damn sight more attractive than those skinny fashion models,' murmured Alan. 'Who's the blonde one swigging out of a hip flask?'

He moved across to speak to her. The blonde smiled and Eva saw her offer the flask to Alan. Something in the way his body leaned in towards hers sent ripples of fury surging through Eva.

'You can put that flask away now,' snapped Zoe. 'Rehearsal starts in two minutes.' She turned to Eva. 'You just sit and rest this time – I'll put them through their paces.'

Eva sat on a stool by the counter. As Zoe took the girls in hand Alan came back to stand beside her and watch. After a time he looked down at her.

'You're not saying much today, Eva. Cat got your tongue?'

Eva spoke quietly. 'Did you know Chantal put up the money for this place?'

'Yes, I knew.'

Eva looked him directly in the eyes. 'We agreed to borrow from the bank, against Luc's inheritance.'

'That's what he let you think.'

Eva stared. 'What the hell for?'

'Bank's interest rate was too high. Chantal thought it was silly. She doesn't want any interest.'

'But why weren't we told?'

'Chantal and Luc thought you might be too proud to take the loan.'

Zoe came to lean against the counter alongside Eva who was calculating. 'So if there's no interest, we've paid off more than we thought.'

'That's right,' agreed Alan. 'So you're not angry, are you?'

'So long as Luc never keeps things from me again,' said Zoe.

'I'm furious,' said Eva. 'The only time in my life I'll ever get an interest-free loan and I wasn't able to enjoy it.' She glared at Alan. 'And you knew all the time.'

'Luc knew how you'd set your heart on it. We agreed to keep it quiet, for a time at least.'

'I see,' said Eva. 'You're very good at keeping things secret.'

Valerie Bartram-Bates eyed her daughter askance.

'You're in love with him! You've fallen for your boss, just as you're about to take up this American job!'

Fay blushed. 'Don't be silly, Mummy – just because he's handsome and a bachelor –'

'Just because nothing! You've been mooning for days – how blind of me not to realize it before! At least you'll be able to twist him round your little finger.'

'That's just it – I can't. He's strong, Mummy. I want to stay near a man I can admire.'

'So what will you do? Will you still take the American job?'

Fay sighed. 'I suppose I'll have to. Isn't it just too stupid for words? I thought I'd got things all worked out . . .'

The fashion show was a success, every table in the restaurant crammed with heads bobbing excitedly to watch the novel display of well-coiffed heads of Mayfair matrons alongside pony-tailed teenagers. Now the last of the diners had gone and the chaotic confusion of clothes and shoes and rails and hangers had been cleared away and the celebration party began. They sat around a candle-lit table, Eva and Zoe exhausted but exhilarated. Champagne corks popped.

'Going to the Dior and Balenciaga houses was never like this,' murmured Chantal. 'How clever you are, *mes chères*.'

'They got everything from Arabs to the Bisto Kids!' raved Rita to Reg. 'Fan-bloody-tastic!'

'So smooth and trouble-free,' said Alan. 'I was impressed.'

'You didn't see us sitting on that blonde Veronica backstage – she was too sozzled to go on,' grunted Eva.

'So Annie had to wear that number, and she's a size larger. Thought she'd split the damn thing,' muttered Zoe. 'Still, all's well that ends well.'

Louis came to join them, hand outstretched. 'Reg – you enjoy the show?'

'Course,' said Reg. 'Now, we got business.'

'Business?' said Louis, brightening. 'Something for the lady, yes? Maybe we do special price for you.'

Rita dimpled. 'Me and Reg is getting married!'

'Oh, congratulations,' said Zoe.

'He gave me this ring – look.' Rita held out her left hand, a diamond the size of a marble catching and reflecting the light from the candles. Louis's eyes grew round.

'It's beautiful,' said Eva. 'I hope you'll be very happy.'

'And I want you to make my wedding dress – something really sexy that'll make Reg's eyes pop out.'

Reg grinned and gave her a slap on the bottom. 'You do that all right, darling.'

'Reg's got me the most fabulous stuff you ever saw – fell off the back of a lorry, he says.'

'Shut your pretty trap, sweetheart,' muttered Reg.

'Seems to be a lot of lorries around with stuff falling off,' Rita went on. 'You think they'd do something about it.'

Louis lifted a bottle. 'Let us drink champagne to celebrate your betrothal. Good stuff, I heartily recommend it.' He poured wine into glasses until they overflowed, murmuring as he did so, 'A man needs a good wife.' He began to drink and then suddenly he stopped and looked around. 'Hey, princess – where is my Rosa?'

Zoe threaded her fingers between Luc's. 'In the kitchen, Papa – why don't you go to her?'

'A good woman,' he muttered, the wine spilling over as he rose.

Chantal turned to Zoe. 'Why don't you and Luc come back with me and stay a few days at Les Pommiers? Such changes I have made to the château – it is so beautiful again.'

'I'd love to,' said Zoe. 'But I've got one or two things to sort out first.'

'Like what?' asked Eva.

'Natalie. I gather it's been suggested she sets up her own shop – isn't that right, Fay?'

Fay sighed. 'I did moot the idea, and it's my guess she probably will one day.'

'You wanted to take her away from us?'

'I thought you weren't very keen on her, darling, but I'm not really concerned now. I'm off to America soon.'

'America?' said Alan. 'On business?'

'Yes – my boss has landed me a plum job as English correspondent for *Vogue*. I'll be flying out to see the editor soon.'

'Gosh, you must have got that boss of yours round your little finger,' said Zoe.

'And if you're good I'll write about you,' said Fay. 'Young British trendsetters, I shall call you, daring and original.'

Alan looked across the table to Eva. 'That's what you are, daring and original. Let me take you out to eat for a change one night. I know a good place.'

'I'll think about it,' said Eva.

'That's right,' said Fay. 'Keep him dangling.'

Eva twirled the wineglass between her fingers and kept her tone casual. 'Like you did?' she murmured.

Zoe squeezed Luc's arm. 'That's right, we ought to teach men their place.'

'A woman's prerogative, darling,' said Fay. 'But I've got fresh fields on the other side of the Atlantic. It's up to you two to beat them at their own game now.'

It was one of the ritziest, most expensive restaurants in town. Eva looked around at the debonair, deferential waiters, the lush carpets and glittering crystal wineglasses.

'I'd offer to pay my share but I couldn't raise the mort-gage,' she remarked. Alan smiled.

'I've been wanting to do this for a long time. You deserve something special. What'll you have to eat?'

Their heads bent close as they deliberated, and Eva watched his profile as he read each item from the menu, the short patches of hair where it had been burnt, his frown as he considered, then the sudden flash of pleasure irradiating his face when he became aware of her scrutiny. She felt joy in his closeness, and then a shadow of uncertainty dispelled the joy . . .

'I think I fancy the roast beef – what about you?'

She sensed he too was watching her as she read, and was glad she had taken the trouble to wear a dress he'd be sure to like, with a demurely high neckline slashed almost to the waist so that nothing was revealed but which held out the prospect that at any moment something might show.

'With new potatoes,' he added. 'I like new potatoes, don't you, smothered in butter? Round and white and succulent.'

She could swear his eyes flickered towards her cleavage and she felt the tingle of excitement those dark eyes always aroused in her when they held that slumberous look. Alan would always awaken that excitement in her, she knew, but she was equally well aware that she would never be quite sure of him . . .

'You're out of luck,' she said. 'New potatoes are out of season.'

Alan grinned and changed the subject. 'I'm glad to hear Natalie's joining Urchin – you certainly unearthed a treasure in her.'

'Yes, she's terrific.'

'You can't go wrong, Eva. You'll have to work like hell, but the world's your oyster now.'

They were talking about anything but the question that burned in Eva's mind. She resolved to steer clear of it just as he was doing.

'Anything worth doing is worth doing well. David Maynard said that to me once.'

'Ever hear from him now?' Alan's tone sounded casual enough.

She shook her head. 'Don't want to either. He was married. I didn't know.'

'And lonely. I can't blame him for wanting you. I do.'

Eva felt the blood rush to her cheeks. Bank managers, wholesalers, awkward customers she could handle, but a compliment from Alan . . .

'You'd fancy anyone in a skirt,' she teased. 'I heard you chatting up Natalie, and the drunken blonde.'

'It's a game, that's all, chatting up pretty girls. They like it – I think they expect it.'

'But how does anyone know if you're serious?'

Alan shrugged. 'It's the way I am.'

'I used to fancy you once. Who didn't?'

'Used to?'

'Until Fay. That was unforgiveable, hurting my friend.'

'Which one?' There was amusement, teasing in his eyes now.

'Fay, of course – who else?'

'Oh – I thought you might mean Zoe.'

Eva's mouth widened. The waiter placed a bowl of soup in front of her. 'Zoe? You don't mean – she never said – oh, Alan!'

He grinned as he sprinkled salt on his soup. 'I'm betraying no confidence – she wouldn't let me near her. Any more than you would, worse luck. But I don't give up easily.'

She watched his mouth open and close around the spoon and wondered at the ferocity of her own feelings. Envy? Possessiveness? She could not hold her tongue any longer.

'No, you don't. You kept pestering Fay, didn't you? Long after we all thought it was over.'

311

He laid the spoon down and his eyes were serious as he looked at her. 'It was over, Eva. At least, I thought it was. Then suddenly Fay started showing interest again. She fascinated me.'

'I know. I saw you with her.'

'And then she told me to shove off, she was only teaching me a lesson.'

'She's changed. Good for her.'

'Going after what she wants? You do too, Eva.'

She leaned across to him.

'You're a trier too – you don't give up on what you want. Just look at the restaurant – it's going great guns.'

'No, I don't give up – I want you, Eva. I realized what you meant to me long before that fellow kidnapped you. I wanted to kill him. The light would have gone out of my life without you.'

The sombre intensity of his tone touched her heart. What was it Zoe had said of Luc? *In him I live and breathe and have my being.*

'And Fay?' she asked quietly.

He smiled. 'I still wanted you.'

Eva changed the subject. 'That kitten Louis brought you – what'll you call it?'

He thought. 'Ginger?'

'That's boring.'

'Copper then. She has the same colouring as you.'

'I beat up a girl once at school for calling me Coppernob. Try again.'

'Marmalade.'

'That's silly. Zoe could do better than that.'

'Have you heard from her?'

'Just a telegram to say she'll be back tomorrow. What about Shandy, Sherry, Amber . . . Hey, what about Gipsy? She looks like a vagabond. I rather like Gipsy Finch.'

'Or Urchin, like you.'

'Did I tell you Maddie saw the gipsy fortune-teller at the Gooseberry Fair? She told her the baby would be a boy. And you know something? It's due to be born in late April or early May – that's the time Maddie's mares always foal.'

Alan was smiling at her. The waiter took the soup bowls away. Eva jutted her chin. 'It's a good sign, that, whatever you think. I think it's highly significant.'

'A good omen?'

'Yes.' She leaned on her elbows and a serious look crossed her face. 'You know, we've got so much to learn about each other still. It'd take years.'

'I've got the time.'

'I don't know what happened to you in the army – did you fight?'

He threw back his head and laughed. 'I was poised ready to go into action in the Suez crisis but somebody called it off and I didn't get there. Very disappointing.'

Eva cocked her head to one side. 'You've experienced much more than me.'

He leaned forward on his elbows. 'You're already wise in an innocent kind of way.'

'I don't get you.'

'Strange contradiction, you are. Whizz kid and idiot, all mixed together.'

'Roast beef, sir?'

Alan sat back, and Eva could feel his gaze on her while the waiter served the main course. When he had gone Eva held out the dish of vegetables. 'Sprouts, or carrots?'

He did not answer at once. She looked at him enquiringly. He was grinning at her. 'I was dying for a helping of luscious, tempting new potatoes, but I can wait.'

*

313

It was Alan's suggestion that they should walk home along the Embankment instead of taking a taxi. The breeze off the river struck chill but Eva was soon unware of it, with Alan's arm around her waist. Across the water lights reflected in a million shattered fragments; London's traffic hummed in the distance and Eva felt contentment.

'It'll soon be Bonfire Night again,' Alan remarked. 'Will it bring back rotten memories for you?'

Eva did not answer at once. It was hard to tell even Alan how often memory, bringing with it remorse, had returned. She took a deep breath.

'Not any more. I think somehow Kath's forgiven me.'

'I'm sure of it. She knows it was an accident anyway.'

'I'm sorry for that crazy boy. He really cared about her in a peculiar kind of way. Not normal at all.'

'Wasn't it Freud who said, show me a normal man and I'll soon cure him?'

Alan stopped walking to lean on the parapet, looking at the river. Eva had a sudden, irresistible urge to lighten the mood. Ignoring the high heels of her shoes she scrambled up on the ledge and stood, swaying, laughing down at him.

He smiled. 'You never could resist a challenge, could you? You were always the first to take on a dare.'

She was teetering along the wall away from him, feeling the cool breeze blowing on the bare skin under her skirt. She knew Alan was following on the pavement.

Then a high heel caught on the edge of a coping stone and she slipped, swaying to try and regain her balance. As she lost control and fell, Alan's arms held her. He set her down on the pavement and for long seconds she stood there, revelling in his closeness, the feel of hard, warm strength. Then a thought flashed into her mind. Fay had lain in his arms. Eva broke away.

'Race you to the bridge!'

She had a head start, taking him by surprise, but as she tore along the deserted pavement, handicapped by high heels, she could sense him catching up. Excitement danced in her and laughter rippled as he drew level and snatched her in his arms.

'That's what I love about you, Eva – the child in you.' The sparkle in his eyes faded. Under the light of the lamp she could see hunger in his eyes. 'And the woman,' he added, and brought his lips down on hers.

For the first few seconds Eva held herself stiff, and then gradually she melted into his embrace, savouring the pleasure of him, responding. Everything about him gave her delight, the smell and feel of him, the gentleness and at the same time strength. This was a man she could enjoy and love forever . . . But would he stay forever?

He straightened at last, still looking down into her eyes. 'I meant what I said, Eva,' he said softly. 'I want you.'

She looked directly into that searching gaze. 'And I want you. But I don't want to be one of your fly-by-night conquests, Alan.'

He shook his head. 'I've grown up, Eva. I play serious games now. I play for keeps.'

There was a gust of noisy laughter sweeping up the steps from the restaurant. Alan stood outside the shop with Eva.

'Coming up for coffee?' Eva invited.

'I'd better sort this out first – the restaurant should have closed ages ago.'

Inside the window the ginger kitten was clambering up Zoe's carefully-draped netting, leaping off and darting underneath. Eva giggled and pointed. 'Just look at that – she gets everywhere!'

'I know. When I took the rubbish out to the dustbin yesterday, guess what I found when I took the lid off? Look,

315

I'd better go down – Louis must be having problems. You go on in – I'll see you later.'

Eva let herself into the shop and, taking a reluctant kitten from the window, went through to the back room. The kettle boiled, she brewed coffee and waited. Downstairs the sounds of laughter and merrymaking continued.

Half an hour passed. The coffee was cold and the kitten fast asleep on Zoe's empty bed. Eva sighed and began to undress.

'What's going on? Couldn't you get rid of them, Louis? It's long past closing time.'

Alan peeled off his coat, ready to do battle. Louis's eyes were huge with apology and explanation.

'It's Reg Fowler, Alan – he's got a party going on. Business associates, he says, and they're spending money like water.'

'But the time, Louis – we shouldn't be open at this hour. What if the police come?'

Louis's plump face broke into a grin. 'Just look over there.'

Alan followed the direction of his finger. In the far corner, illuminated by the light of the candles on the table, sat a genial Reg Fowler and around him, sprinkled among the other guests, sat three uniformed figures. Alan sighed. This was going to take time.

At last they had all gone. Alan locked the front door and glanced at the clock. He could at least go up and see if a light was still burning upstairs.

The steps out of the kitchen up to the back yard were littered with crates of empty bottles and cartons of rubbish. As his head rose above ground level he saw the light from the back room. She was still up.

As he neared the window he could see her, and the breath caught in his throat. She was lifting the skirt of that dress which had teased him all evening and pulling it up over her head. Arms at full stretch she paused, wriggling her head through the neck opening, and he saw clearly the breasts standing high and rounded in their natural beauty.

Her head came free and she dropped the dress on the bed, then stepped out of her pants. Half-turned from him, he could see the sheen of light on the under-curve of her breast, the tiny waist above the gleam of her hip, the swell of her buttocks and the long, slender legs. She tossed the glorious mane of red-gold hair, arching her neck backwards. Drawing a deep breath Alan waited and watched. God, but she was beautiful! He could watch her all night and find joy in the beauty of her.

She crossed to the sink and ran the tap. As she bent to put the plug in he could see the sway of her breasts, and the longing in him surged. She took up a flannel, soaped it, and began smoothing it over her body with slow, easy strokes. It circled her breasts, and Alan's lips went dry. When she lifted one foot and placed it in the sink, slithering the flannel down to caress her thighs, he could bear it no longer. He came close and tapped at the window.

'Eva?'

Her head turned, her eyes wide in surprise, but she did not take her foot out of the water. From beyond the closed window he could hear her voice.

'God, you made me jump!' she said accusingly, then suddenly her eyes began to twinkle. 'Are you going to make a habit of coming to my window?'

'Only till you let me in,' he answered.

She lifted her foot out of the sink. He could see droplets of water sparkling as they fell. She came across and unlatched the window. 'Come on in.'

As he climbed over the sill she took up a towel. Wet footprints marked the floorboards where she walked, and Alan felt a lunge of tenderness for her mingle with desire.

'Here, let me,' he said, and took the towel from her. She stood like a child on bath night, letting him rub her body as if she were unaware of his roughened fingertips; no embarrassment showed on her lovely face, and he loved her the more for it. Tenderness gave gentleness to his hands, and he saw her smile.

'You make me feel cared for, Alan. You make me feel loved. I wish it could last.'

There was no sadness in her words, but he was filled with the same aching sensation he always felt when he listened to a haunting Bessie Smith blues number. He would take a pallet on any floor, endure any hardship, to be close to this woman . . .

'I love you, Eva. I love you with all my heart. For always.'

He let the towel fall and she turned to him. As he took her in his arms she smiled up at him.

'I've always wanted to hear you say that.'

'I mean it.'

'I know.' For the moment at least, she knew he did.

Alan was stripping off his clothes when the telephone shrilled. Eva frowned.

'Who the hell can that be at this time of night?'

'I'll go. It could be urgent.'

Alan went through into the shop and, without switching on the light, picked up the phone. 'Hello?'

For several minutes Eva could hear him listening and then murmuring, and then curiosity overcame her. She followed him into the shop and stood leaning against the doorjamb. By the light of the streetlamps outside she could see Alan's naked back, muscular and gleaming as he held the telephone to his ear. There seemed to be no urgency in his tone.

'Right. I'll tell her . . . See you tomorrow then . . . yes, I'll be sure to give her the message.'

'Who was it?'

'Zoe. She's just got back. She wanted to let you know she's staying at her father's.'

'Zoe? *In him I live and breathe and have my being.*'

'She said France was wonderful. No Algerians this time. She'll tell you all about it tomorrow.'

Alan's fingers touched her hair. 'She's at Louis's – we've got the rest of the night together.'

'*Till the day break and the shadows flee away.*'

'Oh, I nearly forgot,' Alan added. 'She said Louis had a phone call from a chap who wants to do business with you. Chap by the name of Cavendish.'

'Who?'

Alan wound his fingers through her hair and pulled her gently down on to the floor.

'You set fire to his newspaper. Now it's my turn.'

Eva closed her eyes, willing away the doubts. Strong arms around her and a sense of belonging here . . . '*With the right man it's wonderful.*'

Maybe it would last, she was willing to take the chance. . .

In the window a kitten's ginger head appeared behind a purple embroidered blouse, huge green eyes half-filling her face. She looked down to where a small puddle was gradually seeping out from under a pile of sea-shells. She had just added another major fact to her growing store of knowledge – sea-shells were not the ideal material to cover her embarrassment.

She lengthened her neck to peer into the gloom of the

shop where two naked humans lay intertwined. They did not seem concerned. Philosophically the kitten forgot the problem of the puddle and, crawling into the subterranean cosiness of the purple sleeve, curled into a ball to resume her sleep.